CAME

Elizabeth de Guise is the a... , shortlisted
for the Romantic Novelists Association Award, *Flight of the
Dragonfly* and *Bridge of Sighs*, recently published in hardback by
Macmillan. Born in Kenya, she has travelled widely all over the
world, living in Andalusia for more than a year. She now lives
and writes full-time in Pembrokeshire.

ELIZABETH DE GUISE

Came Forth The Sun

PAN BOOKS
LONDON, SYDNEY AND AUCKLAND

First published 1991 by Pan Books Ltd
This paperback edition published 1992 by Pan Books Ltd,
a division of Pan Macmillan Limited
Cavaye Place, London SW10 9PG
Associated companies throughout the world

1 3 5 7 9 8 6 4 2

ISBN 0 330 31278 2

Phototypeset by Intype, London
Printed in England by Clays Ltd, St Ives plc

For Lucien again
and for Daphne
who takes in my dogs when I'm away
and treats them as her own.

My thanks are due to my favourite *bodega* of Williams & Humbert Ltd, Nuno de Cañas, 1, Jerez de la Frontera, Cádiz, Spain. In particular to Señor Don L. Eduardo Jacobs, who showed me round and answered all my questions some twenty-five years ago, and Mr Thomas V. W. Spencer of the Public Relations Department today. One can but marvel at the many changes that have taken place in the intervening years, but the kindness and the courtesy of sherry makers is happily what it always was and always will be.

My thanks are also due to the *bodegas* of Montilla-Moriles who, despite our difficulties with language and the heat of the day, gave me more of their time than they could easily spare, as well as a great deal of wine and laughter.

How often the cup has clothed the wings of
darkness with a mantle of shining light!

From the wine came forth the sun. The orient
was the hand of the gracious cupbearer,
and my loved one's lips were the occident.

From the Diwan of Principe Marwan
(963–1003).

Prologue

It was 24 October 1833 and the whole of Spain seemed to be waiting for the fateful pronouncement. Behind the balcony of the Ayuntamiento of Madrid an uneasy collection of men had gathered, most of them dressed in the historic uniforms of their offices.

'There'll be trouble over this, you mark my words!' one of them muttered in an aside to the High Sheriff. 'How are we going to explain ourselves to Don Carlos when he gets here?'

'*If* he gets here —'

'*If* he gets here!' the Dean of the Town Hall snorted. 'Doña Isabella may be our rightful queen and all that, but she's still a three-year-old girl with a foreign whore for a mother, a whore moreover who plans on being Regent no doubt and who, as likely as not, will bring us all to ruin. The uncle would make the better monarch, whatever one may think of his claim. And who's to say he's not right, for we may be subject to the Salic law in Spain – there was a great deal of talk about it a few years ago!'

'Talk is talk. Unfortunately Don Carlos won't leave it as just talk! He insists his brother meant him to follow him on to the throne.' He sighed heavily. 'Our lives may be forfeit for what we do today! Have any of us thought of that?'

The most senior of the four Kings-at-Arms raised a

13

tired smile. 'It's too late to change our minds at this hour,' he rebuked him. 'Doña Isabella is undoubtedly the eldest daughter of our late liege lord Fernando VII and, as she is without any legitimate brothers, that makes her Queen of Castile and all the Spains, whatever her uncle has to say about it. Whatever our personal feelings, we are obliged, as we believe in God, to do what is right.'

'It'll mean war,' the first man said gloomily.

'Everything means war in Spain these days!' the High Sheriff retorted. 'The Salic law is a *French* law. If we accept the French writ here, gentlemen, we might just as well not have fought the War of Independence at all.' He considered the matter for a moment. 'The British may decide to back the claim of our little Isabella – especially if the French declare for the other side!' he added cynically.

The other gentlemen nodded grimly. The War of Independence, which the British called the Peninsular War, had cost them all dearly and the gains had been fragile though they had finally succeeded in expelling the unwelcome French – with the help of the almost equally unwelcome British. Now, with a female child mounting the throne and her uncle disputing her inheritance, with an army at his back and a large portion of the country supporting his claim, it looked as though they were back where they started.

The Dean sniffed. 'It's time, gentlemen. Shall we begin?'

A straggly crowd had gathered below the balcony. When the doors opened there was a half-hearted cry of approval, hastily silenced by a fear of the unknown and, even more, a fear that Don Carlos would count them as traitors for welcoming the proclamation of his niece as the rightful Queen of all the Spains. They could all feel the civil war coming, the first of many that were to tear Spain apart for the whole of the next century to come.

The Dean of the *ayuntamiento*, the High Sheriff and the Standard-Bearer followed the four Kings-at-Arms out on to the balcony, none of them relishing the task that was ahead of them.

'¡*Oíd, oíd, oíd!*' shouted the senior King-at-Arms. 'Oyez, oyez, oyez! Castile, Castile, Castile, for Queen Doña Isabella II!'

A ragged cheer greeted the proclamation.

'At least she bears the right name,' someone remarked. 'The Catholic Isabel did well for Spain!'

'God's blessing be with the child!' a woman prayed.

'Ay, she'll need all the help she can get!' another worthy muttered in agreement and spat accurately into the gutter below the balcony.

Book One

Enemies and Lovers

Let us now praise famous men and our fathers that begat us

Ecclesiastes 44, 1.

'El Draque *will get you if you're not good.'*

Common saying in the Province of Cádiz, even today, in memory of the time Sir Francis Drake 'singed the King of Spain's beard' in 1587, carrying away with him 2,900 pipes of wine.

Chapter One

Madrid, Winter 1833

Colonel Thomas Harris, faced with the prospect of visiting Spain once more, had set about his preparations with all his usual sang-froid. A soldier went where he was sent and he didn't waste time arguing about his orders. That much he had learned in his first few days in the Royal Horse Artillery. An officer did his duty first, last and all the time, his own preferences coming a long way further down the list of his priorities. And, even while Thomas Harris had long since made the transition into politics, representing a convenient constituency in his own native Hampshire, he took his political responsibilities as seriously as he had his military ones; and if the government required a first-hand account of what was actually going on in Spain now that the child-queen Isabella II had ascended the throne, then that is what he would provide them with, no matter what the cost to himself and his own feelings.

Thomas Harris's first battle had been the Battle of Salamanca in the Peninsular War where he had fought under Wellington himself. It was there that his first and best military friend had been killed, sickening him of war for all time . . .

He had seen Edward Nightingale a short distance away

and had raised a weary hand to him. Nightingale, still looking remarkably fresh, had come trotting over towards him. Together they had set off after the retreating French, only to find that the Spanish garrison who were supposed to be guarding the ford across the river had pulled out at the very moment they were most needed.

Clenching his teeth, Thomas had ridden off to find his commander to break the news to him, leaving Edward Nightingale to line their gun up on the departing French. He had heard the crack of a nearby musket and had looked back to see what had happened in time to see his friend slip slowly from the saddle, a tell-tale stain of blood discolouring the blue of his jacket. One part of his brain knew what had happened at once, another couldn't believe that death could come in such an ordinary guise, as casual as a handshake, without any warning or fanfare, a silent ending, lacking even the drama of being tossed off one's mount.

'My God, Edward!' he had cried in disbelief.

He had wheeled his horse round, galloping back to his friend, his feet hitting the ground long before the animal had come to a stop. He had already known it was too late.

'Dead, is he?' his bombardier had asked.

Thomas Harris had turned a shocked face in the man's direction. 'He can't be! He was enjoying himself! He knew we'd won, you see. The French are beaten!'

'Ay, sir. But they've still got their guns *and* their ammunition. If you don't mind my saying so, you'd best leave him! Can't do him any good now, can you?'

There had been sense in that. Thomas had closed the staring eyes and had eased Nightingale's body into a less contorted position. He had crouched down beside the inert figure for a long moment, not thinking of anything at all. Then he had looked down at himself and had been unsurprised to see that he had wet himself, a great stain of fluid down the muddied legs of his once white pantaloons. His greatest urge had been to find himself a woman and empty his despair and great longing for life deep inside her; for that moment he hadn't cared what woman, any woman who had been warm and alive and whom he could have pressed close against himself and felt the beat of a living heart next to his own. He had been shocked by the strength of his own need; shocked because he should have been thinking of his friend, not of himself. He had felt a great anger and distaste for the whole business of war and the waste it brought in its wake. He had wanted to shake the life back into his friend, almost hating him for dying, and hating Spain for being the venue of his own loss.

'Oh my God!' he had whispered through cracked lips. 'Is Spain – is anything – worth the death of any man? I'll never again believe it can be so!'

. . . Facing the Duke of Wellington across the room so many years later – why it must be more than twenty since he had first fought under the old man's command – Thomas Harris had remembered his friend and his own reluctance ever to return to Spain. The Duke of Wellington was no longer the King's first minister, but such was the regard in which he was held by both establishment and monarch that Thomas thought it was only a matter of time until he would be back, holding the reins in his inimitable manner. The new French Revolution of 1830 had shaken the old man, not that Wellington would even consider that the British might rise against their government in a similar manner. Not even the burning down of the Houses of Parliament, though that was now known to be an accident, had altered Wellington's opinion of the British people. Nor had his opinion of the French altered one jot since that glorious day on the battlefield of Waterloo.

'Is it the Spanish you want to know about, or what the French are up to now in Spain?' Thomas had enquired, striking an elegant pose beside the window. He preferred to place himself where he could see rather than be seen by the other people in the room.

'Both!' Wellington had muttered, as bluff as he always

was when he was not actually on the battlefield. 'But beware! I don't want them to know we're watching them, you understand? You must have a good reason for visiting Spain. Think you can manage that?'

Thomas Harris had already had his friend's mother, Mrs Nightingale, in mind. The two of them had maintained their friendship after Edward's death and Tom Harris's subsequent visit to the Nightingale estate to tell her in person how her son had died. She no longer lived in the old house, of course; that had gone with the rest of the estate to a distant relative of her dead husband's, but she had been allowed to make her home in the dower house on the edge of Home Farm, and Thomas admired the way she had come to terms with her double loss of son and position in the West Riding of Yorkshire.

'I wonder if Edward Nightingale's mother would accompany me to Madrid,' he had mooted thoughtfully. 'A very charming individual and she has long wanted to see for herself the country where her son died.'

'Mrs Nightingale? Yes, I do remember her! Has a way of finding out a great deal more than you mean her to know! Is that the lady?'

'It is indeed!'

The Duke of Wellington had never lost his eye for the ladies. 'Pretty woman in her day!' he had said with satisfaction. 'I remember dancing with her once at Carlton House. Great shame, her losing first her husband and then her son like that! Edward was a friend of yours, was he?'

'Yes, sir, he was.'

'Before Waterloo, I take it?'

'He was killed at Salamanca.'

Wellington had sighed in sympathy. 'So many good friends were lost against the French that we can't afford to lose yet more through carelessness in finding out what they are up to now, what?'

Even after all these years, Thomas could see again that awful moment as if it were yesterday, when Edward's body had slid out of the saddle and on to the ground, the victim of a stray French bullet. Mrs Nightingale had had some idea that Thomas should marry the pretty young daughter of their nearest neighbour in Edward's stead but, whilst Thomas had liked her well enough, he had been far from ready to marry anyone and settle down in those days and after Waterloo nothing had mattered to him for a long while, only the guilt he felt at being still alive when so many of his friends had died and been buried abroad, having given their all for their country. The slaughter of the officers on the field that day had been directly responsible for his preferment, together with two commendations on his actions from Wellington himself, one a Mention in Dispatches after Salamanca, as Edward had predicted, and again, at Waterloo. There Wellington had personally promoted him colonel on the field, an honour that had led directly to his political career. It had been good, too, that Old Nosey, as his men referred to him, had been created Duke of Wellington – he had deserved it for the services he had rendered the whole of Europe – but Thomas couldn't help hoping the old man would never be called on to serve his country in that capacity ever again.

'I suppose Mrs Nightingale could manage such a journey?' the elder man had asked.

Thomas had suppressed a grin. 'Better than either one of us, sir. She has always wanted to see something of the world and where better to start than Spain —'

'Will you tell her why you are taking her with you?'

'She is more trustworthy than many a soldier I have had to do with. We have already spoken about the Spanish disturbances and she knows my opinion that they are never happy, any of them, unless they're fighting one another! I ask you, if any civilized nation put a female child of three, or four, on the throne, it would arrange a proper regent for her, not a scandalous mother like hers! And as for Don Carlos, even if the niece is deprived of the throne by that Salic law nonsense that disallows any female from claiming their legitimate inheritance, the man is still a savage! Very proud and well bred, and full of dramatic, grand gestures that serve his wholly selfish insistence on his supposed rights, whatever becomes of Spain. There's nothing to choose between them in my opinion!'

'Very likely not if Spain were all we have to consider. Everyone in this country is too involved with the Irish wanting their independence to see further than the end of their noses but, in my experience, it always pays to keep a wary eye on the French.'

Thomas had laughed out loud at that. 'It was always the depth of your intelligence that set you apart as a military commander, sir! What do *you* think is really going on in Spain?'

Wellington had turned his head so that Thomas had a good view of the famous profile by which he was known throughout the land.

'Damned beautiful country! Good hunting in the winter months too! Pity to let the French have their way with it. The trouble with you, Thomas, is that you always were half in love with the country and didn't want anyone to know it! Never went back, did you?'

Thomas had given the Duke a thoughtful glance. 'No, sir, I never did.'

Mrs Nightingale was, Thomas Harris had always thought, a very handsome woman and, if anything, she was even more so in old age than when he had first seen her on his first visit to Yorkshire in Edward's company. Having no immediate family of his own – only a bachelor uncle who had little time for the interests and concerns of his orphaned nephew – Thomas had been grateful for Mrs Nightingale's continued interest in him, long after the death of her son. She had become a frequent visitor at the house he had recently acquired near Winchester, taking into her own hands much of the new decoration he had set in train, making suggestions here and there, but never imposing her will once he had told her what he wanted.

'You know, Thomas, your wife should be doing all this for you, not an old woman like me!' she had said to him more than once. 'Don't leave it too late, dear boy. A man is not too old at forty, but at fifty —? Your children are the nearest I shall ever come to having grandchildren and I shall be very disappointed if you don't provide me with at least one to spoil in the days to come.'

But Thomas still had no plans for marriage. The young women he knew bored him. The traditional beauties were insipid to his eye and those who might have caught his interest seemed cowed by the stronger characters of their Mamas intent on marrying off their daughters before they could be considered to be at their last prayers. Mrs Nightingale had taught him that the mistress of any household was the person who set the tone of its whole atmosphere and he frankly shuddered at the thought of having to go outside his own home every time he wanted a little peace . . .

He had chewed on his lip thoughtfully, returning his thoughts to the business in hand.

'Is Don Carlos right in thinking the Salic law should apply to Spain?' he had asked the Duke suddenly.

'Probably. No one in their right mind could think a three-year-old girl is the answer to their problems, especially when one looks at the mother! However, there is no doubt that the Doña Isabella is her father's legal heir according to their own law. Salic law is a *French* law, imposed by them. Fernando VII probably had an opinion, but he changed his mind so many times that Don Carlos certainly can make out a grievance against him and would probably make a better monarch than that poor child ever will! The point is that if these civil disturbances continue the French will be back in charge before we know it and our own influence will count for naught. We hold Gibraltar, but that won't be worth much if France holds all Spain. We'll be back where we started before Badajos, Salamanca, Vittoria or any of the battles in what they're pleased to call their War of Independence.'

'Does our own government appreciate that?' Thomas had asked, with just a touch of bitterness, for he had long ago despaired of getting most of his fellow countrymen to take a proper interest in the affairs of Europe as a whole.

Wellington's whole aspect had changed. Gone was the country squire, with his eye for the ladies and his bluff manners. In its place had appeared the military man, his strategy dependent always on the very latest and best intelligence, his tactics flexible and frequently inspired.

'They will have to when you bring back your report. No one doubts your integrity, Colonel Harris, no matter if he supports our party or not, and that makes you a valuable player in the game. If our government has chosen to forget all about Spain, you are just the man to remind them of its existence. Shall we drink to that?'

Thomas had been flattered, colouring up as if he were much younger than his forty odd years. Besides, if the old man was right in thinking Spain was on the boil again, he could also be right in thinking Thomas was more than half in love with the place. He had found himself remembering the golden, spectacular scenery that had first taken his eye: the blazing sun and the glare that came off the white houses and the white streets, slashed by the black of shadows, and the blues, yellows and especially the scarlets, of the flowers that grew on every window sill. This business with the Irish had done nothing to lessen his dislike of their superstitious religion yet, as with the Irish, he couldn't help but admire the devotion it seemed to inspire in both the powerful and the insignificant. All in all, he thought, it would be good to go back and see again the country where he had lost so many of his friends. After more than twenty years he thought he could look on both land and people with a kinder, more mature eye than he had as a young man still in his teens. In an odd way, he was even looking forward to it.

Mrs Nightingale hadn't hesitated in accepting his invitation to accompany him to Madrid. 'Why, Thomas, what a very kind thought!' she had said at once. 'You know how much I have always longed to see the country where Edward met his end. Oh yes, my dear, I know I've never said anything to you, because I have always felt you took a dislike to Spain because of the silly circumstances in which he died, but I'm told the Spanish have a saying that to die well and bravely is the "Moment of Truth" that sums up a whole lifetime. I have gained great comfort from the thought and I would like to know more of any people who can think like that.'

'There's another purpose to our going,' Thomas had told her, uncomfortably, because he had no time for any such sentiments himself. Dying had very little to do with the living as far as he was concerned. 'We need to find out all that we can about the quarrel between the Doña Isabella and her uncle.'

Mrs Nightingale's steady gaze had made him wonder briefly what her husband had been like. Edward had never been serious for two minutes put together, but Mrs Nightingale seldom laughed although he had never known her be less than cheerful.

'I see,' she had said at last. 'Don't tell me any more and then I shan't be tempted to betray any secrets.' Then suddenly she had giggled, looking like a naughty little girl and much more as he had remembered Edward. 'Oh, Thomas, I do believe you are going to Spain as a government spy and I am to be your *cover*! How clever of you to think of it! I vow I never thought to play such a romantic role! What fun to listen to everyone's conversations and try to decide what they are getting up to!'

Thomas had favoured her with a reluctant grin. 'Yes, but nobody must guess what we're up to!' he had told her sternly. 'It's all very unofficial.'

Her eyes had danced, spoiling the effect of her meek expression. 'It wouldn't be any fun at all if it weren't a secret mission, I assure you! I vow I never thought to be asked to play such an important part!'

Belatedly recognizing that he was being teased, Thomas had said nothing more on the subject and, as she herself had never referred to it again, he half-hoped she had forgotten all about the real significance of their journey.

Indeed, he was very well satisfied with his choice of fellow traveller. Mrs Nightingale had made the intelligent, delightful companion on their journey that he had known she would. Her French was as nearly perfect as was anyone's of his acquaintance, and so she was easily able to make her own way in society without his having to be on hand all the time to find suitable partners for her, or to make sure she was being properly entertained.

'Don't give me a thought, Thomas, if you have things to do!' she pleaded with him. 'I find the Spanish to be quite charming and not at all the proud primitives you have always claimed them to be.' She smiled, plainly amused by his reception of this piece of information. 'Don't look so worried, my dear, who wouldn't like to be found *simpática* by the handsomest men in Europe, even at my advanced age?'

'You're a breath of fresh air in any society, ma'am. I was about to ask you to accompany me to a ball, as I have hopes General Ramón Cabrero is to be one of the guests. I am told he is about to take up arms in the Carlist cause, but if you are engaged on more pressing matters —?'

Mrs Nightingale's laughter died away. 'Oh dear! Do you really want me to come with you?'

'If you won't mind being something of a wallflower for once? A great many people of note will be there and I'm hoping their ladies will be sufficiently bored to be indiscreet. There is little time for talking whilst one is dancing, don't you find?'

'I understand exactly. What fun! But, Thomas dear, have a care, won't you? Something tells me it's better if you don't commit yourself to either side.'

'Oh?'

She shook her fan at him. 'You know very well what I'm talking about,' she complained, 'so don't pretend you don't! Men are not nearly as discreet in the company of women as they imagine! – and I am quite sure you didn't come all this way only to hear one side of the question?'

Thomas gave her a sharp look. 'Have you heard anything about Cabrero?'

'Nothing to his credit, and I don't imagine he is called "the Tiger" for nothing. In fact terrorizing anyone who doesn't agree with him seems to be his chosen method of going on altogether. But I admit to a certain prejudice in favour of that poor child! Fate has dealt her an impossible hand and, somehow, she doesn't *look* lucky, poor little thing. She's going to grow up into a plain, dumpy female, and I have the horrid idea that that is the one thing for which the Spanish will never forgive her! They are the most *elegant* people, don't you think? Even the peasants begging in the street have an air about them. And to think I used to think the French were chic, let alone the first circles in London!'

Thomas Harris knew better than to ignore her warning. 'Do you still mean to go on to Salamanca?' he asked her. 'The ball is not for several weeks yet.'

'I do. But you're not to worry about me, Thomas! Someone from the Embassy is going to escort me and that's how I prefer it. Edward would have disliked it very much if I were to cry all over his grave with his best friend looking on. The Nightingales were never ones to wear their hearts on their sleeves!'

Thomas was glad he was not to be asked to escort her to Salamanca. He wondered if she knew how he still felt about the suddenness and the sheer lack of necessity for Edward's death. Since that terrible day he had had other friends die and had mourned them as deeply, but it was only the memory of Edward Nightingale's demise – and of his own humiliating reaction to it – that brought the bitter taste of disillusionment into his mouth. What had that bombardier thought of him, shaking him by the shoulder and pleading with him to get up and play the man? It was not something he liked to dwell on, even now.

Generally speaking, Thomas was pleased with the way

their visit to Madrid was going. As someone from the British Army who had done so much to gain Spain the victory in their own War of Independence, he had expected to be made welcome and he was not disappointed. Both he and Mrs Nightingale had been invited everywhere, Mrs Nightingale's Spanish improving daily, although most of the people with whom they mixed spoke both French and English as well as their own language. If he had felt a twinge of anxiety when she had guessed what their mission in Madrid was to be, he had had reason to be glad that she knew ever since. Her discretion was admirable and her methods impeccable so that he began to think she received more confidences than any other lady in Spain. He missed her quick wits and her calm good humour more than he thought possible when she finally made her pilgrimage to her son's grave at Salamanca. All the while she was away, he felt more exposed to his enemies than he had thought possible and he realized all over again what a valuable ally he had in this charming woman.

Mrs Nightingale returned from Salamanca barely a week after she had taken her leave. Thomas thought she might have been saddened by the experience, but she arrived dry-eyed and full of plans for a hectic season in Madrid.

'I've done with being sad for the time being,' she told Thomas, 'and now I mean to enjoy myself. Did you obtain tickets for the ball?'

'They're waiting for us at the British Embassy. Does your escort to Salamanca mean to take you to the ball as well?' Thomas teased her.

Her glance was serene. 'Unless you mean to take me yourself? Mr Fanshawe is a very charming gentleman and knows simply everyone in Madrid. He remains on good terms with the families of both sides and that is somewhat unusual, as I'm sure you'll admit?'

Thomas's slow smile answered her. 'I'm curious to meet a certain Señorita Francisca Urquiza —'

'*Thomas!* You've fallen in love at last!'

'I've never met the lady!' he denied.

Mrs Nightingale abandoned the idea reluctantly. 'Why else should you want to meet her?'

'She used to be affianced to General Cabrero. I have to admit to a certain curiosity about her. It seems that while he has declared for the uncle, *her* family is standing by the Doña Isabella.'

Mrs Nightingale's laughter fell away from her. 'Cabrero again! The man's a monster, if all I hear about him is true. Don Carlos will lose any friends he has if he doesn't call that man to heel! It isn't only I who am revolted by his methods, the whole Embassy is worried by him. What if the other side were to retaliate in kind? Civil war is always nasty, but this would be beyond anything!'

'He is, as you say, a monster,' Thomas agreed.

'Is that why you're interested in him?'

'I'm told he is the kind of soldier who will do his duty to the end,' Thomas said wryly. 'I shouldn't like to come up against him.'

Mrs Nightingale managed a light laugh. 'One of the few advantages of being a woman is that I shall never have to meet him on the field of battle! It will be bad enough if I have to meet him on the dance floor!'

The day of the ball began quietly. Mr Fanshawe called in the morning, eager to put his name against the first and last dances in Mrs Nightingale's card, as well as gaining her permission to take her down to supper. Thomas was surprised to find the 'charming Mr Fanshawe' was barely five feet tall, as round as a ball, and with a waspish sense of humour that made most people respect him more than they actually liked him. Mrs Nightingale was as calm and serene as ever in his presence, smiling at his jokes and making up her own mind as to his assessment of the Spanish amongst whom he mixed as often as he did with the visiting Britons from home.

As they were readying themselves to leave for the ball, Mrs Nightingale tapped Thomas on the arm with her fan. 'You needn't worry that Mr Fanshawe will distract me from my real task, my dear. To tell the truth, I think he may be of the greatest value to us both. Fear of getting on the wrong side of that tongue of his gets him into houses where few foreigners are invited.'

'I shouldn't imagine you have anything to fear from him,' Thomas rejoined.

'Good heavens, no! My life is an open book for anyone to read. One has to have a great many secrets for Mr Fanshawe to be any danger to one's reputation. Besides, I rather like the man!'

Thomas grinned. 'There's little doubt that he returns that sentiment. You have a conquest there!'

Mrs Nightingale raised an eyebrow, unperturbed. 'I hope I've made a friend. I'm too old for conquests – which you are not! If you'd only set your mind to the matter, I'm sure you'd have half the females there tonight in a flutter! You're far too serious, Thomas, and if no one else will tell you so, I shall!'

It took nearly an hour before their names were announced to their host and hostess. As they slowly mounted the stairs, both of them took the opportunity to look about them and see who else was there.

'I notice your General Cabrero hasn't arrived yet,' Mrs Nightingale remarked when they had finally gained the ballroom and she had seated herself amongst the dowagers, with whom she was already on the most friendly terms, agreeably chaperoning at least two young ladies while their mothers and aunts amused themselves with a game of cards in another room.

'No, he is already turning the country upside down over by Valencia.' Thomas tried not to let his disapproval of the man to show in his voice. He did not consider it was part of any officer's duty, no matter in what cause, to murder or rape women, still less little children, as rumour had it were the methods of Cabrero, and which were bound to lead to similar atrocities from the other side sooner or later.

'Did you know he trained to be a priest at one time?'

Mrs Nightingale went on, never taking her eyes off her young charges for a single moment.

Thomas froze. 'That would explain everything!'

Mrs Nightingale shook her head at him. 'Or nothing at all! It may explain a certain rigidity of purpose, but it doesn't explain his cruelty. You shouldn't believe all you hear about the evils of the Papist Church, my dear. Much of what we believe of them can be put down to politics of one kind and another, and their beliefs about us Protestants likewise.'

Normally Thomas would have agreed with her. He knew himself too well not to be aware that one man's devotion was another's superstition, yet all through the Irish question in the House and in all his other dealings with the Roman Catholic Church, he had found their pretensions remarkably difficult to deal with, nor did he like the way so many of them put their allegiance to Rome above that which they owed to anything or anyone else. He knew they would claim to be putting God first, but he thought that to be an illusion. He hadn't noticed the Pope putting God first when it came to the details of how he ruled the Papal States in Italy.

He looked round the crowd, seeking anyone who resembled the description he had received of Francisca Urquiza, and was struck again by the beauty of the Spanish women. Unlike their English counterparts, Spanish ladies weren't restricted to the pastel shades in their dress. Many of them favoured scarlet, strong blues, and even the black of their elders if they should be in mourning, and there were few dressed in the pale pinks, the creams, or the unflattering white in which all the young English girls he knew draped themselves before marriage.

It was then that he noticed the most beautiful girl he had ever seen in his life. She wasn't particularly tall, but she held herself so proudly she could have been the tallest woman there. Her hair was black and dressed with a comb the value of which he could only guess at. Her complexion was creamy and her expression one of pure enjoyment.

She was a born dancer, he noted, tapping her high heels on the few occasions when her admirers allowed her to rest for a few moments, as if she were as reluctant as they to miss even a few moments of the music.

'Why don't you ask her to dance, Thomas?' Mrs Nightingale suggested, noting his interest with approval. 'Shall I introduce you?'

Thomas reddened. 'You know her?'

'She's in my care while her friend's mother is otherwise engaged. The friend she is staying with is Francisca Urquiza, by the way, whom you also wanted to meet, I believe?'

'Never mind that now! Who is the other one?'

'The *Señorita* Doña Pilar Morena. Beautiful, isn't she?'

But Thomas was beyond answering. More than anything, he wanted to feel that slim body in his arms, to speak with her for a while to find out if her whole person was as enticing as its exterior. He wanted her for himself, no matter what the odds against her – or even more her family – ever agreeing to such a match for her. He was quite suddenly out of his depth, head over heels in love with her, uncaring that she was little more than a child, while he, he supposed, was old enough to be her father, or very nearly.

He stood, hearing nothing of the introduction, seeing only the proud way she held her head and the mischief in her eyes as she looked at him.

'I had always heard the English didn't dance,' she mocked him, courteously slowing her speech to make it more comprehensible to him. 'We speak English, yes? My English is better than my French. My French is very bad because I never listen to my lessons.'

He smiled, delighted. 'What else have you heard about the English?'

Her laughter was a delicious, husky sound that made him tingle from head to foot. She peeked up at him through her lashes, trying to look far more sophisticated and experienced than she was. 'Why that they are all *espadachíns* – impossible to live with! That as husbands they are *tiranos odiosos* –'

He laughed along with her. 'Do I look like a roistering bully?' he demanded. 'I am the mildest of men! And, as for being a tyrant, you could twist me round your finger any time you chose!'

She was demure and thoughtful after that. 'One day I shall find out if you tell me lies to make me like you! I am told the English are great liars – and braggarts!'

He felt her slight withdrawal as she stood back to see how he would take such an accusation. He watched her complete the complicated steps of the dance, moving away from him and returning once again. His hands tightened on hers.

'It can be dangerous to call an Englishman a liar!'

A flirtatious gleam escaped her demure expression. '*Embastero!*' she whispered, the tip of her tongue appearing between her lips. '*Insensato!*'

His urge to kiss her was almost unbearable, but the dance had already taken her from him again, looking back at him over her shoulder, well pleased at having had the last word.

Thomas Harris returned her to Mrs Nightingale with reluctance. 'May I have another dance later on?' he asked her.

She looked sadly back at him. 'It wouldn't be proper, *Señor Inglés*, for us to dance together more than once. In Spain, we have to be very careful how we behave, not at all like your English ladies who do as they like and have a great many lovers, no?' Suddenly she was laughing again. 'If you wish to see me again you must learn the custom of "plucking the turkey". It would be very romantic if you come to Córdoba –'

' "Plucking the turkey"? I've never heard of the custom.'

'No,' she explained, making a face at him, 'but that is because you do not take we women at all seriously. Your

Mrs Nightingale tells me you are not married – 'ave never been in love! It is sad, no?'

'And what if I do come to Córdoba?'

She shook her head, her eyes big and tragic. 'You have no time for the Spanish courtship! First, you must walk backwards and forwards outside my house. Then you must seek my father's permission to write me a note. Then, perhaps, he will give his permission for us to speak together through the window-grille. After a year, you may be allowed to call and see me face to face – in the presence of both my mother and my father, you understand?'

'I understand why it's called "plucking the turkey"! The miracle is that any of you ever get married at all!'

'You must not mock our customs, *Señor guerrero*! It's reasonable our parents should take care their daughters don't marry with pirates and brigands. It is better we should know something about each other, and that our families should know each other —'

'Will your family assent to your marrying an Englishman?'

She was embarrassed by his forthrightness. 'I don't know – I think not! They are in Córdoba, *señor*, and I am here! Who knows how anyone's fate may turn out? My friend, the *Señorita* Francisca Urquiza was the *novia* of a great Spanish gentleman and he has abandoned her to fight the Carlist cause! Never mind, she would not wish to marry with a traitor, but who else will want to marry her now?'

'You are not affianced to anyone?' he asked urgently.

She shook her head again. 'Perhaps I am waiting for you to come to Córdoba! Will you come?'

He had no chance to answer as a thrusting young man, so like the girl in his appearance that he could only have been her brother, moved purposely between them, his hand searching for the hilt of his sword.

'My sister's card is full, *señor*. She is too young to dance outside the circle of her family's friends – even with a gentleman as highly recommended as you are by Mrs Nightingale.'

Thomas Harris inclined his head, resenting the young man's dismissal of his hopes. 'Perhaps I may be allowed to call on your parents some day soon?' he enquired pleasantly.

'You would have to travel to Córdoba to do that, *Señor* Englishman. With the roads in the state they are, with robbers waiting to steal from the unwary at every corner, you would be better advised to remain in Madrid. There is no shortage of other beautiful women in the capital. You have but to choose and I shall introduce you to her Mamá myself!'

Thomas Harris refused with all the freezing dignity at his command. The young man seemed not even to notice.

'She is very young, Thomas,' Mrs Nightingale sought to console him.

Thomas sat down stiffly beside her. 'Young and beautiful,' he agreed.

Mr Fanshawe, who had been entertaining Mrs Nightingale with a series of stories about the other guests, clapped Thomas sympathetically on the shoulder, amused that a man of his mettle should be so obvious.

'The Doña Pilar Morena is bound to be closely protected by her family, my dear sir. You must be very careful where such young ladies are concerned, I warn you! She is of true aristocratic blood and has probably been promised to some other young blade since she was in her cradle. Her family comes from Córdoba' – he raised his eyes to heaven ' – and there the women are even more closely guarded by their families than they are here in Madrid. You have no chance there, no matter how highly you are regarded at home. The Lord only knows, the Spanish are a stiff-necked people at best!'

'Pilar,' Thomas forced himself to say. 'What a strange name!'

'Why strange? *La santísima Virgen del Pilar* guards the spirit of the Holy Faith here in Spain. It's much the same

Came Forth The Sun

as when our countrywomen claim the patronage of the
Mother of Our Lord by being called after her. You don't
object to that, do you?'

Thomas mumbled that he didn't. One might, he
supposed, conclude that a Mary might have come by her
name that way. Nothing wrong with Mary as a name
after all! Pilar, however, was all of a piece with the
incomprehensible superstition with which the Papists
chose to lace their religion. Doña Pilar Morena! He would
remember her for many a moon, he thought, and
wondered if the entrancing, beautiful young girl had
thought to enquire what *his* name was from any of her
friends. If he thought there was any chance of his fixing
his interest with her, he might have tried to persuade Mrs
Nightingale to accompany him on a visit to Córdoba, but
he already knew that any romance between the two of
them would be over before it began. He didn't need her
brother's thrusting hip to tell him what her family's
reaction would be to his suit. He doubted they would
allow him inside the door of their family home, no matter
how willing the girl herself might be.

He danced several times more during the evening, but
none of his partners meant anything to him. It was the
Doña Pilar Morena who had taken possession of his mind
and heart, no matter what difficulties were put in his way,
and he could think of nothing else but the way she had
smiled at him and every word she had said to him. She
was the only woman he had ever wanted to marry, and
the only woman he ever would want to marry, and
somehow or other, sooner or later, he meant to find a
way of marrying her, despite her family and everyone else
who would try to keep them apart.

Mrs Nightingale saw his preoccupation, but wisely held
her own counsel. To every appearance she was scarcely
attending to Mr Fanshawe's long discourse on how the
English and the Spanish were natural enemies, and how
the dreadful General Ramón Cabrero was a major reason
of why they always should be. She was listening to his

every word only for what she could pick up that might be useful to Thomas, even while, with another part of her mind, she was wondering if she would ever now see Thomas married and hold his children in her arms. She called the Spanish girl to her side in unfriendly tones but, seeing the bleak look in the girl's black eyes, her heart softened towards her.

'Come and sit beside me for a while, Doña Pilar,' she invited her. 'And don't look so tragic, child. Thomas Harris is not a man to be easily defeated, as I have good reason to know.' And she went on hurriedly, telling the young girl all about her own son who had died for Spain so many years before, and was not at all surprised when Pilar said at last, 'Yes, it is very sad, but it is this Tomás who is alive and who is like a son to you, and it is much better to be alive than dead, no? Will you please tell Tomás I said this, and that to live well is a duty one owes to God, man or woman!'

Mrs Nightingale fluttered her fan. 'I'll certainly tell him, but I'm not sure I understand —'

'Tomás will understand,' Pilar told her with simple certainty. 'He will understand exactly, because I don't think we shall ever see each other again. And because he is a good man – even if he is an abominable Englishman, with no manners and no finesse! And I shall do my duty also because that is the way it has to be.'

Mrs Nightingale gave her charge a startled look. For an instant she saw the Spanish girl through Thomas's eyes and wished she had a magic wand to wave that would bring the two of them together. She only hoped this dignified Spanish girl wouldn't have spoilt Thomas for ever marrying anyone else, but she thought she could understand it if she had.

Chapter Two

Madrid/Toledo, Spring 1834

Civil war is invariably nasty and this, the first of a long series of struggles between uncle and niece and their descendants, was nastier than most. Thomas Harris and Mrs Nightingale remained in Madrid for the whole winter; the former because he hoped to find some excuse that would take him to Córdoba, the latter because she was enjoying herself better than she had for many a year.

'My dear Thomas, I simply can't understand your doubts about the Spanish. I can't remember when I've had a more delightful time. What is it about them that makes you so prickly in their presence?'

Thomas Harris was finding it difficult to make up his own mind why he distrusted everyone who had any power in Spain, from the Royal Family downwards. He couldn't rid himself of the idea that the men thought, and very often behaved, like women, and he had never been one of those who professed to understand anything about the weaker sex, not even the smiling woman who had been such an asset to him ever since their arrival in the Spanish capital.

'They make too much over too little,' he answered.

'If you think that, then I should avoid Córdoba over Easter,' Mrs Nightingale recommended calmly. 'I'm told the processions anywhere in the south are too gruesome for words, though magnificent in their own way, of course.'

The Colonel brightened. 'Córdoba? Perhaps you would wish to see these processions, ma'am? I'd be pleased to escort you there.'

'Yes, I'm sure you would, which brings me to what I am about to tell you. Now, please don't ask me to tell where I heard the story because I haven't the least intention of telling you, but I'm very much afraid it may be true. You remember the so-called Tiger, General Cabrero?'

Thomas grunted his assent.

'I am told his mother has been taken hostage to try and put an end to the worst of his atrocities. It won't work, for the Tiger strikes me as being completely ruthless and his revenge will be truly terrible if they do assassinate her, which is what they are threatening him with.'

Thomas smiled ruefully. 'Now you know why I feel prickly, as you call it, when it comes to Spanish politics! No civilized people would threaten to kill old ladies, no matter what kind of son they had been unfortunate enough to mother!'

'It's a long time since we had civil war in England. When we did, Mr Cromwell saw no reason why he shouldn't slaughter every inhabitant of some of the towns he took in Ireland and merely because it was cheaper on the public purse! Thomas, dear, if I can forgive the way Edward died, why can't you?'

Thomas shrugged, reluctant to abandon an old prejudice which had served him well in the past, when the truth was he had come to like and admire a great deal of what he had seen in Spain.

'Are you afraid to risk the roads to Córdoba?' he asked with a slight smile.

'Oh no, not if you are making the arrangements. The thing is, Thomas, I fear it would be a wasted journey on your part, because I really don't believe you are interested in religious processions, no matter how magnificent! That is the second thing I have to tell you —'

Thomas shut his eyes. 'Has something happened to *her?*'

'No, my dear. If that had been so, I should have told you of it quite differently, I assure you! It is only another of these rumours that fly round Madrid and probably has as little substance as all the others, but it is being said that Cabrero is seeking revenge for his mother by holding Doña Francisca Urquiza and several of her friends. If the Cristinos – as the Queen's supporters seem to be called, I suppose after the child's mother – kill Cabrero's mother, he'll have all the others executed also – and, I must say, it's just the sort of repulsive thing he probably would do!'

Thomas felt as though he had been delivered a body blow. 'Are you telling me Doña Pilar is still with Francisca Urquiza?'

'Yes, dear. It was thought too dangerous for her to travel about Spain just now and so the Urquizas took her home with them. If it's true that Cabrero is holding the Urquiza girl, he must have captured your Pilar also and – Thomas, where are you going?'

Thomas paused, turning in the doorway. 'I suppose your informant didn't tell you where Cabrero is now?'

Mrs Nightingale sniffed. 'It was Mr Fanshawe, if you must know. He's *always* so reliable about what the Carlists are up to that one might almost suppose him to be one of them! It would seem there has been much talk about Cabrero hoping to make his headquarters at Morella, one of those border frontier towns between Castile and Valencia, but I don't think anyone really knows where he is, or Mr Fanshawe would undoubtedly know about it. Perhaps the General is hoping for greater success there than he had close by Madrid?'

Thomas made an explosive noise in the back of his throat. 'Will you be all right, ma'am, if I leave you on your own in Madrid for a few weeks. I shall inform the Embassy and all our friends —'

Mrs Nightingale's eyes shone very blue. 'Need you ask,

my dear? I shall still be here when you bring her back with you. You will need me then – and she may need me even more! I share your dislike of General Cabrero to the full. If he is the best Don Carlos can find to lead his followers, the sooner someone puts an end to his cause the better! Really, I have no patience with either of them! Nor with whoever it was who was stupid enough to threaten to murder the old lady! I should have thought she had been punished enough – unless she is more like her son than we've been told!'

Thomas rocked back and forth on his heels. 'That could well be. I've heard they're the most devoted mother and son.'

'Then it must be true that he plans her revenge. Official sources must be much more reliable than the kind of gossip I am able to pick up!'

Thomas smiled a wintry smile. 'My dear ma'am, it has been most salutary to see what a pair of sharp ears, coupled with an intelligent mind, can pick up in society. Believe me, you know more of what is happening in Spain than the whole British Embassy.'

He could have said much more on the subject for he had come to value this clear-sighted English woman more than he had ever thought he would. Over the winter he had learned that her judgement was far more to be trusted than the view of Spain as seen through the eyes of the British Embassy, most of whom would have preferred to have been posted anywhere else rather than in Madrid.

It didn't surprise him, therefore, that no one at the Embassy had heard of the *Señora* Cabrero's capture, and that no one cared if she lived or died.

'The Cristinos are as barbaric as the Carlists,' they opined wearily. 'Spain will always be the same. If it weren't for French ambitions where they're concerned, we'd do better to leave them to it! Madame Regent is more concerned about her lovers than the country!'

Thomas buttoned his tongue, reflecting how close Britain was to suffering much the same fate as poor, decadent Spain. He had heard for himself the King speak of his determination to stay alive until his niece was of age in order to keep her mother from ever being Regent in England. King William, the Sailor King, was by no means a popular monarch – it was only the other day he had been spat on in the streets by some of his own subjects – but it was doubtful that the British monarchy would survive if Victoria's mother should ever get her hands on the levers of power, not with republican unrest everywhere on the Continent, and plenty of radicals at home looking for any opportunity to sow the seeds of revolution. Were the British, then, to be considered a barbaric nation also?

Realizing he wasn't going to get any help from anyone in Madrid, Thomas laid his own plans for travelling east to where Cabrero had last been sighted. He travelled alone, keeping himself to himself and avoiding the more frequented roads, hoping thus to avoid the robbers who were reputed to outnumber the respectable citizens who risked their lives and possessions getting from one place to another in this huge, golden, restless land.

He caught up with Cabrero's men on the borders of Castile. He had heard that the Carlist cause had found little support in Madrid amongst the aristocracy and he saw the results in the lack of officers to control the worst excesses of the rough men. Cabrero's army seemed more like a rabble than a disciplined body of men in the chaos they left behind them. When the villagers spoke of them, it was with ill-concealed enmity. Neither their crops nor their daughters were safe, according to the peasants he spoke to asking about Cabrero's whereabouts.

'If you're thinking of joining him, you'd do better with the Devil himself!' the local innkeeper told him. 'I have no time for people who don't pay their bills – whoever they may be!'

'What is General Cabrero doing here?' Thomas asked the man, not really expecting an answer.

'He's taking revenge for his mother's death.' The man

laughed a cruel laugh. 'They say Juan Pórtigaz is the unlucky one who has been chosen to tell him that the Cristinos have executed his mother! I wouldn't be in his shoes for anything – nor in those of the young women he is holding up there in the castle. They say one of them was his own *novia* before all these troubles, yet no one expects him to spare her.'

'Is there any chance of seeing General Cabrero?'

The man shook his head. 'He is intent on revenge, *señor*. For such a one, revenge is better than war, or any cause! We shall be thankful when he and his army have left our town for good. Meanwhile, all we can do is wait and pray for the souls of the young women —'

Thomas muttered a few choice expletives in English. How typical of the Spanish temperament, he thought, that they should accept death so lightly when they made such a fuss about everything else. They would pray – oh yes, they would storm heaven with their prayers! – but they would do nothing practical to save any of the young ladies from General Cabrero's fury. Well, thank God, he was made of sterner stuff and, if there was a way to save Doña Pilar, he was determined he would be the one to find it. He had to be, because if anything were to happen to Doña Pilar Morena, the whole of life would have lost its savour.

He planned his campaign with the same eye for detail he had learned from Wellington himself. There was little chance of carrying off all the women that he could see, but to save one of them – the one he wanted for himself – that was a different matter. Surprise them! That was the best form of attack! He considered his plan again with increasing satisfaction, quite sure in his own mind that one Englishman was the equal of any number of Spaniards in the field. If he had any doubts, it was because nothing had ever mattered to him more than what he was about to do now.

Rather to his surprise, the priest he consulted – the local *cura* of the village – agreed immediately to render what aid he could. If he had any doubts about having dealings

with an English heretic, he kept them to himself. The
Doña Pilar Morena was known to him; indeed, he had
already made it his business to ask the General for
clemency on her behalf on the urgent recommendation of
her usual confessor. When he had taken her the news of
his failure, he had been impressed by her fortitude and
piety and, more than any of the others, his heart had been
warmed by her example and the pride with which she was
comporting herself.

'I will do anything I can to help,' the priest offered at
last, 'but promise me one thing, *Señor* Englishman, if we
succeed in getting the young lady safely away, you will
marry her according to the rites of her own Church. I will
not help to save her body only to have her lose her soul!'

'She may not wish to marry me,' Thomas pointed out.

'She will have no choice once her family gets to hear of
your part in her escape. She has family in Córdoba, and
some in Madrid, and it will be several days before you
can reach either city. Don't fail me in this, *señor*, or you
may consider her to be your wife, but she will know
herself to be no better than your whore —'

Thomas was frankly impatient with such an idea. 'Of
course she will be my wife!' he exclaimed.

The priest smiled, but he made his point all the same.
'In the sight of God – perhaps. In his wisdom, he decreed
that a husband and wife should administer the sacrament
of marriage to each other, but we Catholics, as a matter
of discipline, are obliged to marry in the presence of an
ordained priest before we give way to our desire for one
another. The Doña Pilar may one day want to return to
Spain; you wouldn't want to dishonour her in the eyes of
herself and her own people, would you?'

'Heaven forbid!' Thomas responded. He did not want
to antagonize a valuable ally by suggesting that the services
of his own Church would serve as well as any papist
flummery. Besides, he knew the priest was right and that
Doña Pilar would only be happy if she had the blessing
of her own rites. He had been suspicious of the *cura* before

he had met him, as he would have been of any member
of a breed he regarded as corrupt, superstitious, and
historically given to attempts to subvert the precious
freedoms of England, but he had soon found himself liking
the man and, long before he had left the presbytery to
prepare for his own part in the proceedings, he knew there
was a sympathy between them he would always value.

Thomas spent the rest of the day crawling up and down
the cliffs with the aid of a couple of boys the priest had
recommended to him. Together, they had laid the ropes
by which he hoped he and the Doña Pilar would make
their escape. It was easy enough to keep out of sight of
the fortress, for the boys seemed to have a natural ability
for keeping out of the way of any authority that threatened
their happy-go-lucky existence, supported half by thievery
and half by what work they could find in one of the poorer
villages of Spain, running errands or begging from the
Carlist soldiers. They were strange, ragged boys who
smelt of hunger and the 'catch as catch can' way of life
they led. Colonel Harris had met their English equivalents
in the Ragged Schools of London, acting as boot blacks
on the city streets, or as matchgirls, if they were lucky
enough to find such a job to keep themselves from
starving.

Because he thought he understood the way his young
helpers were thinking, Thomas didn't trust them to buy
the second mount he was going to need for Doña Pilar
and went about the task himself, choosing a small Arab
mare which was a trifle more mettlesome than he would
have liked, but which would be strong enough to make
the dash to Madrid, or even to Córdoba. The boys were
left to attach the ropes he had brought with him to trees,
or to anything they could find that would take the double
weight of a man and a woman, waiting until after dark
before they tested their work, shinning down the ropes to
the safety of the valley below.

They were eager enough to mount guard over the horses

and bring them to the foot of the cliff at the right time. They took the Colonel's money with dignity, and waited until they felt themselves to be unobserved before looking to see how much he had given them.

'There will be a gold piece for each of you tonight,' Thomas promised, pleased by their restraint. He knew many men for whom he had less respect and whom he would have trusted less as a consequence. 'See you at midnight, *muchachos*!'

Harris took up his own position at the foot of the fortress walls, marvelling at how the Spanish were able to build on the most inaccessable places, be it a monastery or castle. He supposed that right from the days of El Cid they had had practice in the art, just as they were well practised in fighting each other, hardly needing the excuse of the present war.

Looking up the steep walls of the fortress of Valderrobes, Thomas imagined that he could hear General Cabrero's cry of 'Pórtigaz, I wish to die! No – to live to revenge her death!' when he had heard of the murder of his mother. A short time later, the order had been given that four of his own female hostages were to be shot, among them Francisca Urquiza and the Doña Pilar Morena. Unless he could prevent it, they would be shot at sunrise the next morning. That was the civilized way, the *cura* had said bitterly, giving the victims time to say their prayers that they might meet their Maker properly shriven and fortified by all the rites of Mother Church. Was it murder, or was it war? Thomas no longer professed to know. As long as he could get the Doña Pilar safely away, he would leave such questions for others to solve. The only thing that mattered was that she should not die! He could taste the fear he felt for her on the back of his tongue in a way that he had never had for himself, not even in the worst moments of battle.

The time passed slowly. Thomas nervously waited for the priest to play his part, still not quite sure that he would, when it came down to it, entrust a good Catholic girl into the hands of a man he considered a heretic. But there he was wrong. The *cura* was doing exactly as he had promised. He had hidden a length of rope beneath his robes and had gone about the business of hearing the condemned women's last confessions with a heavy heart, wishing they could all be spared seeing the new day dawn that was to be their last.

When he came to Doña Pilar, he spoke roughly to the guard, telling him the girl needed a breath of fresh air and that he would stand surety for her safety. Such a young woman should be treated gently to make a proper assessment of how much she had loved God in her short life. She needed time and space in which to remember what sins she had committed, for wasn't she the youngest of them all, brought up in a *hidalgo* household and kept at a distance from all that might distress such a tender conscience?

The guards were indifferent to anything the priest might do, knowing it would be certain death to fall from the great height of the ramparts outside. The *cura* touched his lips with his forefinger to ensure the girl's silence. She watched with wide, frightened eyes as he went to the edge of the ramparts and uttered a piercing whistle that was no doubt meant to sound like the cry of a bird. Then he unwound the rope from beneath his habit, tying one end to the nearest solid looking pillar and the other round Doña Pilar's waist.

'Pray to your Patroness that the pillar holds!' he hissed close to her ear, and then more gently, 'Come, girl, take courage and I'll lower you as far as the rope will take you. After that, you must slip out of the harness and hope the man down below will catch you. *Vaya con Dios!*'

She swallowed convulsively, suddenly almost more frightened of escaping than she was of death. But the dawn was already showing a faint gleam over the hills even while they dallied and from inside the fort they heard the first firing squad going about its dastardly business. The priest gestured for the girl to hurry, beginning the

Came Forth The Sun

prayers for the dying women under his breath, commending their souls into the hands of God as the first of the shots rang out.

'Why me?' Doña Pilar interrupted his prayers.

'Only God knows that!' the priest answered shortly. 'Go quickly, child!'

It was a terrifying journey down to the bottom of the ramparts. Doña Pilar could see the shadow of the man below, but at first she couldn't recognize him. It had taken a supreme effort to resign herself to the death she had been about to suffer by a bullet and she had thought herself to have conquered her fear as a true Spanish aristocrat should, yet now that circumstances had changed so abruptly for her and she was more likely to die from falling on to the rocks below, she felt herself to be more afraid than ever. Nor did she enjoy barking her shins against the walls as she was lowered down them. It hurt, it might even have hurt more than any single, well-aimed bullet would have done.

The pain served to make her angry, however, and she had worked herself up into a fine passion of rage by the time she had to undo the precarious harness and let go of the rope, and she was as mad as fire when she finally found the necessary courage to make that leap into the unknown.

Strong hands caught her, holding her tightly against a hard body that reeled backwards at the impact of her fall and they landed in a tangle of limbs and skirts, bruised and breathless, but both of them very much alive.

Doña Pilar sat up, a flood of Spanish on the tip of her tongue. None of it was ever uttered. Her rage vanished the instant she recognized the man who was embracing her with more enthusiasm than she considered proper, even given the circumstances.

'Oh, it's you, *Señor* Don *Inglés!*' A tremor of laughter came into her voice. 'How convenient for me that you should still be in Spain! Where are you taking me?'

He held her more tightly than ever, silently saluting her bravery.

'To England! Will you marry me, *querida*? It's been a rough wooing, I'm afraid, but I promise I'll look after you for the rest of my life – you'll never want for anything!'

In his agitation he spoke in English, still holding her tightly against him. She was smaller than he remembered and, despite her days in the fortress, smelt as sweet as a flower. She leaned even closer against him, her breasts brushing against his hand.

'*Toda mi vida!*' she translated. 'Oh, *sí, sí! Toda mi vida!*' And she reached up to kiss him, a gurgle of laughter at the back of her throat. 'But that won't be very long, *Señor Inglés*, unless we go, no? How do we get down from here?'

They rode right through the heat of the day. Thomas would have spared her the last few miles if he could, she looked so pale and drawn, but not once did a complaint cross her lips.

'*Claro*, we must go as far as possible from that horrible place,' she shrugged, when he tried to explain to her why he was pushing on into the gathering darkness.

'You must be tired and hungry,' he went on awkwardly.

Her dark eyes caught fire. 'I'm alive!' she said simply. 'Tomorrow, or the next day, there will be time to be – *fatigarse! Es claro, no?*'

Soon after that the Arab mare stumbled, throwing her young rider on to the dusty road and, to Thomas's dismay, Pilar burst into tears, speaking such rapid Spanish that he had no hope of understanding her.

He dismounted and gathered her into his arms, only to receive a sharp kick on the shins. His infuriated love rose to her feet, caught the Arab mare by the mane, hurling abuse at the poor creature until the mare stood, shivering, beside her, then she threw her arms round the animal's neck, crooning to her and blowing up her nostrils.

'Good!' she said at last. 'Now we understand each

other.' She turned to Thomas. 'Please to help me get on again!' she commanded. One dainty foot was put on his joined hands as he threw her up into the saddle, amused when she blew him an imperious kiss as she rode off, not waiting for him to remount his own gelding.

Used as he was to bivouacking in the most uncomfortable circumstances, Thomas would have liked to have found somewhere more secure for Doña Pilar than the broken-down farm shed that seemed the only place available. She looked pale, he thought, and her straight shoulders drooped a little when she thought he wasn't looking.

'My poor little love,' he sympathized, 'you look fit to drop!'

'I am quite well, thank you,' she responded, glaring at him. '*Nada me duele!* If it is necessary, I am able to ride many more miles. It is *you* who wishes to rest, no?'

He made no answer, lifting her off her mare and depositing her on the bale of hay he had spread in the barn for their use. He left her only a few moments while he saw to the horses, glad that they, at least, could fill their stomachs with some of the hay from the barn and water from a nearby stream. There was nothing that he could see that was fit to offer Pilar to eat, nor did he want to leave any clues as to their route for any would-be pursuers.

By the time he returned to her, she was already asleep, one hand tucked under her cheek, the other still grasping the kerchief he had loaned her to cover her head from the ·dust. He spent a long time, seated beside her, watching her sleep, marvelling that anyone so female and so physically tiny could match any soldier he had ever known when it came to courage. He was exhausted by all they had gone through and yet he had still to hear a single word of complaint on her lips. He had not thought it possible to love any other human being as much as he loved her!

With a deep sigh, he eased himself down beside her, putting his arms about her sleeping body, not expecting to sleep himself in case anyone should arrive to disturb her slumbers. Yet he must have slept for the next thing he knew was the light of the rising sun in his eyes and a pair of lips exploring the planes of his face, two black eyes alight with the delight in her discovery of how easy it was to arouse her *Señor El Draque*, as she chose to address him.

In a matter of seconds he had reversed their positions and it was his lips that were exploring her face in their turn. At their first kiss, his senses flamed. His fingers tore at the bottom of her bodice, to be slapped away by hers as she undid the fastenings herself, baring her flesh to his eager gaze.

His whole body shook with the need to possess her, to make her irrevocably his own, without benefit of any prayers said over them, just a man and a woman together, making their own commitment to one another.

She was willing enough. He felt rather than heard her quick intake of breath as he took her breasts in his hands. She eased herself more comfortably against him, making no protest when he explored still further, revealing the secret parts of her body to his touch. Far from being shocked at the effect she had on him, it gave her the greatest satisfaction to know that she could bring about these changes in his body, increasing her own pleasure in the contact between them.

'You want me very much!' she gloated. 'Very well, I am yours, because I love you very much, *mi esposo!*'

If she had not called him her husband, he undoubtedly would have made love to her with all the abandon that she seemed to want from him, but he was very conscious that he was not yet her husband and even more so of the promise he had made the priest who had helped effect her rescue the day before. He groaned with frustration.

'I cannot! I promised the *padre* that before I touched you I would marry you first according to the rites of your own Church —'

She was immediately matter-of-fact. 'You must keep

this stupid promise?' she demanded. 'It is a matter of honour?'

He nodded helplessly. 'I'm afraid so.'

She was silent for a long moment, pulling her clothes together and sucking in her cheeks to hide her irritation at the stupidity of this male concept. Then, after a while, the smile was back in her eyes and the jauntiness back in her movements.

'Very well, *Señor Inglés*, if your promise means so much to you, it is to be hoped you will also keep those promises you will make to me, no? *Mire!* This pleases me very well. But I think it is not good for you to wait many days to marry me, so we shall ride straight to Toledo where I have a Dominican cousin who shall marry us as soon as it can be arranged and then we can make love together whenever we wish, which will be very nice for me too, because I want very much to be your woman. *Bien*, we must go on at once! Is it agreed?'

'Agreed,' he said.

Only once, along the way, did Thomas try to justify himself to the straight-backed girl by his side, to be answered by a worldly-wise smile as old as Eve.

'But I understand exactly how it is, Tomás! It is necessary that the Doña Pilar Morena, a member of one of the oldest aristocratic families in Spain, should be able to hold up her head in honour when she visits her mother and her brothers – that she has nothing to be ashamed of in her dealings with the *Señor* Pirate *Inglés*, to whom she owes her life and all her future happiness. This is what it means to be Spanish and hidalgo and it makes me happy an Englishman can understand that, when I have always been told English heretics understand nothing that matters to anyone of honour. But for me, for the *muchacha* Pilar, all my honour is in being the woman of Tomás 'Arris, who could have had any English lady he chose, but who prefers to make love with me, and who means everything to me, because I want to make love with him also, even if he is the *tirano odioso* that all English husbands are said to be!'

Thomas's own tiredness fell away from him as he laughed out loud. There was nothing coy about this girl of his! She spoke her mind with all the frankness of a seasoned soldier and he liked that! Better still, he appreciated her quick understanding of what society, Spanish or English, would find acceptable behaviour and what it would not. If he had been at all worried that she might find it difficult being a Spanish wife in a country not noted for its love of foreigners, he was worried no longer. He was convinced that nothing could quench her spirit, the freshness of her beauty, not even the shock of being transplanted to the cold, greyer climes of his homeland.

To Thomas, Toledo was famous because of its steel and for no other reason. When he first saw it, pausing on the bank of the Rio Tajo below the city to allow the horses to drink their fill, he couldn't believe anywhere could be more beautiful, situated as it was on a granite hill, surrounded on three sides by a gorge carved out by the river, the Alcazar and the cathedral surmounting the Gothic and Moorish walls that completely surrounded the narrow streets of the city.

'But of course,' Pilar murmured. 'We have very beautiful cities in Spain. Toledo has many things that would interest you, such as the most important cathedral in Spain and many, many paintings by El Greco, but you must not like it too much because Córdoba is *my* city and that is more beautiful, more everything, with flowers and sun and much dancing and music! One day we shall go there and I will show you the very heart of Spain.'

He spurred his horse into fording the river, keeping a firm hand on the reins of her mare to make the tired animal keep pace with his own, stronger mount.

'I already possess the heart of Spain!'

'*Me?*' She was delighted by the compliment. 'It is true

I am very Spanish. I like to dance and sing, and I like pretty things, but I shall like to make love with you better than anything! You will see how Spanish I am then! I will be much, much better for you than any of your cold English women, which is what I shall tell Padre Gregorio when I ask him to marry us —'

'I don't think it will be my happiness he will be worrying about,' Thomas said drily.

'But he will, Tomás, as soon as he sees that your happiness is mine. He is family as well as being a friar and that means a great deal in Spain, I assure you. Perhaps he will not be *quite* so concerned about our happiness as I told you, but he will concern himself very much that I have been with you alone for three nights, and then he will marry us very quickly because he will not want my brothers shooting him dead because he has allowed me to be dishonoured by a pirate Englishman!'

Thomas put a hand on her knee. 'Doesn't it matter to you at all that I'm a heretic in the eyes of your Church?' he asked her.

She was surprised that he should ask. 'God knows the English have no proper religion and know nothing! We poor Spaniards have done our very best to convert you — we send ships, soldiers, our king married one of your queens, and the next queen would have nothing to do with him! And what is the result? If you do not change your minds perhaps it is because God doesn't want you to change, no? We are taught that faith is a gift of God, not the gift of the Spanish, and God's patience is infinite, so why not leave everything to him? I shall pray for you, and I shall be a very good Catholic so that God will forgive you and allow you into heaven for my sake, which he will surely do. So why should it matter to me that you are a heretic?'

Padre Gregorio saw his cousin's future in a less rosy glow. Deciding Pilar to be the weak link in the proposed relationship, the argument between them became more and more heated, but Pilar, despite her exhaustion, showed no signs of giving way. Dirty and tired out with her adventures she might be, but nothing could shake her determination to marry her Englishman, if necessary in the sacristy of one of the minor churches of Toledo, because she could see for herself that her beloved Colonel could not be married before the High Altar as a Catholic would be, but she preferred a public ceremony in the sacristy of the cathedral itself, with all El Greco's portraits of the saints, modelled on lunatics from the nearby madhouse, in attendance. Thomas Harris, his Spanish quite inadequate for the task of keeping up with the argument, was astonished to hear a great deal about *El Draque*, a name she had called him once before. Belatedly, he realized him to be none other than the Elizabethan mariner Sir Francis Drake, and that his was a name to frighten Spanish children with, much as Bonaparte was used in England. It was equally obvious that Doña Pilar was not in the least bit frightened. On the contrary, she was plainly determined to marry her own English pirate as soon as the arrangements could be made. A lift of the chin, a slight tap of one heel, and her cousin was prepared to agree to almost anything.

Finally, Pilar turned to Thomas, hands on hips, triumph written all over her face.

'It is all arranged!' she announced. 'We marry tomorrow in the afternoon. You must find a friend to be your witness, and the nuns from the convent where I shall spend the night will be my witnesses. It must be the afternoon because I need the morning to find something to wear that is clean and respectable, or they will not allow us in the cathedral. Do you have such a friend?'

Thomas nodded. 'Mrs Nightingale.'

Pilar was pleased to learn that he had the mother of his dead friend close by in Madrid. 'That will please Padre Gregorio more than anything because he is worried there will be no respectable female to help me when we go to England. How kind you are to me, Tomás!' With another change of mood, she held out her hand to him, watching

57

with her head on one side, as he bowed over her fingers.
'You will be there tomorrow?' she asked him anxiously.

'Nothing and nobody will be able to keep me away!'
he promised.

Pilar threw herself into marriage and her new life in
England with all the zest she brought to everything she
tackled. She had only one regret and that was that after
the birth of their daughter, Petronilla, she was unable to
bear her husband any more children. In this one respect
only she felt that she had failed him despite his frequent
assurances that providing he had her for his wife he had
no regrets at all.

When, after nearly seventeen years, the news came that
Pilar's widowed mother had died, she began to wonder if
the time wasn't coming for her to go back to Spain to
make proper arrangements for the management of her
inheritance herself. Both her brothers had given their lives
in the endless civil strife that had plagued Spain, and there
was now only her great-uncle left to manage the estate
that had now devolved on her as her parents' sole
remaining heir. Despite her many years in England, she
had a Spanish woman's idea of freedom when it came to
dealing with her own property and it never occurred to
her that as an English husband, Thomas might think that
everything which was hers rightfully belonged to him, for
that was not the Spanish way, where ladies retained their
own names and their own property even after marriage.
Besides, what did he know about winemaking and *bodegas*?
Nothing at all! The fact that she knew very little more
simply didn't occur to her.

She began to dream of the Spanish sun, the smell of
orange blossom, and the deep black shadows that cut
across the vivid white of the buildings, everything that
went to distinguish that beautiful, golden land from her
adopted country. She allowed herself to dream of her own
traditions: for Madonnas who wept real jewels that were
the eternal tears of weeping Spain; for Spanish notions of

honour that made of death a moment of truth that revealed the whole quality of the life which had gone before, a concept she doubted her beloved husband would ever be brought to understand. It was a knowledge that had been bred into Pilar, along with the correct way to use her fan, or drum her heels in the strange gypsy dances of Andalucía. Suddenly she was homesick and, although she loved her husband more than life itself, she found she wanted to return to her own home once again before she died and she began to make her plans accordingly, plans which naturally included her daughter quite as much as they did herself, for although Thomas Harris insisted Petronilla to be an Englishwoman through and through, Pilar secretly knew her to be every bit as Spanish as she was herself.

Chapter Three

'Papá!'

A grunt answered her.

Petronilla dropped a small curtsy towards her father's rear view. It was all she, or anyone else, had seen of him for at least a week now. Colonel Harris was a determined man. His family called him stubborn more often than not, but they were proud of his modern ideas, or they would have been if they had really understood much about them. Since becoming a Member of Parliament, the Colonel had steered clear of the remnants of the hard-facts men – his wife had taught him that there was more to life than plain statistics and an economic view of mankind – but he had been completely won over by the idea that hygiene was the key to curing bad housing, poverty and most of the illnesses that beset the population, especially small children. Clean water was his battle cry and the topic of most of his speeches in the House. It said much for him as a man that few sighed and wriggled in their seats when he rose to his feet; fewer still wasted their time in futile attempts to persuade him that it was uneconomic to waste such luxuries as clean water on the undeserving poor, for Colonel Harris had another side to his character that was universally respected. His knowledge of foreign affairs, especially those of Europe, was without parallel on the back benches, and it was well known that he remained there from choice and not from lack of talent, political or otherwise. In these times the Government was teetering on the brink of disintegration, what with all the fuss over the Papal Aggression, as it had been dubbed after a letter from the Prime Minister had been printed in the *London Times* when the newly restored Cardinal Archbishop of Westminster had chosen to celebrate his arrival in England by a singularly ill-judged statement saying that England had been restored to its rightful place in the firmament, thus upsetting just about everyone who didn't share his own enthusiasm for the papal connection. Added to which there was what Mr Disraeli called 'the unhappy quarrel between town and country', meaning the division of interests between on the one side landlords, and the 'old money', and on the other manufacturers, and the 'new'. All in all, an upright man of truly independent views was all the more to be valued.

'Papá!'

Her father muttered something unintelligible into the lavatory bowl he was busy installing. 'What is it?' he added only a little less belligerently.

Petronilla hid a smile. 'Why don't you allow Partridge to help you?' she suggested.

Her father grunted again. 'The best way to teach is by example,' he muttered, 'not by giving orders to others! Besides, Partridge only gets in the way!' He stood up, standing aside for her to get a better view of the magnificent polished mahogany frame and cover, in the centre of which was now seated a porcelain bowl, the interior of which was painted with the prettiest flowers imaginable. All that remained to the task was to fit the lever that, when pulled upwards, would flush the bowl, and to turn on the piped water that had now been successfully laid all over the house.

'Your mother's bathroom is only waiting for me to finish here and for the water to be turned on! She won't be able to believe her eyes when she sees such luxury! Not many other houses in England have a bathroom at all yet, I warrant!' he said with such obvious satisfaction that Petronilla found herself smiling again. 'It's a pity she won't have time to get used to the convenience of having her own water closet before she goes to Spain,' he went on, glaring at his daughter through bushy eyebrows to see what her reaction would be.

'To Spain?' Petronilla repeated. It was the first she had heard of her mother paying a visit to the land of her birth. 'Does Mamá know she is going to Spain?'

Her father sighed. The daughter was very like her mother and he loved them both dearly, but they were but women and the truth was sometimes best kept from them in their own interests. Yet he had to admit that Petronilla had more sense than most despite her tender years. He pulled at his whiskers.

'I'd rather you didn't say anything to your mother, Petronilla, but she has been feeling rather homesick lately, ever since we heard her mother had died – family property and all that! – and, anyway, I think it better she should be out of England just now.'

'Why now, Papá?' Petronilla had never heard her father say such a thing before.

'I don't want there to be any trouble over your Mamá's religion on Guy Fawke's Day —'

'My religion too, Papá.'

'I know that, child! Your mother is still very Spanish, however, and, like all her people, she is all fire and brimstone when anything that's dear to her is attacked. She has never learned the value of silence —'

'Papá!' Petronilla's level gaze mocked him. 'How can you say so? Only just the other day you were trying to worm out of her what she is giving you for your birthday, and I don't believe she has told you, has she?'

'Humph,' said the Colonel, 'neither God nor Spain was involved in that!'

He sounded so unexpectedly wretched that Petronilla

saw he was genuinely concerned for her mother. 'Why don't you tell me all about it downstairs,' she suggested gently. 'It's cold up here with all the doors open. Let's go to your library and Partridge shall bring you one of your favourite drinks and you can make up your mind what is best to be done if there really is going to be trouble.'

Thomas Harris gave her a sharp look. 'I've already made my decision, Petronilla, and you're not going to change it about to suit yourself! Your mother goes to Spain!'

'Then I shall go with her,' Petronilla said calmly.

'That would probably be best,' her father admitted. 'I shall be happier to know you are both together. I'd come with you if I could, but the Prime Minister would never forgive me if I were to leave the country just now – not that he is guiltless himself, stirring the pot whenever it suits him! I wish I could persuade him that upsetting the Irish and their supporters is not the way to stay in power when your majority is as paper-thin as his is, and, of course, the papers are having a field day, doing their best to rerun the anti-Catholic riots, as if they were doing everyone a favour! And as for your Archbishop Wiseman! What a misnomer his name turned out to be!'

Petronilla made no answer. She never made any reference to faith and religion in her father's hearing if she could help it. It was not a subject on which they could ever hope to agree, though she was more than prepared to admit there had been a great deal of foolishness on both sides, most of it brought about by historic misunderstandings from long ago which had successfully divided Europe, making enemies out of those who had no other reason not to be perfectly amicable together.

Her father sighed with contentment as she settled him in his favourite chair when they reached the comfort of the library. It was called the library, not because of the few leather-bound books he had inherited from one of his more bookish relations, but because it was here where he did most of his homework, preparing for the speeches he made in the House. In this activity Petronilla took her full share. There was always a pile of blue books, the latest Parliamentary reports, neatly bound in hard blue covers from which their name derived. For more than a couple of years now, Petronilla had helped her father much as a male secretary would have done, sorting through the facts and figures far more easily than any of his other assistants ever did, selecting those she thought would be of use to him and putting the others on one side in case they should ever be needed in the future. The forties had been the hungry years in Britain, and she had been inwardly appalled by the evidence of poverty and crime that fell out of every page.

'I can see no difference between the deserving and the undeserving poor!' she had declared violently on one occasion. 'They all need our sympathy, or so it seems to me!'

'There will always be those who will help themselves and those who have to be driven to make an effort on their own behalf,' he had responded thoughtfully.

'And those who are too poor and hungry ever to be able to manage to look after themselves without help!' she had snorted.

She had never been able to convince him of that, however, but nor had she ever given up trying to point out that many people were inadequately provided for, not through their own faults at all. They both enjoyed these political jousts; of course, being a woman she felt her reasoning probably lacked much of the polish that a man's would have had, but it was more than enough for her that he didn't dismiss her arguments out of hand as every other father she knew would have done.

When Partridge, their manservant, had placed the Colonel's glass of shrub and water by his side, and she had seated herself on the footstool at his feet, she gestured to Partridge to place some more coal on the fire before he left, and gave it a thoughtful poke, enjoying the sensation as the fire blazed into life, bringing a warm glow to her face.

Anti-Catholic feeling had been growing in the country by leaps and bounds in the last few weeks, but it hadn't occurred to Petronilla to worry about it before; she had too many other things to think about and she was accustomed to any number of tactless and disparaging remarks on her religion, even in the new magazine *Punch*, and such newspapers as *The Times* and the *Morning Post*. Nor could she remember a time when she had not been wise enough, in deliberate imitation of her father, never to take any remarks that might be made by friends and neighbours personally. The same could not be said for her volatile Mamá who went out of her way to take them very personally indeed, and would fire up, screaming Spanish abuse in return until everyone collapsed in helpless laughter, for no one could stay angry with Doña Pilar for long, not even the most stiff and starchy of her English neighbours. No, she had to agree with her father that it would be absolutely fatal to give her mother so much as a hint as to why he had suddenly become so amenable to her plan for visiting Spain.

But her father lost no time in discussing with Petronilla the full extent of his worries, explaining the intricacies of the political realities to her, just as if she had been a boy and had understood what would be of concern to the serious practitioners of power, especially of those who had every intention of hanging on to that power. With Peel's death, and Lord John Russell's administration – which depended on such disparate groups as the Irish MPs who were deeply offended by any anti-Catholic legislation, and the radical English who were equally offended by a Government who refused to take any measures against the representatives of the Pope, whom they saw as a foreign power rather than as an authentic religious leader – it was only a matter of time before the Government would fall. Everyone was hoping it would be later rather than sooner because, with the Great Exhibition being held in the following year of 1851, nobody could be doing with a General Election just then. Certainly not the Queen and

Prince Albert, and certainly not Colonel Harris, not over such an issue as this, not with a voluble Spanish papist for a wife, as well as a Catholic daughter, which might be enough in itself for him to lose his seat if he were opposed by someone who would use his family against him.

'Much better not to say anything to Mamá,' Petronilla agreed soothingly. 'You'll never get her to admit that the Pope, or even Cardinal Wiseman, might be wrong about anything!'

Her father smiled a wintry smile. 'That's not to say the two of them haven't taken leave of their senses with this latest display of rhetoric. Here, read the fellow's pastoral letter for yourself!'

Petronilla obediently cast her eye over the offending paragraphs in the newspaper, her slightly raised eyebrows her only reaction. It was indeed a singularly tactless letter, beginning with the announcement that he was 'Nicholas, by the Divine mercy of the Holy Roman Church', that 'at present and till such time as the Holy See shall think fit otherwise to provide, we govern and shall continue to govern, the counties of Middlesex, Hertford, and Essex, etc.'

'It seems to me more a manner of speaking,' she said at last. 'Surely Lord John doesn't imagine he is setting himself up as an alternative administration to the lawful government of England?'

'Shouldn't be surprised! The whole business has got completely out of hand! "England has been restored to its orbit in the ecclesiastical firmament, from which the light has long vanished" indeed! And as for "the silver links of that chain which has connected their country with the see of St Peter", how does the fellow expect to be understood?'

As Petronilla had nothing to say to that, he pulled on his whiskers some more, his agitation increasing by the minute. 'Who would have thought we would have trouble in the streets over such a matter these days? I don't mind telling you I'm afraid for your mother's safety. I don't want her involved in any unpleasantness —'

'I should hope not!' Petronilla agreed, horrified. 'Though surely no one would attack even the most obvious papist today, in the nineteenth century. It was different two hundred years ago —'

'We had trouble in Knightsbridge, at St Paul's, the other day, and the next best thing to a riot in Pimlico, where Mr Bennett of St Paul's is busy setting up a church for the poor. The police had to be called, just as if Mr Bennett was about to convert to Rome, which he isn't, not that anybody was in the mood to listen to what he is about! It isn't as though your mother has enough sense to keep out of trouble!'

'No.' Petronilla chuckled. 'She'd enjoy the excitement, quite sure that no matter what happened you would arrive in time to rescue her! I quite see why you think this is the right time for her to visit Spain, only, if you're not going to tell her anything about this stupid so-called Papal Aggression, what are you going to tell her?'

'Oh, something quite different! Nothing but the truth, mind you, but not that kind of truth, that's for your ears only! Fortunately, I have other, equally valid reasons for sending you both to Spain right now. I have to remember how much older I am than your mother and that she is likely to outlast me by a good many years. If you had been a boy everything would be different, of course, for my grandfather saw fit to entail every penny of his fortune in the male line. When I die, much of what I have will go to your cousin, whose intentions towards my widow will be honourable no doubt, but probably not over-generous as they have little liking for each other. It won't do for her to have to be beholden to him for the rest of her life—'

'Do you blame her for that?' Petronilla demanded fiercely. She wasn't in the least bit worried about her own future for life had been a delightful business so far and she saw no reason for it to be less happily disposed towards her in the future, but her mother was a different matter.

Her father grunted. 'They arrange these things better in your mother's country, though she herself would say *differently* – and, with both your uncles killed in the Carlist rebellions, the vineyards and *bodega*, and everything else that belonged to your grandfather and great-grandfather has come into her keeping in trust for yourself. Your great-uncle writes that he is keeping an eye on everything for her, but I should prefer to have the whole business tidied up and put on a firmer footing because it may be when your mother is alone she will choose to return to her own country and people, and I want to have both your futures settled long before that.'

Petronilla stretched sleepily in the heat from the fire. 'That won't be for years and years, so I refuse to worry about it now. I'm sure Mamá will feel the same way. What on earth would we do with a *bodega*? You don't even care for sherry-wine much, do you? Besides, I don't believe she will go to Spain without you, even if she's inherited the whole country!'

Colonel Harris took a long, hard look at his daughter. The picture she presented pleased him immensely. She had her mother's black hair and dark, dark eyes – as dark as bitter chocolate – and the same amused lift to her brows that was somehow completely un-English, especially in one who was so young and who had never been far from her native Hampshire, except for the occasional trip to London.

'There is also the question of finding a husband for you,' he went on with resolution. It's hard to believe you are grown up already, or almost so, but we mustn't be selfish and keep you at home with us too long. There are few enough likely young men around for you to choose from and it is more than time for you to widen the circle of your acquaintances. So, you see, it is your future we are talking about as well as hers!' His face puckered thoughtfully. 'Though, without wishing to hurt your mother's feelings, my dear, I should not like to see you married to a Spaniard —'

'Why not a Spaniard?' she demanded. 'I'm just as much

Spanish as I am English. More, I sometimes think! I didn't know you disliked the Spanish.'

'Spain is so far away!' he grumbled. He met the laughter in her eyes and shrugged slightly. 'You are far too level-headed to pass as a Spaniard, though you have some of your mother's beauty and wit. If you think I'm in too much of a hurry, it's because you forget how old I am. It should have been your grandfather, not your father who fought in the Peninsular War! Your dear mother was little more than a child when I married her, no more than the age you are now, and, though I think she has been happy enough —'

'She adores you, Papá, and you know it!'

'Well, that's as maybe, but I've seen a side of Spain I hope neither of you will ever know anything about, and I would much rather my darling daughter were married to an Englishman, even one who lives in Spain, someone you'd know with whom you were dealing, if you understand me? The Spanish are a superstitious, priest-ridden people, forever quarrelling amongst themselves! Take their present troubles. Both your uncles killed fighting the Carlists, as your mother very nearly was before them! You'd think there was something wrong in having a Queen, though poor Isabella will never be the woman our Queen Victoria is, not having a man like Prince Albert to guide her, or any proper man at all if the French have their way! However, that isn't the point! The point is that the Spanish as a whole will never accept her!'

'They won't accept her uncle either,' Petronilla said flatly.

'Exactly! Every Spaniard I've ever known should be king in his own estimation. Spanish men think far too highly of themselves to make comfortable companions. Impetuosity is all very well in a woman, but in a man it is frequently tiresome.'

Petronilla took that with a pinch of salt. She stretched again, enjoying the sensation of being warm and

comfortable and having her father's attention all to herself
for once.

'I'm too young to be married,' she yawned. 'I have no
mind to leave you and Mamá quite yet and, thankfully,
there can't be many English men who would want to take
me on just now.' She sat up, laughing, pleased to have
found a good reason for putting him off. 'I share Mamá's
priest-ridden religion as well as her blood and, if all you
say is true, that doesn't make me a very good match, does
it?'

Her father chuckled. 'Pilar will be most disappointed if
you don't make a creditable marriage, my dear. She has
her heart set on the matter.' He put an arm round his
daughter's waist. 'Your mother has never understood my
reservations over you having much to do with your
Spanish kin, but they did precious little to help her when
she was in danger of being executed by Ramón Cabrero!
A Spanish husband could sacrifice you just as easily on
the altar of some cause or other! Death means very little
to them – even your mother was as cool as you please in
the face of her own demise! Astonishing in a woman!'

Petronilla said nothing. She thought it must be much
the same whether it were a man or a woman faced with
certain death, but she knew better than to try and persuade
her father of such an idea. He had a romantic notion that
her mother was a fragile, angel-like creature standing in
need of his unremitting protection from the more
unpleasant aspects of life. The truth was that Doña Pilar
had always been her husband's emotional sheet-anchor,
making most of the major decisions in their joint life
together and never for a moment allowing him to suspect
that he wasn't completely and in every way master of his
own household.

'Yes, my dear, a *very* brave woman!' he insisted, as if
she were about to argue the point with him. 'I can never
forget that she left everything that was dear and familiar
to her to come to England with me. I don't know any
other woman who could have managed half so well in a

foreign country, with nobody even to speak her own language with her.'

'I speak her language, Papá!'

'I'm glad you do. That will make it easier for you when you accompany her to Spain.'

Petronilla gave him a sideways glance. 'I wonder if I shall like Spain? I may *look* like Mamá but, thanks to you, Papá, I am very much English bred and I shouldn't at all like to be held hostage as she was and, as for their politics, they seem quite mad to me!'

'Quite right, they are! But I don't see why that should worry you, Pet. The quarrel split whole families when it was at its height, but Isabella has kept her throne these last years and the Carlists must be beginning to lose heart.'

'Are all Mamá's family loyal to the Queen?'

'I believe not. She has cousins who declared for Don Carlos just before that last skirmish when her second brother was killed. I never heard why and I didn't ask because I didn't want to revive the chagrin she felt when she first heard of their defection. You'll like Spain well enough, my dear, but it's a more black-and-white world than we have here in England and you have to make allowances for that in everything. Still, I don't suppose anyone will be asking you your opinion about anything as divisive as the recent unrest and, if they do, I hope you're sensible enough not to have any opinions on the subject.'

Petronilla nodded her head in that quick, decided way she had. 'I wish you were coming with us all the same, Papá. It won't be half as much fun without you!'

'Well, it won't be until after Christmas. I'd like to have got you both away earlier than that, but we are to have a visitor and, as he is coming to see you and your mother, you had both better be here to receive him.'

Petronilla judged by her father's expression that he hadn't entirely made up his mind whether he approved of this unknown visitor or not and this intrigued her, making

71

her think he might be more interesting a visitor than he was telling her.

'Is he something to do with Mamá's inheritance?'

'In a way. I believe Mr Arbuthnot is also in the sherry business.'

'Mr Arbuthnot? That doesn't sound very Spanish!'

'Mr Arbuthnot is a Scot, I am told. Another of your mother's co-religionists – which is probably why he finds it more convenient to live in Spain!' he added bitterly.

Petronilla's brows rose. 'That sounds like one of your prejudices. There must be something more interesting to know about him? Mamá says lots of Britons are involved in the sherry trade – and making their fortunes in it, too.'

'Humph, a great many disaffected Irish have ended up in Spain over the years, but Scots have less reason to make their livings overseas. We need them here – more than ever with this Great Exhibition of our own and the world's achievements arranged for next year.'

'One Scot isn't going to make much difference to its success! Besides, from all I hear, Prince Albert is doing everything himself anyway!'

'Naughty puss!' her father chuckled. '*I* never told you anything of the sort! Wherever did you get such an idea?'

Petronilla presented an innocent face. 'It must have been Mrs Nightingale. She is the only other person with whom I discuss these things – you know that!'

Mrs Nightingale had come to live with them some years before, made welcome by the whole family, especially Doña Pilar and Petronilla who both adored her. To Petronilla, she was the grandmother she had never had; to Pilar, she was the person who had done most to ease her way into English society, who never minded accompanying her on the dullest visits, and who – together with Miss Fairman, who had been Petronilla's governess and who now acted as her chaperon when need arose – had become her closest intimates. They would sit chatting together as they worked on a patchwork quilt together, Doña Pilar's tiny stitches learned in her convent school coming into their own, while the other two cut out the patches, arguing amicably as to the colour scheme and the general pattern they wanted to achieve.

'Don't forget Mr Arbuthnot is partly coming to see you,' Thomas Harris warned, busy with his own thoughts. 'You will make him welcome?'

'Yes, of course, Papá!'

Doña Pilar was more forthright than her husband ever was in telling Petronilla all she knew about Mr Arbuthnot's proposed visit.

'Has Tomás told you this Mr Arbuthnot is a good Catholic, despite being British —'

'Am I supposed to like him the better for that?' Petronilla demanded.

'*Ay de mí*,' her mother responded in Spanish. 'If you don't like him, *pequeña*, we'll look elsewhere for you. There is no hurry for you to make up your mind. Most English girls wait until they are much older before they think of marriage – they are children when they are in their twenties!' Her dark eyes twinkled irrepressibly. 'But you are Spanish, like your Mamá, and already a woman, no? So you will be nice to this Scot your father has found for you and think seriously whether you like him or not. Is it agreed?'

Petronilla nodded in silence. That he was a good Catholic might be important to her mother but she wanted to know a great deal more about him than that. She knew better than to push for more information from her mother, however, for she doubted if Pilar knew much more about him than she did herself.

Doña Pilar gave her an approving look. 'And what about Spain? Are you pleased to be going there at last? Imagine it, to be warm again! If only your Papá were coming with us, everything would be perfect!'

Petronilla had her reservations about that. Life was good, yes, but seldom perfect. Nevertheless, she shared her mother's love for the sun and her hatred for the snow.

'Papá will come later on,' she murmured. 'It will be

much worse for him, left alone here in England with only Mrs Nightingale for company. Will he stay at his club in London, do you think?'

Doña Pilar shrugged, her mouth pulled down in distaste. 'Boodles, where the food is terrible! Perhaps Mrs Nightingale can persuade him to go to Crockford's from time to time to have a decent dinner.'

Mother and daughter looked at each other in perfect understanding. It never even occurred to Petronilla to wonder how her mother should know such intimate details of the exclusive gentlemen's private and gaming clubs. Somehow or other, Doña Pilar always knew everything to do with her husband and yet she never showed the least curiosity about his public and political life, or indeed anything he did on the rare occasions when he was away from her.

'Is life in Spain very different from here?' Petronilla asked at last.

Her mother considered the matter, giving it her full attention. 'Yes,' she said at last, 'it is different in many ways. But it is also wonderful! I hope you will learn to love it as much as I do!'

'I hope so too,' said Petronilla.

The game of Snapdragons was proving to be a great success. Petronilla had made all the arrangements for the small, select party her parents were giving for their guest. Her mother had been far too busy preparing for their journey to Spain and the invaluable Miss Fairman had taken to her bed with a cold. Only Mrs Nightingale had been available to help with the invitations and she was quickly tired these days and so everything else had been left to Petronilla. And she was very well pleased with her efforts. Never one to hide her light under a bushel, she had soon informed anyone who would listen that they had her to thank for the delightful programme she had arranged for them and now even the rather stiff Mr Arbuthnot was deep in the foolish nursery game of trying to snatch burning raisins from a bowl of flaming brandy and eating them while they were still alight.

To tell the truth, Petronilla was quite impressed with Mr Arbuthnot's tactics in winning the raisins from her side of the bowl, and she liked him a whole lot better when he fell about laughing at her shameless cheating, because she too liked to win, and to win by a handsome margin.

'Do you attend functions like this when you are in Spain, Mr Arbuthnot?' she asked him when all the raisins had finally been consumed.

'Not up to now.'

'Then what do you do?'

Mr Arbuthnot's earnest manner returned to his reddened, freckled face. He was quite unlike most of the young men Petronilla knew, lacking much of their ease of manner, though he more than made up for that in her opinion with his broad shoulders, his slow, rare smile, and his unusual eyes and hair. His hair reminded her of a fox that had escaped from the hunt once, and which she had nursed back to health, before releasing it, much against her father's wishes, somewhere down by the river.

'I don't have much of a social life in Spain yet, Miss Harris. There's time enough for play when I've made my fortune.'

'In the sherry business?'

He nodded. His whole face changed at the mention of the fortified wine from Jerez de la Frontera, his eyes lighting with enthusiasm as he spoke of his plans for the future.

'I began working as a wine merchant, buying from all the best *bodegas* and shipping it back to England, but now I think I can find my way to procuring my own *bodega*. It will be hard work at first —'

Petronilla eyed him curiously. 'Do you like Spain so much?' she enquired, a little surprised that it should be so.

'I suppose I do,' he said.

'Is it because of Mamá's *bodega* you are here?'

He was a long time answering. 'Not entirely.' He hesitated. 'How much do you know about your family's *bodega*, Miss Harris?'

'Very little.'

'I suppose you have always lived in England?'

'Of course. My father is an English Member of Parliament and both Mamá and I hate being away from him for any length of time. We are to go to Spain now, however, Mamá and I, on a long visit to Córdoba and Montilla. Perhaps we shall see you there?'

'You may rely on it,' he answered, which pleased her very much, although she was inclined to the opinion that he was a pompous, over-serious young man when compared to the carefree sons of her father's friends with whom she had teased and romped her way through childhood. By comparison, Mr Arbuthnot seemed to be weighed down with the cares of the world, probably because he was faced with having to make his own way in the world, with no parents to fall back on, it seemed.

'Do your people have land in Scotland?' she asked him, anxious, as always, to get to the bottom of the matter at once.

'My parents died when I was still a boy.' He smiled a rather superior smile. 'I have no family expectations, if that is what you want to know, Miss Harris,' he added.

She was not at all put out of countenance. 'I haven't either,' she confessed frankly. 'Papá's estate is entailed to the nearest male in the family, and Spain belongs to my mother and is too far away to count!'

'Too far away from where?'

She thought it a trick question and refused to answer. Mr Arbuthnot might have grown accustomed to living in Spain and all things Spanish, but Petronilla knew from her father that there was no nation as foreign in their ideas, or as barbarous in their treatment of one another, with the single exception of her mother; she, where Thomas Harris was concerned, was the one exception to every rule, who had somehow managed to escape the excesses of pride and indifference to suffering that he considered to be the hallmark of every Spaniard.

Petronilla gave him an amused look. 'Too far away from the way we look at things in this country,' she said.

His eyes narrowed, obscuring his usual good nature. 'Have you ever thought that the British aren't always right about everything?' he countered. 'Your mother, Doña Pilar, strikes me as a very great Spanish lady, with all the virtues of her race, and with all the pride and fire of Spain in her veins —'

Petronilla laughed, enjoying this romantic picture of her mother, even while it surprised her a little. Her mother was her mother where she was concerned and not typical of anything, except when it came to dancing, about which she could be fanatical in her enthusiasm.

'She certainly loves to dance!' she told him. 'If you know any Spanish dances, do dance them with her. She's forever telling Papá and I that no music speaks to the heart like *flamenco* does. She's been in England years and years but she still misses it.'

Mr Arbuthnot understood this better than Petronilla could have imagined. No one there knew how to play *flamenco* music, of course, but he led Doña Pilar out on to the improvised dance floor for nearly an hour, the Spanish woman remembering old steps she had long forgotten. She sparkled like a young girl, returning to her husband's side at intervals in an attempt to include him in her pleasure.

'I haven't danced like this in years!' she exclaimed. 'Almost that young man could be a Spaniard!'

Petronilla giggled. 'He doesn't *look* like a Spaniard, Mamá!'

Doña Pilar exchanged a tolerant smile with her husband. 'It is how a man feels that is important, *pequeña*, and how he makes other people feel inside themselves. *Mire*, he makes me feel very Spanish and that is good manners, no, because I like to feel Spanish? He has a kind heart.'

'I like him,' Thomas Harris agreed.

Petronilla liked him well enough herself, but he didn't make her feel anything particular inside, neither Spanish nor English, not even that she particularly wanted to dance with him. He was nice, but she had other fish to fry, half a dozen other young men whom she had known all her life, who danced the same dances that she was accustomed to dancing and who laughed at the same things that she did herself. It had been fun playing Snapdragons with him earlier, but she was too much her father's daughter to approve that he should go abroad to earn his living, even though he had chosen to live and work in her mother's country. England was the best place to live in the whole world! It had to be, because nowhere else was as safe and secure, with none of the rebellions, revolutions and civil disturbances that beset the rest of Europe, wherever one looked on the map. But, like her mother, Mr Arbuthnot didn't seem to have noticed this obvious fact, or, if he had, it didn't appear to matter to him. Yet he didn't look the adventurous type. Besides, it was Petronilla's considered opinion that any young man in search of adventure should join the Army as her father had in his youth. He had managed to see enough of the world to content the wildest spirit and, if anything, he appreciated his native land all the more because of it.

She made no objection, however, when Mr Arbuthnot asked her to show him her mother's rose garden in the morning. She pointed out to him that all gardens looked pretty dreary by the end of November, but she had to admit that in the autumnal sunshine, the trees golden with leaves not yet fallen, and still the occasional bloom pretending that summer was not yet over and gone for another year, it did look beautiful.

'How long are you going to be in Spain, Miss Harris?'

She watched him crumbling a clod of earth between his fingers, exactly as their head gardener always did, as if he were testing the soil to see what could be made to grow in it. She wondered if he knew he was doing it and why he should bother. Gardening bored her, as she was on the point of being bored by him.

'Not for very long I hope,' she answered him.

His sherry-coloured eyes were warm and kind. 'You don't really want to go at all, do you?'

She shrugged. 'I'd be looking forward to it if Papá were coming with us! Mamá hates being separated from him even for a few days – and so do I! It wouldn't be necessary for us to go right now if it weren't for all this business about the Papal Aggression and so on.' Her shoulders sagged as she thought of the latest letters on the subject in the morning papers. 'Is it because you're a papist that you live in Spain?

He gave her a startled look from beneath frowning brows. 'I've never given it much thought. It's the sherry business that interests me more than anything else. There's a lot of us British in and around Jerez, you know.' He grinned suddenly, disarming her with his enthusiasm. 'The British are always to be found where good wines are grown all over the world. I happen to think sherry is the best wine of them all, that's all.'

'No wonder you get on so well with Mamá!' she sighed. 'I prefer politics to wine – like my father!'

It was much to his credit that he didn't laugh at her, or show in any way that he thought it an unsuitable interest for a female. Instead he changed the subject, picking one of the late roses and handing it to her with a gallantry she didn't know how to accept.

'I think we'd better go back inside,' she said stiffly.

He walked beside her in silence, opening the french windows for her so that she could precede him into her father's library.

'Don't worry,' he said as her skirt brushed against his leg, 'you'll soon feel as much at home in Spain as you are here. You have the advantage of being half-Spanish —'

She looked at him over her shoulder. 'Is that an advantage?' she snorted.

'*I* think it is,' he said gravely.

It was very strange, but something in the way he said it made her heart thump in the most peculiar way. Her eyes widened, her limbs feeling suddenly so heavy that she couldn't move away. His head seemed to come towards hers in slow motion, as if she had been caught up in a dream – or was it a nightmare? She licked her lips, instinctively waiting for the touch of his against hers. The feel of his mouth sent shivers of excitement up and down her spine; the pressure of his tongue against her own brought an implosion of desire somewhere in her middle, shocking her into an awareness of needs she had never known she had.

'Why?' she heard herself asking.

'Because the Spanish know how to live,' he breathed in her ear. 'They have a zest for life the English lack. And living, my lovely one, is what life is all about!'

He stood back then, allowing her to pass, a lop-sided smile on his face making her think that he knew more about her than she did herself, which was ridiculous! She marched into the library, doing her best to clear her mind of any thoughts of him. She was probably hungry, she decided, and the faintness she was feeling had nothing to do with him at all! It was with relief that she saw Mr Arbuthnot hadn't followed her into the house, choosing instead to walk round the garden again on his own. And a good thing to, she thought, glad not to have to worry about him any further.

She disappeared into the kitchen, meaning to ask Cook for some of her 'cut and come again' cake, only when she arrived breathless a few minutes later at the pantry door, she didn't feel hungry at all, just tearful and filled with an odd nostalgia she couldn't understand in herself. It was all very silly and not at all how she liked to see herself, but there was something about Mr Arbuthnot that had managed to make her feel very young and insecure and not at all the grown-up, level-headed young lady she had previously known herself to be, who could never be put out of countenance by the flirtatious ways of any of the young men she knew – though none of *them* had ever dared to kiss her on the mouth for all the world as though there were some kind of understanding between them! And it was this last that was the most terrifying thought of all, for she didn't know – more, couldn't even guess at – exactly what it was that he did expect of her and for once, she knew, it was not something she could run and ask her father about.

Book Two

Montilla and Amontillado

'Las niñas y las viñas dificiles son de guardar.'
Girls and vineyards are both hard to keep an eye on.

Old saying in Jerez de la Frontera, the town that gave its name to the fortified wine, known in Shakespeare's day as Sack, but now as Sherry.

Chapter Four

Petronilla had not expected to be homesick, but as soon as England had fallen away, out of sight of her longing eyes, she had been sorely tempted to jump overboard and swim back as fast as she could. It was all the more ridiculous because she didn't even know if she was able to swim. She longed for England and all things English and, if she couldn't have the real thing, she saw no reason why they shouldn't take refuge in the nearest British territory.

'Mamá, why must we disembark at Cádiz? We could just as easily go on to Gibraltar, which is nearer Córdoba, and where I'm sure we should have a very good reception!'

Doña Pilar looked down her nose. 'Me, I will never set foot in that place! It is the one subject on which your father and I will never agree, and you would be wise not to enter into the argument! No Spaniard can countenance Britain's claim to what is rightfully Spanish!'

Petronilla had never had the slightest doubt that Britain was entitled to the whole world if it came her way.

'It suits a great many Spaniards that Gibraltar should be British. It's a well known hotbed of contraband, serving both Spain and Morocco!'

'Naturally!' Doña Pilar retorted. 'The English have always been pirates!'

'Mamá!'

'Ah, you are taught nothing of *that* in England, but we have always known all about it in Spain, let me tell you! All my life I have known that most of the Barbary corsairs were Englishmen. Who else would be willing to lose their souls by turning Mohammedan in such a cause? If, after all these years, the Spanish have begun to learn from them, it is only right the British should have the headache of dealing with them, no? Besides, these smugglers are only *pancistas* – the Bread Party – of whom there are always some in every nation!'

'Is that why contraband is a Spanish word?' Petronilla scoffed.

'As is tariff! Where else does that come from but the city of Tarifa? And where is Tarifa? Just down the coast on the Straits from Gibraltar! You may say what you like, *pequeña*, Gibraltar is ruining the economy of the whole of Spain! Even your father will admit that a third of all the tobacco entering Spain is smuggled through Gibraltar!'

Petronilla had heard her father railing about the illicit trade on which Gibraltar lived on many an occasion, but she wasn't going to admit as much to her indignant mother. Besides, it didn't seem much of a reason to her for not going on with the ship as far as the nearest piece of British soil. 'What is there at Cádiz?' She asked crossly.

Her mother's indignation gave way to amusement. 'All Spain, my darling daughter! More particularly, there is Seville quite close by, where we have many relations waiting to meet you. Seville will be much more amusing for both of us than that *Piedra Gorda*!'

Petronilla abandoned the Fat Rock with regret. Instead, she concentrated on how they were going to travel from Cádiz to Seville with the minimum of fuss and bother. On enquiry, the officer at whose table she sat on board ship, told her of the steamers that plied their trade up and down the River Guadalquiver as far as Seville. He handed her a card with the address of the shipping offices on one side: No. 168 Ce. del Molino. 'Anyone will tell you how to find them, Miss Harris, if you should need their services. However, your mother seems to be expecting to be met by a Mr Arbuthnot and I'm sure he will see to everything for you.'

It was the first Petronilla had heard about it. Neither she nor Doña Pilar were accustomed to travelling without a male escort and, although Petronilla was doing her best to carry out her father's detailed instructions as to how she could best look after her mother's comfort, she thought she would be rather pleased to see a friendly face, especially if it were someone who would lift the burden of their travel arrangements from her inadequate shoulders.

She did not, at first sight, like the look of Cádiz at all. Doña Pilar was reluctant to disembark until nearly everyone else had gone, claiming that the port area of any city was no place for two ladies on their own. When Petronilla did finally persuade her, she found herself even more upset than her parent by the audible comments from the old men who seemed to have nothing better to do than to watch the world go by the cafés, where they sat drinking small cups of coffee spiked liberally with Spanish brandy.

'*¡Que polvo tiene!*'

Petronilla cast an outraged look at the speaker. How dare he say such a thing to her? How bedworthy indeed!

'No no, pretend you haven't heard!' her mother whispered in English.

Petronilla was more indignant still. 'Do you mean such comments are *customary*?' she demanded.

'It is a compliment – of sorts,' her mother tried to explain.

Petronilla stared at her in disbelief. There was something different about Doña Pilar that she couldn't quite fathom. It wasn't just her helplessness in finding a suitable carriage to transport them to the best hotel in Cádiz; it was something in her whole deportment which made her look more completely Spanish then she had ever been in England.

'You're enjoying all this!' Petronilla discovered.

Her mother's eyes flashed as another man called out, '*¡Mira la mujer de bandera!*'

'He called you fat!' Petronilla exclaimed. 'What an impertinence?'

Her mother suppressed a smile Petronilla could only describe as smug. 'Why not fat?' she said placidly. 'All Spanish men, like their Moorish ancestors, like fat women.' She laughed happily in the back of her throat. 'As your father does now he is no longer a young man. As one grows older, one likes to be comfortable —'

'Mamá!'

Her mother laughed again. 'We're not in England now,' she observed. '*En nombre de Dios*, I had forgotten so much! Oh, how happy I am to be in my own land again!'

Petronilla was not at all happy. The inn was no more than comfortable though even she had to admit it was pretty enough with its whitewashed walls and hanging flowers of all sorts, and they seemed eager enough to serve their foreign guests when it came to finding a suitable room for them and plying them with food, quite sure in their own minds that they would have had nothing fit to eat since leaving England. What was more difficult was finding anyone who would take a message to the shipping offices and book their passage on to Seville.

'I will find a boy shortly, *señorita*! Calm yourself! There is plenty of time for everything!'

'*Mañana*, I suppose,' Petronilla returned coldly.

'When God wills it!'

There was no arguing with that so Petronilla did her best to possess her soul in patience and follow the example of her mother, who was in her element sitting under a parasol in a shady corner of the inner courtyard of the inn, picking her way through the plate of sweet biscuits that had been placed at her elbow.

'Do stop fussing, Petronilla,' she smiled. 'Mr Arbuthnot will be here soon enough and he'll see to everything for us. Here, have a biscuit and try some of this delicious wine.'

'But, Mamá, we'll never get to Seville at this rate! It says here that the poop where the best cabin is situated, costs five reals, and the *proa*, which must be a lower deck, only three reals. Which would you prefer?'

'Mr Arbuthnot will have seen to everything —'

'Then why isn't he here?'

Doña Pilar watched her daughter with placid indifference as she marched back and forth across the patio, keeping a tight rein on her temper.

'He'll be here soon. Your father thinks him a most reliable young man!' she said languidly.

Petronilla drew herself up, about to tell her mother exactly what she thought of anyone who would abandon two helpless women to their fate in a foreign land, when she noticed that Doña Pilar was relishing every minute of the delay. She looked exactly what she was, every inch of the *hidalguía* class of Spanish lady, with her mantilla drawn back from her face and her fan of the very finest lace resting lightly on her knee. Doña Pilar was as Spanish as her surroundings and far more at home than she had ever been in England.

Accepting defeat, Petronilla sat down beside her, helping herself to one of the what were indeed excellent biscuits and a glass of wine. She became aware of her mother's amused gaze watching her and she began to relax.

'Papá would have managed things much better!' she excused herself.

'Yes, but happily you are not your Papá, but only a young girl abroad for the first time – and a little lost, no?'

'A little. The streets are so narrow and dusty, though I must admit that the flowers are pretty. Did you see those great piles of what looked like snow?'

'Salt. Cádiz is a working city and smells of the sea, but it is still beautiful! I shan't mind if Mr Arbuthnot doesn't come at all today! Tomorrow will be quite soon enough for worrying about how we are to travel to Seville!'

Petronilla managed a small, weary smile. 'If you say so,

Mamá. It's certainly pleasant to be off that ship for a while. I shall never make a good sailor, I'm afraid.'

What she would have liked would have been an early supper and bed, but it was ten o'clock before the girl came to lay up the table in the patio for their meal and later still before an enormous dish of chicken bedded in saffron rice was brought for them to try. Petronilla was beyond hunger by that time, though she did her best to make polite conversation to her tireless Mamá who wanted first one thing and then another until Petronilla was dizzy with all her commands and counterdemands. The only dessert was the huge oranges that came in answer to one of her mother's queries, and they were the best Petronilla had ever tasted, quite unlike any she had eaten in England, and her spirits rose, beginning to think there might be more to Spain than she had thought.

It was then, at this late hour, that Mr Arbuthnot made his appearance. He made his bow, apologizing all the while that his horse had thrown a shoe and that he had to come the last few miles on foot because of it. His smile was jaunty rather than repentant, however.

'A good night's sleep will set you up for tomorrow's journey, ladies! I have arranged for you to go by chaise to Sanlúcar, before you have to set foot on another steamer!' He turned his attention fully on Doña Pilar. 'I thought you might like to sample one of the local wines on the way. There are one or two I think you might like and I shall value your opinion of them.'

Doña Pilar accepted the offer graciously. 'We're in no hurry now we have arrived in Spain. I hope you haven't forgotten you are coming to visit my family's *bodega* at Montilla when you have the time, Mr Arbuthnot. We have some very good wines of our own.'

'I've heard as much, even here in Jerez.' His grin grew broader. 'I may take you up on your invitation quite soon because the possibility of my giving up buying wines for someone else's profit in London and founding a *bodega* of my own may come to fruition sooner than I thought. I have had an offer of a small *bodega* here in the Jerez area, together with an option on some vineyards but, even so, I shall need to eke out my own production with wines from Montilla, or something similar, in the first instance. I very much hope we will be able to do business with one another?'

Doña Pilar shrugged elegant shoulders. 'You are very welcome for yourself, but if we can do business together, that will suit us very well, won't it, Petronilla?'

Petronilla was almost asleep. She had been embarrassed to meet Mr Arbuthnot again, remembering very much against her will the feel of his lips against hers, but she had soon forgotten any awkwardness in the struggle to keep awake, good manners insisting that she should make him at least as welcome as her mother was doing. She started at the sound of her name, her eyes opening wide. 'I am so sorry, I wasn't listening.'

Her mother was immediately all concern for her. 'Go to bed, my child,' she instructed her. 'Mr Arbuthnot and I will excuse you and, if we are to go wine-tasting in the morning, you will need all your wits about you for that!'

Petronilla dropped a curtsy to them both, wondering if she should take a lamp up with her to her bedchamber or if there would be one waiting for her upstairs.

'She misses her father – as I do!' she heard her mother say with a sigh. 'I forget that although she is now out in society, she is still a child in years.'

'A sleepy child,' Mr Arbuthnot agreed.

'A child today, but a woman tomorrow, Mr Arbuthnot. You know that the *bodega* will be hers one day?'

'So Colonel Harris told me,' he said. Which was very odd, Petronilla thought, for it was quite unlike her father to discuss his family's affairs with anyone, let alone a man much younger than himself, whom he had only just met. Perhaps Papá had liked Mr Arbuthnot more than he had told her, or perhaps it was just that he recognized the younger man knew infinitely more about winemaking than he did for, if the *bodega* was now her mother's, it

was also his as her husband, and he would be quite justified
in finding out all about its possibilities before he decided
what to do with it.

Their visit to Sanlúcar de Barrameda was a great success.
Petronilla, who had decided this corner of Spain to be
without any particular appealing features, was impressed
by a whole flock of flamingos feeding on an inland lake.
After that, she began to notice other things which had
previously escaped her attention and, what had at first
seemed so flat and uninspiring took on a haunting beauty
of its own that was difficult to ignore, especially for one
who had always possessed an urge to draw and paint, an
urge unfortunately not matched by any real talent – at
least, not in her own opinion.

'It was from Sanlúcar that Ferdinand Magellan
embarked on the very first circumnavigation of the world,
on the 10 August 1519,' Mr Arbuthnot broke into her
reverie. 'Only the one ship, the *Victoria*, made it back
home. Poor Fernando was murdered by savages in the
Philippines.'

Petronilla shuddered. 'Imagine being cooped up on a
ship long enough to go right round the world!' she
exclaimed.

'Ay, imagine it!' Mr Arbuthnot agreed with a grin.
'Give me the land any day!'

'Me too!' she confessed. 'Mamá was as right as rain,
but I suffered from *mal de mer* from the moment we left
England until the moment we came in sight of Spain!'

'A glass of wine would have settled your stomach, Miss
Harris. I find it an excellent cure for most ills.'

By the time he had settled both her and her mother at
what he claimed to be the best inn in town, the *Fonda
del Comercio*, and had brought them both a glass of the
manzanilla wine that was the local speciality, and which
was frequently passed off as sherry in London, she was
enjoying herself more than she would have thought
possible the day before. The name *manzanilla* was

supposed to describe its light camomile flavour, but Petronilla wasn't sufficiently a connoiseur to be able to detect any difference from any other sherry she had tasted. She enjoyed it, nevertheless, rolling it over her tongue in the way her mother had taught her long ago, shocked that English children were taught so little about the good things in life, amongst which she naturally included the golden wines of Spain which were her birthright.

'The sooner you make your visit to Montilla the better,' Doña Pilar told Mr Arbuthnot, one eye on her daughter. 'Our wine is as good, or better, than this!'

'And what do you have to say to that, Miss Harris?' Mr Arbuthnot enquired.

The look in his eyes, so very like the wine she was drinking, brought the colour to her face. 'I shall be very pleased if you can come,' she said stiffly. 'I know very few people in Spain,' she added, 'so I shall like to see a familiar face. Will you buy some of our wine?'

His eyes smiled at her. 'I can't promise you that, Miss Harris. It depends how my plans go for buying a *bodega* of my own. Would you object to going into some kind of partnership with me?'

Petronilla looked away. 'It isn't for me to say, sir,' she whispered.

'I shall come anyway to see you,' he said.

It was hard to know whether to be pleased or sorry when Mr Arbuthnot announced that it was time for them to drive to Bonanza where the steamer would be waiting for them. It was only a small hermitage by the side of the river but a great many people from Sanlúcar seemed to be there, seeing their friends and relatives off to Seville.

'Why Bonanza?' Petronilla asked.

'It was built by a South American company in honour of Nuestra *Señora* de Bonanza, Our Lady of fine weather,' he told her. 'Cheer up, you won't notice the motion of the steamer on the river you know, and the eighty miles to Seville only takes about six hours.'

'Are you sure?' Petronilla groaned.

'Absolutely. No more then eight hours at the very most!'

Petronilla smiled back at him. 'If it takes longer than eight hours I may never speak to you again!'

'That would be a terrible fate now that we have decided to be friends,' he agreed. 'I'll have a word with the captain and tell him my whole reputation rests on his transporting you to Seville as quickly as possible. Will that do?'

She chuckled, liking him much better than she had done in England. 'Have you noticed how *Spanish* Mamá looks in Spain?' she asked. 'It makes me feel more of a foreigner than ever.'

'You look as much at home here as she does!' he assured her, dropping a light kiss on the back of her hand. 'Your Mamá will tell you that only married ladies have their hands kissed,' he went on shamelessly, 'but don't you believe her. *Vaya con Dios*, Miss Petronilla.'

Petronilla also expected to receive some kind of rebuke from her mother for flirting so obviously with Mr Arbuthnot. No such remonstration was forthcoming, however, though Doña Pilar did find an opportunity shortly afterwards to tell her daughter that as Spanish women wore their wedding rings on the right hand, as she did herself, it was the ring that men kissed, acknowledging their married state, and not the woman herself. But she laughed even while she was speaking, rubbing her own wedding ring with a finger.

'How well do you like Mr Arbuthnot, Petronilla?'

'I hardly know him,' Petronilla retorted.

'I hardly knew your father either,' Doña Pilar sighed and, much to her daughter's relief, changed the subject by telling her of all the people she would be meeting in Seville, while Petronilla thought her own thoughts and decided Spain was much nicer than she ever could have imagined.

Travelling by train was something of a novelty for the Harris ladies. Colonel Harris sometimes made the journey

between Winchester and London by train, and Miss
Fairman had frequently been known to travel by what was
known as the 'Parliamentary' because of the law which
had been passed in 1845 compelling all the railway
companies to run on each of their lines daily a passenger
train that charged no more than 1d a mile. Petronilla could
count her own train journeys on one hand, however, and
she was all the more excited to be travelling from Seville
to Córdoba by such novel means.

Doña Pilar had insisted they should have a carriage to
themselves, with the servants who were to accompany
them sitting in a small compartment on the other side of
the kitchen which was to provide them with meals and
any drinks they might wish to refresh themselves with.
They were quite private, therefore, with more than
enough time to discuss the great, rolling, golden landscape
outside as well as what Petronilla could expect when she
met the greater part of her mother's family in Córdoba.
She felt she had already been introduced to at least a
hundred members of the clan – and it had felt like three
hundred when everybody had come to see her mother and
herself off after their brief visit to Seville.

Nothing her mother had ever told her about her
homeland had prepared Petronilla for Seville. The Spain
she had been told about had always seemed a part of
Europe, but Seville belonged to another continent; a
strange, exotic place, where orange trees grew in the
streets and many of the buildings were left over from the
days of the Moors, as beautiful as the lace Petronilla had
seen some of the black-clad old ladies making as they
gossiped together in the sunshine. Even the huge
cathedral, its enormous censers hanging directly from the
roof and requiring several people to pull them back and
forth, was built according to a foreign conception, with
its intimate yet magnificent choir and the uncluttered body
of the huge church providing ample space for the great
processions of Holy Week.

Other people might have been more impressed by the

tomb of Christopher Columbus· Petronilla was enchanted by the famous *seises* in their Renaissance costumes, who had the privilege on certain feasts of the year, after an introductory song, for they were also the cathedral choir, and making their obeissance to Our Lord, of replacing their hats and dancing to the beat of their castanets. It was in the cathedral that Petronilla had met her Spanish heritage head on and had begun to understand she was not as English as she had always thought herself to be, for she had been completely at home there from the moment she set foot inside it, and she knew her father would not have been. Colonel Harris was easily made uncomfortable by such an intense atmosphere and he never would have understood *dancing* in the House of the Lord!

'How many relations do we have in Córdoba?' she asked, smiling, when Doña Pilar declared she was glad Seville was behind her and that they would soon be home.

'Not many that need worry you,' her mother reassured her. 'Your great-uncle, and a few cousins. They won't mind you being more English than Spanish, not when they get to know you. You have very pretty manners, and you are my daughter as well as your father's!'

Petronilla had already met so many relatives that she was beginning to think her father remarkably clever to have succeeded in marrying Doña Pilar without any of them having been present except the distant cousin who had married them. She thought it even more clever of him to have rushed his bride off to England before any of them had come to hear about it and so escape their endless questions and the blatant disbelief that anything good could come out of England, a country they regarded with as much suspicion as England did Spain, despite their joint experience of the Peninsular War.

It was with some reluctance, therefore, that she stepped down from the luxuriously fitted carriage after her mother, faced with at least another hundred strangers all claiming close kinship with them both. She was afraid her Spanish would desert her, though it never had before, and her mouth was dry with a painful shyness that was also new to her.

Her great-uncle was very tall and thin, exactly her idea of Don Quixote, but he was kind and welcoming in a dismissive way, concentrating most of his attention on Doña Pilar, just as if Petronilla were still a child. Nor was his wife any more attentive. An unhappy looking woman, dressed entirely in black as if she were a widow, her face was grey and the set of her mouth bitter. She pecked Doña Pilar on the cheek, nearly did the same to Petronilla, somehow managing to avoid any actual contact at the last moment, and then retreated, making disparaging comments on the appearance of both ladies to anyone who would listen. Doña Pilar was too busy laughing and greeting cousins she hadn't seen for years, but Petronilla began to listen for the acid criticisms until she could hear nothing else that anybody said to her. They must think her a fool, she thought to herself, as she asked yet another person to repeat what they had said to her, or else that she was out of her depth in the buzz of Spanish going on all around her.

Yet, once their luggage had all been stowed away on a handcart and Don Ambrosio had assigned them to the chaises awaiting their custom outside the station, she found herself amongst the younger members of the family and was soon feeling completely at home with them as they pointed out the sights of the city Doña Pilar had spoken about as her own ever since Petronilla could remember.

It was very much as her mother had described it. The narrow streets; the blindingly white houses, their doors often left open so that one could glimpse the flower-filled courtyards within; the blackness of the shadows; and the way the breeze lazily lifted the dust as it blew fitfully from one cobbled pavement to another with each passing carriage. Then there were the secret squares, most of them dominated by a crucifix or the statue of some saint, and all of them decorated with hanging pots of yet more flowers, a blaze of scarlets, pinks and golds that dazzled the eyes.

'Over there is the Roman bridge,' a young cousin who had introduced herself as Teresa, told Petronilla, 'and those are the old Moorish mills – those great wheels along the bank of the river. And now you can see the Mesquita, the great church of the city. It's a beautiful cathedral built in the middle of an old mosque. You must go and see it some time. I'm sure you have nothing like it in London!'

Petronilla could only agree that there was nothing comparable anywhere in England.

'Tío Ambrosio will never allow it, but what you should really do is to walk through the old Jewish Quarter to the Mesquita. I do it all the time, but I am not asked to live in the same house as Tía Consuelo thankfully! *Nothing* pleases Tía Consuelo! According to Mamá, nothing ever has!'

Few of the people who had come to meet them were actually living in the family home. Apart from her great-uncle and his wife, there were a few maiden aunts, a visiting cousin from South America who departed almost immediately, and a great many servants who, compared with their English peers, were extraordinarily familiar and noisy, singing as they worked, or clattering over the marble floors, and frequently answering back in a way no English servant would have dreamed of doing.

Tía Consuelo was always polite, but Petronilla could tell she avoided ever being alone with her.

'Have you said or done something wrong to anger her?' Petronilla asked her mother when, for once, they were alone together.

Doña Pilar languidly flapped her fan. 'An unhappy woman, that one! She always was! Don't concern yourself about her! I want you to enjoy your visit with your Spanish family, no? That poor soul never enjoys anything very much, I'm afraid.'

Petronilla was amused despite herself. Every day her mother became a little more Spanish and a little more foreign to her. She wondered what her father was going to make of this transformation and smiled inwardly to herself, knowing he wouldn't care at all as long as his beloved wife was happy.

'I think it's more that she doesn't like me, even though I am your daughter,' Petronilla complained.

'Oh, England is the old enemy with her. We Spanish never went to the Crusades in the old days, you see, because we had our own crusade here at home to fight. That was the true reason for the Armada. Our king, Philip II, was a very devout man and he wanted only to bring heretical England back to the True Faith. He would have done it, too, if the weather hadn't turned against him, scattering his ships all over the seven seas!'

Petronilla gave an outraged gasp. 'Mamá! You know it wasn't like that at all!'

'It was exactly like that from the Spanish point of view,' her mother said. 'Spain and England should always have been friends and, but for the religious question, we always would have been. To me, it seems very strange that anyone should suppose the good Lord would have us all kill one another because we wish to follow him a little differently, but there it is! Here, your father is the heretic; in England, it is we who are thought to be the danger, as we saw before we came away. It is quite stupid, no?'

Petronilla could only agree. She understood much better after that the curious questions with which the black-clad aunts plied her whenever they were able to get her by herself and, although she still avoided the subject whenever she could, she no longer thought they were deliberately looking for a quarrel when they wondered aloud that her father could be so blind as to have a good Spanish Catholic for a wife and yet remaining outside the Church himself.

It was a fortnight before Doña Pilar could drag herself away from her relatives, for she fell easily into the comfortable ways of the other ladies who were quite content to spend their days in interminable gossip, the opening and closing of their elegant fans punctuating the talk, in a constant flow of sound that was always to remind Petronilla of Spain thereafter.

'How wise of you to seek a husband for your daughter in Spain!' The aunts nodded their heads in unison. 'Have you anyone in mind?'

Doña Pilar managed to look smug and regretful at the same time. 'Whatever my ideas, Petronilla will naturally need her father's approval as well as mine before she chooses the man she will marry. She is young yet, so there is no hurry for her to make any decision.'

'No, indeed!' the aunts chimed in. Then one of them, braver than the rest, added, 'We thought you might be thinking of one of her cousins?'

Doña Pilar shut her fan with a snap. 'Colonel Harris had other plans for her, I believe.'

It was after that exchange that she decided it was time for her and Petronilla to complete their journey to Montilla. In a whirl of activity that left her daughter breathless, Doña Pilar went herself to the local horse market and came back with two superior hacks that she had been assured had been broken in to a lady's saddle. She chose the larger of the two *jacas* for herself, inviting Petronilla to try out the pretty chestnut with a cream mane and tail that was so long it practically swept along the ground behind.

Doña Pilar sat her horse as if she had been born in the saddle. She watched her daughter bring her animal up beside her with a critical eye.

'Your father should have seen to it that you ride as well as you drive! Relax a little, *pequeña*, or you will be in a sorry way by the time we have gone a few miles!'

Don Ambrosio marched between them, adjusting Petronilla's stirrup with his own hands.

'She may not ride as well as you do, Pilar, but she sits the horse well. Almost she could be Spanish!' He smiled at the younger woman. 'I am very well pleased with my new niece!'

Doña Pilar laughed. 'Of course she is Spanish! She is *my* daughter! She is a little bit English too, but that is a mere nothing now I have brought her to Spain!'

She was still laughing over her shoulder at Petronilla when they finally moved off, the guard her uncle had provided for them falling in behind them in a cloud of dust.

Petronilla pulled her mantilla more closely about her face, glad that she had given in to her mother's insistence that she should follow the Spanish custom while she was in Spain of wearing a comb in her hair and the mantilla whenever she went out. 'Not only to hide away from people,' her mother said, 'but Spain is a dusty place and one soon learns the advantages of not swallowing too much of it!'

The men were all wearing Córdoban hats, the wide brims shading their eyes from the sun. Rich and poor, they all dressed very much alike, especially when it came to shoes. There was not a Spaniard who didn't insist on being able to see his reflection in his polished boots. They said it was the first sign of a gentleman – but then, in Spain, they also said that every man is king, and even the poorest of the poor would often behave as such.

Petronilla was astonished by the beauty of the land all round Córdoba. It seemed to sweep away from the city as far as the eye could see in any direction. There were the high hills on one side and the rounded fields on the other, fifty, a hundred times as big as any field she had seen in England. Nor were there any little villages, their welcome steeples or belltowers standing out in the distance, a guide to the way to the nearest human habitation. Here there was nothing, only space, where nobody seemed to live at all, and where the fields as much as the edges of the road were thick with wild flowers encouraged by the rainy season that hits Spain at the turn of the year.

'It's beautiful!' she whispered, pausing to ease herself in the saddle.

'Yes, it is beautiful. But beauty can also be cruel, as Spain is cruel. The hotter the sun, the deeper the shadows. The grey skies of England are kinder to the complexion. My people don't understand that grey is sometimes better than black and white. We are always afraid that to compromise is also to bring dishonour. Death, we say, is the moment of truth. It was your father who taught me that living could be better than death, that not everything is solved by the grand gesture, that some things are better considered at length, with a cool mind, before doing something that can never be undone again —'

For a moment Petronilla thought her mother was joking. 'Like eloping with Papa?'

'I thought I was to be executed in the morning.' She shrugged. 'My best friend did die that morning. She died with courage, as sure that she was right as was the man who ordered her death. Do you think I was a coward to run away from death?'

'Certainly not!'

'It took a long time before I could be sure,' her mother went on. 'It was enough that your father was sure, but me, I was certain of nothing! How one dies can be more important than how one lives, or so I thought, and here I was still alive!'

Petronilla squinted between the ears of her mount. 'What changed your mind?'

'Marriage to your father. Something my cousin said when he married us. Many things. Then one day I thought, would it have made the Queen more secure on her throne if I had died? The idea was ridiculous! Riding down this road brings it all back to me – how gentle your father was with me, and how he thought I would never stop crying, not at the time, you understand, but afterwards when we were safely married and there was no further danger of death for me. He told me it was sometimes the same when a man survives a battle in which his comrades have all been killed and that no woman should know anything about things like that! Even so, I only began to feel better when I realized that having me alive meant more to him than it did to me. I am sad to be here alone now. If Tomás were here, it would be perfect for all of us. It means much to me, you see, that you should love my country as much as you do England, and he would have explained how we must live much more intensely, whether we are enjoying a glass of wine together, or preparing ourselves for eternity. It is something he understands very well in me, even while he laughs at me and tells me nothing is as important as I think it is. I think I would have managed my life very badly without him, so it is a good thing that it was a sensible Englishman who rescued me from being shot, no?'

A town appeared in the distance: the white buildings, their wrought-iron security bars on the windows; the orange-red tiles of the roofs; and the lofty façade and tower of the church crowning the hillside on the left side of the road. As they turned their horses off the dusty track and into the narrow, cobbled streets that led up to the central plaza in front of the church and the *Áyuntamiento*, it was easy to dream of a future that would be every bit as romantic as her mother predicted. Why shouldn't it be so, when Spain was just as beautiful as Petronilla had been told it was, and the sky as blue as it only was on the most perfect days in England? Why shouldn't she be happy when everything about her seemed designed to make her so?

Petronilla was tired from the long ride to Montilla. Her mother was as straight-backed as ever, her dancing glance noting every tiny change that had taken place since she had last seen the town of her birth. With her whip, she pointed out the surrounding vineyards, telling her daughter which ones belonged to the family and which to some other family. Petronilla hadn't realized how much her mother must have missed the easy-going, dance-and-wine-filled years of her childhood. Rubbed raw from the saddle as she was, she made up her mind that nothing should spoil her mother's homecoming if she could help it. She could feel the suppressed excitement and the obvious joy in being reunited with her own soil coming from her in waves. Funny, how she had always thought of her mother as a rather formal person, reserved in her affections despite her occasional bouts of fiery temper, and always a little distant from the rest; now, seeing her in her own environment, she was astonished and amused to find she was really quite a different person. She seemed to know the whole town by name, every detail of their lives committed to memory. She was able to ask after parents, brothers and sisters, children and grandchildren, with the greatest of ease and as though the answers really mattered to her, and she gave each person her whole attention while she was speaking to them in a way she never did in England. There was nothing of the formal, prim and proper English wife in this warm, vital Spanish lady. Was this the way Thomas Harris saw her? Petronilla remembered the deep affection between her parents and thought it probably was. She was only sorry that she had never before seen her mother that way herself, as she saw her now and would always remember her in the future.

As they clattered over the cobbles, she remembered Miss Fairman, scarlet in the face, saying, 'How fortunate you are to have such a mother, child! I have never known any employer who took such an interest in a mere governess's future. Most people would consider me to be quite beneath her notice, but she has always treated me as a friend more than anything else! I don't believe she would mind at all if I were to marry into her own circle! Not that I should of course! I have always known my place in this world!'

Petronilla had only wondered what her governess was talking about at the time, though her mother had cast some light on the matter.

'Truly, that Miss Fairman is her own worst enemy!' she had exclaimed crossly one day. 'Sometimes I think she prefers being a governess to becoming a married lady! Mr Dowle would be the ideal match for her, for they are in close agreement on every subject under the sun! Then what must she do but shy away from him when he finally pops the question, making fun of him and *laughing* at the poor man! Learn from her experience, *favorita*, that no man can be expected to show any humour when it comes to his own consequence! I despair now of ever finding a husband for that governess of yours and so I told her this morning!'

There had been a glimpse of this Spanish side of her mother on that occasion, Petronilla thought, for her interest in Miss Fairman's future had continued unabated, forever pushing the governess under the noses of every single gentleman who came her way, determined to rescue her from what she considered a most unattractive future for anyone gently born.

'They talk about the Gran Capitan all the time in Córdoba, but it was here that he was born!' Her mother's voice cut across her thoughts. 'He was my greatest hero when I was a child!'

Petronilla had never heard of the Gran Capitan. Her mother's laugh broke out, seeing her daughter's blank expression. 'He was the commander of the forces of the Catholic Kings. Would that the second Isabella had such a fine man on her side. Isabella and Ferdinand had only the Moors to fight against, not their uncle and half their own countrymen!'

The civic dignitaries stood stiffly to attention outside the town hall, their chains of office gleaming in the late sunshine. Petronilla followed her mother down the line, trying to ignore the slight headache that had formed at the back of her eyes. It was the constant glare from the white buildings and the white earth that nurtured the vines, following on from their long ride from Córdoba that had sapped her strength, and she could only marvel at the light way Doña Pilar stepped down from her *jaca*, as if she had only just this minute risen from her bed and a good night's sleep, taking it as only her due that the entire town should have turned out to greet her.

'How lovely it is to be home!' Doña Pilar cried out happily. She accepted several bouquets of flowers, exchanging a laughing comment with each of the donors. Then, each time, she drew Petronilla forward and presented her as her English daughter, come to Spain for the first time. 'She will soon know all there is to know about winemaking and then the famous Morena *bodega* will be hers!'

Petronilla ignored the whispered comments, pretending she hadn't heard their ill-concealed doubts that anyone with English blood in her veins could possibly settle down in Spain, let alone have any real appreciation of all that goes to make a great marque of wine. It was hard to ignore their whispered comments of: Is she married? She looks too like a Morena to be English! The Doña Pilar is as beautiful as I remember! After all these years! Why, her daughter must be as old as she was when she left Montilla!

Doña Pilar watched her daughter make her curtsy for the umpteenth time, before giving her a quick nod of approval and saying in English, 'It won't be long now, *hija mía*, before we'll be home and you can slip into a hot bath. You have the headache, no?' Her eyes shone as she lifted her chin disparagingly. 'Just like your father! The English have no stamina!'

Petronilla's jaw dropped, her hackles rising as she sought the words with which to defend her absent parent. Then, almost immediately, her mother caressed her cheek with one hand, adjusting her mantilla with the other, laughing once more. '*Just* like your father! Why must the English always be as good if not better than anyone else? Sometimes to be Spanish is best – as you will find out!'

If Petronilla had thought she had met all the Morena family in Córdoba, she soon found out how wrong she was, there were plenty more of her mother's relations waiting to meet her at the old *finca* homestead that stood at the heart of the family *bodega* and vineyards. The house was so beautiful that Petronilla was astonished. There was a great horseshoe shaped arch at the entrance, and the house itself had been whitewashed so often that its outlines were blurred and a brilliant white, where the walls were not covered by flowering creepers of all kinds. Built round an internal courtyard, it looked in on itself, a fountain playing ceaselessly in a pool built into the marble floor. All the rooms had verandas above the courtyard, with wrought-iron rails that matched the security bars of the outside windows. The furniture was mostly of wood, heavily carved and black with age. Only the rugs were a riot of colour spread out on the white marble floors that were sometimes outlined in black or green. The lamps were burnished copper and gave out remarkably little light, but no one cared. If the Spanish ambition for turning night into day was not yet achieved, most of them refused to be defeated by the dimness of the flickering flames and went about their business just the same.

'We came at once,' Doña Rosa fluttered, her heavy black mantilla betraying her widowhood, 'so happy to see you again, cousin! How often have we consoled ourselves that you, at least, were safe! It was terrible for your mother, though there was never a word of complaint from her, when all her children were gone from her! She would tell me though, because I was always the closest to her of her first cousins, that to have a daughter in England was almost as bad as having her in her grave – but that was before first one son, and then the other . . . these are terrible days! And now you have brought your daughter back home, and your mother is dead also and will never set eyes on her pretty face! Don Diego ought to be here to receive you, but he is never here when he's wanted —'

'Diego? Our cousin Diego Salcedo y Morena? I haven't seen him in years, when he was just a baby in his mother's arms!'

Doña Rosa sniffed. 'Never would be soon enough for me. I can't think what Tío Ambrosio was thinking about when he put him in charge of the *bodega*! What does a boy like him know about fine wines?' She lowered her voice to a whisper. 'His side of the family are all Carlists! I was never so ashamed in my life as when our Cousin Tomás went to stay with Cousin Diego's family in Granada and came home with the news that he had declared for Don Carlos! I was thankful your mother never knew about it, not after all *she* had suffered in the Doña Isabella's cause!'

'I expect he wanted a bit of adventure,' Doña Pilar replied, shrugging off the knowledge that her cousin was a traitor and beneath the contempt of the loyal members of her family.

'*Adventure?*' Doña Rosa repeated with disapproval.

Doña Pilar hugged her indignant cousin. 'What else did my brothers want? What else did *I* want when I went rushing off to visit with Francisca Urquiza when I did?' She smiled a secret smile. 'Never did I think to find all the adventure I wanted with an Englishman! And now, instead of being in my grave these many years, like poor Francisca, I am very much alive and a respectable matron, with everything I need to make me happy!'

'Nevertheless, you would have died for our rightful Queen!' Doña Rosa insisted, not bothering to hide her confusion.

'As I hope Don Diego won't die for his rightful King,' Doña Pilar answered gently. 'Too many of us have died already.'

All the ladies were able to agree with this sentiment. 'It is sad that the whole *bodega* should depend on the female line! Who have you in mind for the Doña Petronilla, Cousin Pilar? Tío Ambrosio is anxious to find her a Spanish husband while she is here, though he needn't expect any help from Tía Consuelo in that direction – as we all know what she thinks of the English! As if your daughter isn't just as modest and as well-mannered as if her father had been a Spanish Grandee!'

It was the first time Petronilla had ever heard herself referred to in the Spanish way and not as Miss Harris, or even as Miss Petronilla by those who knew her well. *Doña Petronilla!* She hugged the title to herself with glee, her fatigue falling away from her. There was so much she had never known about Spain, or about the Spanish side of herself, hidden beneath her English upbringing. Seville and Córdoba had awakened her to the beauty of Spain, but here, in the old farmhouse where her mother had spent her childhood, she felt as much at home as she did in her father's house in Hampshire. In an odd way she, as much as her mother, had come home.

Chapter Five

Doña Pilar declared herself exhausted by the journey and refused to do more than sit in one of the internal courtyards of the *finca*, fanning herself from time to time, and exulting that she was warm from head to toe instead of suffering the colds and snows that go to make up the English winter.

'To be Spanish is to be *alive*!' she told her daughter.

Petronilla regarded her with some amusement, not for a moment deceived by her mother's fatigue. She was like a cat purring in front of the fire, but anyone who had seen Doña Pilar on a horse, or dancing the night away while those half her age fell by the wayside, would have taken her present claims with a pinch of salt.

'Then I'm glad I'm half-Spanish and half-alive,' she answered with a smile. 'But, Mamá, don't you want to have a look round the *bodega* and the vineyards and see what changes have been made?'

'You go, dear. If only your father were here I'd be completely happy. How sad that he couldn't come with us straight away. I never feel complete when I am parted from him! I shall sit in the sun and gossip with Cousin Rosa, like the widow I almost am!'

Petronilla kept to herself any idea that if her mother were to occupy herself with something more strenuous than gossip the time would pass more quickly while they were waiting for Colonel Harris to join them. She knew from experience that it would be useless. Doña Pilar had never subscribed to the view that the Devil would find work for her idle fingers; she didn't feel herself to be on sufficiently intimate terms with him for him to bother. Besides, she had always regarded with astonishment the English obsession with keeping busy. Other people might feel a certain guilt when they succumbed to reading a romantic novel, or some other work of fiction, in the morning, or at some other unsuitable time of day. Doña Pilar read all such books in a single gulp, ignoring everything else as she did so, and didn't feel either decadent or that her time might be better occupied in some other way. Why, she would ask, should one time of day be better than another for such things? It was wholly incomprehensible to her and, although Miss Fairman had seen to it that Petronilla should very well understand the importance of being properly occupied at all times of the day, neither lady was prepared to try to convert Doña Pilar to a more disciplined way of life.

'Well,' Petronilla said, 'I mean to ride round the vineyards today. I had hoped you would come with me and explain it all to me.'

Doña Pilar settled more comfortably into her chair. 'What is there to explain? The grapes grow in this glorious sun and then we make them into wine. *¿Claro?*'

Petronilla gave up the unequal struggle. 'Very well, I'll go alone!'

Her mother nodded contentedly. 'Take a Córdoban *sombrero* with you to shade you from the sun. It is unbecoming to get over-heated, and you already have too dark a complexion to be fashionable in England.'

Petronilla did as she was told. For the last two years she had employed all the latest creams and potions to try to rid herself of the honey-coloured tone to her skin, which had always singled her out from her fairer friends. In vain she had longed for the pink and white complexions and golden hair of the others; she remained an exotic flower of more southern climes – as her father would have it! She took one last, scandalized look at her idle parent, half-wishing she could look as beautiful and be as indifferent to the prejudices of others as she was. And yet, she thought with a sudden rush of affection, her father had only to clear his throat to bring his wife to his side, as eager to support him now as she had been on the morning when he had rescued her from certain execution.

Her new mare seemed to recognize her, accepting the carrot she was offered with a dignified curl of the lip, very much aware she was the beautiful and valuable animal she was. Petronilla led her to the mounting block, talking to her all the while, first in English and then in Spanish when she saw she was getting no response. The mare sidled away from the block, snorting through widened nostrils, but a calming pat and a few more Spanish endearments, and she allowed Petronilla on to her back, apparently as pleased to be out and doing as was her new owner.

At first, she thought it was her inexperienced eyes that found the vineyards to be a disappointment. The plants were in a wretched state, badly tended and with many of them trailing in the dust when she should have thought they would have been pruned back before the turn of the year. It was the rainy season – not that she had seen a drop of rain so far – and she would have supposed there would be workers in the fields ensuring the water was conserved long enough to reach the wilting vines: indeed, she would have supposed there would have been some workers somewhere but, once she had left the homestead behind her, she could have been alone in the world.

She was hot, tired and dusty by the time she got home. Doña Pilar came running out to meet her, a manservant in hot pursuit relieving Petronilla of her sweating mount and walking the *jaca* briskly away to the stables. The Spanish woman met her daughter's quizzical look with raised eyebrows.

'Were you lost?'

Petronilla hugged her, shaking her head. 'It didn't take

you long to get all the servants running to do your bidding,' she teased lightly, gesturing towards her vanishing horse. 'You'll have to work your magic outside as well sometime – if you can find anyone to work on our land!'

'Poor pet!' her mother responded. 'Come and sit down and José will bring you a cold drink. Didn't I warn you about staying out in the sun for hours together? I'm not surprised you are feeling out of sorts and a bit scratchy, my love, but you'll soon feel better if you sit quietly for a while and recover yourself.'

'Mamá, I'm not in the least in need of quiet and meditation, though I will gladly accept a cold drink. Tomorrow, you must ride out with me and see the vineyards for yourself! I can't believe Tío Ambrosio can know how neglected the land is. As soon as I've had a rest, I mean to have a look at the books and see what kind of a vintage we produced last year —'

Doña Pilar clutched her daughter's arm. '*¡Querida!* Are you sure you know what you're doing?'

'Quite sure, Mamá!'

'Oh dear,' her mother fussed. 'How well I know that stubborn look of yours! So like your father's! And what do you intend to do if you find everything to be as bad as you think it to be?'

Petronilla frowned. 'Make some improvements – with your consent, of course.'

Doña Pilar covered her face with her hands. 'There are men to do these things! Tío Ambrosio will be most displeased if you interfere with your cousin Diego's decisions, and Diego himself has always been known for his short temper! I beg you not to get on the wrong side of both of them before you've given yourself time to learn something about winemaking!'

Petronilla gave her a meaningful look. 'Mamá dear, it doesn't need a qualified vintner to see what is happening here! The place is dying on its feet!'

'The vintage is over —'

Petronilla gratefully accepted her drink from a silver tray brought to her by José and took a sip, smiling her approval.

'Will you speak to the foreman —?'

'No, my love, I will not! It is understandable that you should want to take an interest seeing your father and I have decided that the *bodega* will be a part of your dowry when you marry, but I can't be expected to worry myself about such things as the vines which are being planted —'

'Or not planted!' Petronilla interposed bitterly. Seeing that she had finally gained her mother's full attention, she pressed on quickly. 'The foreman whom I saw is a man called Rodriguez – he said he thought you might remember him?' Her mother's quick nod confirmed that she did. 'He says all the grapes used to be Pedro Ximenez, and some Palomino, but such replanting that has been done, which isn't much, is a grape called Tintilla de Rota which, according to Rodriguez, is much better grown nearer to the coast. Apparently, the young lord thinks it will make a good Communion wine!'

Doña Pilar was beginning to feel as appalled as her daughter. She might pretend to know nothing of the workings of the *bodega*, but the growing and making of the wine for which the area was famous had been a part of her growing up. She might not have given her old home a thought for years, but nothing could erase her instinctive love for the land and its produce.

'Ridiculous!' she exclaimed aloud. 'We have always grown Pedro Ximenez! Such a romantic grape, I have always thought, though I can't remember enough of the old stories to tell you why. What I do remember is that they are two of the greatest vines grown anywhere in the world! Communion wine, or not, it is desecration not to replant such vines in this area!'

Petronilla pounced. 'Will you tell Tío Ambrosio so?'

Doña Pilar acknowledged the trap with a faint smile. 'No! *You* may go to Córdoba and speak to your uncle but, first things first, you will need to know a great deal more about the *bodega* than you do now. I will teach you all I can, but that is very little for I have never had anything to do with the day-to-day business of the *bodega*. Nor is Rodriguez the man to teach you – we must find somebody else. I suppose we still have a *capataz*?'

'I don't know,' Petronilla admitted. 'What does he do?'

'He's the foreman of the *bodega*. Without him, nothing can be done. It is he who makes the wine, who knows exactly when the fermentation is done – everything! A good *capataz* is an artist as well as a scientist; he is born, not made, you understand? When I was a child the *capataz* was a man named Fernandez, but he was an old man and my mother wrote to me that he was retiring and she was making him a pension from her own resources.' She made a regretful face. 'My brothers were not known for their generosity, which was understandable because they were always off fighting somewhere, and it is expensive to fight battles – even for one's Queen!'

Petronilla felt only irritation at her uncles' lack of interest in the source of their income. Like her father, she had no time for those who lived on trade and yet despised the very enterprises which provided them with the greater part of their income.

'Then you'll ride out with me tomorrow?'

Doña Pilar looked sufficiently comfortable never to move again. 'If I must. But I am telling you now, Petronilla, that *nothing* will induce me to go over the books with you! Oh yes, don't pretend that isn't what you have in mind for me next! Well, I won't do it – and it wouldn't help you one bit because I have never understood how to make such things add up, apart from which, I don't *wish* to know! It is understood?'

'*Claro*,' Petronilla murmured. 'Happily I don't need you to look at the books because Papa taught me how to do that myself. But only you can remember how things used to be organized here and compare that with what is going on now. Tío Ambrosio won't listen to me unless I go as your messenger. Mamá, you know that to be true!'

'I have said I will go with you tomorrow. Now, may we please talk of other things at table tonight? Something that will interest Cousin Rosa lest she thinks we mean to neglect her entirely while she is with us.'

Petronilla hid a smile. 'How long is she staying with us?' she asked innocently.

Doña Pilar shrugged. 'Who knows? Don't think badly of her for she has few enough amusements in her life. She was widowed very young, poor thing, and everyone has made use of her ever since. She will enjoy being an honoured guest for once and, in return, she is telling me all the gossip of the family that I have missed all these years. It's a fair exchange, don't you think?'

'As long as you are enjoying her company.'

Doña Pilar spread her fan, admiring the fine lacework between the spines. 'There is something to be enjoyed in everyone if one can find the time for them. Cousin Rosa was always a talented mimic when we were young and she has not forgotten anything of the art. Her husband was no one in particular and people have fallen in the way of ignoring her presence, tucked away in her corner and saying nothing. If they knew half of all the secrets she has overheard, they would pay her a great deal more attention – though she is never unkind, which is something I have always liked in her! She has even been known to find something nice to say about Tía Consuelo, who has always treated her abominably in return! Me, I shouldn't like to be a spare relation in that one's household!'

Petronilla resigned herself to Doña Rosa's presence at the *finca* for the forseeable future. 'Papa wouldn't like it if you let her tease you by constantly hanging on your sleeve —'

'She won't do that! To tell the truth, Petronilla, I am glad she is here because I am missing your father even more than I thought I would!' She was silent for a moment, then she said, 'Really, it is she who is doing me the kindness of consenting to stay on here for a while. I could never persuade her to make the journey to England, but perhaps you may be able to reassure her that not every English person is obliged to tuck his tail into his trousers every morning!'

Petronilla laughed. 'Mamá, really! Where did you come by such an expression?'

'From your father, where else? He read it out to me from a magazine, only it was referring to the Holy Father, saying he wore a mitre to hide his horns and had to tuck in his tail every morning before he could go out amongst ordinary men.'

Petronilla laughed again. 'I'm sure he wouldn't have wanted you to repeat it to anyone else!'

For a moment Doña Pilar was affronted and then she laughed also. 'Since when were you anyone else? I shall say what I please to my own daughter!'

They were still laughing when Doña Rosa came to join them, her exquisite embroidery carefully folded and held in one hand. Her first concern was to find Petronilla safely returned after her long, hot day in the sun.

'I was thinking as we rode out here from Montilla yesterday that all was not quite well with the vineyards and, when you were so long in coming home today, I did hope you hadn't found something that wouldn't wait for your father's arrival to be put right.'

Petronilla was thoughtful. 'Do you know much about winemaking, Cousin Rosa?'

It was Doña Pilar who answered. 'Cousin Rosa's husband was the best *capataz* in the district.'

'Yes, he was,' Doña Rosa agreed gently, 'the very best.'

Petronilla leaned forward. 'Don Diego is supposed to be managing things here, but all he seems to want are Communion grapes. Do you think Tío Ambrosio knows about that?'

Doña Rosa spread her embroidery out on her knee. 'Oh dear! I don't *think* Tío Ambrosio would be much interested in what goes on here. He always thought very poorly of

Cousin Pilar's father for not employing someone else to make his money for him. Tío Ambrosio is very proud of his blue blood – and, it's true, he does have a very white skin!'

'Because he never goes out in the sun?' Petronilla asked, confused.

'No, no, because one's veins only look blue if one has a white skin,' Doña Rosa explained. 'I think the saying came about because the Moors, and the Moriscos after them, didn't have blue veins, or, rather didn't have skins white enough to make their blood *look* blue. It's only a saying, my dear, and a rather silly one I've often thought.'

'Nevertheless,' Petronilla persisted, 'Tío Ambrosio chose to put Don Diego in charge of the *bodega* —'

'Well yes, dear, he did,' Doña Rosa interrupted, 'but not for the reasons you imagine. Don Diego is a very lively young man and I did hear it said that he was in need of some kind of an income to keep him out of trouble. *That* is something that would concern Tío Ambrosio very nearly for, although it is rumoured that Don Diego is as likely as not to fight for Don Carlos as the Doña Isabella, his uncle would prefer not to believe it. Family means a great deal to him and there aren't many men left to carry on all the traditions and everything. You do understand, don't you? Cousin Pilar has a husband to look after her and you're not *entirely* family, are you?'

Petronilla could follow the logic of that. She was a Harris and, when she married, would belong to her husband's family, more even than she would have done as a Spaniard. Then she would have retained her father's name, adding to it that she was so-and-so's wife – as Doña Rosa did, who was still Rosa Morena, the widow of Juan Canovas, her children, if she had had any, taking first their father's name and adding their mother's name to it: Canovas (*y*) Morena.

'That would be tolerable if my cousin had used it for that purpose!' she said with some asperity. 'It's the sheer neglect which is so distressing, whoever is supposed to be reaping the benefits.'

'Oh dear, yes, I do see what you mean,' Doña Rosa babbled on. 'The only thing is that Tío Ambrosio is more likely to agree with Don Diego that to take up arms for whatever dubious cause is a more worthy occupation for someone of his rank than the making of money. He would really prefer him to live on thin air – as I have reason to know!'

This came as a revelation to Petronilla. For the first time, she took a closer look at the quality of the material of Cousin Rosa's dress. She had not thought that Rosa might be a wealthy woman: she had not thought much about her at all, she thought with real penitence, but had supposed her to be a poor relation such as would have found refuge with a wealthier member of her family in England, to be treated as little better than a drudge, without interest for anyone.

'You don't agree with him?' she said carefully.

'I never did!' Doña Rosa made a fluttery gesture. 'Tío Ambrosio may order much of the way I live now, but I am thankful to say, I have never been obliged to rely on his generosity for my material needs, or I should be poor indeed!'

Doña Pilar gave a lazy chuckle. 'How true! And if only Tomás were here, Tío Ambrosio wouldn't dream of interfering with his decisions, whatever benefits he wants Diego to have, and then Petronilla wouldn't have all these worries!'

Petronilla looked askance. 'Does Papá know anything about wine?'

'Nothing at all!' her mother retorted blithely.

Doña Rosa smiled a kindly smile. 'Just remember, my dear, that Tío Ambrosio may be the head of the family, but the *bodega* is your mother's property, not his. If your parents wish it to be a part of your dowry then he has no choice but to give way – and the same goes for Diego!

Such a charming young man – ' She smiled again. 'You will find him quite irresistible, I am sure!'

Doña Pilar's eyes flashed. 'Is he charming to you, Cousin Rosa?' she enquired.

'To me? Oh, dear me, what would he have to gain by being charming to me? He has no reason to notice me at all.' She embroidered a few stitches with frenetic energy, unpicking them again and redoing them to her greater satisfaction. 'The younger members of the family all admire him greatly, as I'm sure you both will when you meet him. He has a strong look of your father, Cousin Pilar, which he must have come by from his mother, Tía Juana, but his ways are those of his own father, or so everyone tells me, and he is probably none the worse for that.'

Doña Pilar muttered something under her breath which neither of the other two ladies caught. 'Should I go with Petronilla to Córdoba, do you think?'

Doña Rosa peered down at the intricate stitches. 'I think, if I were you, I would write to Colonel Harris. It will delay your having to make any decision that might be unpopular in the family and if Cousin Petronilla can meanwhile persuade Tío Ambrosia to allow her to make a few changes, then nothing will be lost, will it?'

'Nothing at all,' Doña Pilar agreed and, shutting her eyes, proceeded to lose all further interest in the conversation.

When Petronilla ordered the horses to be brought round first thing in the morning, she was surprised to find her mother already dressed and anxious to inspect the ruined vineyards before she wrote her letter to her husband.

'Should we take a picnic, do you think?' she said doubtfully, casting an impatient look at Petronilla's half-filled cup of coffee. 'Me, I drink chocolate at this hour of the morning, which is much better for one's digestion. You drink far too much coffee, as I am forever telling you!'

Petronilla paid no attention at all. She buttered a piece of freshly baked bread, spread some apricot jam on it, and handed it to her mother, doing another for herself.

'That sounds fun,' she agreed. 'Perhaps Cousin Rosa will join us?'

Doña Pilar made to say something, changed her mind, putting some more jam on her crust instead. 'I will arrange something,' she said abstractedly, 'while you finish your breakfast. You ate so little yesterday evening, you must be hungry!'

'I find it difficult to do justice to a meal in the middle of the night!' Petronilla confessed. 'My thoughts are more on my bed than my stomach at that hour.'

'At your age?' Doña Pilar's lip curled scornfully. 'Why, when I was your age, nothing pleased me better than to turn night into day!'

'I daresay I shall grow used to it in time,' Petronilla returned, undismayed. 'Until I do, José is going to bring me a sandwich in the late afternoon. I don't think he approves of such a display of weakness —'

'I should think not! I wonder you should have persuaded him you need to be fed every other hour like a baby! He probably thinks it some strange, English custom!'

Petronilla took another sip of coffee. 'He thinks I am very much my mother's daughter, if you must know! He likes doing things for me!'

'Then let's hope he won't mind bringing our picnic out to us. I'll go and speak to him about it.'

Doña Rosa declined the long ride, having no ambition to spend a long day in the saddle. If her cousins had no objection, she would remain behind and entertain herself as best she may, and no, she wouldn't join them for the picnic either as she was far more comfortable where she was and they would manage very much better without her. And so Petronilla and her mother rode out alone, accompanied only by a couple of grooms mounted on two of the thinnest horses Petronilla had ever seen.

'At least he could have seen the animals were properly fed!' she remarked to her mother.

'I expect he would have done, if he had been here to notice they were being neglected. Don't think too badly of your cousin – I don't suppose he has any more interest in growing vines than Cousin Rosa has.'

Petronilla, noting her mother's set expression, was content to leave things in her hands. She even began to enjoy herself, finding it much more interesting than she had the day before, with Doña Pilar briefly pointing out the quality of the soil and all the other things that went into the cultivating of a fine sherry grape.

'It's many moons since any work was done around here,' her mother said after a while. 'The earth should have been prepared for the new vines as long ago as August. I can remember when one of the vineyards had to be replanted; first the old vines were grubbed out, and then the land was planted with some cereal crop to give it a good rest before the new vines were put in. There's always the chance that the ground may hold a disease left over from the old stock and it pays to disinfect the soil as best one can. If that had been done, we could be harrowing the ground and dressing it with manure, before marking it off for the new stock. It angers me to see such waste, and so you may tell Tío Ambrosio!'

'Are you sure you wouldn't like to tell him yourself?' Petronilla pleaded.

Doña Pilar shaded her eyes from the glare that came off the *Albariza* soil which held much of the secret of the successful cultivation of the sherry grape.

'As far as the family is concerned, I gave up my rights to their consideration when I married an Englishman. If my mother were still alive, she would smooth my path for me and perhaps I might be forgiven, but even my brothers couldn't understand why I hadn't preferred death to marriage with your father! If they had had their way, the vineyards and *bodega* would never have become mine. Fortunately, your grandmother survived them both and she had a mind of her own – as well as having a soft spot for your father! – which is why the property was tied up for me and, ultimately, for you. It's much better you should go to Córdoba because I have no wish to quarrel with Tío Ambrosio if there's no need to do so, and he won't bother to quarrel with you as he won't expect you to display the same family feeling.'

'It would be better still if I knew what I was talking about!' Petronilla complained.

Her mother gave her a complacent look. 'I thought those books you were studying all last evening were going to tell you all you needed to know?'

'They told me enough to know you needn't expect any income from the *bodega* this year, nor next year either!'

But Doña Pilar was still not convinced that any figures written in a ledger could reveal anything of consequence about the welfare of the *bodega*. 'At least you use your eyes to some purpose when you look about you. The whole place is, indeed, abominably neglected and good for very little but the plough, just as you told me yesterday. Never mind, *mi hija*, while you are away in Córdoba, I will take on some labour here and see what can be done to rescue our fortunes!'

Her mother seemed to cheer up after that. She turned her horse's head towards a delightful, well-treed valley, where a rampaging stream forced a passage through its rocky bed, swollen with the rains that had fallen up in the hills but were yet to reach Montilla itself.

'Our picnic should be waiting for us close by,' she said, giving the grooms instructions to go ahead and help put up the chairs and table that she had given José orders to bring with him.

Petronilla had not expected the grand meal her mother had ordered. Out of an enormous hamper José produced a fruit cordial; a thick, cold omelette, stuffed with cooked potatoes, chopped up bacon, peppers and onions; a variety of cold meats; and more of the freshly-baked bread they had eaten for breakfast, which was now past its prime and no longer warm from the oven, but still an extremely welcome part of the feast.

'I hope something was left behind for Cousin Rosa?' Petronilla observed, lifting an enquiring eyebrow in her mother's direction.

'Cousin Rosa didn't suffer from *mal de mer* for more than a fortnight, and then pick at her food for days together, either because it was strange, or because it was served at a strange hour! Eat, *pequeña*, and put a little flesh on your bones! I'll not have you looking like a skeleton when Mr Arbuthnot gets here, or he'll think we are starving you – like the horses – to death!'

'Does it matter what he thinks?' Petronilla asked lazily.

Doña Pilar nodded with a determined jut to her chin. 'He understands growing wine as nobody does around here! I shall be glad of his advice, for although I was practically brought up in a vineyard, that was all years ago and it's a very different thing having to order what is to be done to make it pay. I was never trained for such a task! Indeed, my Papá would have been horrified by the very idea of my showing more than the most superficial interest in everything he was doing. Mamá could understand my boredom at being kept inside and sewing a fine seam much better than he ever could, but even she was deeply shocked by the results of my determination to have adventures just like my brothers. Being here with you, in my old home, reminds me of how *my* mother and I used to chatter and giggle together, far more than we have ever done. The English are very prim and proper, don't you think?'

'I suppose we are,' Petronilla admitted. 'I don't feel at all prim and proper, but you're the best judge of that!'

'You are as much Spanish as English,' her mother hastened to soothe her.

Petronilla thought there was some truth in that. 'I'm surprised at how quickly I feel at home here,' she agreed, helping herself to another portion of the Spanish omelette with a sigh of content.

Doña Pilar smiled and nodded. 'Of course you do! Vineyards are peaceful places, no? Remote and undisturbed, showing nothing of the ceaseless work that is necessary to maintain them. Mr Arbuthnot understands that very well also. He may not be a Spaniard by birth, but he is by adoption. I only wish he were here now!'

'So you said, Mamá!'

'You like him well enough, don't you?' her mother repeated sharply.

Petronilla refused to answer. She didn't want to think about Mr Arbuthnot, or anyone else, just at that moment. She had eaten enough to be slightly uncomfortable and was hoping she wouldn't regret it later. Even so, she still managed to wonder if she could find room for another almond biscuit and, catching her mother's interested look, took the last two with a rebellious shrug.

'Wasn't the idea to put some flesh on my bones?' she muttered.

'As long as your *jaca* can carry you home, eat every last crumb and welcome, my child!'

That was the comfortable thing about her mother, Petronilla reflected. She had friends whose parents were forever having fast days and days of family humiliation in the interests of one cause or another. Her mother had always found such practices unhelpful and unnecessary.

'We fast for Lent; we abstain from eating flesh at least once each week; and we do it for the benefit of our own souls, because the Church tells us we must. It is enough! I refuse to discipline myself at the whim of some politician!'

And absolutely nothing would move Pilar, not even the strictures of her husband who submitted to her Church's fasts and abstentions with such ill ease that she would occasionally order a side dish to be put on the table especially for him and bid him eat to his heart's content, knowing full well that he only did so as a gesture to his Protestant conscience.

Petronilla nibbled on the last biscuit. It was unexpectedly pleasant being alone with her mother for a while, for in England there had always seemed to be someone else there, either Miss Fairman, or even her father. She couldn't remember when they had last been absolutely alone, and she blessed Cousin Rosa for tactfully remaining behind and thus giving them time together.

As they meandered homewards towards the *finca* homestead, giving their horses their heads to take whatever route they wanted, Petronilla was surprised all over again to find how much they had in common, she and her mother.

'The most fascinating thing about the way we make wine here is the *solera* system. The word doesn't come from the sun, as you might suppose, but from the Latin *solum*, meaning floor. In England, whenever I thought about my old home, I would think of the silence of the warehouses, known as "cathedrals", where the casks of wine are stored and matured, some small part of the oldest vintage being mixed with the next, and so on, so that all the wine is exactly the same, year after year. It takes immense skill to know exactly when to mix the wine – there isn't a set date of the year, or anything like that. I can remember the excitement that would build up to the great day, and how we children would watch the *capataz* taking a sample out of each of the giant casks. It's the atmosphere of the *bodega* which I remember best!'

It was getting dark by the time they had walked through the giant sheds, the tang of the Spanish oak and the maturing wine still in their nostrils and the awesome atmosphere still seeping into their thoughts.

'I'll never be able to explain the importance of the *bodega* to you to Tío Ambrosio!' Petronilla exclaimed, once more seated on the back of her mare.

'I shouldn't try,' her mother advised drily. 'I wanted you, not Tío Ambrosio, to understand something about me! Wine is in my blood – and, one day, it will be in your bloodstream too! That, my darling, is your inheritance from my family. Until today you have always been a

Harris, but now, in Spain, we shall add "y Morena" to your name. Is it agreed?'

Petronilla was touched. 'I shall be very proud to use both names,' she said.

Chapter Six

Petronilla wrote to Tía Consuelo proposing herself for a visit in about a fortnight's time. Her aunt sent a message back at once, suggesting she should come a few days earlier as her cousin Don Diego would also be in residence and it was more than time that she made his acquaintance – such a delightful young man, as she was sure Petronilla would find out for herself. She quite understood that her niece was finding it a little dull in the country, but nobody could make that complaint around Diego, though, if Petronilla would take her advice, she would not stress her English blood in his presence, nor flaunt her mother's heroism in front of his eyes as he was of the opinion she would have done better to have died with her friends.

Thoroughly annoyed by this missive, Petronilla would have changed her mind about going at all if the matter hadn't been so pressing. José brought it to her when she was having a mid-morning cup of coffee with Doña Rosa, who shared her preference for the beverage and who obviously enjoyed the treat of having someone to chatter with while she drained the one cup she pretended to allow herself each day.

'My dear, what is the matter?' she asked, as Petronilla smoothed the single sheet of Tía Consuelo's colourful writing paper on the table beside her, trying to dismiss its contents from her mind.

Petronilla handed it to her cousin in silence, annoyed to see her fingers were trembling with suppressed anger.

'Ah,' said Doña Rosa, 'if it's from your Tía Consuelo, I don't need to read the actual words. She can't help herself, poor soul! She's so unhappy herself that she can't bear anyone else to be content with their lot. If she sees her barbs have found their mark, she'll never let go.'

Petronilla realized she was speaking from experience and that she undoubtedly knew what she was talking about.

'I don't mind her thinking I should be ashamed to be English, but I won't have her criticizing Mamá to me!' she said flatly.

'Certainly not! I shouldn't worry, my dear, she'll soon have something else to think about with you under the same roof —'

Petronilla's eyes twinkled appreciatively. 'Are my manners so very foreign and disagreeable?' she asked.

Doña Rosa was horrified. 'Oh, no! What an idea! I didn't mean —' Her gentle voice trailed off in the face of the amusement in her young relative's eyes. 'You're a wicked tease,' she reproached her, accepting the last of the coffee against her better judgement. 'It takes me back any number of years to when your Mamá and I were young! I missed her sorely when she went away. But there, I knew she had found happiness with her Englishman in England, and life goes on.' A sudden anxiety came to her. 'She has been happy, hasn't she?'

Unaccustomed to assessing her parents' happiness or otherwise, Petronilla gave the matter her serious consideration. 'They are the happiest *couple* I know,' she answered finally. 'I think Mamá missed Spain – her home – everything – more than even she realized, but she would rather be with Papá than anywhere else in the world.'

'That's how it should be. Just think, my dear, if Tía Consuelo had been happily married, how much the rest of us would have been spared!'

Petronilla determined not to waste the ten days she had before she was to leave for Córdoba. Despite her mother's protests that what Tío Ambrosio knew about the production of wine could be written on the back of a postage stamp, if she wasn't touring the vineyards in order to acquaint herself with every detail of their neglect, she was poring over the books and trying to make sense of the desultory efforts at bookkeeping that were apparently all that her cousin thought necessary.

It was hard work, not made better by the fact that nobody else could see any need for it.

'You're as brown as a berry!' her mother complained. 'What would your father say if he could see you now? You look less and less like an English lady every day!'

Petronilla dropped a kiss on Doña Pilar's brow. 'And more like a Spanish one?'

Her mother rose to the bait, her outrage visible. 'Spanish ladies do not spend their days toiling under a hot sun, let me tell you! Nor do they spend their evenings adding up figures as if it were the only thing left in the world for them to do – just as if Cousin Rosa and I were not here at all!'

Petronilla chuckled. 'What do they do, Mamá? What did you do when you were young?'

Her mother sniffed. 'Cousin Rosa would make you a better example! *She* manages to occupy herself all the day long without having to burn herself to a crisp!'

'Sewing a fine seam,' Petronilla agreed meekly.

Doña Pilar eyed her suspiciously. 'She was always better than I with her needle. I remember when the holy nuns were trying to show us a new stitch, she was always able to do it right away. I am not a natural needlewoman.' This manifest untruth fell on deaf ears.

'Nor am I!' Petronilla mocked her. 'It's sad, isn't it, how we prefer something more adventurous than wielding a needle! And the blame is more yours than mine, Mamá dear, for I have always tried to live up to your example of how a great lady should behave in all circumstances.'

'*I* don't rush about in the sun, tiring myself out; nor do I think myself as good as a man around the *bodega* – I leave all such things to those whom God intended should be the ones to worry about them, and that doesn't include you!'

'Oh no, you don't, Mamá! You're just biding your time until Papá comes, but you don't feel any better about Don Diego's efforts than I do! Who said she is going to be hiring some labour while I'm in Córdoba? And who has been making enquiries about the old *capataz* Fernandez, just in case he is still alive and able to train up someone to your exacting standards? You don't fool me, mother dear!'

Doña Pilar flounced into the nearest chair. 'I have a husband, you have yet to find one, my dear, and that makes all the difference!'

Petronilla looked at her in astonishment. 'I never thought to hear you say such a thing! I'm not looking for a husband!'

'You're a little young as yet,' her mother conceded. 'But we shan't be in Spain for ever and, once your father arrives, he'll be making that sad face of his whenever you *talk* to a Spaniard, and I have never seen anyone in England with half the address and the pride of we Spanish. Only your Papá could make my heart beat faster, the rest – are like Mr Gladstone and not at all the kind of man one would wish to be one's husband!'

'I'm not about to marry poor Mr Gladstone –'

'That is it exactly! Me, I do not wish my husband, or my son-in-law, to be referred to as *poor* Mr So-and-so!'

'Well, if it's any comfort to you, neither do I!' Petronilla assured her. 'The only thing is, I'm not sure Tío Ambrosio and Tía Consuelo would think of someone like Mr Gladstone as *poor* Mr Gladstone, they'd probably see him as worthy Mr Gladstone, or clever Mr Gladstone –'

This had obviously not occurred to Doña Pilar. 'Perhaps I should come with you to Córdoba after all.'

'Why? Is Mr Gladstone going to be there?' Petronilla teased her.

'Mr Gladstone is too old to interest you, but who knows

what other young men may come calling when they hear you are in Córdoba? If Cousin Rosa was going to be there, there would be nothing to worry about, but Tía Consuelo is not the person I'd have chosen to be your *accompañadora*, not if you are to enjoy yourself!'

'It's Tío Ambrosio I want to see!' Petronilla insisted. 'And if Don Diego is there, all the better! I have a great many questions to ask of both of them!'

'Petronilla, I beg you, leave it until your father comes! Do try to remember you are only a young girl! Tío Ambrosio is an old man and he won't enjoy being reproved by you, no matter how just your case! Please be very careful how you go about things!'

'I'll do my best,' Petronilla promised.

As the day for her departure grew nearer, however, she began to share some of her mother's doubts over her ability to make her great-uncle understand how neglected everything was. She was not her father's daughter for nothing though, and far from changing her mind about the projected visit to Córdoba, she applied herself all the harder to mastering every detail of the way the *bodega* had been managed and the changes she wanted to make.

Taking the books to the patio closest to her bedroom, she settled herself there, meaning to make the most of a quiet hour or so before she changed her dress and went to sit with her mother and Cousin Rosa over a glass of sherry, a ritual that was observed every evening by all three ladies with all the more pleasure because they were guiltily aware there were no men present to serve as an excuse for their indulgence.

Within the homestead there were several courtyards, with greater or lesser privacy from the rest of the house. This one was Petronilla's favourite. A fountain played lazily at one end of an oblong pool and there were four orange trees, one in each corner of the cobbled floor, which at the moment were in flower, their scent pervading her bedroom as well as the still air inside the courtyard. It was peaceful there, marvellously peaceful, with only the occasional burst of birdsong, or the buzzing of an insect to break the silence.

She sat herself on a wooden bench, letting the atmosphere seep into her very bones. She felt more like dropping off to sleep than opening the books and making a last attempt to understand what was written there. She had learned that the vineyards were divided up into three types: *Albariza*, which has a chalky soil, *Barros*, which has a clay soil, and *Arena*, which has a sandy soil. It was the *Albariza* which had the greatest value, for it was the white, chalky soil that produced the best grapes for the fortified wine the *bodega* made. Each vineyard had its own section in the records, where every vine's grapes were weighed and recorded every year. It made dismal reading to see how it was the same story of a declining vintage in each of the last five years, ending in the last year with a few entries made in an illiterate hand, blotched and illegible, but nevertheless bearing the same message of decline as all the former entries.

She was puzzling out the final entry, which ended in the middle of a word as far as she could see, when José appeared at her side. Expecting her promised afternoon sandwich, she looked up expectantly, but the only thing on the silver tray was a single gentleman's visiting card.

'Isn't my mother in?' she asked.

'The gentleman asked for you – the Doña Petronilla.'

Petronilla picked up the card and looked at it. The moment she saw the name on it her heart began to thump painfully against her ribs.

'Please show him in,' she said to José.

Mr Arbuthnot was taller than she remembered. She had time to remind herself of his foxy-coloured hair and his sherry-coloured eyes; she remembered, too, how when they had played Snapdragons together she had first noticed that his beard and moustache were a lighter red than the rest of his hair. And how, later on, they had kissed.

She offered him her hand, giving a quick instruction to José to bring them both some refreshment.

'So, you've taken up my mother's invitation and come to see us?' she said.

He looked round the courtyard with appreciation. 'How are you enjoying Spain?' he asked.

Her eyes followed his. 'More than I imagined possible.'

'I hoped you would.'

'Because it mattered so much to my mother that I should?'

'I thought it might matter to you too. I feel at home here; I hoped you might as well. Your mother must have missed living in this lovely house!'

'My father's house has much to recommend it also,' she pointed out. 'The new plumbing for a start! There is nothing out here like the water closets my father has installed!'

He seated himself on the wooden seat beside her. 'I hadn't realized such luxuries were so important to you.'

Afraid she had disappointed him, she abandoned trying to pretend she was other than completely fascinated by her new environment. If she felt faintly disloyal to her father because of it, she smothered the feeling back down where it belonged, and smiled happily at her unexpected visitor.

'They're not,' she admitted frankly. 'I love it here, every minute of it, and you're a most welcome visitor! I think Mamá means to pick your brains over what we should do about our vineyards and *bodega*. I can't think why José didn't tell her you're here —'

'I wanted to see you first,' Mr Arbuthnot interrupted her.

Petronilla tapped the card she still held in her left hand. *Charles Arbuthnot*, she read, *Shipper of Fine Sherries, Jerez de la Frontera, Cádiz, Spain*. She turned the card over and found the same message written in Spanish. Even the Charles was written as Carlos.

'I'm not sure my mother will approve of my receiving you alone,' she demurred. 'Are you sure I shouldn't send José to fetch her – or Cousin Rosa?'

'I beg you will not quite yet,' he insisted gently. 'I don't want to get you into any trouble, but it would be a great kindness if you would hear me out before we tell your mother that I'm here. It's a business matter, you understand, which, if your father is to be believed, is more in your line than hers.'

Petronilla looked doubtful. 'My father flatters me because I have helped him from time to time in writing his speeches for the House, but don't underrate Mamá! She knows more about Papá and every detail of his career than I ever shall, and all without looking as though she's taking the least interest in anything that smacks of politics!'

'That's because she loves your father. She is probably as fiercely loyal to all the members of her family.'

'Of course.'

'That's why I wished to speak with you first. I do want to talk to you both about the *bodega*, but there is something else I wish to discuss with you first.' He paused as José came back into the courtyard with a tray laden with cold cuts of meat, bread and butter, some of the local crisp white wine, and some cordial for Petronilla.

'May I bring you anything else, sir?'

Mr Arbuthnot waved him away, turning his attention back to Petronilla with a thoughtful air.

'I came by way of the coast, through Gibraltar. I hadn't realized your mother's family was so well known throughout Andalucía – and not always for the quality of your wine.'

This wasn't at all what Petronilla had expected. 'What have you heard about us?' she demanded. She made an impatient gesture, wondering why she should feel responsible for anything the Morena family might choose to do, and then equally cross with herself for trying to deny she was one of them, even if it were only to herself, and only for a moment. 'I haven't met everyone in the family yet,' she added.

'Not your cousin Diego Salcedo Morena?'

'I'm paying a visit to my uncle Ambrosio next week in

Córdoba and I hope to make his acquaintance then. Did you meet him in Gibraltar?'

'No.'

Petronilla gave him a bewildered look. 'Have you ever met him?'

'No.'

She frowned. 'Then what are we talking about?'

'I just wondered what you knew about him. I was surprised a cousin of yours should be a follower of Don Carlos, knowing how your mother was nearly executed for being on the other side, but civil wars often divide families as much as they do the country concerned, and there is frequently right on both sides. There was something else I heard that I thought your father ought to know, if you won't mind including it in your next letter to him?'

'Something to do with Don Diego?'

'With Gibraltar. Just tell him the "ragged rascals" are busier than he thought, or so it is said in the neighbourhood. Will you do that?'

Petronilla helped herself to some cordial. 'Is it important?'

'I don't really know, but I think your father will want to be told anyway. Do you mind being used as postman?'

'Of course not!' Petronilla disclaimed. 'What has it got to do with my Cousin Diego?'

'His name was mentioned, that's all. His family has estates close to Granada, don't they?'

Petronilla was obliged to admit she didn't know. 'According to Tío Ambrosio, he's supposed to be overseeing the *bodega* and vineyards here,' she said drily.

'Which is why you're going to Córdoba next week?' he concluded. 'Why doesn't Doña Pilar go with you?'

Petronilla ignored the question. 'If you came up from the coast, you must have seen our vineyards on the way. Mr Arbuthnot, would you have time to ride out tomorrow and tell me what you think should be done to set things right? Mamá and I have been hoping you would come – she will tell you as much herself at dinner! You will stay the night, won't you?'

'Thank you, but I've already booked a room at the inn in Montilla as your father isn't here. Perhaps I might do myself the honour to call on you and your mother in the morning?'

Her nervousness of him was gone. In England, she remembered, until he had kissed her she had felt completely comfortable with him – and not only when they had been playing Snapdragons together.

'My mother will be very pleased to see you any time,' she responded, a twinkle appearing in her dark eyes. 'You're already a great favourite with her, as you know, but if you'll talk wine with her and give her some proper advice as to how we should go about reclaiming the vineyards, she'll be your friend for life! I'm afraid she has very little faith in my efforts to persuade Tío Ambrosio that something has to be done if Mamá is to receive any income from the winemaking in the future.'

He grinned, his formality disappearing in the sudden lightening of mood. 'It'll be my pleasure! I'd understood, though, that the *bodega* was yours?'

She nodded slowly. 'Part of my dowry, but I shan't be marrying anyone for ages yet and, until then, it's a family affair. Mamá is the real owner, however. Her mother's will saw to that, not that I expect Tío Ambrosio *or* Cousin Diego to pay much attention to her wishes, if at all.' She lowered her voice to a conspiratorial tone. 'She married an Englishman and, worse, *I* am an Englishwoman!'

'What a terrible fate!'

'Well, you'd certainly think so if their hints and sideways glances are to be believed. The trouble is that we feel exactly the same about *them* back in England! It's all so stupid!'

'Maybe it is, but it goes back a long way. You know yourself how many people in England think our loyalties are suspect because we are Catholics.' He gave her an amused, sidelong glance. 'Your own father isn't free from that particular prejudice, I imagine?'

'No, but for Papá religion is merely a part of politics, and not a particularly interesting part at that!'

'There's an element of truth in that, wouldn't you agree?'

'I suppose so,' she sighed. She uttered a naughty chuckle. 'God proposes and man disposes, something like that?'

'If you believe man is free to choose right from wrong, and so on, you have to put up with the mess he sometimes makes of it,' Mr Arbuthnot agreed.

Petronilla tried to imagine herself having this conversation with any of the other young men she knew and failed. Somehow, it seemed quite natural to discuss such things with him. Men might philosophize between themselves, but women were not expected to be able to make any worthwhile contribution to the world of ideas.

'It's always men who make all the decisions,' she said aloud. 'I'm sure Tío Ambrosio doesn't know a quarter of what Mamá does about making wine and yet we can't begin to clear up the mess that's been made of the *bodega* without his consent!'

'Your father might have something to say to that!'

'He has other things on his mind,' she replied sadly. 'Besides, by the time I write to him and ask him to intervene, and he tries to sort something out – because he doesn't even drink sherry wine, bless him! – we might as well wait for him to come to Spain, which will undoubtedly be too late anyway!'

'As bad as that?'

She gestured towards the books. 'Worse!'

He was silent for a moment. It was a comfortable silence, although she could almost see the wheels going round in his brain as he considered what she had told him.

'Well?' she prompted him.

He was amused by her impatience. 'Perhaps I should wait until I see your mother in the morning —'

'You have a plan!' she marvelled.

'An idea that might benefit us all,' he temporized. 'No more than that.'

She jumped up, laughing at him over her shoulder as she danced over to the fountain and back again. 'Mamá was quite right when she said you'd know the answer! I'm so glad you came today!'

After he had gone, she was still hugging herself with glee when she went to tell her mother of his visit. Whatever his solution, she was sure it would be practical and that, if Doña Pilar would allow him, he would lift the weight of the *bodega* off their shoulders no matter what objections Tío Ambrosio cared to make.

But Doña Pilar was far from pleased at her news. 'What were you thinking about, Petronilla, receiving him on your own – and practically in your bedchamber, for that patio is only just outside! Really, it is too bad! Spain is *not* England, as I am forever pointing out to you!'

'I know that, Mamá —'

Doña Pilar closed her eyes in distress. '*Cada país su ley y cada casa sus costumbres,*' she quoted. And then translated the saying in case her daughter hadn't understood what she was getting at. 'Each country has its own law and every house its customs. Let's hope Mr Arbuthnot doesn't speak of this to anyone else.'

Petronilla thought there were rather more important things in the world than whether she and Mr Arbuthnot had spent ten minutes alone together.

'He couldn't see anything untoward in it because he *asked* for me!' she said, aggrieved. 'Papá had nothing to say about it when I showed him the gardens in Hampshire. I was just as much alone with him then!'

'That isn't the point, my love. We were all within call and both of you knew it. Here, you could have been in real danger and I shouldn't have heard a single sound! If you have no sense of propriety, Mr Arbuthnot should have known better! And so should José! He wouldn't have dreamed of showing a strange man into your private patio if you had been a Spanish young lady! And so I shall tell him! The very idea!'

Petronilla glared. 'I thought you liked Mr Arbuthnot?'

'What has that to say to anything? Of course I like Mr Arbuthnot! I hope you do too! But you must learn to be more circumspect, *pequeña*, because, although your father treats you as his unpaid assistant in his political work, you are still a young girl and must learn to behave as such! Most of this is my fault! I'm as bad as your father, expecting you to worry about all kinds of business much better left to the men of the family. The concept of *vergüenza* is the most important thing to any Spanish lady. It's more than virtue – more a sense of shame. To be found *sin vergüenza*, to put one's family to the blush, is the worst fate that can befall any of us! When I think what Tía Consuelo would make of your behaviour, I feel quite faint!'

'But, surely —' Petronilla began to object.

'But nothing! You're in Spain now, my love, and there's not the least use telling me things are different in England, because I have more reason than most to know that they aren't in the least bit different! A woman's honour is her most precious possession until she has a husband to guard it for her and that is true all over the world! I beg you will not do such a thing again!'

'I'll be very careful,' Petronilla promised.

Her mother eyed her suspiciously, unconvinced by this display of filial obedience. 'I am sure you will be,' she returned warmly. 'It would be very rag-mannered to upset all your new relations for such a silly reason, no?'

Petronilla's moment of rebellion crumbled. She knew the great emphasis her mother laid on good manners and, up to a point, she agreed with her.

'Darling Mamá! I'm sorry I displeased you, but you won't hold it against Mr Arbuthnot, will you? He means to come and see you tomorrow to talk about the *bodega*, and even if you do think Tío Ambrosio to be the head of the family I can't help thinking Mr Arbuthnot knows a great deal more about wine and will be of much more use to us!'

'I won't argue with you about that!' Doña Pilar smiled. 'Next to your Papá, I can't think of anyone I want to see more, if only to keep you out of the hot sun for a few days! I hope Mr Arbuthnot didn't remark that you looked more like a peasant girl than an English young lady!'

'I don't think he looked at me at all,' Petronilla replied. 'If you ask me, he has plans of his own or he wouldn't have come anywhere near us.'

Doña Pilar's eyes snapped with amusement. 'How young you still are sometimes! And very English! Me, I always knew when a gentleman had his eye on me, even before I could walk!'

Petronilla blushed, resentful that her mother should be able to embarrass her over anything as silly as what she truly believed to be her parent's own wishful thinking.

'What makes you think I don't?' she asked crossly. 'I know enough to know that Mr Arbuthnot has only one love in his life and that's the wine he buys and sells! It certainly isn't me!'

'*Ay de mí*! Almost you persuade me!' her mother teased her. 'We shall see which one of us is right when your Mr Arbuthnot comes tomorrow. What time did he say he would be here?'

'He didn't say, but as he's spending the night in Montilla he may be quite early.'

And early he was. Petronilla had already changed her dress twice by the time José announced him. She couldn't have explained her eagerness to look her best for him and, fortunately, her mother was too tactful to draw attention to her daughter's distracted behaviour. Cousin Rosa had faded into the background long before breakfast was finished with a skill born of long practice. Even Petronilla, busy with her own thoughts as she was, felt obliged to try to draw her back into the family circle, but it was like encouraging a character in a shadow play to take life and speak and sing for herself. Long habit had made her a specialist in fading her personality into a grey as deep as the shadows that marked her chosen background, a faded gentlewoman who was of no further interest to anyone now that she no longer had a husband to speak for her. Only Doña Pilar's gentle insistence that she should make some contribution to the general conversation drew her out sufficiently to make Mr Arbuthnot aware that she was there at all and that her English was practically non-existent.

'You should have spoken up before, Doña Rosa. All of us speak Spanish as easily as we do English and we have no secrets we are trying to keep from you.'

Doña Rosa bridled happily, beginning to enjoy herself. 'I know nothing of the vintner's art, *señor*. My husband could have been some help to you, but I'm afraid I have very little knowledge of such things.'

'Her husband was the greatest *capataz* of his generation,' Doña Pilar put in smiling. 'My father used to say he was the greatest of them all!'

There was no doubt but that Mr Arbuthnot was far more impressed by this information than he would have been to hear he had been the greatest Grandee in the land.

'Then it must grieve you as much as it does your cousins to see how neglected the vineyards are here,' he said eagerly.

Doña Rosa peered up at him. 'It's all the fault of that scallywag, our young cousin Diego. My uncle Ambrosio is now the head of our family, because both Cousin Pilar's father and mine are dead, you see. Well Tío Ambrosio doesn't know any more about the wine trade than I do, but he does understand that Diego's branch of the family lost everything when they declared for Don Carlos and then went on to lose the only battle they actually bothered to fight for him. The trouble is that Diego doesn't understand anything about winemaking either.'

Mr Arbuthnot looked from one to the other of the three ladies. 'I see,' he said at last. He cleared his throat. 'I was under the impression the *bodega* belongs to Doña Pilar?'

'So it does,' Petronilla answered immediately. 'I told you how it was yesterday.'

'I know you did.' His eyes met Doña Pilar's and he flushed a little. 'I – er – I hope you didn't object to my calling on Miss Harris before I made my presence in the neighbourhood known to you?'

Petronilla's mother looked down at her hands, neatly folded in her lap. 'I did think it ill-advised of her to receive you alone, Mr Arbuthnot. I hope you won't mind my speaking frankly but, with Petronilla being a foreigner in Spain, all her Spanish relations are looking for an opportunity to find fault with her manners and general behaviour, and should they ever learn that a young girl of her age has been receiving gentlemen callers, without any kind of chaperon being present, there would be little I could say or do to retrieve the situation.'

'I understand, ma'am. I am sorry I presumed too much. Miss Harris has nothing to fear from me!'

Doña Pilar raised her eyes. 'You and I may know that, Mr Arbuthnot, but until Miss Fairman gets here, I am obliged to fulfil the role of my daughter's chaperon, which is not a task I relish in the slightest, and for which I have very little talent, if the truth be known! I'd prefer it if you could contrive to make as easy for me as possible and give me your co-operation – as well as Petronilla's – in future?'

'Yes, of course.' Mr Arbuthnot's face fell. 'The blame is all mine – not your daughter's, ma'am, for I gave her no choice in the matter. Colonel Harris – we – er –'

Doña Pilar gave him a warning look. 'Shall we talk about the vineyard? My daughter gave me to understand that you have some plan that might rescue it from total dereliction. Is it possible? To be honest with you, I am in flat despair as to what will become of it!'

Mr Arbuthnot looked relieved to be on firmer ground. With a conspiratorial glance at Petronilla, he forgot the dressing down he had just received and seated himself opposite Doña Pilar, rubbing his hands together in enthusiasm.

'The thing is, Mrs Harris —'

'In Spanish, Charles, if you don't mind?'

He flushed absurdly with pleasure that she should have forgiven him sufficiently to use his given name and, at the same moment, a ray from the sun caught his hair, giving him a burnished look that was momentarily dazzling. He turned at once to Doña Rosa, making her a handsome apology that she accepted with what Petronilla thought was excessive calm when one considered how most people ignored her altogether.

'Yes, do let's listen to Mr Arbuthnot's plan!' Petronilla said aloud. 'We are all ears, aren't we, Cousin Rosa?'

Her Spanish cousin threaded her needle with aplomb. 'Indeed we are,' she agreed at length. 'Please, do go ahead!'

Mr Arbuthnot chewed on his lower lip. 'I must begin with myself, though I know you are more interested in your own vineyards. As you know, up until now I have been engaged in buying sherry in Spain and selling it through various outlets in England – London mostly. When I last saw you in Sanlúcar, I confided my hopes of buying my own *bodega* and starting my own brand of sherry.' His excitement grew visibly as he went along. 'I've made an offer for just the place! There is a vineyard attached, but it isn't nearly big enough for my needs because I have hopes of supplying all my old customers, most of whom have been kind enough to say they will recommend my product to all their outlets. I must confess I had hoped to come to some arrangement with you and use your wine to augment what I shall be producing myself in Jerez. I hinted as much in England, you may remember, but I'm now in a position to make you a provisional offer of some kind of partnership, though nothing is finalized as yet. I know there are people who refuse to admit that any wine grown outside the Jerez area is a true sherry, but it is frequently done and not always for foreign sales. I mean to sell only the very best wines from both areas. The very best!'

'Yes, but the vineyards here are in ruins!' Doña Pilar objected.

Petronilla looked anxiously from one to the other. 'If I were allowed to —' she began darkly. 'Still, I must say your coming is the next best thing to being allowed to take charge myself!'

Mr Arbuthnot positively glowed. 'I took the liberty of riding round most of the vineyards when I left here yesterday. They are neglected, it's true, but not beyond redemption. I came to the conclusion that whilst those vineyards that are easiest of access have been replanted with inferior vines – if not left to rot away altogether – there are other vineyards hidden away that are far from being neglected. I spoke to some of the men who were working on them and they admitted they had been selling the grapes to another local *bodega*, or keeping them for their own use, until such time as either Doña Pilar or Doña Petronilla came home again.'

'But the books —?' Petronilla protested.

'None of them can read or write, Miss Harris,' he explained awkwardly, 'and they were afraid the foreign lady would think the less of them because of it!'

'Is that what they call me? The foreign lady?'

'*La inglesa,*' he nodded. 'The English lady.'

Doña Rosa looked up from her sewing. 'I can't believe the wine will be of a very high quality without an experienced *capataz* to oversee its production,' she murmured. When she found that all three were listening to her, she grew flustered. 'Oh please, don't pay any attention to me! I know nothing of these things, nothing at all! Only, my husband always used to say that a good wine could only be made by a true artist – which he was, as even the most reactionary members of our family were wont to admit!'

'Indeed yes!' Doña Pilar agreed.

Mr Arbuthnot nodded impatiently. 'There is a *capataz* here —'

'*Señor* Fernandez?'

'I fancy this man is the son of the *capataz* you remember,' Mr Arbuthnot told her. 'Fernandez tells me your mother was the one who made him *capataz* here. I'm sorry to tell you he'd have nothing to do with your cousin's plans for the *bodega*.'

'Yet he had no hesitation in telling you his troubles?' Doña Pilar said doubtfully.

'There is no doubt about his loyalty to yourself!' Mr Arbuthnot answered quickly.

'Well, I don't know. How is it he hasn't come forward to tell us any of this? He must have seen Petronilla riding round the vineyards and, as everyone else in the district has come to call, he must have known by this time that I am in residence.'

Mr Arbuthnot gave an embarrassed smile. 'Don Diego is your cousin, ma'am. You may have wanted him to continue to run the *bodega* —'

'And none of them will work for him, is that it?' Petronilla interrupted impetuously. 'I'm not sure I should either! He may be a very fine soldier, but he's completely useless when it comes to wine!'

'Hush, dear!' Doña Rosa rebuked her. 'You'll like him well enough when you make his acquaintance. Everybody does! I do myself!'

But Petronilla was nothing if not persistent. 'Is that what I'm to tell Tío Ambrosio,' she demanded, 'that nobody will work for him? Shall I tell him that Papá has agreed to Mr Arbuthnot —' She broke off, dismayed by her mother's doubtful expression. 'I must tell him *something*!' she pleaded.

'Yes, of course, dear. I think it might be better not to mention Mr Arbuthnot to your uncle just yet, however. All you need say is how disappointed we are to find the vineyards in such a condition and that, if he has no objection, we are going to seek advice as to how to put matters right.'

Doña Rosa put down her needle with unusual decision. 'All Tío Ambrosio wants is a settled income for Diego.

Why don't you tell him the *bodega* belongs to you and have done with it, Cousin? Mr Arbuthnot will soon have things back to normal, which seems to me a most satisfactory solution to all your problems, particularly if he and Cousin Petronilla —'

'Oh do hush, all of you!' Doña Pilar said crossly.

Petronilla sat up very straight. 'What about Mr Arbuthnot and me?' she asked in a tight little voice.

'You're far too young!' her mother stated flatly.

Mr Arbuthnot took Petronilla's hand in his. 'I spoke to your father when I visited you in Hampshire and we all agreed you're too young to be thinking in terms of marriage quite yet, Miss Petronilla, but I hope I wasn't quite wrong in thinking you were pleased to see me yesterday, was I?'

Petronilla felt a tight constriction round her chest. Marriage? With Mr Arbuthnot? She peeped up at him, enjoying the feeling of power this new knowledge had given her.

'I was a little bit pleased to see you,' she admitted demurely.

His eyebrows rose in mute enquiry, bringing an unwelcome glow to her face. 'Only a little bit?' he quizzed her.

'I was *very* pleased to see you!' she amended, not quite meeting his eyes. 'Will that do?'

His smile warmed her, relieving her embarrassment. 'For now it will do very nicely,' he said.

Chapter Seven

By the second day of Petronilla's visit she was sure Tío Ambrosio was avoiding her, not that she blamed him for he must know that, from his point of view, she was about to be extremely difficult. Tía Consuelo, on the other hand, seemed unwilling to leave her alone for a minute.

'I hardly got to know you at all the last time you were here,' she explained herself. 'We were so busy welcoming your mother home, I'm afraid we neglected you. Never mind, my dear, we have all the time in the world now you are on your own with us. Did you meet your Cousin Teresa when you were here? She is very excited to have a foreigner in the family and has volunteered to show you around Córdoba, such as it is – I'm afraid we have few of the entertainments of Seville here, but with so many of us in the family it hardly seems to matter.'

Petronilla was glad of Teresa's company. Neither of her parents had ever encouraged her to giggle about nothing and to make silly jokes, for both of them thought such adolescent behaviour tiresome, and Petronilla wasn't sure that she didn't find it so herself. But although Teresa giggled all the time, finding something funny in whatever was said to her, she was no fool underneath this lighthearted exterior, as Petronilla already knew, and she was soon advising her English cousin to say very little to Tío Ambrosio about the *bodega*.

'Cousin Diego is coming to Córdoba in a day or so and you'd do much better to ask him direct. Poor Tío Ambrosio feels, as the head of the family, he ought to know all the answers about all of us, but the truth is that he doesn't. He doesn't even recognize me when he comes across me in his own house!'

Petronilla laughed. 'Nevertheless, he is the head of the family and something must be done to rescue the *bodega* at Montilla from any further depredations. I really must speak to him about it sooner or later. Valuable planting time is being lost!'

Teresa giggled. 'You sound as though you care for such things?'

'Well yes, I think I do.'

Agog, Teresa stopped laughing, twisting the tassel on her fan between her fingers instead. 'I don't understand you,' she said at last. 'Perhaps it's because you're English you think the way you do. I don't know whether my parents are rich or not, or anything about that side of our life. Neither my father, nor my mother, would *dream* of my setting myself up against Tío Ambrosio's wishes, no matter how much they might like to! They'd tell me I'm only a young female with no possible interest in such things – and I must say I think they'd be right. How can you know better than the menfolk about making wine and things like that?'

Petronilla only smiled. 'Even a complete ninny could do better than Cousin Diego seems to have done!' she declared.

Teresa, looking quite serious for once, spread her fan and closed it again with a snap. 'You don't understand,' she said at last. 'Everybody *likes* Cousin Diego! He's exciting, and even the dullest event is fun when he's staying. It isn't his fault that he hasn't any money. Why should you care what happens to your mother's *bodega*? Neither of you will go hungry, will you? You don't even belong here!"

'The *bodega* belongs to my mother —'

'Who married an Englishman! *She* doesn't need it either!'

But Petronilla was not to be persuaded. 'Whether any of us need the *bodega* to live isn't the problem,' she tried to explain. 'As it is, it will soon be more desert than vineyards, and that doesn't help anyone, does it?'

Teresa was unconvinced. 'You'll upset everyone if you insist on making trouble for Cousin Diego,' she declared.

Petronilla tried to divert her young cousin's attention. 'Surely you don't admire someone who's declared for the Pretender King?' she teased her.

Teresa sighed heavily. 'It doesn't seem to matter where Cousin Diego is concerned!' She fanned herself with energy, frowning sulkily as she did so. 'You'll see when you meet him for yourself!'

Petronilla didn't believe her, but she said nothing more on the subject. What was the point? Teresa couldn't help her.

When she did finally meet Don Diego Salcedo Morena it was evening. She had become accustomed to waiting until gone ten o'clock for her evening meal – she had even come to enjoy the formality with which the entire family went into dinner. Tío Ambrosio preferred the old-fashioned seating, with the women on one side of the table and the men on the other. It must have been a hundred years since the British had followed the French example and introduced what was still sometimes known as 'promiscuous' seating, but it was now normal in that country and, before coming to Spain, she had never seen the older custom and had presumed that men and women were always seated alternately in these times.

Tía Consuelo, still unsure of Petronilla's English origins and therefore presuming everyone else to be equally as doubtful, had determined her niece's place as far away from herself as possible. Even Teresa had been granted a superior position in the order of things, although she was not a house guest as such and was not yet 'out' in society, as Petronilla was known to be. But Petronilla enjoyed her lowly position, well away from her aunt, whom she liked less and less the more she saw of her, and in amongst all the most interesting visitors to the family household, including a visitor from South America who had a fund of strange and improbable stories about her indigent servants that kept the whole of the centre of the long refectory table in fits of laughter.

That evening, Petronilla was sorry to see that the South American lady, whose sister had been staying during Petronilla's first visit to her uncle's household in Córdoba, had gone, and that she herself was expected to move up one place, one of Teresa's younger sisters taking her place as the lowest of the low. She was a little late because she had thought her old governess, Miss Fairman, was to arrive that day and had taken the trouble to go personally to meet the late train from Madrid in case she should have been on it. After making a breathless apology to Tía Consuelo, who had merely sniffed by way of response, she had seated herself in a flurry in her allotted place before looking about her to find out who her neighbours for the evening were to be. It was then that she had first seen Don Diego.

He was, without doubt, the most handsome man she had ever seen. His profile was classical, his eyes almond shaped and beautifully set in his head, his nostrils proud and flaring. He was the ideal Spanish grandee, only his expression was more lively and his dress a trifle more careless than was acceptable amongst the most elegant of the old noble families. On Petronilla it had a devastating effect, making her warm to him at once and in a way which she couldn't quite explain to herself.

'Cousin Petronilla, at last!' he greeted her across the table.

'Cousin Diego,' she responded demurely.

He leaned forward, eating her up with his twinkling, yet surprisingly cold, eyes. 'How come that all I've been told about you is that you're English, when there are so many more important things – like your beauty, and that you wear your mantilla like a true Spanish lady? What did Tía Consuelo tell you about me?'

Petronilla glanced at him and away again. 'Nothing.'

He was deeply offended. '*Nothing?* After all the trouble I've taken to ingratiate myself with her so that she would tell the world about her favourite nephew, she tells you nothing at all about me?'

'Absolutely nothing.'

'Then I'll have to do the honours myself! Where shall I begin?'

Petronilla raised her brows. 'At the beginning?' she suggested.

'That's easy!' His mouth tightened and, for a moment, she thought that he could probably be as cruel as he was charming. She didn't think her father would like him, but she, herself, felt the pull of his attraction and was excited by the novelty of his approach. 'I was born into the wrong branch of the family,' he went on, a vicious note underlying his amused tones. 'My mother's dowry was – shall we say – overlooked, and my father has very little of his own. That is how I became a soldier of fortune —'

'Under Don Juan's banner?'

'Ah! So you do know something about me! Well, I make no apology for pledging my loyalty to our rightful king. The Salic law prevents the Doña Isabella from ever being the Spanish queen. One can't make and remake laws to suit one's politics. Besides, we need the firm hand of a man, not the whims and fancies of a female who is no better than she should be, just like her mother before her!'

'She remains the lawful queen,' Petronilla responded gently. 'Both my Spanish uncles died in her cause.'

'We all have to die sooner or later! They were my first cousins, too, not that I ever had anything much to do with them. My mother's marriage was disapproved of by both of them, as was everything else about me, but my father's family are more enlightened. They have always been loyal to Don Juan, as I am.'

'Oh, I see!' Petronilla smiled. 'Fortunately I don't have to take sides, though I must admit my sympathies are all with the Queen. I claim English neutrality!'

'The English are never neutral, any more than are the French! I cry pardon, cousin, for boring you with our politics, however. The fair sex have no love for such topics of conversation. Public life is not for them under any circumstances, I know! Your minds are fashioned for other things – like gossip and the endless fascination of who loves whom! Am I not right?'

'My father is an English Member of Parliament,' Petronilla warned him.

'Then I shall definitely avoid boring you with our Spanish politics – you would soon find out that I am nothing more than a soldier of fortune and despise me accordingly! Instead, I shall take you to see one of our famous bullfights and you will fall in love with me, no?'

'I doubt it,' Petronilla said drily. She was intrigued by him all the same and, as she turned back to her neighbours, feeling she had neglected them long enough, she had already half decided that she would go with him to the bullfight, just as soon as she could persuade Miss Fairman to chaperon her on the expedition. She had a delightful vision of Miss Fairman being revolted by it all and neglecting her charge shamefully! That would give her the opportunity to get to know her cousin better, as well as finding out what he intended to do about her mother's *bodega* and vineyards. It would be quite an experience!

Tía Consuelo tapped her on her shoulder with her fan. 'Petronilla! I have been trying to attract your attention for the last five minutes! It doesn't amuse me to have to interrupt my dinner because you are too busy making eyes at all the young men rather than paying proper attention to your elders! That may be the way you carry on in England, but here, in Spain, we expect more modesty in a young lady! Your governess has arrived! Kindly move up

and give her your place! Perhaps she will have greater success
in moderating your behaviour than we have been able to
do!'

Petronilla's delight in seeing Miss Fairman overcame
her chagrin at such a public dressing down from her aunt.
She apologized handsomely, rising to her feet as she did
so and flinging her arms about her ex-governess's slender
figure.

'When did you come? I met every train all day long and
you weren't on any of them! Oh, I am so glad to see you!'

'So it would seem!' Miss Fairman responded to the
warm embrace with a slanting eyebrow. 'Your aunt
doesn't seem to share your enthusiasm?'

'No. Partly it's because you're English, of course, but
mostly she treats everyone the same way. Cousin Rosa
says it's because she hasn't had much happiness in her
life —'

'Cousin Rosa? Is she here?'

'She's staying in Montilla with Mamá. You'll make her
acquaintance soon enough, but first you must rest from
your journey here in Córdoba and take things very easily.
Papá wrote and said you were coming through Paris. Why
didn't you come by sea?'

'I wanted to see what Paris is like. I may never have the
opportunity to travel abroad again. How lovely Spain is!
Though I can't approve of everything I've seen since I
took the train to Madrid. I should imagine life can be very
cruel here if one is poor, or not particularly well born.'

'True,' Petronilla agreed carelessly. 'One is either rich,
or poor. There isn't any middle class such as we have in
England.'

'You mean I wouldn't exist?' Miss Fairman said,
blinking short-sighted eyes.

Petronilla gurgled with laughter. '*Exactly*, only we all
know you to be related to half the landed gentry of
England —'

'Indeed? Whoever told you that?'

Petronilla put her face closer to her governess's. 'Mamá,'

she whispered. 'Who else would know, you keep it such a fast secret, almost as if you were ashamed of your birth! Darling Miss Fairman, will you chaperon me to a bullfight if my cousin remembers that he invited me to go with him?'

'I'll think about it. I'm not sure I should *enjoy* seeing a poor dumb animal being tortured and butchered to make a Roman holiday.'

Petronilla wasn't convinced that she would either; it didn't alter her determination to go, however.

By the end of dinner, she had introduced Miss Fairman to most of the more immediate members of her Spanish family. She left Don Diego to last, not wanting to attract her great-aunt's ire all over again.

'You will have heard Mama speak of Don Diego Salcedo Morena,' she said carefully, knowing Miss Fairman spoke little, if any Spanish. 'Cousin Diego, may I present Miss Fairman who used to be my governess and who is now my friend?'

The young man smiled and nodded curtly across the table. '*Encantado!*' he murmured.

Miss Fairman eyed his patrician profile with appreciation. 'Have you long been an *aficionado* of the bullfight?' she asked him.

'Since childhood. Are you a fellow admirer of the art?'

Miss Fairman denied that she was. 'You must know I have never been outside of my native shores before, sir, and we don't have bullfights in Britain.'

'You are the losers,' he said gravely. 'There are Spaniards who dismiss bullfighting as a pagan rite. If it is, give me the Old Religion every time!'

He paused for her to express her shock and dismay at such an attitude, but Miss Fairman did nothing of the sort. She merely sat quietly waiting for him to go on as if she had heard such sentiments every day of her life. When he said nothing further, she prompted him gently,

'I expect you're a literary-minded gentleman? Were you an Englishman, I'd put you down as a follower of Mr

Coleridge. What is it about bullfighting that so appeals to you?'

Don Diego resented being pigeon-holed in this way. He particularly resented it because he had never heard of Mr Coleridge and had a suspicion that this dowdy English spinster was well aware of it. He had known from the moment she had sat down that she didn't approve of him and he thought that to be an impertinence in itself. He glared at her across the table.

'The "moment of truth", madam. To a Spaniard, there is no greater moment in life than the one when a good matador delivers the death blow with his sword and the bull falls to the ground like a clap of thunder. If he has done well, who would take that moment of triumph away from a truly brave man? Imagine how he feels as he makes his *vuelta al ruedo*, his triumphal march round the ring followed by his *peónes*, accompanied to a flutter of white handkerchiefs! To have experienced such a moment is to have lived! I don't expect a foreigner can understand how we feel.'

'Oh I don't know,' Miss Fairman returned pleasantly. 'Some deaths, like martyrdom, we all know to be a hard-won honour, and many of us hope that our death will be the culmination of our life, though in that we are often sadly disappointed; but to rejoice in another living creature's death does seem strange to me.'

'The bull is more powerful than the man,' Don Diego muttered sullenly, looking rather less handsome than he had. 'Many matadors are gored and sometimes killed before the end of their careers.'

'And does the bull have his triumphal march?'

To Petronilla's relief, her governess didn't wait for an answer but turned her attention to her other neighbour, looking as short-sighted and as vague as she always did. Don Diego's face took on a sneer as he transferred his attention back to Petronilla.

'My sympathies, cousin! Shall we persuade one of the other aunts to chaperon you to the bullfight instead?'

Petronilla sat up very straight. She was unused to being the object of such open approval and, truth to tell, she was a little embarrassed by it. She lowered her gaze to the table to disguise the fact that she was unsure of herself – and of him!

'I should prefer to have Miss Fairman with me,' she said.

His nostrils flared, reminding her of a dangerous stallion. 'Very well, little cousin, on your own head be it!' And then he was smiling at her and she was overwhelmingly relieved that he wasn't offended by her preference for someone he considered beneath his notice. When he got to know Miss Fairman better, he would understand how her mockery was as much a part of her as the colour of her eyes, and that she had no intention of giving offence to him or anyone else. In the meantime, Petronilla herself felt torn between the two of them in her anxiety that they should be friends. She had become much more Spanish herself in the last few weeks, in the way she thought and in the way she was living, and Miss Fairman was a reminder of her home and her father in England. Sadly, she wondered if her difficulty would always be in translating one side of herself to the other. The English side was comfortable and familiar; the Spanish new and exciting, and often as unexpected to her as it would be to any other English person. She wasn't at all sure what her own reactions to a bullfight would be, but she was agog to see the spectacle and to know if she too would rejoice in that mysterious 'moment of truth' that somehow, to her, would always be inextricably bound up in the challenge her handsome cousin presented to every female at the table – except Miss Fairman, and that had to be because she was English and of a certain age and therefore past noticing such things.

Tío Ambrosio finally agreed to discuss the *bodega* with Petronilla on the morning of the bullfight. Seated behind an enormous, highly polished desk, he looked more like a walking skeleton than ever. Petronilla, bursting with excitement at the expected treat of the evening, managed to sober her stride to a walk as she obeyed her great-uncle's bidding and joined him in his study, making her curtsy as she approached the desk.

'Well, well, child, are you enjoying your visit to your family in Córdoba? Your aunt tells me that in most respects you are as Spanish as we are ourselves! That will be your mother's doing. I remember her as a child, always wanting to have adventures like her brothers! I hope you have a less wilful nature and are more amenable to the direction of your elders?'

Petronilla managed a small smile. She was not accustomed to being patronized because of her sex, for her father seldom did so unless he wished to tease her into an unwise retort, but on this occasion she had to remember she was her mother's emissary and she had no intention of failing her by antagonizing this old man by a display of English independence.

'I hope I have some of my mother's courage!'

The old man grunted. 'You have her looks. I was surprised to see her looking so well and as elegant as ever after all her years in England. It must have been a difficult time for her!'

'She is very happy with my father,' Petronilla felt obliged to say. 'She hates being away from him, as he hates being parted from her.'

'Ah yes, your father. The English Colonel. Is it true he fought under the Duke of Wellington in our War of Independence?'

'Yes, at Salamanca and later on at Waterloo —'

'There were many battles,' Tío Ambrosio cut her off. 'We all fought for the same cause at that time and knew the true nobility of taking up the sword in the service of the right! Truly, life was more simple in those days!'

'My father would agree with you,' Petronilla said at once. 'Which is why I have come to you about the dreadful neglect we have found in my mother's vineyards. I have all the facts and figures —'

'My dear child, it is not your business to dabble in such things! You can't possibly understand how the accounts are kept, or what is needed to keep the vineyards in order. It isn't work for any female!'

Petronilla tried to conceal her irritation without much success. 'I am very well equipped to deal with the books, Tio,' she assured him in frosty tones. 'My father often makes use of my services when he needs to look up the facts and figures when he is writing one of his speeches. I assure you that it is all too easy to understand what has been happening at Montilla. Look, you can see for yourself, if you'll allow me a moment to fetch the books and show you what has been happening in the various vineyards and in the *bodega* itself!'

Tio Ambrosio was horrified. 'No, no, I have told young Diego he can keep the income if he keeps an eye on the place and I must keep my word to him until your father comes to look into the matter for himself.'

Petronilla made a conscious effort to keep her temper. 'Don't you care that the proceeds are more likely to be keeping Don Juan's cause alive in Andalucía?' she asked sharply.

'I know nothing of that! And neither do you, *sobrina*! What could you know of the rival claims to the Spanish throne – you an Englishwoman! Don Diego's mother is my own sister, my youngest sister, who didn't see fit to marry a foreigner and leave her inheritance behind whilst she had everything she needed for herself in a foreign land! Let me hear no more of your complaints! If you'll take my advice, you'll forget all about it and spend the rest of your visit enjoying yourself! Why, you may even find a husband for yourself amongst your cousins, and then he can see to the whole business of finding a new *capataz* and foreman for you! Meanwhile, until your father's arrival, Don Diego is my choice to look after the *bodega* and that's an end of the matter! Understood?'

'Very well,' said Petronilla, 'I'll write to my father and see what he has to say about it. I should tell you, Tío, that my parents are agreed that my mother's estate should form a part of my dowry and neither of them are likely to be pleased if it turns out to be a valueless property through sheer neglect.'

Her uncle didn't care for such plain speaking. He pulled his mouth in and tapped the top of his desk with irritated fingers.

'Neither of them saw fit to consult me about its future – or yours! Your mother chose to be an *English* lady, what right has she to criticize my stewardship of her *Spanish* estate?'

'Nobody is criticizing *you*, Tío! Please believe me! What we want is your permission to replant the vineyards, and so on, now that my mother is back in Spain for a while. Cousin Diego knows nothing of the vintner's art, as I'm sure he'd be the first to tell you, and the whole place is going to rack and ruin!'

'Your cousin is a soldier, a true *hidalgo*! What should a fine fellow like him know about trade, even the wine trade?'

Petronilla tried to ignore the trickle of pleasure that afflicted her at the sound of his name. It was an affliction because she couldn't *approve* of her cousin, any more than Miss Fairman did, yet he still made her blood run faster in her veins, as a leopard, or some other splendid wild animal might if she met it in the domestic surroundings of her uncle's household.

'I know his mother is your sister, but surely you're not responsible for his future? He has declared for Don Juan, hasn't he? Doesn't that make him some kind of a traitor?'

Tío Ambrosio let the question drop into a long silence, then he said, 'Don Diego's family is older in this country than that of the Doña Isabella, or that of Don Juan. The throne has become a plaything of the foreign powers. Who am I to call him traitor because he prefers one foreigner to another?'

Petronilla admitted defeat. She felt sorry for the old man rather than angry with him. Anyway, what was the use of arguing with him any more: she had the feeling that he hadn't really understood a single word of what she had been saying. He was an old man, of the *hidalgo* class, proud of his calling in life, and who was she to berate him for his lack of interest in anything as mercenary as the making of wine?

She changed the subject, smiling prettily at her uncle across the vast expanse of polished wood. 'Don Diego is taking Miss Fairman and me to the bullfight this evening. I wish you were going to be there to explain the finer points to me. We don't have anything like it in England!'

He was pleased by her pleasure in the excursion. 'I'm glad you mean to be friends with your cousin,' he commended her. 'He's a fine young man, even if he is wrong-headed about some things! Does your aunt know where you are going?'

'I don't know,' Petronilla admitted.

'Ah well, if Miss Fairman is accompanying you I don't suppose it matters, but your aunt is a stickler for correct behaviour in the young. I would advise you to consult her as to what you should wear – things like that! These bullfights are very public affairs and it's well known that your mother's daughter is staying in Córdoba.'

'Yes, it surprised me how well everyone remembers my mother here, she was away so many years.'

Tío Ambrosio looked disapproving all over again. 'As your aunt would tell you, popularity has nothing to do with a good and virtuous life, my dear. Remember that, if you should ever be tempted to elope with some foreigner instead of remembering your duty to your family!'

'Yes, uncle.'

He unbent a little. 'Your mother always had the most pleasing manners – even as a child. If you take after her in that, as well as in your looks, your aunt Consuelo won't have anything to complain about. Run along, child, and enjoy the bullfight!'

*

Miss Fairman was properly sympathetic that her ex-charge had got nowhere with her great-uncle.

'Never mind, dear, your mother will think of something.'

Petronilla sighed. 'We'll have to wait for Papá to arrive, that's all. The poor love doesn't know the first thing about wine, and doesn't want to, but at least he'll listen to Mamá and me! Best of all, he'll listen to Mr Arbuthnot, who does know what he's talking about, and that'll be the end of our worries – at least I hope so!'

'What about Don Diego?'

Petronilla's face lit. 'Do you like him?'

Miss Fairman raised a brow. 'Do you?'

'I'm not sure. He reminds me of a wild animal, beautiful but unapproachable.'

'As long as you don't think it your destiny to tame the beast, I'd say that was a very good description of him,' her governess agreed.

Petronilla chuckled. 'So you do think him attractive?'

Miss Fairman shook her head. 'Not at my age, my love. At my time of life one needs more than animal charm to make one's heart beat faster.'

Petronilla nodded, her dark eyes full of laughter. 'I hope you don't mean that boring reverend gentleman who visited last year and never preached for less than an hour at every service? He almost converted poor Papá to Catholicism!'

'I remember!' Miss Fairman said drily. 'I may be of a certain age, but I am not yet in my dotage!'

'Then we must *both* look our very best at the bullfight! I mean to put on my prettiest Spanish dress, what about you?'

Miss Fairman blinked. 'I mean to look my ordinary English self, as always! And you be careful, *pequeña*, that young man has claws unless I'm sadly mistaken!'

'Like Byron! Didn't someone once say of him that he was "mad, bad, and dangerous to know"?'

'So were the Lambs, my dear, which was why I always

took the greatest care never to get involved with any of their set!'

'You weren't old enough to have been involved with them,' Petronilla objected.

'I most certainly didn't go around half-naked, damping down my clothes to make them cling better, or anything outrageous like that, but I remember being told all about it —'

'In the nursery?' Petronilla opened her eyes very wide, her mouth trembling with laughter.

'Never you mind! It was an awful warning to me – a warning I am passing on to you!'

'*¡Claro!*'

'Then see that you remember it, pet!' Miss Fairman kissed her charge fondly. 'Now, shall we get ready for your beastly bullfight?'

Petronilla kissed her back. Thank goodness, she thought, it was Miss Fairman who was going with her as her *accompañadora* to the bullfight and not Tía Consuelo! And she kissed her again, her mind already skittering over the promised treat that was to come, wondering if the mantilla she was wearing wasn't a little too much for such a *small* bullfight, and her fan a little too elaborate. Tía Consuelo had gone out of her way to tell her that the real bullfights only started after the High Masses on that holiest day of the year, Easter Sunday. Before that, they were mostly small corridas, where the hopeful *toreros* of the future earned their right to go on to bigger and better things. It was a long and rigorous training, beginning as small boys when they would take it in turns to pretend to be the bull, or drive a cart decorated with horns to make the exercise more realistic, and to tempt the animal in the direction they wanted him to go with no more than a cape held out across a single piece of wood.

A few minutes later the two ladies were being handed up into Don Diego's own carriage. Petronilla had only time to note the elaborate crest on the door, before the already restive horses started forward, throwing her up against Miss Fairman. Don Diego grasped his whip, whirling it above his head and bringing it down sharply on the gleaming rump of the leader. The horse reared and bucked, jolting the carriage back and forth. Furious, Petronilla grabbed Don Diego's right wrist, trying to prevent him from doing any further damage, but he threw her off, his face contorted with blind rage against the offending animal.

' "*How art thou fallen from heaven, O Lucifer, son of the morning!*" ' Miss Fairman quoted beneath her breath.

Petronilla's knowledge of the Bible was not great, a fact she put down to the Latin of the Mass, but she recognized the meaning of the reference without any difficulty and found it well chosen. Lucifer, the Shining One, did suit her cousin as a description, and, like the Devil, he knew how to tempt any defenceless female who came within his range. If she weren't extremely careful, she thought he might even tempt *her*. But that wasn't a thought to dwell on, she reproved herself, knowing herself to be far too sensible to have her head turned so easily. He might be as beautiful as Lucifer himself, but he was not for her!

Her immediate concern, however, was not for herself, but for the horses between the shafts of the elegant carriage as Don Diego drove them through the narrow, deeply shadowed streets, where they brushed the terracotta pots of flowers off their perches and broke the palms and other plants that had been set out on the cobbles for the enjoyment of passers-by. His horses might be strong and mettlesome, but he was as careless of them as he was of himself, pressing them on to an intemperate speed in such a confined space, paying no attention at all to their metal-shod hooves slipping on the rough cobbles.

All in all, she was glad to see the circular building of the bullring before them and to know that the breathless chase through the streets was coming to an end. They came to a halt with a final gliding protest from the horses. Thankful that neither of them had broken a leg, Petronilla jumped lightly down, without waiting for Don Diego, and turned herself to help her governess down beside her.

'Well,' said that lady, 'we seem to be here – and in one piece! For a moment there, I didn't think we were going to wait for the bulls!'

Petronilla suppressed a giggle. Safely back on her own two feet, she could begin to find excuses for Don Diego's driving methods, beginning with the undoubted truth that they weren't any of her business, to the undeniable fact that they had arrived intact, despite her worst fears, and that therefore there might not have been anything to worry about in the first place.

Thus, thoroughly restored to her normal self, she shut out of her mind the picture of Don Diego wielding his whip and the sharp, terrified whinnying of the lead horse, and gave herself up to a real enjoyment of being escorted into the box next to the President's on Don Diego's arm and knowing that every head in the place had turned at their entrance. True, the place wasn't exactly overcrowded, but the atmosphere was wholly Spanish and she was wholly a part of it and she meant to enjoy every minute.

Miss Fairman, equally determined *not* to enjoy the spectacle, or any other part of the corrida if she could possibly help it, sat on the edge of her seat and shut her eyes with such determination that even her nose wrinkled with the effort of it.

'Don't bother to tell me what's happening,' she begged, 'I don't want to know!'

Petronilla was only too willing to oblige. She was Spanish enough to appreciate the elaborate ritual of the corrida and to be excited about it. She regretted that the bulls must die, but she was realistic enough to know they had been bred from the best and had lived pampered lives for longer than their cousins, the store-cattle bred for the table and not for their courage. More than that, she knew from her mother the skill that was involved in fighting the bulls and she too could appreciate that their death was the culmination of everything they had been born for. Besides, if anything went wrong, it might be the matador lying on the ground, his blood seeping into the sawdust, and not the bull.

The trumpets sounded and one of the gates of the arena opened to admit two *aguaciles* at a canter, dressed in black velvet and the large white collars that were worn in the reign of King Philip IV. They went straight to the President's box, saluting him, before turning their mounts and cantering over to another gate, through which the *toreros* were about to enter.

Even Miss Fairman opened her eyes when the stirring sounds of the *paso doble* started up and the whole gorgeous procession entered the ring: first the three matadors walking side by side; followed by their *banderilleros* and, behind them, the *picadors*, followed by the *monos sabios* and the caparisoned mule teams, the *areneros* bringing up the rear. Slowly, they marched across the ring, each rank of performers saluting the President in their turn. When everyone had left the ring again, one of the *aguaciles* took the key of the bull pens from the President's hand and carried it over to the bull-pen keeper, after which they both cantered out again.

A great hush came over the audience. Even the women's fans were stilled and silent, the familiar clack of their opening and shutting in abeyance as everyone held their breath waiting for the drama to unfold.

It was soon obvious to Petronilla that Don Diego was on the most friendly of terms with the President of the corrida. He spent a great deal of his time exchanging pleasantries with the President's party and with the President himself. He made no effort to introduce either herself or Miss Fairman to any of the ladies enjoying the scene from the most privileged place in the ring, however. Her brow creased a little as she wondered why not. It seemed to her the height of bad manners to make no effort to bring the two parties together and, after a while, she drew the matter to her ex-governess's attention.

'Is it because we are foreigners, do you suppose?'

Miss Fairman sighed a patient little sigh. 'No, dear. You did tell me this was a *little* bullfight, didn't you? Perhaps that reflects on the President. I shouldn't be surprised if he weren't *quite* respectable, putting our hero into a quandary because they obviously get along very well together.'

'Yes, don't they?' said Petronilla. She was a little put out that Miss Fairman should laugh so easily at her handsome cousin. She was enjoying being dazzled by his good looks and his obvious admiration for his English cousin. And Don Diego, what of him? She doubted he was any more serious than she was. It was a delightful flirtation such as she had never indulged in before. It made her feel grown up and sophisticated in a completely new way and she resented Miss Fairman's belittlement of this splendid creature who was, if only for this moment, filling her horizons.

The three *peónes* of the first of the three matadors spread themselves round the ring, each one of them waiting behind one of the screened entrances of the arena for the first of the bulls to enter. One by one, they stepped out from their hiding place, teasing the bull into making a pass at them, deliberately showing off the animal's strengths and weaknesses both to the expectant audience and the ever-watchful matador, the man who was ultimately to pit his strength against the bull in single combat. The capes waved, the *peónes* appeared and disappeared, baffling the angry animal, until the President decided the matador had had enough opportunity to size up his quarry, and showed his handkerchief. The trumpets sounded and the matador himself made his appearance in the ring, the *picadors* riding in after him and taking up their stations near the *barrera*.

Then came the part of the bullfight that Petronilla liked least. As the *picadors* tempted the bull to rush them, each placing his sword in the beast's back just behind his shoulder blades, she shuddered with anxiety lest they should miss and the bull savage one of the horses on which they were mounted – horses who, it seemed to her, had no stomach for the charges that frequently ended in their being bowled over completely, the more maddened and frustrated the wretched bull became.

Lazily watching the matadors taking it in turns to distract the bull between each bout with the *picadors*, Don Diego tried to persuade his guest that the horses enjoyed their part in the affair.

'Horses are remarkably stupid animals!' he drawled indifferently. 'I doubt they notice much of what is going on.'

Petronilla gave him an outraged look, before looking back down into the arena to see what was happening now. The matadors still in the ring, were taking a rest while the *banderilleros* took their turn in further weakening the bull. Each *peón* took his turn, a *banderilla* held in either hand by the tips of his fingers, first attracting the bulls' attention and then running in a curve across its path, placing the two darts between the animal's bleeding shoulder blades, six darts in all.

The trumpets sounded once again and the President waved his handkerchief for the last act. The first of the matadors, resplendent in his 'suit of lights', took his sword and *muleta* in one hand and his *montera* in the other, and swaggered across the arena towards the President's box, saluting him. His eyes travelled round the audience, his eye falling on Petronilla. He took a step towards her, coming right up to the *barerra* just below her.

'I dedicate this brave bull to the most beautiful lady here!' he announced. His eyes glittered, his whole body poised and ready for anything. Petronilla nodded her head in assent, thrilled to bits by the compliment. The young man turned his back and sauntered back into the centre of the ring, throwing his *montera* over his shoulder and into her lap.

Don Diego bent his head towards her. 'Perhaps he'll present you with the ears!' he muttered, not quite sure he liked anyone else but himself being the centre of attention.

But Petronilla was no longer listening. She scarcely heard the trumpets announcing the *faena*, literally a 'job of work', so intent was she on the minimal movements of the matador below her. He scarcely seemed to move at all each time the bull charged, yet by some miracle his body had swerved from the path of the animal, his *muleta* guiding the maddened bull as it thundered past him. She was no longer conscious of anything, not of her companions, not of the sufferings of the bull, nothing but the grace and beauty of the combat below.

When the final moment came, she even forgot to breathe. The matador stood some three yards away from the beast, his *traje de luces* smeared with his opponent's blood. He held his *muleta* across the front of his body, raising the *estoque* to eye level and taking careful aim. Then, suddenly rising on his toes, he plunged forward, driving the sword home into the base of the bull's neck, his right arm passing between the beast's horns as the sword was pressed home. The bull swayed and dropped to his knees, the thud of the heavy body meeting the ground resounding round the arena.

Petronilla shut her eyes tight, the English side of her nature distressed by the moan of appreciation that went through the crowd. But the other side, the Spanish side, found the atmosphere as cathartic as did the most fanatical of the *aficionados* around her. She made a gesture towards her cousin and saw his eyes light up in triumph. In that moment, it seemed to her, there had grown a bond between them that nothing and no one would ever be able to break. Then she remembered that they were cousins and it was probably no more than the tie of blood between them that made her feel that way. On her father's side, her cousins were all a great deal older than she and she had never felt particularly drawn towards any of them. But, as her mother had pointed out, to a Spaniard the family was everything and nobody was ever excluded from the muddled, magic circle of distant relationships, not even a Byronic, traitorous cousin who bore a close resemblance to Lucifer himself. It was another, not unpleasing reminder that she was a great deal more Spanish than she had thought.

Chapter Eight

'My dear girl, I have absolutely nothing against the young man! So handsome! So well set up in his own conceit! I ask myself who would dare to dislike him? Certainly not I! And quite obviously not you! Enjoy yourself with a little light flirtation by all means, if that is what you want to do, but be wise enough not to take him seriously. He is one to wear in your buttonhole with pleasure, not to allow into your heart.'

'Oh really!' Petronilla responded. 'You'll be telling me next that "handsome is as handsome does"!'

Miss Fairman, who never missed an opportunity to play verbal games (to the despair of her employer who regarded it as another of the governess's defensive ploys calculated to put off any man in the vicinity) snapped back, 'There's many a true word spoken in jest!'

Petronilla sniffed. 'Don Diego is a man, not a flower,' she objected. 'I've never seen anyone as beautiful before. Did you notice how his skin gleamed in the sunlight when we were at the bullfight?'

Miss Fairman nodded. 'Lucifer, the Shining One, in the flesh. But then the Devil wouldn't be the Devil if he weren't attractive. Rather like a sugar plum, one wouldn't want to have to deal with him every day, but one is forced to admit the sparkling exterior is superficially attractive.'

'You don't like sugar plums,' Petronilla pointed out.

'No, I don't, do I?' the governess laughed. 'I did once, but I ate too many of them and they gave me a revulsion for them which has lasted ever since. I think I might grow bored with the Devil if I ever got to know him at all well for much the same reason.'

Petronilla was unimpressed. She thought Miss Fairman far too easily bored by the opposite sex. She was forever having to prove herself their intellectual equal, taking a peculiar pleasure in making them ridiculous, just as she was laughing now at Diego. Petronilla was not laughing. If anything, she was hurt that Miss Fairman should dismiss her cousin so lightly when he had gone to so much trouble to entertain them by taking them to the bullfight, and who never failed to compliment his English cousin on the beauty of her appearance and the elegance of her wit. He was the first man outside of her family she could ever remember who treated her as a grown-up all the time and not as a child to be indulged at one moment and put on one side the next. Even Mr Arbuthnot thought she was too young to have any serious thoughts on her own future.

As always when she thought of Mr Arbuthnot, she thought of the kiss he had stolen – she preferred to call it 'stolen' in her own mind, because she was still quite unable to decide how much part she had had in the incident. She liked the rush of feeling the memory inspired in her, a memory all the more precious because it was a promise of things to come. She *liked* Mr Arbuthnot, especially when he wasn't being stiff and gave her his full attention without expecting her to play second fiddle to her mother all the time. Petronilla adored her mother, but it was fun to be someone in her own right for a change and there was no danger of Don Diego making up to one as settled and middle-aged as the mother, if the daughter were available as a recipient for his compliments and flirtatious remarks. Besides, her mother wasn't there, and she was beginning to wish that Miss Fairman weren't there either if all she could do was criticize and make jokes at Don Diego's expense.

'You're not bored with Córdoba, are you?' she enquired of her companion, knowing that Miss Fairman spoke little Spanish and that the other ladies, led by Tía Consuelo, refused to speak anything else, deliberately trying to exclude her, considering her to be more a servant than another guest in the house.

'I am never bored!' Miss Fairman averred. 'Your mother has frequently told me how beautiful her country is, but I never realized what she was talking about – perhaps one never does until one sees a place for oneself! I am *fascinated* by everything I see! I could spend a week in the Mesquita alone – isn't that what they call it? You can say what you like about those Mohammedans, their buildings are as intricate as lace and yet as simple as any religious buildings I have ever seen. The cathedral in the middle shows an abominable lapse of taste on someone's part, but perhaps if they hadn't put it there they would have torn down the whole place instead. Your father is always telling us about the benefits of progress, but it has an arrogant face at times which more sensitive souls must always find depressing.'

'I believe the cathedral to be quite old,' Petronilla said darkly. It wasn't that she admired the heavy baroque features of the cathedral, but she was in a mood to be argumentative.

'I suppose every age had its progressive element,' the governess returned calmly. She thought her charge to be tired and over-impressed by her cousin's attentions, but she had great faith in Petronilla's good sense and she hesitated to rein her in when the poor child was doing no more than enjoying herself. Her own youth had been spent chafing against the restrictions genteel poverty imposes on any woman of birth and breeding who unfortunately has no fortune to support her pretensions. Only when she had found employment with Doña Pilar had she known again the joy of being able to relax sufficiently to enjoy life instead of merely enduring it. It had left with her a determination not to quench the spirit and hopes of anyone in her charge, having found it such a daunting experience herself, with the consequences that she had been a better governess than she ever would be a chaperon.

Petronilla knew this very well. 'The thing is, Miss Fairman,' she confided, 'I am not ready yet to leave my uncle's roof. Nothing has been decided about the *bodega* —'

'If you haven't found an opportunity to tell your cousin what you think of his management by now, you never will!'

'There always seems to be something else to do,' Petronilla explained. 'You don't mind, do you?'

Miss Fairman gave her a level look. 'Your mother is expecting us, as you know. How long do you mean to keep her waiting?'

Petronilla shifted uncomfortably. 'Not very long. We'll leave quite soon, I promise. I've been invited for a picnic —'

'Oh?' The governess's tone was cool.

Two spots of colour showed on Petronilla's cheeks. 'It's to be quite a small picnic, but I should like to go. Apparently there was once this gorgeous palace not far from Córdoba. It was called the Medina Azahara, after Abd al-Rahman's favourite, and was the most beautiful palace in the world. It had a Royal Salon that had a pool of mercury —'

'My dear, however do you know such things?'

Petronilla modestly averted her eyes. 'Don Diego said it would make a perfect setting for me. Wasn't that kind of him?'

'Marvellously kind! *That thou, light-winged Dryad of the trees, In some melodious plot* of broken stones and tumble-down walls. Are we to picnic in fancy dress? You as Azahara, he as Abd al-Rahman, and I as the court jester?'

But Petronilla was not to be diverted, not even to the pleasing allusion to herself as nightingale. True, it brought Mrs Nightingale to mind, and she had no doubt at all that her adopted grandmother would have been as quick as her father to condemn Don Diego as a *poseur*, striking attitudes like some romantic hero, and not to be taken seriously by anyone.

'Diego says it's to be a surprise, but I expect it to be a party of young people – I expect Cousin Teresa will be there – and others too! We can all chaperon one another, so it will be quite respectable.'

'And I am to be consigned to the company of your Tía Consuelo?'

'You don't mind, do you? I don't think you would enjoy the outing. It's bound to be very strenuous and Don Diego always rides as if the Devil himself were after him. You'd only get hot and tired —'

'And cross? Dragging you back to your uncle's house long before you're ready to leave? That's all very well, Pet, but I doubt your cousin's notion of respectability and mine are quite the same thing —'

'You don't like him, do you?'

'I don't know him very well – and I'm not your age. What concerns me more is whether your mother would approve of my staying home. What do you think?'

'Mamá isn't here to mind!'

'Exactly!' her governess said drily. 'I knew you'd see the point sooner or later!'

Petronilla acknowledged the thrust with a reluctant smile. 'I think she trusts me – more than you seem to do!'

'Oh, I trust you, my sweet! I'm not sure how much I trust your chosen escort! But there, I don't see what harm can come to you on a picnic. I keep forgetting that all these young people are part of your family and can hardly be considered foreigners by you as they are to me. Only, don't let that young man take you out of sight of the others, no matter what attraction he dreams up to show you. There's safety in numbers, as the saying goes!'

'I'll remember,' Petronilla promised dutifully.

Inwardly, she felt only a vast impatience that she should have to ask Miss Fairman's permission at all. Don Diego had laughed at her when he had heard she still had a governess, even if she was now her chaperon, and he treated the older woman with a lack of respect that, at first, Petronilla had found upsetting, for Doña Pilar had always insisted Miss Fairman should be treated as one of the family, her opinion on everything consulted, and the contribution she made to the household duly noted. Miss Fairman showed no sign that she noticed his barbs, however, as her cousin had predicted.

'Servants are made like animals,' he had told her, 'to work and not to have opinions.' And then he had thrown back his head and laughed at her. 'Are you always so serious?' he had asked her.

'Always,' Petronilla had responded, trying not to smile.

He had stopped laughing, his mouth twisting into a cruel, bitter line that made him look more attractive to her than ever. Her heart had gone out to him that he should have known so much unhappiness in his life, whilst she had known nothing but happiness in hers. More than ever, she had wanted to wipe away those lines of bitterness for ever, sure that his true nobility would be revealed if she could only find the dark secret that drove him and which made him so different from the rest of her Spanish family.

'I am never serious,' he had bitten out savagely. Then he had begun to laugh again. 'Except about myself! A nobleman needs some means of support, wouldn't you agree? To restore my fortune requires more than any dowry you are likely to have, so your worthy chaperon may mind her own business as to my intentions towards you! We are both young and healthy and in need of some fun. Surely cousins may be permitted to do that much for each other?'

Petronilla had seen no objection then and she could see no objection now. Picnics in England were frequently rather damp affairs and the novelty of being able to plan such an event, days away in the future, and know that the sun would be shining in all probability, appealed to her more than a little. She had not ever experienced that *frisson* of awareness of the past that ruins were supposed to give one, but she had made up her mind that the ghost of Azahara would undoubtedly walk the ruins of her own palace, and her expectations had been aroused accordingly. Indeed, the only displeasing thought was that her Cousin Teresa would undoubtedly giggle and make fun of everything and that Azahara might take offence and not make her presence known to Petronilla, but that didn't bear thinking about and so she turned her mind to other things.

The morning of the picnic was overcast, but Petronilla wouldn't listen to any suggestion that the treat might be put off until the next day.

'The sun will soon burn off the haze and it will make the ride out cooler,' she dismissed Miss Fairman's objections.

The governess adjusted her charge's Córdoban hat to exactly the right jaunty angle with a sigh. 'A little less determination in a female would be more becoming, my love. Perhaps your Don Diego will cry off!'

But Don Diego was ready and waiting for Petronilla, complaining that the horses were restive and the sooner they made their departure the better. He helped Petronilla up into the saddle, watching as she adjusted her habit and settled herself more comfortably, her back straight, and her excitement lighting up her dark eyes.

'Where are we to meet the others?' she enquired as they trotted along the road towards the Sierra Morena. 'You have certainly allowed plenty of time for exploring the ruins, cousin, if it's only four miles outside the city.'

He turned his head towards her, his profile proud and distant. 'I wish you wouldn't address me as cousin,' he complained. 'The relationship between us is far too distant.'

Petronilla thought it sufficiently close to be recognized in the ordinary way. However, she had no ambition to antagonize him. 'What shall I call you?' she asked with all her usual directness.

'My name is Diego – as you are very well aware!'

'*Señor* Don Diego, is *Cousin* Teresa to be one of our number?'

'No, she is not!'

Petronilla bit her lip. 'Then who —?'

His glanced crushed her fleeting thought of rebellion. 'That dragon who has charge of you would never have allowed you to come with me on your own! She sees you still as a schoolgirl, someone who has to be watched and kept on leading-strings like a baby. That isn't how you see yourself though, is it, Petronilla?'

'No,' she agreed.

'Then spare me the female hysterics! We're going for a picnic, two adults together. What's wrong with that?'

Petronilla frowned, still not wishing to upset his precarious good humour. On this day of all days, she wanted only his approval. 'I can't imagine our families consenting to my —'

'Do you need their consent?'

The mockery in his voice made her feel more foolish than ever. She had no doubt in her own mind that she was able to decide matters for herself, and that Diego meant her no harm, being much more concerned with his own amusement than whether it was a suitable entertainment for her. Besides, although he had asked her not to address him as cousin, he *was* her cousin and, therefore, a perfectly proper companion with whom she could ride out with an easy mind.

'I think it may cause comment, that's all,' she said defensively.

'There's an easy remedy to that – don't tell anyone!' he advised. 'You shouldn't let a pack of women nag you to death for doing no more than what they would have liked to have done themselves at your age! You don't want to end up like Tía Consuelo, do you, without hope of ever having had an adventure of your own?'

Petronilla did not. Neither did she think it in the least likely that she would ever be old and bitter and resentful of the pleasures of others.

'How much I wish I'd been born a man!' she exclaimed. 'It must be marvellous to go where you like, think what you like, and know anybody who takes your fancy!'

Don Diego's eyes narrowed. 'A *hidalgo* must always remember the responsibilities of his birth. If he has no money to support his station in life, what is he to make of his life?'

Petronilla's lips hinted at a smile. 'Take up the Carlist cause?'

'Most people think that dead and buried years ago!'

'But you don't?'

'Not while that female and her mother are allowed to make such a mess of Spain. There was an uprising in Madrid in '48 which they put down without much trouble. It won't be the last. The Catalans are always disaffected. Barcelona is where the Carlos cause will be won or lost in the end. What's needed is to spread dissention in the rest of the country so that the Catalans get some support when they do rise. The rest of the world will only sit up and take notice of Spain when we have a man ruling us and show ourselves strong enough to rid ourselves of petticoat government by both women and the Church!'

Petronilla slanted her head thoughtfully. 'You believe in progressive politics, cousin?'

Don Diego's mouth tightened into an ugly line. 'I'm sorry if I was boring you. I forgot females have no taste for serious conversations, or does being English make you different?'

'I think it might,' Petronilla conceded. 'I have no brothers, you see, so my father talks to me more than most. I would judge our politics to be more practical than those of Spain, however. The English find great causes rather wearying at the best of times.'

Don Diego's smile was as charming as she could have wished. 'No wonder you have fallen in love with your mother's country! Shall I make you fall in love with me?'

Petronilla could be as haughty as her mother. She held

her head high, growing longer in the neck as she disdained to make any reply to this ridiculous suggestion.

'What is that monastery I can see up in the hills?' she asked in freezing tones.

'San Jerónimo de Valparaíso. If you take fright, cousin, I'm sure the good fathers will take you in and hear your confession before returning you to the bosom of your family.'

'Ah, but, cousin, I don't intend to have anything to confess!' she retorted, pinning a sweet smile on to her face. 'Is the palace far from here?'

'Just below the monastery.'

He increased the pace of his mount until her own smaller mare had to break into a canter to keep up with him. The dusty track had large stones embedded in the cream-coloured earth and Petronilla was afraid the horses might stumble. This was not the moment, she thought, for her pretty mare to break a leg, or suffer some other injury. *That* was something her mother certainly wouldn't understand, even while she might accept the picnic as a harmless bit of fun on her daughter's part.

She slowed, keeping her eyes on the track ahead, and so she wasn't aware at first that her escort had left the track and was forcing his mount down a steep bank to the left. She paused, watching him, dismayed by the loneliness of the location. As far as she could see there was no palace to be seen anywhere, not even a few crumbling walls for them to inspect while they tried to imagine how it once had been.

'Come on!' Don Diego urged her over his shoulder.

'I'm not sure that I should,' she replied. It was one of the loneliest places she had ever seen.

He turned his horse, came back up the bank, seized her bridle and forced her mare down beside him, giving her a sharp whack from his whip as the little mare objected strenuously to such treatment, tossing her head and digging her hooves into the soft earth.

Petronilla was furious. She lifted her own whip and brought it down on her cousin's thigh.

'Never do that again!' she commanded him. 'I am more than capable of guiding my own mare where I want her to go! Nor do I approve of a needless use of the whip! Let me tell you, cousin, that no hunt in England would let you ride with them if you showed such a display of bad temper with any animal!'

Don Diego said nothing at all. He dismounted, his face purple with fury as he turned on her, dragging her off her horse with angry hands. She was only just in time to ease her right leg free from the pommel that held her securely in the saddle, before he pulled her close up against the hardness of his body, bringing his mouth down on hers in a burning kiss that made her senses reel. It was not at all like the way Mr Arbuthnot had kissed her. She wasn't even sure that she approved of Diego's violent approach, even while she had to admit it to be exciting.

'*Zorra!*' he whispered.

She knew that *zorra* meant vixen; she was almost certain it also meant what her father would delicately refer to as a 'fallen woman'. Was that the impression she had given Diego of herself? Surely not! He was the one who had claimed to have progressive views, not she! And most people of that turn of mind were always demanding that women should have more liberty as well as men. Perhaps that wasn't what it meant in Spain? In Spain, married women could own property and do all sorts of things women couldn't do in England. And yet there were so many things they couldn't do, and one of them, Petronilla was reasonably sure, was to ride out alone with an unmarried man who had already shown he had only contempt for the family relationship between them. He would not call her a prostitute twice!

'I want to go home!' she said aloud.

His exasperation made him more handsome than ever. 'You should have thought of that before you decided to cross swords with me, my lovely cousin! No woman takes a whip to me and gets away with it!'

'You shouldn't have beaten my *jaca*!'

'Another female in need of being taught a lesson. You make too much of it! I thought you wanted to come on a picnic with me?'

'I did – I do!' she amended. 'Did I hurt you?'

'Devil a bit! I'll have my revenge yet, don't you worry. Let's go and find a place out of the sun and see what my man has put us up to eat.'

She was subdued and thoughtful as she followed him further down the hillside, looking about her for any signs of the ruined palace she had come to see. The kiss she had received had shaken her more than a little. If she allowed herself to dwell on it, she thought, she would have some difficulty in walking at all. A man's chest was much harder than she had imagined, and his arms stronger. She couldn't have escaped Diego's hold had she wanted to, not when he had held her tight up against him. Was that how a man usually held a woman when he kissed her? Mr Arbuthnot hadn't put his arms round her at all, yet there had been an excitement in his kiss, a teasing temptation that had been wholly lacking today.

'You know, cousin —' she began.

'I told you not to call me that!' he ground out. He tied the reins of their horses together to a branch of a tree. Petronilla noticed that neither animal could reach down to the grass and stepped forward to ease their restraint, but Diego was there before her, putting an arm about her waist and bidding her mind her own business. 'Do all English women spend their time telling us menfolk what to do?'

'Only when we're given cause,' she returned.

'What cause have I given you?'

She seated herself gracefully on the rug he had spread in the shade of the tree, leaning her back against the silver trunk. He sat down beside her, the picnic hamper on his knee, fiddling with the buckles between his fingers.

She gave him a speculative look, not quite as sure of herself as her demeanour proclaimed. 'I came to Córdoba to tell Tío Ambrosio how disappointed my mother and I are in your management of the *bodega*,' she began.

'The old boy won't listen to you!'

'He suggested I speak to you about it,' Petronilla insisted. 'You're not really interested in sherry-making, are you?'

'*Me?*' His outrage was almost funny. 'Tío Ambrosio thought I might gain an income from the vineyards and *bodega*. He knows as well as anyone that I'm a soldier and not a *capataz*! Your grandfather didn't mind dirtying his hands in the soil, but I was born to better things!'

'My uncles thought like you,' Petronilla said sadly. 'My uncles died.'

'Better dead than dishonoured – for a man.'

The last words were said reluctantly, as though he didn't really believe them but had remembered, belatedly, that some things were better left unsaid. Perhaps he had remembered the fate of her mother, but Petronilla didn't think so. He had added the last bit to distract her from the rest. But did she believe it? Was it better to be dead than dishonoured? Was she Spanish enough to believe that?

'Some women would think so too,' she said aloud.

'Are you one of their number?'

She shook her head. 'I don't believe one can be dishonoured, one can only dishonour oneself.' She dropped her eyes, refusing to meet his hard, self-interested gaze. 'I expect you think that that is to think like a man, but that is what my father has always taught me.'

He opened the picnic hamper and put it down between them. 'Eat,' he bade her. 'We have plenty of time to amuse ourselves afterwards and I would not have you say your Spanish cousin has no manners!'

She ate a piece of chicken, picking at it, not really enjoying it at all. He poured himself some wine and lay back, leaning up on one elbow, staring at her every movement through overbright eyes.

'I wish you would not look at me in that way!' she complained after a little while.

'Like what?'

'Like some wild animal waiting to be thrown his breakfast!'

He laughed, without any resentment that she could detect. 'What kind of wild animal? I hope you have me marked out as a tiger, or one of your English lions —'

'Alas, we have no lions in England. The only lions we have are heraldic ones. I don't think you'd fancy being one of them.'

'A tiger then. I have always thought the tiger to be a beautiful animal, haven't you?'

'Oh yes!'

It was apt, she thought. He too was a beautiful animal, the most beautiful she had ever seen, but what lay behind that beauty and that charm? She had yet to discover though if she liked him half as much as she liked to look at him, which was odd for she usually had no such difficulty in deciding how she felt about anyone. On the contrary, her father had told her many times that she was far too decided about everything, an unattractive trait in any woman. She turned away, dressing him in her mind in a 'suit of lights' such as a bullfighter wears, and trembled inwardly with a sudden gush of excitement that she was close enough to touch his warm flesh and to see the drops of perspiration that gleamed where his side-whiskers met his shaven cheeks.

The word 'matador' meant killer! She didn't know how the thought had arrived in her mind and she did her best to dismiss it as quickly as possible. The bullfight had been a marvellous, brilliant experience, and it wasn't surprising that she should connect it with Don Diego as he was the one who had taken her to see it. But she had not thought what matador meant the whole afternoon they had spent at the bullring. Not once!

'Some wine?'

She accepted, still without looking at him again. She dared not! To look was to want to touch and, if she touched, who knew what that would lead to?

'How English you are sometimes,' he mused. 'That's wine you're drinking, not English ale.'

That amused her. How did he know the English drank ale? She twisted round to ask him and was startled to find he had put the picnic hamper to one side and was kneeling up beside her, his eyes brighter than ever.

'I don't drink ale. My father is a great believer in the properties of clean, potable water. I was brought up on it.'

'Perhaps that accounts for the softness of your skin.'

'Don't be ridiculous!' she rebuked him, not ill pleased. 'Thanks to your lack of care for our property, I have been forced to ride out in the hot sun practically every day since we arrived in Spain. I am burned to a crisp!'

He assessed her gravely. 'It adds a ripeness to the English pink and white complexion your compatriots prefer.'

She accepted the compliment with a thoughtful look of her own. 'Are you going to show me these ruins now?' she made herself ask.

He shrugged. 'What's there to see? There are other things I'd far rather show you – far more pleasurable things for both of us!'

What did he mean? Could he be meaning to kiss her again and would she object if he did? She felt confused, young and uncertain, and bitterly resented that he should be able to throw her off balance as if her feelings meant no more to him than those of the butterfly that was encircling his head.

'I – I'd rather explore the ruins!' she insisted.

He sat back on his heels, his expression darkening. '*Dios*, do you think I went to all this trouble to be alone with you only to show you some ruins?'

'No,' she said honestly.

'Then why did you come with me?'

She put her head on one side. 'I don't know. I shouldn't have come though, and I'm sorry that I did. Please take me home.'

He reached out a hand and pushed her mantilla away from her face, removing the jewelled comb that held it in place, throwing it carelessly down on the ground beside them.

'I'll take you home when we've had our pleasure; nothing to hurt you, my lovely cousin, just a taste of the delights known to every woman since Eve. Isn't that what you really want too?'

All she knew was that she was afraid, though more of herself than him.

'I don't think we should stay here any longer.' She felt his fingers in her hair and felt the same delicious tremble go through her as she had when he had kissed her. She forgot that she had disliked his violence, remembering only the excitement she had felt. 'Diego, I shouldn't have come!'

'But you wanted to, didn't you?'

He didn't wait for an answer, pulling her close up against him and kissing her with an urgency that scattered her thoughts and made her blood run like quicksilver in her veins. The whole world tip-tilted itself and centred itself on Diego. Her own hands felt the roughness of his cheeks where his beard had already grown since his valet had shaved him that morning and she laughed in the back of her throat. He was like a glorious, warm statue, as hard as wood, but alive! Splendidly, gloriously, fantastically alive! She wanted more of his kisses, more of him altogether.

His fingers found the knot that fastened the cord that held her bodice together. He pulled at it, wrenching it apart with impatient hands. She was afraid he would tear her clothing, but with an effort he controlled himself, undoing the fastenings one by one as if it were the only thing in the world that mattered to him. She herself was frozen into inactivity, unable to move a muscle in the face of the onslaught of emotion in which she was slowly drowning.

When he touched the bare flesh of her breasts, her breath rasped, recalling her to reality.

'Diego, we can't do this!' she pleaded.

'Don't you like it?'

'You know I do,' she admitted, 'but that doesn't make it right.'

'What harm are we doing?'

Petronilla shook inwardly. If he didn't know, she didn't think she could ever explain it to him. Nor did she want to. She wanted to be closer still to him, closer than she had ever been to any other human being – except her mother and the last person she wanted to think about just now was her mother! Doña Pilar would be so disappointed –

Diego kissed her again. He lifted her skirts, making a bracelet of his fingers round her ankles, then moving higher, and higher, smiling to himself as her skin responded by coming up in goose flesh as if she were suddenly cold. When he reached her thigh, she angrily denied him, swishing her skirts round her knees.

'This is wrong!' she burst out.

'Because we are both enjoying ourselves?'

She stood up shakily. 'I can't!'

He stood up also. 'Then why did you come?'

The tears began to flow down her cheeks as she bent down and searched for her comb, pinning her mantilla back into place and crying the harder because she couldn't manage even that without making a mess of it. Without a word, she plunged forwards towards her mare, plucking at the reins and moaning under her breath when they didn't give way to her touch.

'Petronilla! Please stay!'

'I can't!' she said again.

'Nor can you ride back looking like that,' he interposed, pushing her hands away from the reins. 'Be reasonable, Petronilla! You can't run away now!'

She looked at him with unseeing eyes. He was as beautiful as he had always been and she felt empty and betrayed. The excitement had gone and her mind was full of other things: how matador meant killer; and how disappointed Doña Pilar would be in her daughter for wanting to lie in the dust with her own cousin – for that was what she had wanted. She had wanted that beautiful, living animal for herself. She still did. He stirred emotions inside her she hadn't known she possessed. She couldn't stay, but she would never be quite the same person again.

'I must!'

'Petronilla, I want to make love to you! Don't you understand that?'

'Oh yes,' she said.

'You want it too! You can't deny it!'

She straightened her back, shutting her eyes against the sight of him. 'Wanting has nothing to do with it, Diego. There are so many other things to be considered —'

'What things?' he asked savagely, but she was beyond being afraid of him. 'We may never have such an opportunity again!'

'You wouldn't understand,' she said wearily. She felt very old and tired – and disappointed.

'What do you want from me?' he roared at her. 'Promises to love you until the day I die and beyond? I can't do that —'

'I know you can't.'

'— because I have nothing to offer you!' he ended. 'You and your mother are even taking the *bodega* away from me. I have only my cause, one which you despise because your uncles threw away their lives too cheaply on the other side. Is that why you won't stay with me?'

She swallowed noisily. She had thought she had reached the bottom of the well of unhappiness the day would bring, but now she knew it was only just beginning.

'I have to go.'

She took the reins from his hand and led the little mare to a convenient rise in the ground, only realizing when she got there that this was one of the buried walls of the ruin she had come to see. She settled herself into her saddle, arranging her habit over her knees. Her hair was a mess and her bodice was still flapping open. She tried to repair the damage as the *jaca* clipped along the dusty trail back towards Córdoba. It was surprisingly difficult to do and her spirits drooped still further accordingly.

When she heard Diego's horse thundering along after her, she quickened her own pace. If he were to catch up with her, she would be lost, she knew, for she had no more arguments to offer him. She was running away because she was her father's daughter: had she been her mother's daughter only, she thought she would have stayed and be damned to the lot of them!

Nobody saw Petronilla as she entered her uncle's house by the back way. She had almost reached her bedchamber when Miss Fairman discovered her.

'Child, whatever happened to you? I knew I should have gone with you!'

'I wish you had,' Petronilla answered. Another voice could be heard in the small withdrawing-room from which her governess had emerged. 'Who is that?' she enquired.

'It's Mr Arbuthnot,' Miss Fairman hissed. 'You'd better go and change your dress —'

Mr Arbuthnot appeared in the doorway behind the governess. His eyes widened as he took in Petronilla's appearance, licking his lips, and blinking at her as though he couldn't quite believe his eyes. She felt a vast impatience with him and couldn't prevent her toe from tapping impatiently on the marble floor.

'What are you doing here, Mr Arbuthnot?' she demanded.

'I came to see you,' he began and stopped. Female footsteps sounded at the other end of the corridor. Petronilla felt his hand on her arm and she was dragged into the small room behind him, his forefinger on his lips bidding her be silent. 'Your fearsome aunt is asking after you!'

'Tía Consuelo?'

'Is that her name? Where have you been, Petronilla?'

She felt as though her heart would burst within her. That *he* should be here was the final humiliation in a humiliating day! She lifted her chin and gave him look for look.

'I went on a picnic – with my Cousin Diego!'

The sherry-coloured eyes held none of the condemnation she was steeling herself to expect from him. 'Alone?' he asked mildly.

'Yes, alone.'

Her aunt's footsteps came relentlessly closer. Mr Arbuthnot turned his back to the door, put his arms about Petronilla's slender form and held her tightly against him, hiding her face in his shoulder.

'Petronilla! Petronilla, are you in there? Answer me, girl! Teresa is here, knowing nothing of this picnic of yours! And your *dueña* most certainly wasn't with you!'

Mr Arbuthnot smiled over his shoulder at the angry woman. 'My *novia* is with me, Doña Consuelo. Miss Fairman is here also.'

It was unfortunate that at that moment Diego appeared, angry and as dishevelled as Petronilla, brandishing his riding whip in his hand.

'Petronilla!' he cried out. 'No one, but no one, ever runs away from me and gets away with it!'

'Aha!' exclaimed Tía Consuelo. 'Now we have the truth of the matter! Well, Miss *English* Petronilla, the sooner you return to your mother's care the better I shall be pleased. As for you, Miss Fairman, your employer may condone such laxness on your part, but in Spain we keep a better watch on the young and silly girls in our care! I shall be giving my niece a report on this whole incident! The very idea of a young woman under our roof going straight from the arms of one man to another, as if she were no better than she should be. I told Don Ambrosio he could expect nothing more from one who can hardly be considered Spanish at all! The English are known to have no morals and the proof stands before us! I won't hear another word on the subject! Tomorrow you will return to your own home, miss, *if* your mother sees fit to receive you there!'

Mr Arbuthnot gave Petronilla a warning squeeze. 'Hush, love, let me do the talking!'

Miss Fairman cast a harassed look about her. 'Oh dear!' she groaned.

Only Diego refused to be cast down. He threw back his head and a great roar of laughter came out of his throat. The sound ran through Petronilla's veins like a flash of lightning streaking across the sky. For her, at that moment, there was no one else there.

Chapter Nine

'*Frailty, thy name is woman!*'

Doña Pilar gave the governess a freezing look that effectively reduced her to a jelly.

'Yes, but you have yet to hear the worst!' Miss Fairman fluttered, determined to get that worst over as quickly as possible. 'Don – Don Diego made no effort to hide what had happened! It is all *most* unfortunate!'

Doña Pilar frowned. She looked positively majestic as she sat, straight-backed, considering her unfortunate daughter and the wretched governess.

'It would seem frailty's name is man,' she said at last. 'This Don Diego person is not only careless of my vineyard, but careless of my daughter as well! Very well, what is done is done, though I am at a loss to know how you, Petronilla, could be so foolish —'

'I'm sorry, Mamá.'

'So am I,' her parent went on sardonically. 'Have you read Tía Consuelo's letter? It's bad enough the old hag should have witnessed your return from this – picnic with your cousin, but that she should write in such terms about any daughter of mine is something I will not permit. You may be sure I shall be telling her so, and Tío Ambrosio also, but first I want to hear exactly what did happen. That this woman should say she will not have *my* daughter darken her door until she has made a respectable marriage, of which the family can approve, is nothing short of insolence!'

'*Most* unfortunate!' Miss Fairman sighed. 'As Thucydides said, a woman should *show no more weakness than is natural to her sex, and not to be talked of, either for good or evil, by men.*'

Doña Pilar was outraged. 'Miss Fairman, you will please not tell me what some silly Greek may have said thousands of years ago. What has that to do with Petronilla now?'

'I should have known!' Miss Fairman moaned, shutting her eyes against the disaster fate had dealt her charge. '*The man that lays his hand upon a woman, Save in the way of kindness, is a wretch Whom 't were gross flattery to name a coward.*'

'That is enough! I don't wish to hear about any more old Greeks —'

'John Tobin wasn't Greek,' Miss Fairman murmured unhappily.

'Whoever he is, I have never heard of him! And what is more, I do not wish to hear of him again,' Doña Pilar informed her with decision. 'If you can't say something more to the point, it's best not to say anything at all, no?'

Miss Fairman subsided, not at all put out by her employer's strictures. Her thoughts were full of Don Diego's shining exterior, which she felt was more than enough to dazzle the most sensible young woman, though she hadn't expected Petronilla to be taken in by him. It was easy to forget her erstwhile charge was too young to be amused by such posturing and to take such heroics at their face value, but how to explain it to Doña Pilar who, in Miss Fairman's opinion, was always more practical than she was romantic?

'Perhaps Petronilla would prefer to explain herself in private,' she said at last. 'Such a beautiful young man! I blame myself for not making certain there were other young people going on the picnic, but we both, Petronilla and I, confidently expected *Señorita* Teresa to be there, as well as half-a-dozen others.'

'But she was not there,' Doña Pilar said tartly.' Nobody was there. What I do not understand is why Petronilla didn't return home as soon as she found she was alone with Don Diego?'

'Cousin Diego, Mamá,' Petronilla hazarded hopefully.

'You may call him cousin, child, but did he behave towards you as a brother, or cousin, might be expected to do?'

Petronilla shook her head. 'He doesn't feel like a cousin to me either,' she said in a rush. 'Miss Fairman likened him to the Shining One, and that's what he is, Mama. I don't even like him! Yet, when he's there, I can't think about anything, or anyone else. I can't explain it. I know I shouldn't have been alone with him, but I can't regret it either!'

Miss Fairman crept away, leaving mother and daughter alone together. She would have been happier if Mr Arbuthnot had returned to Montilla with them, for she had formed a very favourable opinion of him one way and another and she had every expectation that he would rescue Petronilla from this unfortunate predicament – and a good thing too! *Somebody* should make a push to distract that girl from wanting to have anything further to do with Don Diego. Miss Fairman had done her best on the ride from Córdoba, which had wearied her body as much as it had her spirits, but nothing she could say had had the slightest effect on the child. It was almost as though she were enclosed in an enchanted circle, and who better than Mr Arbuthnot to play the prince who would awaken her with a kiss. It was a solution that pleased the governess, for she couldn't really believe that anyone as basically *sensible* as Petronilla could fail to see the empty selfishness behind the splendid façade her cousin presented to the world.

Left alone together, Doña Pilar and Petronilla could think of nothing to say to one another. Doña Pilar broke the silence, flapping Tía Consuelo's letter in front of her daughter's face.

'How could you place me in the position of receiving a letter like this from someone I despise? That she should call a daughter of mine *sin vergüenza* or, even worse, *cara dura*, hard-faced, which, let me tell you, is a hundred times worse than to be called thick-skinned in England! She is not a generous woman, poor soul, and you may be sure she will do all in her power to shame us both.'

'I am sorry, Mamá.'

Doña Pilar's face crumpled, her lips trembling. 'I know, *pequeña*, I know! If only Tomás were here, he would know exactly what to do. I am lost without him!'

They both were, Petronilla acknowledged, she as much as her mother.

'Mr Arbuthnot was there —'

The colour drained from Doña Pilar's face. She was still in her middle thirties but suddenly Petronilla could see her as she would be when she was an old, old woman.

'Charles Arbuthnot. Did he speak to Tía Consuelo?'

'He did his best to put her off, Mamá. He was shocked when he saw my appearance, I know he was, but he did his best to hide me from Tía Consuelo and he would have succeeded, too, if Diego hadn't come roaring after me, first angry because I had run away from him, and then bursting into laughter because fate was living up to his expectations and casting him as villain. He's a spoilt little boy, who only thinks he's a man with the whole world against him. I – I can't dislike him, Mamá.'

But Doña Pilar was scarcely listening. 'Mr Arbuthnot, what did he have to say about it all?' she demanded.

'He told Tía Consuelo I was his *novia*. He was holding me so tightly against him I could hardly breathe —'

'His *novia*?' Doña Pilar's spirits began to rise. 'Despite this picnic with Don Diego, he still called you his *novia*?'

'Only to Tía Consuelo.'

'And to you? What did he say to you?'

'Very little,' Petronilla remembered sourly. She had been hurt by the speed with which Mr Arbuthnot had

taken his leave, even if he had been kind during the short
time he had been there.

'But he must have said something!' her mother objected.

'He said he hoped I would go picnicking with him some
day.'

Doña Pilar smiled at her daughter's despondent note.
She was beginning to feel far more optimistic about the
eventual outcome of this affair than she had at the
beginning.

'He is a good man, Petronilla.'

Petronilla gave a weary sigh. 'I know he is, Mamá.
Would Papá's goodness have been enough for you?'

Doña Pilar relaxed into happier memories of the past.
If Thomas couldn't be beside her, helping to deal with
their recalcitrant daughter, what better than to remember
how it had been with them, that first time she had seen
him and danced with him.

'For me, it was a choice between your father and death.
Tomás is also a good man and not at all romantic except
where I am concerned. I have never thought of him as a
knight in shining armour, or I should have been
disappointed every day of our life together. It would not
be comfortable to have this armour in bed with one all
the time. It is better to like the man one marries than to
have romantic dreams about him. I am fortunate to have
known both with your father, but I know which I should
choose if I could only have one or the other! Romance is
for fools and the very young! What I wish for you, my
love, is real life.'

Petronilla chewed on her cheek, wishing she could
explain better how her cousin seemed much more like real
life to her than Mr Arbuthnot ever would.

'Don Diego would never be dull!' she complained.

Doña Pilar laughed. 'Do you find Mr Arbuthnot dull?
You didn't when he kissed you in the library in England!'

Petronilla's face burned. 'I didn't think you knew!'

'¡Claro! You may hoodwink Miss Fairman whenever
you please, it would seem, but I am your mother, and

many men have wanted to kiss me – even before I knew your father! So, now you have been kissed by two men and you think to compare one with the other, no? Did you think Mr Arbuthnot unromantic when he kissed you?'

'No, it was exciting,' Petronilla admitted.

Doña Pilar flicked her fan open, lazily stirring the air, her composure completely restored. 'But Don Diego excited you more?'

'It – it wasn't the same!' Petronilla sought for some way to explain the difference. 'Diego treats me as an adult with a mind of my own —'

'Does he now! It doesn't sound like the same Don Diego whose only interest in his mother's family is that he might get an income from them; who neglected the *bodega* because it was beneath his dignity to dirty his hands with honest labour as my father did to support his family; who won't allow a woman to follow her father on to the throne of Spain because women are no better than children and should never be in the position to govern their male subjects! Say what you will, my love, I cannot forgive him for treating my daughter's reputation as carelessly as he did my vineyards. Did he try to do more than kiss you? Is that why you find him more exciting? A dishonourable man is not romantic! Oh, he may be a temptation to silly girls, but imagine how it would be to live with someone whose only interest is to satisfy his own pleasures! I shall tell you something, *hija*, something known only to your father and me – and to God – and that is that he never laid a hand on me until after we were married, not because I wouldn't have given myself to him there and then, but because he had promised the priest who helped me get away. Your father is a man of honour and he wouldn't go against that promise. He has always treated me with honour and that is the measure of his love for me. He put his obligation towards me before his own pleasure. Would Don Diego do the same for you?'

'You know he wouldn't,' Petronilla admitted. 'We both

know he wouldn't, but, oh Mamá, when you see him you'll understand —'

'I understand now, *querida*. The point is, do *you* understand how it would be to live with a man who cared nothing for your honour, or his own where you're concerned? Not even your Papá and I could redeem you in society's eyes, however hard we tried! I am not saying that no man could be worth losing one's place in the world for, but I think you are still too young and too inexperienced to make such a decision, no?'

Petronilla knew only a black despair. She felt cold inside and out. She could even admire the deft way her mother had put an end to her dreams, leaving her no room to do other than to put all thoughts of her cousin out of her head. She only hoped she could do it. Don Diego might be as wicked as the Shining One himself, but he was also a lonely, misunderstood man with a great deal of good in him – and he was *exciting*!

When Doña Pilar spoke again, her voice was so gentle, so *kind*, that Petronilla cast herself into her arms.

'There's one more thing, my darling, something you didn't know about your cousin. Tía Consuelo writes he is engaged to be married to Fabiola Ensenada y Lopez of Granada and is only waiting until she is old enough to marry her. He can never be yours.'

He would never be anybody's, Petronilla answered silently. A wild animal would always walk alone, wary of every snare baited to trap him. An arranged marriage would never contain him, but she thought she might have come to terms with him if she had loved him enough and had allowed him sufficient freedom. As it was, she didn't envy the girl who had been chosen by their families for the honour of being his wife for, sooner or later, her heart would be broken as Petronilla's was breaking now. She had no illusions that her cousin would number kindliness amongst his virtues. She knew he would despise it as a weakness in himself, and she was not so besotted that she couldn't see this to be a flaw in his character that even the most partial of his admirers would be foolish to ignore.

Petronilla wandered into the noisiest of the *bodega*'s sheds, the cooperage, casting a gloomy look at the small fires over which skilled men laboured, hammering the sherry butts into shape. In the last few weeks she had become thinner than ever and had kept Cousin Rosa and Miss Fairman busy taking in her dresses in a vain effort to lessen Doña Pilar's distress over her daughter's lack of appetite. The excuse that dinner was served too late at night for her to have any appetite was no longer available as José brought Petronilla a tray of tempting dishes from the kitchen whenever he saw her slumped in a chair, chasing her thoughts like a squirrel in a cage.

The cooperage was an expense the *bodega* could have done without. Only the evening before, in an effort to stir herself out of her lethargy, Petronilla had tried to discover some way of making the butts last longer than the two trips to London which they did now. Made of American oak, they were expensive to make, having to be soaked in water for six months and in wine for three before they were ready to be shipped anywhere, and it was scarcely worth it for the quality of wine they were producing these days. It was hardly worth the cost of transporting that to the nearest port down on the coast!

She watched the foreman as he oversaw a new lad who was washing out the once-used butts, making them ready to be used again. The young man's muscles bulged as he lifted the heavy chains into the butts already half filled with water. A few weeks ago she wouldn't have noticed such a thing, she thought, mocking herself because she saw such things always in terms of Diego and her memories of him. Would she ever be able to forget?

The chains clanked as the butts were thoroughly shaken and she lost interest in them, turning her attention to the rhythmic clang of the hammers as the coopers knocked the metal bands neatly into place to keep the young wood bent over the heat of the fires into their required shape.

'Your mother was in here earlier,' the foreman told her. 'Doña Pilar always understood wine as her brothers never did. It's a pleasure to see her back amongst us.'

Petronilla nodded, half of her attention still on the new lad, stripped to the waist, his skin as smooth and as golden as that of Diego and his muscles rippling as he worked. If she had tried to answer him, she would have had to shout above the noise and, as she had nothing in particular to say, she waited for the foreman to go on. He too was watching the youth, critical of his every movement in case he should be less than thorough for, with any wine, the most important thing is cleanliness, sherry being no exception.

'Now you can do that again with wine instead of water,' the foreman instructed the young man. He turned back to Petronilla. 'It looks as if it may rain later on, *señorita*. That'll lay the dust and give the grapes a chance to get started.'

'I hope so,' Petronilla responded.

She might have said something further, for she and the foreman had done their best to keep up each other's spirits recently, but there was nothing left to say that hadn't already been said where the vineyards were concerned. They both knew the replanting would have to wait for the new season and that what there was already in the ground would scarcely be worth the picking come the autumn.

'I suppose the rain will make the roads impassable,' she said dully, realizing that he was expecting something from her.

'As likely as not.'

So Mr Arbuthnot's coming would be still further delayed. Petronilla didn't know whether to be pleased or sorry. She had no idea why he had come looking for her in Córdoba. Whatever it was, he had gone on his way without telling her. She had passed on his previous

message to her father and had received a reply that he
hoped Europe wasn't on the boil again as it had been in
1848. Then there had been rebellion in Madrid, in Paris
Louis-Philippe had been forced to abdicate, giving way to
the Second Republic, which had turned out to be too
extreme even for the revolutionary French, and in England
there had been the Chartist meetings, making everybody
quake in their shoes in case what had previously been a
Continental fervour should make its appearance in
England. As it was, Queen Victoria had withdrawn to
Osborne and the Duke of Wellington had stationed troops
and guns at the approaches to Westminster. Her father had
made no bones about it that he thought such precautions to
be a mistake, but he had gone on one of his journeys
shortly after that and had come home full of promises that
he would take his womenfolk to Italy as soon as things
had settled down again and, if they wished it, they might
even have an audience with the Pope, though he had to
tell them that the fellow was making a great nuisance of
himself, worrying far more about his temporal crown than
his heavenly one.

Petronilla supposed it should have been embarrassing to
one of her supposed sensibility to have to face Mr
Arbuthnot again, but she had no fears on that score. He
wore no shining armour, but nor did he waste his time
criticizing what was over and done with. She didn't know
how she knew that, only that she felt she knew him as
well as she knew herself.

She was on the point of leaving the cooperage, when a
disturbance outside made her pause.

'Whatever —?' she began.

She began to move towards the heavy doors of the shed
but, before she could get there, a young girl stepped into
the inferno that was the cooperage, looking about her with
wide, astonished eyes.

'May I help you?' Petronilla asked her, thinking the
visitor to be far too small and dainty to be anywhere near
the heat and the flames over which the men were working.

The young lady raised her chin. 'I am Fabiola Ensenada y Lopez, and this – ' She looked back over her shoulder. 'My *dueña*, my cousin Immaculada Lopez, must have stayed outside. She is never there when one wants her!'

Petronilla's eyebrows rose. 'Shall we go outside?' she suggested. 'It's too noisy in here to converse with any ease. I am Petronilla Harris y Morena, by the way.'

'I know very well who you are,' the young girl told her. 'I have come all the way from Granada to see you. What happens in there to make so much noise and heat?' she demanded, blinking as they gained the sunlight outside.

'They are making the butts to hold the wine,' Petronilla answered.

'Oh? You make wine here?' The girl looked confused. 'I shouldn't have thought Don Diego to be interested in wine,' she added.

'He isn't.'

'No? But he is interested in you. That is why I've come.'

Petronilla's spirits sank. 'Don Diego is my cousin —'

'Ah, there is my *dueña*! Immaculada, we are over here!' Fabiola sighed. 'She is stupid that one! But kind! Why doesn't she come when she's called?'

'Perhaps she can't hear you,' Petronilla put in, trying not to laugh.

'She didn't want to come with me,' Fabiola went on darkly. 'Now she tries to punish me by ignoring me.' She smiled a sunny smile, her mood changing so quickly that Petronilla was hard put to it to keep up with her. 'Where can we talk?'

'Shall we go inside? My mother —'

'No, no! It's *you* I wish to see. Please, may we speak together before we go inside? I shall love to meet your mother afterwards, but she will be more concerned to send me back to Granada and to save my parents any worry to listen to why I came – *Immaculada*! Are you coming?'

Petronilla hid a smile. She felt as though she were in

the company of a butterfly and, for the first time since
coming home from Córdoba, she felt a lift to her spirits
and a desire to laugh. She waited for the stout, kindly
faced Immaculada to catch up with them, holding out a
hand to her.

'Have you come very far today? Do come out of the
hot sun and sit in the shade. I am about to show Doña
Fabiola our "cathedrals", where our wines are put to
mature —'

'Immaculada will wait here,' Fabiola cut her off firmly.
'If someone will put up our horses and deal with the
baggage, we can have our conversation in peace. I am so
glad to be here at last!'

Immaculada Lopez came to sudden life. 'I will not leave
you alone in a strange place, cousin. What would your
dear mother say to me if anything were to happen to you
so far away from home! We should never have come! I
don't know how I allowed you to talk me into such a mad
adventure, really I don't!'

'I can understand it very well!' Petronilla observed,
taking pity on the harassed woman. 'I can't believe you
had any say in the matter – and nor will Fabiola's mother,
so I shouldn't fret about what she will have to say to you
when you return. Shall I have a drink brought out to you?'

Señorita Lopez would not hear of putting her hostess to
so much trouble. She was vastly relieved to have found a
sympathetic ear into which she could pour her troubles,
beginning with the madcap idea that she should
accompany Cousin Fabiola all the way to Morilla, without
benefit of any proper escort to protect them from the
robbers who thronged the roads of Spain. She really didn't
know how they had managed the whole journey without
serious incident. But then, Cousin Fabiola was set to be a
saint and no doubt her prayers had prevailed. There could
be no other explanation, didn't Petronilla agree?

Petronilla was considerably startled by this confidence.
A steel-willed butterfly might prove an interesting friend,
but she doubted Diego's fiancée had come all this way to

offer her the hand of friendship. Indeed, it was a mystery as to why she should have come at all.

Still grumbling, Immaculada Lopez settled herself in a shady corner, fanning herself as if her life depended on it and refusing to go one foot further until she was allowed to greet her hostess and be shown to a bedchamber where she could take the rest that had been denied to her during the sleepless nights she had spent along the way.

Petronilla and Fabiola walked on together towards the nearest of the huge brick-built buildings of the *bodega*. Separated by courtyards in which flowering trees grew with beds of flowers at their feet, the buildings echoed the architecture of the homestead and were individually named and numbered with ornamental ceramic tiles. Petronilla led the way into the first of the 'cathedrals', automatically checking the temperature on the huge thermometer that stood at the end of the middle aisle that ran between the huge butts of wine, piled carefully one on another in three storeys; each one contained wine from past years, from which, every few months, some of the mature wine was drawn off and the remainder 'refreshed' by the young wine which gradually took on the character of the old, thus maintaining the same quality throughout the years.

Fabiola, holding her skirts out of the dust which had blown in through the open door, marched up and down the cool aisles, looking at the incomprehensible signs chalked up on the enormous barrels telling the initiated of the quality of the wine within.

Petronilla waited until she was done, then she said, 'Well, hadn't you better tell me why you've come?'

Fabiola came rushing back. She had grey eyes and a nose that gave her the look of an ancient Greek goddess; Petronilla was not familiar with such persons, but she did wonder if they were not built on far more generous lines than the petite figure of her unlikely visitor.

'You won't be cross, will you?' Fabiola began. 'Don Diego came to see us in Granada and told me all about you.' She hesitated, unsure how to go on.

'Nothing he told you need concern you,' Petronilla tried to help her out. She took a deep breath, furiously angry that Diego had seen fit to tell his fiancée anything about her. Had he no care for anyone's feelings but his own? Or was it that he really cared about her, enough to want to rescue their lost love from the oblivion to which she had done her best to consign it.

'Yes, but it does!' Fabiola insisted. 'The thing is, I don't wish to marry him and I never shall. I keep telling everyone so, but no one believes that I can possibly know what I want, which is very stupid, don't you think, because I have known for many years now that marriage is not for me. I have a vocation to be a nun.' Her smile was sweet, reflecting an inward contentment and confidence Petronilla could only envy. 'I mean to be a Carmelite, though it is very difficult to make my mother believe it is the only way I can ever be happy. As if God would ever let me be anything else!'

Petronilla, whose faith was not of the same order, wondered if she should point out that even the Great Teresa had complained of the way the Christ of her visions treated his friends, but she decided against it as Fabiola went on,

'I knew you would understand! That's why I came to see you. My father thinks that because he betrothed his baby daughter to Diego when I was only a few weeks old that I have to marry him now that I'm grown-up. He says the only possible way for me to have any happiness is to do my duty as a wife and mother; that my first obligation is to my family and to my parents' wishes, and that I have no right to entertain any other notion than to please them. But Don Diego tells me he doesn't wish to marry me either!'

'I see,' said Petronilla.

'Yes, it is lucky, is it not? One can't dismiss lightly one's obligations to one's family, but now the problem has been resolved. My confessor told me it was unlikely the Carmelites would receive me while the betrothal stood and I don't know what I should have done then! I don't wish to marry Don Diego!'

Petronilla felt a lightening of her own heart. 'Surely, your family wouldn't force you into a marriage you don't like?'

Fabiola slanted a smile. 'They have forgotten what it is to be young,' she said ruefully. 'It's the one thing my parents agree on, that one can only be happy by doing exactly as Papá wishes! That's all very well, and I would do as he wants, but I know God has another design for me, so of course I always knew there would be something that would intervene so that there would be no marriage between Don Diego and myself!'

Petronilla was not deceived. 'How very fortunate,' she murmured.

Her visitor gurgled with laughter. 'Well, it is, but it's always as well to give the Lord a helping hand, don't you think?' She became immediately serious. 'Don Diego told me you would marry him if he were free, which is why I came. I wanted you to know you need not consider my claim to his hand, that as far as I'm concerned our betrothal has never been more than a wish between our parents, which neither of us has ever wanted.'

Petronilla was very still. 'Did you tell him as much?' she enquired after a little.

'There was no need to tell him. He rode into Granada like one obsessed, demanding to see me alone and making a great fuss when poor Cousin Immaculada insisted on being there. He had met the one woman in the world for him! An Englishwoman, as reckless as himself, who would nevertheless bring him enough in a dowry to keep him in comfort all his days! I have several sisters, you see, so the extent of my dowry has always been a sore point with him —'

'Tell me, do you *like* Don Diego?' Petronilla burst out.

'Oh yes,' Fabiola assured her, 'he amuses me very much, and he always has exciting stories to tell, though I think he may exaggerate his own part in these tales – just a little!

I am sure he sees himself as El Cid come again to save Spain from poor Doña Isabella, when he is only a sulky boy who was born too late to take part in any of the real Carlist battles.'

Petronilla was silent for a long minute, then she said, 'He took too much on himself if he thought I would marry him, even if he were free. I have obligations to my own family also!'

'Yes, but you are English!'

Nettled by Fabiola's amazement that someone who was English should make any claims to integrity, Petronilla began to wonder exactly what Don Diego had told Fabiola about her.

'I have a Spanish mother,' she pointed out, though she couldn't help thinking that if anyone ground the importance of keeping one's word into her it had been her very English father. 'And I, too, am promised to be married elsewhere.'

Fabiola was astonished. Her mouth opened and shut again while she took in the full import of what Petronilla had said.

'Does Don Diego know?' she asked imperiously.

'Yes, he knows,' Petronilla answered sadly.

Fabiola was shocked and sufficiently disappointed to be close to tears. 'I didn't think you cared a fig for anyone but him!' she exclaimed.

Petronilla didn't know what she would have said to that for, at that moment, the *Señorita* Immaculada came panting towards them, her distress so obvious that Petronilla thought she might have been taken ill while she had been sitting on her own. Immaculada had only one thought in her head, however, and that was to rush her charge inside as quickly as possible.

'Come, child, you've dawdled out here quite long enough! If you want to speak to Doña Petronilla privately, you may do so after we have made the acquaintance of our hostess, can you not? I won't have you seen out here, standing about like a lost kitten, when there are strange men coming and going, someone who might even know us! Come along at once!'

Fabiola looked at her *dueña* with amazement. 'What men?' she demanded.

Immaculada stamped her foot. 'Do as you are told! I have seen him coming. I tell you – not a *caballo*! – not anyone your parents would wish you to meet, I'm sure of that! I'm sure he's a foreigner and a heretic! Perhaps the Devil himself! Come inside at once, child!'

Petronilla looked at the kindly face, now contorted with fear, and wondered how it could have come about that perfectly nice, ordinary people should have been taught to be so afraid of anyone who was unfamiliar to them. Her father would have said it was the fault of their priests, making them frightened of their own shadows in order to keep their control over them, but Petronilla knew how the English felt about the Spanish – and not only the Spanish, the French as well.

She sighed. 'But of course we shall go inside,' she encouraged the older woman. 'José will announce your arrival to my mother and see you are taken to your rooms, so you may be quite comfortable in your mind about Doña Fabiola and not worry about her any more. I should have taken you inside directly myself and can only apologize for not having done so. Please forgive me?'

Thus handsomely applied to, Immaculada's fears began to subside, though she still saw fit to chivvy her charge towards the house as fast as she could go.

'The stranger speaks Spanish,' she whispered to Petronilla. 'He was speaking to some of the workmen when I saw him. Please believe me, I shouldn't have interrupted you except that Don Lorenzo, my cousin and Fabiola's father, is very strict as to whom he will admit to his daughter's acquaintance. It's bad enough that I allowed myself to be talked into – into this mad escapade – I'll never be forgiven, *never*! But that's no concern of yours,' she added on a whisper, 'that is on my conscience for the rest of my life! *¡Ay de mí!* I never thought I'd be a party to such a madcap scheme!'

'I'm sure you didn't,' Petronilla agreed. 'It's easy to see how it came about, though, if Doña Fabiola had anything to do with it!'

Immaculada almost smiled. 'She can talk me into anything, that one! And when she is a saint in heaven, she will talk the good Lord into taking me there with her also!'

Petronilla thought Fabiola far too fond of her own way to attain sanctity as easily as her *accompañadora* seemed to imagine, but she held her tongue, sure that her mother would find the right words to comfort the older woman and would somehow reassure her that she had done the right thing in accompanying her charge all the way to Montilla.

She was giving her instructions to José when the first spots of rain began to fall. There was no chance of their unlikely visitors returning to Granada until the rains were over, not that Fabiola would care much for that, she was very well pleased with herself for having carried out her plan so well – and all by herself, for she wouldn't give poor Immaculada any of the credit for having brought them safely such a long way.

José took charge of the visitors, leaving Petronilla free to go back outside. The rain was pelting now as she peered out towards the gate, trying to see who Immaculada's stranger might be. When she saw Mr Arbuthnot's easily recognizable form dismounting in the yard, she ran out to meet him, wondering a little at her own joy at seeing him.

'Mr Arbuthnot!'

He turned and smiled at her, baring his head to the rain. 'You'll get wet, Petronilla! Go inside!'

She shrugged, holding out her hands to him. 'Who cares?'

A groom came and took his horse, catching the coin Mr Arbuthnot tossed into the air with a quick hand.

'*Gracias, señor!*'

Petronilla watched Charles Arbuthnot untie his saddlebags and ease them off his horse's back.

'I didn't think you'd come,' she said.

'Then you must have a very short memory for I distinctly remembering telling you I would!' he retorted.

She bit her lip. 'You said a lot of things.' She stood very straight, the rain plastering her hair to her scalp and darkening her dress as it worked its way into the material, wetting her to the skin. 'You might prefer to forget some of them?'

He put up a hand, pushing a stray lock of hair back from her face. 'None of them, my love. How are *you*? Did you make your peace with your mother?'

She nodded. 'I behaved very badly,' she began awkwardly. 'But, truly, I didn't know I would be alone with Don Diego.' She turned away abruptly, hiding from him the pain in her eyes. 'His – his fiancée, the Doña Fabiola Ensenada y Lopez, arrived just before you did. She says there's not to be a wedding after all, but I think her family may insist on it.'

Mr Arbuthnot bowed his head curtly. 'I would say she had my sympathy, but I don't suppose you see it that way?'

'No, though I hope I may – one day.'

He seemed satisfied with that. 'I hope you made Doña Pilar my apologies for not escorting you home from Córdoba?' He made an impatient gesture. 'You look peaky! Haven't been fretting, have you?'

Petronilla preferred not to answer. 'Doña Fabiola wants to be a nun, not a wife,' she told him. 'Do you know, I almost envy her!'

He laughed then, turning to face her and taking both her hands in his. 'You'd be wasted as a nun. You'd soon want to get away from those holy hens and have a living, breathing man of your own! Besides, whatever would your father say?'

The mention of her father reminded her of something

else she had to say to Mr Arbuthnot. 'Did you come to Córdoba to give me another message for him?'

'He'll be here, in Spain, soon enough, and then I'll see him myself,' he answered. 'And when I do, I shall be asking him for your hand in marriage, Petronilla, as I hope you told your mother. I believe I know what his answer will be, but I would sooner hear yours from your own lips. Will you do me the honour of consenting to be my wife?'

She bowed her head, thinking how unromantic it all was and how anyone else but Charles Arbuthnot would at least have waited until they were inside the homestead and warm and dry again. Nobody wanted to receive a proposal of marriage with the rain running down the end of her nose! She gave him a vexed look and saw his uncertainty written on his face. Diego would have taken her consent for granted, she thought, and with far less reason, for she had made no move to deny Mr Arbuthnot's claim that she was his *novia* when it had suited her to have some kind of defence from Tía Consuelo's jibes. She owed this man so much, but it was still the hardest thing she had done in her life.

'I shall be proud to be your wife,' she said. Her throat constricted on the words, stiff and sore with the effort of holding back her tears for a lost dream she could not yet force herself to forget.

He bent his head, putting his lips against hers in a gentle kiss that was suddenly not nearly enough for her. She reached up, pulling herself hard up against the wall of his chest, and opened her mouth to his. The saddlebags were left neglected on the cobbled floor as his arms went about her with a groan of pleasure. Confused, she felt her own body react to the excitement of his and wondered how he could still have this effect on her when all her desire since Córdoba had been for Diego. Beside her cousin, honour and kindness, and everything else, seemed to pale into insignificance. Would it always be like that?

When he finally let her go, Petronilla ran before him

into the house. The rain suited her mood, doing her weeping for her, shedding the tears she was too proud to shed for herself. There was only the future to look forward to now that she had committed herself of her own free will to Mr Arbuthnot. She had made her bed and now she must lie on it – but she was still only seventeen years old.

Book Three

Jerez and Sherry

Some English merchants sent from a town in Andalucía called Xeres de la Frontera at least 40,000 butts of wine annually besides eight or ten tons of fruit, which wine and fruit they are not able to consume themselves, whereby they are furnished of above 200,000 ducats annually to provide them for other necessaries, without which they could not live.

Sir Thomas Chamberlain to Queen Elizabeth I, dated 27 September 1561.

Chapter Ten

Fabiola fitted into the household as if she had always been a part of it.

'You don't understand how fortunate you are to be the only daughter,' she told Petronilla. 'If one has sisters, one is only allowed to be as old as the youngest of them. Imagine, my still being confined to the schoolroom at my age! Your mother understands exactly how a young lady should be treated. Me, I find her delightful! *¡Muy simpatica!*'

'Yes, she is,' Petronilla was glad to confirm.

'*¡Muy española!* How has she managed for so long in England? To be away from everyone one knows and loves, it is inconceivable! She must have suffered very much!'

Petronilla stiffened indignantly. 'But England is a delightful place!'

Fabiola gave her a kind look. 'You might think so, because you never knew Spain until you came here, but nothing can recompense the true Spaniard for being exiled from his own land! It is like – it's like being exiled from Heaven!'

Had her mother ever felt like that? Petronilla didn't think so. Doña Pilar loved her homeland, there was no doubt about that! Petronilla had watched her come alive, like a flower greeting the morning sun, and had seen a Spanish side to her she had never even suspected was there, but she also knew how passionately her mother missed her father and that, for her, living away from her beloved Spain was a very small price to pay for being Mrs Thomas Harris of Hampshire, England.

'I have heard Granada is particularly beautiful,' Petronilla commented.

Fabiola's face shone. 'It is the most beautiful place on Earth!'

Meanwhile, Doña Pilar was trying to reassure Fabiola's luckless *dueña* that, as it was quite impossible for her and her charge to return to Granada because, although they had managed to travel from Granada without mishap, no one was going to allow them to return the same way, not with all the robbers that infested the hills and the bands of semi-official soldiers, ostensibly backing one cause or the other, but more often living off the land as best they could, as undisciplined as the real robbers. No, Doña Pilar decided, she had far better stop worrying as to what Fabiola's parents would have to say to her on her return and make the best of the present, where both she and her charge were very welcome.

'Your cousins have every reason to be most grateful to you for bringing Fabiola safely to me,' she insisted with a firmness that even poor Immaculada was beginning to recognize. 'So, you won't worry any more about something neither of us can do anything about! Dry your tears, and thank God that nothing worse came out of this prank! I have sent a message to her parents that the child is with me and that I shall guard her as closely as my own daughter! Now, why don't you and Miss Fairman put your heads together and decide which of these pieces of material we may use to make the patchwork quilt I have in mind for Petronilla's marriage bed. Alas, the *nord-americanos* are artists when it comes to making these comforters, and I am not! I rely on you to advise me as to colours and so on. Will you do that?'

Thus appealed to, Immaculada's self-importance grew daily until Miss Fairman lost all patience with her and

refused to have anything more to do with the making of
the quilt, a decision that came as a relief to them both for,
whilst Miss Fairman was something of a bluestocking, she
had never pretended to being the kind of seamstress that
all Spanish ladies seemed to be by nature.

'That woman would try the patience of a saint!' she
declared to Doña Pilar.

Amusement flickered across Pilar's face. 'As long as she
is kept well away from Petronilla and her Mr Arbuthnot,
I don't care what you do with her! She has some very old-
fashioned ideas about the proper conduct of a modern
courtship and I won't have her upsetting my silly
daughter, not now she has put all that foolish business
with her cousin behind her.'

Miss Fairman, who knew herself to be quite as much
at fault as her erstwhile pupil about all that had happened
in Córdoba, nobly put her own irritation with Immaculada
on one side and, in an agony of self-sacrifice, did her very
best to keep both their visitors busily engaged whenever
Mr Arbuthnot made an appearance at the *bodega*.

'*Alas! when duty grows thy law, enjoyment fades away,*' she
quoted to herself with increasing frequency, adding the
silent rider that Germans always understood these things
better than anyone else, certainly better than the Spanish,
whose ability to make a full-scale drama out of nothing
at all was something that the governess could only deplore.

Fortunately, Doña Rosa's benevolent good humour and
obvious enjoyment in the hospitality of the *bodega* acted
as a brake on the petty squabbles of the other two ladies
for, whilst they might be jealous of each other and of their
standing with Doña Pilar, they were both impressed by
Doña Rosa's unswerving devotion for her cousin.

'The little Fabiola may wish to be a saint in the next
world,' she would chuckle happily, 'but Cousin Pilar has
the good manners to make one feel important in this world
and that is sanctity enough for me!'

Petronilla, when she heard this, couldn't resist repeating
the remark to Mr Arbuthnot. 'Having so many women

in the house makes me appreciate our home in England all the more! I don't know what my father would say to all these female quarrels!'

'He probably wouldn't notice them.'

'Meaning I should not?'

'Meaning I should leave them to your mother who has only to lift her little finger for them all to sing a different tune. The Doña Pilar is the most charming woman I have ever met – and one of the most Spanish!'

Petronilla gave him a dissatisfied look. 'I don't think a person's worth should be judged by how charming they are!' she shot at him.

'Nevertheless, I rate it highly in any woman.'

'And in a man?'

His look was so long and serious that she could feel herself warming beneath it. Besides, she doubted if he found Don Diego charming. Perhaps it was a quality one only saw clearly in a member of the opposite sex.

'Your mother's brand of charm warms and delights everyone around her. I have known such charm in a man, but more frequently he will use it as a weapon in the service of his own selfish ambition.' He smiled wryly. 'The British have always been suspicious of charming men, probably because they seldom aspire to being particularly charming themselves, not in that way at any rate.'

'You make it sound so cold and calculating,' she protested. 'I'm sure it's never that!'

'Some men will do anything for power,' he answered soberly. 'Your mother told me the Tiger himself, General Ramón Cabrero, could be very charming when he wanted something from a woman, and yet he wouldn't have hesitated to execute her along with the rest of them.'

But Don Diego was no Tiger! She longed to say as much, but she knew his name was forbidden between them and that it had been her own choice that it should be so – always! She looked away, seeking a less dangerous topic of conversation, one in which there were no hidden meanings to tear at her conscience. Sometimes, she wished Mr Arbuthnot would be less understanding of her feelings and more revealing of his own, instead of always leaving it to her to make the running between them.

'Tell me about the *bodega* you are buying in Sanlúcar!' she demanded imperiously. 'Is it as fine as ours here could be?'

'It's in the right place,' he began. 'Do you really want to hear all about it?'

His hesitancy made her realize how much she had hurt him and she gave him an impatient look, irritated that he should ask so little when they both knew that he had every right to make whatever demands he chose. Indeed, she wished he would and get it over with, instead of walking around on eggshells, like Agag, or whoever it was that Miss Fairman was forever quoting from the Old Testament as having tried to avoid trouble and death only to have it catch up with him in the end. Very likely, nobody would have noticed Agag either, if he hadn't tried so hard not to offend!

Petronilla made a last effort of her own. 'Of course I want to hear about it! If I'm going to live there, why should I *not* want to hear about it? Or do you think a female should have no interest in her future home – or husband either?'

'I wasn't sure —' he began.

Petronilla stood up, looking every inch as haughty as her mother. 'I'm not going to turn my whole life into an apology, not even to please you, Charles Arbuthnot!' she declared. 'I'll admit I was unwise to go picnicking alone with my cousin Diego, but that was the whole extent of my guilt, and I refuse to go about in sackcloth and ashes, doing penance for something which was not really my fault!'

For a long moment he stared at her open-mouthed, while her irritation with him grew until she would have flounced away from him, leaving him to his own devices, if he hadn't reached up and caught her by the hand, pulling her back to his side. Then he threw back his head and began to laugh in great, infectious bursts until curiosity overcame her annoyance and she found herself wanting to laugh also, though she couldn't for the life of her see that there was anything to laugh about.

'What's so funny?' she demanded.

He was still grinning. 'You are!' He put his hands on her shoulders and gave her a great, smacking kiss on the mouth. 'Welcome back, dear heart! So you want to know all about my *bodega*, do you?'

'You know I do!'

'I wondered,' he admitted. 'You haven't shown much interest in what has been going on here recently. You haven't even asked me why I've stayed on here for such a long time.'

'I've noticed you and Mamá with your heads together often enough!' she answered with some asperity.

'Neither of us have any secrets from you. We would have welcomed your opinion on the replanting of the main vineyards.'

Petronilla sniffed. 'My mother knows much more about these things than I do!'

'She was a child when she was living here. She never thought to inherit the *bodega* with two brothers living. I'd like to stay longer, to help her put the place in some kind of order, but I must soon be getting back to my own affairs. However, it will be something to have the main vineyards planted and the foreman should be able to keep things going without much supervision during the summer.'

'The workmen like you,' she told him reluctantly. 'Mamá does too!'

'And you?'

She wondered how she did feel about him. The strength of his fingers against hers were comforting and she had liked his kiss. For an instant she had longed to return it, pressing close up against him and trying to obliterate from her memory those other kisses from Don Diego that she could still feel on her lips, even in her dreams. Mr Arbuthnot's body had a hard, masculine quality that her cousin's had lacked. Diego was the more beautiful, there was no doubt of that, with his dancing movements and his natural agility, but there was something secure and reassuring to have her own curves and softer outline complemented by the solid qualities of her future husband. Don Diego had the dazzling quality of a firework, but she couldn't *like* him half so much as she did the Scotsman. And liking would have to be enough for her, she thought soberly. Many women, pressed into marriages with men they hardly knew, found they didn't have the slightest affection for their partners and yet they lived out their lives without a moment's complaint. How fortunate she was to like the man she was to marry!

'I'll try to be everything you want in a wife,' she said awkwardly.

'Will that make you happy?' he insisted.

She shut her eyes. 'Of course,' she said.

He brushed his knuckles against her lashes in a movement that touched her to the quick. 'You wouldn't be happy with *him*, but I think you know that. He not only has no feeling for wine but, if all I hear about him is true, he'll end his life dancing at the end of a rope, either as a traitor to Queen Isabella's line, or as a *contrabandista*, lining his own pockets instead of his master's. Ask your father, if you don't believe me!'

'What interest could such a man have for Papá?' Petronilla asked.

'You will have to ask him. He seems to know more than most what is going on here in Spain.'

Petronilla sighed. 'It probably has to do with Gibraltar. I could easily hate that place as much as Mamá does! She says it's the cause of most of the trouble between England and Spain, and it's certainly the only thing she and Papá ever quarrel about! I refuse to take sides!'

Mr Arbuthnot laughed. 'Very wise.'

'Yes, but Mrs Nightingale says they're both on the same

side really and, if anybody knows what my father is up to, it will be she! If she wasn't so old, she'd have loved to come to Spain for a last visit, but she seldom stirs from her suite of rooms in Papá's house these days. She's always been like a grandmother to me and I must admit to missing her clever words of wisdom from time to time.'

Mr Arbuthnot said nothing. He seldom had anything to say on the subject of the enquiries he carried out for her father, Petronilla had noticed, except on the rare occasions when he asked her to send some message to her parent and then he said as little as possible.

'Will she come out to see you married?'

Petronilla shook her head. 'I doubt it. She's the oldest person I know.'

'Some people never grow old,' Mr Arbuthnot observed. 'I think you'll like my Doña Louise from whom I'm buying my *bodega*. I'm sorry that she's returning to England as soon as the sale goes through because her many friends will miss her from the district —'

'Returning to England? Is she English?'

'Yes, though her husband was Spanish. He died in the cholera epidemic of 1834. They had no children and she never married again, which is why she is selling out now. It isn't a very big *bodega*, but the vineyards are in good heart. In fact they are on the very best *albariza* soil, between Jerez and Sanlúcar de Barrameda, so I couldn't ask for a better situation.'

'Is there a house?' Petronilla inquired, more interested than she had thought she would be.

He nodded. 'A family house,' he said with satisfaction. 'The vineyards are too small for me to be able to fulfil all my contracts in London but, if your mother's wines come up to scratch, I hope to mix the two and produce a very creditable sherry that my customers will like. I have every intention of being a famous name in the wine trade before I'm through.'

'I'm sure you will be!' Petronilla said warmly. 'I know Mamá thinks very highly of your capabilities.'

'That means a great deal to me,' he confirmed.

Her mother's opinion meant a great deal to Petronilla also, but she would have liked it better if he had asked her what *she* thought of his plans, especially as they concerned her more nearly than anyone else.

She might have asked him a whole lot of other questions about the house, and about how the English widow had managed all on her own for so many years but, at that moment, Fabiola came outside to join them, her face bright with suppressed laughter.

'I shall never forgive you if you tell Cousin Immaculada where I am,' she greeted them. 'I have told her I am going to my room to make my devotions!' She produced her prayer book from a pocket in her voluminous skirts. 'It is not very exciting, however, praying alone, when everyone else is doing something else. Why do you never pray, Petronilla?'

Petronilla kept a perfectly straight face. 'I read somewhere that when one prays, one should go into one's chamber and shut the door on outside distractions, not hurry out to see what gossip one can hear from those who have nothing better to do with their time!'

Fabiola giggled happily. 'But me, I love to gossip!' she exclaimed. 'It's different at home where nothing ever happens, but here, you are always doing something new and interesting! Which reminds me, the Doña Pilar wants you both to attend her over by the *bodega*. Do you think she would mind if I came also?'

Petronilla joined in her laughter. 'I'm sure she won't! But what about your prayers?'

Fabiola's face fell. 'Perhaps I should retire to my room and pray, only I should like to know what happens in a *bodega*, because I have never been anywhere near one before and your mother makes it seem one of the very nicest places to visit!'

'Goose!' Petronilla teased her. 'I am sure God wouldn't have you ignorant of the best sherry wine produced in Montilla! Besides,' she added, 'it will please my mother very much if you take a proper interest, as poor Miss Fairman has no palate for any wine, and my father drinks only whisky and thinks sherry to be a woman's drink!'

'She has you to taste the wine with her,' Fabiola pointed out.

'Daughters don't count,' Petronilla riposted and wished she hadn't when she saw the suddenly bleak expression on the other girl's face. 'Or not as much as they sometimes think they should,' she added quickly.

But Fabiola was no longer laughing. 'You have no brothers or you would know how true that is. Daughters are only for marrying and making liaisons with the right families! I am sorry Diego is your cousin, but if my father cared for me at all, he would see how unhappy I should be with such a man! It would be a living death to be in that man's power!'

Petronilla felt more than a little uncomfortable, especially as Mr Arbuthnot could hardly have helped hearing what Fabiola had said. She cast him a swift look to see what he was thinking, but she had no means of telling. He was intent on his own thoughts, or so he wanted her to believe, thus renewing her irritation with him, and so she did her best to ignore him, taking Fabiola's arm as she walked quickly across to the main building of the *bodega* where her mother was waiting for them.

Doña Pilar eyed her daughter with approval as she saw her come in with Mr Arbuthnot on one side and Fabiola on the other. She had heard enough from Fabiola to have forgotten all the embarrassment Petronilla's indiscretion with her cousin had caused her; instead she had been left with a deep-seated concern that Charles Arbuthnot would prove too diffident a wooer to distract her daughter from dreaming over a man who had no heart and few scruples when it came to satisfying his own appetites. Fabiola had been quick to see the cruelty that lay behind the charm, but Petronilla had been exposed to few men other than her father's friends and none of them would have wished her an instant's harm, if only out of the respect in which they held her father. Miss Fairman had called Don Diego the Shining One and had muttered about him falling out of Heaven in the most ridiculous manner, and Doña Pilar, even while she hadn't approved the metaphor, had soon seen exactly what the governess had meant when she had been confronted with Petronilla's bewildered, still-dazzled expression whenever the man's name was mentioned. How much simpler things had been for herself! But she was realistic enough to know, and had been privy to far too many female confidences not to have had that knowledge confirmed, that few men treated their wives with the same respect and loving affection as Thomas Harris had unfailingly brought to their marriage. Charles Arbuthnot was another such man, she thought, which would make it all the more tragic if Petronilla were to think him dull in comparison with her tiresome cousin. If only her Tomás were beside her now, she was sure that he, of all people, would bring about a happy solution for Petronilla, but she knew he wouldn't come while his stupid political masters had work for him to do in England. But, oh, how very much she missed him! She felt only half alive without him!

Pilar was not gloomy by nature, however, and she was quick to distance herself from such miserable thoughts, intent on squeezing the last drop of enjoyment out of the present moment. And there was a great deal for her to enjoy! As a child, she had always enjoyed the day to day working of the *bodega*, even while she had had no responsibility for its workings herself. She loved good wine as she loved good food and, with Charles Arbuthnot's help, she meant to produce the very best.

Eagerly, she danced about the darkened, silent building. 'My dear Charles, you have seen only the worst of our family *bodega*, so today I have made up my mind you shall see the best. Some of this wine dates back to the time of the Armada, some of it I like to think is the best the soil of Spain has ever produced. Today, we are going to taste and see how good it is! It will encourage us to build up the *bodega* again into producing yet more great wine!' She tapped him on the shoulder, laughing openly at him. 'It isn't only in your Jerez that such wines are made, my friend!'

'I'll grant you that,' he acknowledged, 'but is it a true sherry?'

'Taste and see!' she bade him.

Gone was the carefully restrained wife of Thomas Harris; in her place was this vital, intent, Spanish lady, a stranger even to Petronilla, as she rushed from one cask to another, dipping the *venencia* in as if she had done it all her life, and pouring the golden liquid into first one glass and then another.

'You see, this is what we have been making these last few years!' Pilar made a face as she tasted some wine from her own glass. 'It is terrible! It would be a crime to call such a bastardized wine Amontillado, no? But see what we have already bottled from my father's time! Then you will see what fine wines this soil can produce! A gift from the gods, I promise you!'

Petronilla, her tongue curling away from contact with the immature wine she had been offered, shuddered and picked up the *venencia*, wondering how it had come by its name. She dipped the cup at the end of the long stick into the nearest barrel and promptly spilt it on the floor. Laughing, she looked at her mother with a new respect.

'Why on earth is it called a *venencia*?' she asked.

Doña Pilar took it from her, demonstrating its use with a flick of her wrist. She handed it back to her daughter, impatient at her ham-fisted attempts to follow her example.

'You will learn! You *must* learn, for *venencia* comes from the word *avenencia*, meaning a bargain. It is used for taking the samples with which one bargains for the sale of the wines. Perhaps one learns better as a child!' she added, clucking impatiently over the spilt wine.

Petronilla handed the *venencia* to Fabiola. 'You try!'

To her relief, the Spanish girl's efforts were no better than her own.

'Your turn!' she said to Charles.

But Mr Arbuthnot had long ago learned how to wield the strange sampling cup. He successfully transferred the wine from butt to glass without spilling a drop, grinning at Petronilla all the while.

'I had to learn when I became a wine buyer,' he said. 'All it takes is a little practice!'

'A lot of practice!' Doña Pilar contradicted him darkly. 'But then, I was very little when I learned! What else could I do with two brothers taunting me that I was too little and too silly to learn anything useful! I soon decided that they could learn to fight with swords if they wanted to, I should learn how to sample our Papá's wines!'

However she had learned, she had learned well. She knew exactly what she was doing although she had been away from the *bodega* for more than half her life. Petronilla watched with some amusement the fierce concentration with which her mother selected the bottles she wanted Charles Arbuthnot to try, taking one from here and another from there with all the ease of an acknowledged expert. Who would have thought it of the elegant Mrs Harris, that she could open a bottle as easily as any man, throwing a small portion of the wine on the floor as she did so, saying it was in case it had been corrupted by contact with the cork?

'Is that why you do it?' Mr Arbuthnot murmured. 'The Jerezanos do the same, you know, making an offering to the earth that produces such a magnificent liquid year after year. They have probably done the same since the beginning of time.'

Doña Pilar gave him an enigmatic look. 'But you should know how one may never be sure of the quality each year will produce,' she answered. 'One must wait and wait to see what grade of wine you have made this year. There are never two years the same! Why should one not keep the spirits of the vineyard sweet with such a small gift of their own produce?'

Petronilla was shocked. Her eyes flew to Fabiola, sure that she would be equally outraged by such pagan thoughts, but the Spanish girl was nodding her head and smiling happily at her hostess. The only thing that bothered her was that the worst of the wine should be considered good enough for Communion, which she thought was less than proper when all good things came from God originally.

'I should prefer the very best!' she claimed hotly. 'You must sell your poor wines elsewhere!'

'No one else would buy it,' Doña Pilar told her, shrugging her shoulders. 'One cannot afford to be too idealistic, especially when most priests are well satisfied as long as the wine is sweet. They are taken away from real life before they have time to acquire good palates!'

'The priests, yes,' Fabiola muttered, 'but God?'

'If God can change water into wine, no doubt he thinks nothing of turning any wine into something as beautiful as his own Precious Blood, no?'

Fabiola remained unconvinced, but she had been brought up never to argue with her elders and so she kept her indignation to herself. Besides, she was Spanish enough to share the same strand of realism that told her Doña Pilar was probably right in her estimation of the kind of wine most of the country priests would prefer anyway. Nor did she have the least difficulty in seeing the Church at one and the same time as the Holy Foundation of God and as a human institution with all the failings and faults that that implied, but she still wondered why the good and the best were so often the questions at dispute and to which there were no tidy answers, rather than the black and white questions of good and evil, to which even she could make up her mind without difficulty.

Doña Pilar poured the wine. 'Now my beautiful daughter will tell me what she thinks of her Spanish heritage! This is the true Amontillado!'

Petronilla allowed the aroma of the wine to creep up her nostrils as she swirled the golden wine round the glass, admiring the purity of its colour. She took a sip, noting the smoothness and the full-bodied taste as it slid smoothly down her throat.

'Compared to the other, this is pure nectar!' she breathed.

'A gift from the sun and soil,' her mother agreed.

Petronilla's brow creased thoughtfully. 'I don't understand why anyone should want to grow anything else!' she said at last.

Doña Pilar's expression changed. 'You must ask your cousin that!'

Petronilla bit her lip. 'Don Diego has no interest in wines. Tío Ambrosio should never have chosen him to look after the *bodega*!'

Doña Pilar said nothing and it was left to Fabiola to remark, 'Don Diego needed the income, you know that! Now you have come home again, he will have to marry great wealth or think of a new way of making a living.' Her lips trembled. 'Me, I would much rather not be the wife of such a one!'

'You don't want to marry at all!' Petronilla pointed out, rattled by this criticism.

Fabiola sipped her own glass of wine. 'I am sure I don't want a husband who is more interested in bulls than he is in me!'

'He's a fine soldier!'

'A traitor!' Fabiola snorted. 'What is so wonderful about that?'

Petronilla had no answer. She felt close to tears, but her pride would not allow her to show that she minded her cousin being cast in a less than flattering role.

'He certainly has no palate for a good wine!' she said stiffly. 'Probably he didn't even bother to find out what was going on here. I think he considers anything to do with buying and selling to be beneath him. So does Tío Ambrosio, but he can afford to live up to his birthright,

Don Diego can't!' She forced a smile. 'Perhaps he will turn matador, or something splendid like that!'

Charles Arbuthnot lifted his glass. 'I think his plans were laid long ago. Don Carlos's cause seems to attract ruthless men. Poor Spain! Civil war seems to be her destiny, though we have a sort of peace at the moment, thank God.'

Doña Pilar produced some other wines and she and Mr Arbuthnot exchanged notes on their merits, the latter doing a number of complicated sums in his notebook as to how much he could afford to buy immediately, and how long he would have to wait until the *bodega* could be brought back into full production.

Petronilla waited for his verdict as eagerly as did her mother. His face was flushed with enthusiasm when he finally looked up. Deliberately, he put out a hand and took a fresh glass of wine, lifting it to both ladies.

'It will be a few years before we make our fortunes, but we've made a good start!' he announced. 'By this time next year we may even be looking for new markets. What do you think of that?'

Petronilla felt the warm affection of his smile and thought again how much she liked the man. She tilted her own glass towards him and returned the smile. Charles Arbuthnot was a good man and she knew she would never find a better husband. She turned away, wishing her father would hurry up and come, so that he could settle the details of the marriage contract once and for all. If she were only married to her Scotsman, she would have no time to dream of any other man, and how glad she would be to be free of that particular madness! She put her hand on Mr Arbuthnot's arm and took a peek at the figures he had written in his notebook.

'Keep still! I can't see!' she commanded him.

He gave way, passing her his notes, smiling at her as she checked his figures. He bent his head very close to hers and whispered, 'You're the perfect wife for me, Miss Harris, and very beautiful besides!'

She wanted to answer in kind, but she could not, so she whispered back instead, 'Marry me quickly, Charles Arbuthnot, if you love me!'

She was struck by the look of sheer delight he gave her and felt the more wretched because of it. She didn't deserve to be happy with any man until she could pluck the image of Don Diego out of her heart. Could one make oneself love to order, she wondered, or would she always be haunted by a sense of failure because this man was far too good for her?

A virtuous woman is a crown to her husband: but she that maketh him ashamed is as rottenness in his bones.

'I shall try to be everything you want me to be!' she said in fright, trying to make the words go away from her mind and be forgotten for ever. 'I want to be a good wife to you!'

His hand covered hers, broad and comfortable. She had always liked the feel of his hands against hers.

'I want *you*, Petronilla, not a woman who'll make me a good wife. Shall we drink to that?'

She clinked her glass against his, pinning a smile to her lips. Her throat was stiff and sore and her tongue felt two sizes too big for her mouth. She tipped a little wine against her teeth, but she couldn't force herself to swallow it. What had she done, what had she ever done, that when she should have been at her happiest all she wanted to do was to burst into tears and cry herself into oblivion along with her lost love?

When Doña Pilar came into the *salon* after changing her dress that evening, she was pleased rather than otherwise to find Mr Arbuthnot waiting to speak to her.

She spread her fan, whipping it shut again with a crack that resounded round the room. 'Is it about Petronilla?'

'Yes,' he admitted frankly. 'Your daughter has intimated to me that she would like us to be married as soon as possible. I realize, of course, that Colonel Harris can't possibly leave England until the House rises and that is still several weeks away—'

Doña Pilar raised her eyebrows. 'You know a great deal about his movements!' she commented. 'He tells *me* that the Exhibition has caused so much excitement everyone has quite forgotten all about the evils we Catholics are supposed to be about to commit. The truth is probably that they have new things to worry about now that they know the results of the census and that there are as many dissenters as there are worshippers in the National Church. Ah me! One wonders why they make so much fuss, but there is no understanding how the Church of England works! Tomás tries to explain it all to me and, because he is a good man, I listen very carefully but it seems to me it has a great deal to do with English politics and very little to do with God!'

Mr Arbuthnot was sufficiently astonished that she should have even heard of the census, let alone have an opinion on the matter. He saw that he had underrated the intelligence of his future mother-in-law and gave her a sheepish grin. Probably she was equally aware of the reasons why she and Petronilla had been sent to Spain in the first place.

'There are politics in every Church, ma'am,' he pointed out.

'Indeed,' she sighed. 'Even in my beloved Spain!'

'The thing is,' he went on carefully, 'that your husband may be detained in England longer than we think. I realize that this is your home from which you have been away far too long as it is, but I wondered if you would consider bringing Miss Harris on a visit to Jerez. You could meet Doña Louise and see her *bodega* and vineyards for yourself before the announcement of our engagement is made.' He coughed, putting a hand up to his mouth. 'Perhaps you won't agree with me, ma'am, but it seems to me that Petronilla is always on edge here – almost as if she were expecting a visit from Don Diego Salcedo at any moment.'

Doña Pilar looked sharply at him. 'Cousin Diego had better not show his face here!'

'Don Ambrosio may send him to explain his stewardship to you. The old man won't take any responsibility himself.'

'No, poor man! That he should be head of our family is something else for which this eternal strife can be blamed. So many dead! And always the best of every generation! Don Carlos should have thought of all that before he rose up against *la reina*! Though not even he could have wished Cousin Diego to declare for his cause. One wishes some intelligence amongst one's lieutenants, after all!'

'Don Diego is far from being stupid!' Mr Arbuthnot said sharply.

'Cruelty is always stupid, my friend.'

'I think him more selfish than cruel, ma'am. But I'm prepared to admit to being prejudiced. Cruelty sounds more romantic – and often looks it too – it gives a glamour to what is often only self-indulgence.'

Doña Pilar was silent for a long moment. 'My daughter will always do her duty, you don't have to be afraid on that score,' she said at last. 'She was more than half in love with you before we ever came to Spain!'

He sucked his cheeks in between his teeth. 'I must be more romantic than I thought! I have the oddest wish *not* to be a duty where she is concerned. I take comfort in the knowledge that she likes me – more than she *likes* her cousin! – and once she is free of all reminders of him, I have hopes she may come to love me too.'

Doña Pilar spread her fan again, swishing it back and forth in irritation. 'Have you discussed this with my daughter?'

He shook his head. 'Some things are better not said, don't you agree?'

'Poor child! I should never have let her go to Córdoba without me!'

'She was bound to meet her cousin sooner or later,' he

pointed out. 'And, little as I like him, I can understand her fascination with him. He has the looks of a hero of a romantic novel – and the "devil-may-care" manner of a spoilt child–'

'Yes, but I should have taken care to reveal his less flattering attributes, not encouraged her to see him as some romantic hero of her imagination! But she is no fool, my daughter. How could she be with Colonel Harris for a father? She will soon see her cousin as he really is! And do you know what gives me most hope?'

Mr Arbuthnot looked enquiringly, thinking it was the mother's daughter he had fallen in love with.

'She says he is cruel to his horses!' Doña Pilar declared triumphantly.

Mr Arbuthnot chewed on his lip. 'Whereas I am invariably kind – and dull!''

Doña Pilar nodded forthrightly. 'Then you must surprise her from time to time, because dull you are not! Some people have called my Tomás dull, let me tell you – and kind too! – but I am the only one who has known him in the marriage bed and me, I have no eyes for any other man! It will be the same for you and Petronilla I have no doubt!'

Mr Arbuthnot wished he were as certain. 'Then you will bring her to Jerez as soon as we can arrange to leave?'

'And what am I to do with Fabiola?'

'Send her home to Granada!'

Neither Petronilla nor Fabiola would entertain the notion of the latter's departure for a moment, however.

'You can't send her home!' Petronilla said, aghast.

'It will be perfectly proper for her to travel in the company of her own *novio*,' her mother declared, not best pleased by this unexpected rebellion.

'Except that Don Diego is *not* my *novio* and never will be!' Fabiola insisted, her eyes wide with fright. 'I refuse absolutely to go anywhere in his company in case it should be thought I assent to this marriage!' She stuck out her lower lip, looking more childish than virtuous. 'I shall go with you to Jerez!'

But on that question Doña Pilar could be equally adamant. 'My dear child, I have a duty to your parents to return you to their care as soon as possible. How can I possibly justify carrying you off with me to Jerez?'

'Very well,' said Fabiola, 'if I may not go to Jerez with you, Immaculada and I will go home, alone as we came!'

'And what about all the bandits on the roads?'

'I prefer the bandits to Don Diego!' Fabiola informed her with a fierceness that lay oddly on such a small person. 'I will go nowhere in the company of any man!' She put a quivering hand out to Petronilla. '*You* convince her how it is with me!'

Petronilla suppressed a reluctant smile. 'It's true, Mamá. You can't make her go with him on such a perilous journey, even if he were to agree to take her.'

Doña Pilar was still undecided. 'It seems to me that someone who claims to have a vocation to be a bride of Christ would do well to learn a little obedience,' she began.

'I will not trust myself to a man!' Fabiola insisted.

'Besides,' Petronilla pointed out flatly, 'no one knows where Cousin Diego is.'

Doña Pilar saw that neither of them were to be persuaded. 'Very well,' she conceded, 'I will write again to Fabiola's parents and explain that I am sending her to Córdoba to stay with my family there. *Señorita* Immaculada will accompany her. This will give your parents time to accustom themselves to their daughter's ambition. But,' she added on a note of asperity, 'understand me well, young lady, only your parents have the right in the end to decide your future and, if they insist on this marriage with Cousin Diego, then it is your clear duty to submit to their judgement, as I'm sure your confessor has already told you!'

Fabiola's eyes danced and her mouth turned up at the corners in a delicious little smile.

'I am in your house, so I hesitate to contradict, but it will be God who will do the deciding in the end,' she said. 'Not even your Don Diego can prevail against him, can he?'

Doña Pilar gave in gracefully. 'Oh, very well, child. I must admit I have no ambition to throw you to such a big, bad wolf, as our cousin has turned out to be, but what your parents will have to say to me for interfering in something which is quite definitely *not* my business, is something which I don't care to contemplate!'

Fabiola gave a little laugh of triumph, hugging her hostess with a familiarity for which no one thought to reprove her.

'But you mustn't call him a big, bad wolf, ma'am. He is no more than a black sheep, no? A lost black sheep for whom we must all pray! Don't you think so Doña Petronilla?'

But Petronilla had nothing to say on the subject. She despaired of anyone seeing Cousin Diego as she did herself, as a man of charm and possible greatness, neither wolf nor black sheep, but a man she could have loved with her whole heart, if she had been allowed to do so.

Chapter Eleven

Seville was buzzing with rumours about the Royal Family. All the talk seemed to be about the unfortunate Doña Isabella and the extraordinary influence a certain Sor Patrocino seemed to be exercising over her royal patron.

Doña Pilar was inclined to make light of the whole affair. 'What does it matter what this Franciscan lady says and does?' she enquired. 'I don't see it has anything to do with anyone else.'

'But it does, Mamá,' Petronilla said at once. 'Doña Isabella thinks she can do no wrong! Why, it is even said that she wears her cast-off shifts as if they were the relics of some saint! It's unhealthy for one in her position to make so much of such a woman.'

'You say that because of the circumstances of her birth!'

'Does anyone really know what they were?' Petronilla countered.

'She was born in some field when her mother was fleeing from the French in 1814. That is understandable, is it not?'

'If it's true. She has other claims to fame, however. People are saying she is a stigmatic, which I take leave to doubt, and that she was transported by the Devil himself to Aranjuez so that she could see for herself the way the Queen's mother chooses to live. That may well be every bit as scandalous as she says it is, but one wonders if she is really speaking from her own knowledge, or whether there isn't someone else pulling the strings to which she dances!'

Nearly a year in Spain had done her daughter the world of good thought Doña Pilar. Gone were the days when Petronilla had despised all female gossip as being beneath her notice. 'You sound just like your father when you take a dislike to someone!' Pilar exclaimed. 'Me, I find all this talk about the Court very amusing! It's said Olozaga, the civil governor of Madrid, imprisoned this woman in the house of a certain Doña Manuela Peirotet, in the calle de la Almudena, for three months. He went to visit her there and fell in love with her, silly man! Some say she refused his advances, but his friends say she succumbed to his charms —'

'Mamá, do you believe that?'

Doña Pilar smiled, reluctant to put an end to her speculations about this peculiar religious sister, unsuitable as they were for anyone of Petronilla's tender years, even though she was now eighteen. 'I believe she was imprisoned, sent into exile, and only allowed back to Madrid in 1844.'

'And now has the ear of the Queen again?'

'It's said she has even more influence over the King-Consort. If he were another sort of man, I daresay they would be calling them lovers too! How could they have married that poor lady to such a man?'

'I'm told he's very handsome!' Petronilla objected. 'Does the Queen dislike him?'

Doña Pilar decided against trying to explain her reservations about Francisco de Asis, Duke of Cádiz, and why she thought him an unlikely husband for anyone. Petronilla might be on the point of marriage herself, but it was still an unsuitable subject for one who had no knowledge of these things. The whole situation angered her, for having once given her allegiance to the Doña Isabella she resented the outrageous activities of the Queen's mother, which were more than sufficient to strain the loyalty of many of the best Spaniards even without marrying the daughter to an effeminate fop who would never father an heir to prop up his wife's shaky throne. Indeed there never would be an heir unless Doña Isabella looked elsewhere for a father for her child and, in view of the scandalous affairs the Queen Regent saw fit to indulge in, that was not a solution that was likely to appeal to anyone. María Cristina was not an example Doña Pilar would have chosen to dangle in front of any young girl, and she had not been surprised when Doña Isabella had been declared to have come of age as soon as she turned thirteen, in order to rid her of her mother's influence – a polite fiction as everyone in Europe had known, since the child had not even come to puberty and probably knew less about adult life even than her younger sister. And now it was the same younger sister who had walked off with a real man and some chance of happiness, while the Queen of Spain knew only disappointment and disillusion in her married life.

'The Queen may not dislike him, but I do!' Doña Pilar said aloud. 'He wouldn't do for any daughter of mine! Shall we go and join the others?'

Petronilla was only too willing. She had been downcast at first when her mother had suggested they should make their journey to Jerez through Seville. She was still confused as to the identity of many of her family there, unable to distinguish between one old lady and another, and sometimes giving the wrong children to the wrong parents in her own mind. She had been doubtful, too, as to what sort of reception Mr Arbuthnot could expect, remembering how suspicious they had been of her own English blood. Since their arrival, however, it had been Mr Arbuthnot who had been welcomed with open arms, smoothing her path for her by his obvious approval of everything she said and did, until she had begun to enjoy herself more than she had thought possible, as pleased with his success as she was with her own.

She had begun to relish the dry, earthy humour that

seemed to be a family characteristic. Better still, Doña Pilar was in her element, as full of life as Petronilla had ever seen her, and such was the relationship between mother and daughter that not for a moment did Petronilla resent her mother's enjoyment of the scene while she was still unsure of herself as a foreigner whose native language was English and not Spanish. Her weeks in Spain had served her in good stead in that respect for she found herself understanding much more than she had during their last visit and was therefore able to enjoy the company much more than she would have done otherwise. It was one thing, she had discovered, to converse with her mother in her own tongue, but another thing to follow the quick banter favoured by the majority of her cousins.

Charles Arbuthnot looked up with obvious pleasure as the Harris ladies came into the patio where the whole family had gathered. With a courtly gesture – one that he could never have learned in London – he found Petronilla a chair and went to get her a cooling drink, as pleased to see her as if they had been parted from one another for weeks instead of a few hours.

'*¡Quel hombre!*' one of her cousins murmured as he made his way back to her. 'The English always have the luck of the devil!'

Petronilla blinked demurely, only the colour in her cheeks betraying her astonishment that anyone should speak in such terms of Mr Arbuthnot. She accepted the drink with a slight smile, looking at him with new eyes, noting the firmness of his mouth and chin and the sweetness of his expression in his sherry-coloured eyes as his fingers deliberately caressed hers as the glass changed hands. His shoulders were broader than Don Diego's, she noted, and he had the same quiet confidence of her father. There was none of the glittering charm she craved, but the warmth of his approval made the misery uncurl inside her, giving way to a contentment she had begun to think she would never feel again.

'Thank you,' she said, and she didn't mean it for the

drink, not entirely, but because she was proud of him as someone who seemed able to make himself respected and at home anywhere. She found she liked being connected to such a man and enjoyed the compliments her Sevillian family showered on him as much as those they were beginning to offer her from time to time.

She sipped her drink, listening with only half an ear as the men, as much as the women, speculated on the more intimate details of the Queen's marriage. It was Doña Pilar who, at length, pleaded for another topic of conversation.

'What's done is done!' she exclaimed. 'Doña Isabella must find her own answers – and if *Señor* Bravo Murillo succeeds in sending that religious woman away from the Court, he will be doing no more than his duty as her First Minister. If you ask me, the poor lady is so starved for affection that she admits such a strange person into her circle. *Ay de mí*, poor Queen! Poor Spain!'

'What would you have us talk about?' Mr Arbuthnot asked her. 'Gibraltar?'

'No, never Gibraltar!' She frowned at him, annoyed that the Fat Rock should be even mentioned, such was her dislike of the place.

'What is there to say, Don Arbootno?'

Mr Artbuthnot smiled faintly. 'I wondered what everyone thought of the new wharfage tolls that have been imposed there?'

'Meaningless! The British are out to ruin our trade, with their Fat Rock and their Free Port!'

Petronilla observed her mother's ire with a grin. 'Gibraltar hasn't been a Free Port since 1827, when an Order in Council put charges on all hulks and pontoons in the Bay –'

'And what were they doing there if they were not smuggling?' her parent demanded.

'Well, the King of Morocco wasn't best pleased,' Mr Arbuthnot put in deliberately.

Doña Pilar ignored him, and it was left to the rest of the family to point out that Gibraltar had never played any part in the affairs of Spain but that of a robber baron who taxed all the lesser thieves while offering them protection from the justice of Spain. No, no; all the while Britain held the Fat Rock there would be strife between the two countries.

'We need it to hold the entrance to the Mediterranean. You don't want the French back, do you?' Petronilla asked indignantly.

They shook their heads at her, but the heat had gone out of the argument. 'All we need to put our affairs in order is a few years of peace in which to grow into a great nation once again, but neither you nor the French will ever leave us alone long enough for that!'

Mr Arbuthnot's eyes narrowed thoughtfully. 'I think myself Gibraltar will always be trouble no matter who holds her,' he said at last. 'I imagine a lot of money can be made running contraband in and out of that harbour.'

'You never said a truer word than that!' they conceded one and all. 'That much has been true ever since the time of the legendary El Cid. What do the British do with all their ill-gotten gains though, that's what we'd all like to know?'

'I wish I could tell you,' Mr Arbuthnot answered with a smile and changed the subject once again.

Jerez de la Frontera, the town where the whole sherry industry that is called after it came into being, was enchanting in the early spring sunshine. The wide avenues and squares were lined with orange trees, the famous bitter oranges of Seville. The city fathers had determined that if sweet oranges had been used, their fruits would have been stolen by all and sundry. As it was, the ex-patriot British sherry-makers could be seen, whenever the wind blew, collecting up the fallen fruit to make their year's supply of marmalade. On the day of Petronilla's arrival, the trees had come into flower and the smell of orange blossom drifted across the little town. Petronilla thought she had never seen anywhere more beautiful, not even in her native

England. How odd it was, that she could take such delight now in a corner of Spain that she had largely dismissed as being dull before.

'Aha! You are beginning to like my country!' her mother accused her. 'It is beautiful, no?'

'Yes, beautiful,' Petronilla agreed.

Doña Pilar and Mr Arbuthnot exchanged satisfied glances, both well pleased with the success of their stratagem to remove Petronilla as far as possible from the orbit of Don Diego. Petronilla pretended not to notice. She wished it were as simple as they supposed. Somewhere inside, she felt older than the two of them put together, that she would never be wholly young and carefree ever again. She was glad she hadn't changed so much outwardly that it had occurred to either of them that since her cousin had kissed her, half tearing her clothes from her, she had been privy to a guilty knowledge of her own sexuality that she had never previously suspected. She was aware of all men as she had not been before, in a way that had nothing to do with love or liking, but which was wholly physical and shaming to someone who had always been kept as ignorant as she was innocent of any relationship between men and women other than that of father and daughter.

Their progress was slow as other vintners recognized Mr Arbuthnot and stopped to congratulate him on becoming one of them.

'Don Carlos! Don Arbootno!' they greeted him, slapping him on the back. 'Doña Louise says you have persuaded her to sell! *¡Bravo, amigo!* We look forward to seeing you at the meetings of the *bodega* owners!'

There was no doubt that the Scotsman was popular in his adopted place in the world. Nobody here thought him dull and he responded in kind, grinning from ear to ear and answering their sallies in such perfect Spanish that Petronilla wondered where he had learned it. How many Spanish *señoritas* had he known, and with what degrees of intimacy, she wondered. It was hard to imagine Charles

Arbuthnot as a lover – or anything other than the kind, undemanding friend who was always there when she needed him. Watching him amongst these Jerezanos though, she wondered if she hadn't underrated him once again. There was a glint of humour in his eyes that would be very attractive to most women. She only wished that it were enough to make her own heart beat faster, but she remained stubbornly unmoved, except that every now and again she would remember his firm, capable fingers against hers and she would wonder how they would feel against her breasts if he were to touch her there as Don Diego had done, frightening her half to death.

Sanlúcar was not as pretty as Jerez. The house, however, was one of those gabled Spanish mansions, enclosed within its own blindingly white wall. Built round two internal patios, both wall and house were topped by orange and green tiles that shone in the sunshine. Citrus trees shaded a straggly patch of grass outside the main portico, some English roses dying of thirst in their dappled shade. Inside, in the patio around which the public rooms were arranged, flowers were massed in pots and window boxes, complemented by the caged yellow canaries whose sound in the morning and in the evenings could be deafening in its intensity. The birds were Doña Louise's pride and joy and she was forever fussing about them, supplying them with fresh water and birdseed whenever she could find nothing better to do. Petronilla regarded them with mixed feelings. At first she thought the sound they made to be exotic and rather exciting, but she soon tired of it, especially as they competed avidly with every human conversation that took place around them, frequently drowning out every sound with their own sharp trills and squawks.

'Sanlúcar de Barrameda has its own interest,' Mr Arbuthnot told her one evening, when he found her reading in the patio, her hands over her ears to aid her concentration.

'Oh?'

'Come and see,' he suggested.

She was glad to get out of the house for a while for Doña Louise and her mother seemed to have nothing to talk about but the coming wedding, spiced with yet more gossip about the private life of Doña Isabella II, both subjects doing little for her jaded spirits.

He led her down to the harbour where they could watch the ships coming and going from all over the world, many of them carrying the wine on which their fortune was to depend.

'When I first came to Spain, I used to come here a lot,' he confided. 'Everything was strange to me and my Spanish was almost non-existent. I was often lonely, lonely enough to wish myself aboard one of those steamers and on my way back to London and everything that was familiar that I had left behind me.'

Petronillà gave him a sidelong glance of disbelief. 'You can't have been lonely often,' she demurred. 'You're far too popular around here for that! And someone must have taught you Spanish!'

He cleared his throat thoughtfully, wondering how to answer. 'It isn't my mother tongue as it is yours,' he admitted at length.

She laughed, pleased by the thought. 'I've always thought of English as being that,' she said. 'A father tongue doesn't sound quite right, does it?'

'Which did you learn first?'

She laughed again. 'You'll have to ask my mother that. I'm afraid I can't remember. My mother taught me well, but I speak much better since I've had more practice. Didn't you find that?'

'Of course,' he said. He was as gentle and courteous as ever but somehow she didn't like to press him further. She respected him the more for not indulging her curiosity, much as she would have liked to know all sorts of things about him that it had never occurred her to wonder about before.

'Ships are such graceful things,' she said instead. 'Only

birds are able to skim along, making the most of the wind in that way.'

'As long as one is only an onlooker and not a participant?' he teased her.

'Indeed, sir! As far as I'm concerned, it's as unnatural for human beings to travel by sea as it would be by air!'

'Our ancestors probably felt the same way,' he smiled. 'Sanlúcar is called de Barrameda because just outside the harbour is a reef which is very dangerous to shipping. Long before Christianity came to Spain, a little pagan temple stood in that forest over there, dedicated to the Morning Star. The title is applied to the Virgin Mary these days, of course, but the idea of seeking protection from the dangers of the sea is the same. I often wonder if Christopher Columbus said a prayer at her shrine when he set sail for his third voyage to the New World.'

'Did he leave from here?' Petronilla was impressed. 'When was that?'

'In 1498.'

'My father says the gold he brought home with him was the cause of Spain's decline. He was much shocked by how much of it was used to decorate the churches of Rome, though Mamá of course thought it only proper that it should end up there where everyone can enjoy it! Papá says it led to such dreadful inflation that the Spanish economy never recovered. Could that be true?'

'Your father would be the one to know that. My gold is a liquid gold – much more exciting than money!'

'That it is!' Petronilla agreed. How fortunate it was, she thought, that no matter what there would always be their mutual interest in sherry to bind them together. 'Your very own sherry from your very own *bodega*!' She squeezed his arm with a greater show of affection than she usually allowed herself, enjoying the ease and intimacy of the moment. 'You must be very proud!'

'Our wine from our *bodega*,' he corrected her firmly. 'Shall we seal it with a kiss?'

She said nothing, but he noted the flash of interest in

her dark chocolate eyes and was well contented with her reaction. He bent his head and put his lips to hers, much as he might have kissed a child. He felt her disappointment, laughed deep in his chest and brought her closer up against him, his mouth seeking hers with such determination that she was caught off balance and had to clutch at him to save herself from falling.

'Charles!' she exclaimed, startled by his fervour.

But he was no longer listening. His palm cradled her head as he pushed his tongue against hers. Then, as suddenly, he let her go, but not before he had felt the quickening of her pulse with a burgeoning passion that was every bit the equal of his own.

'I'm sorry,' he apologized. 'You go to my head quicker than any wine!'

She took a deep breath, a little shocked by her own reaction. Would any man's kiss be the same where she was concerned?

'Shall I take you home?' he offered, once again the self-contained, phlegmatic man of her acquaintance.

She shook her head. 'You go on,' she bade him. 'I think I will visit Our Lady's shrine of the Morning Star, and I'd prefer to go by myself. Do you think any of her other shrines were once pagan too?'

'Probably.'

'In England too?' That she would find very hard to believe. Not that there were many shrines dedicated to the Mother of God in England any longer, whereas they seemed to be two a penny here in Spain.

'I suppose most of the holy wells have pagan origins. Does it matter?'

Petronilla didn't know. She might have discussed it with him further, but she no longer felt quite at ease in his company, not now she knew it wasn't as a friend that he saw her, not even as his wife-to-be, but as a woman he wanted to take into his bed as he probably had those other women, the ones who had taught him to speak Spanish like a native. Good gracious, she thought, was that the quality that was so lacking in the unfortunate king-consort, the Duke of Cádiz. Her eyes widened at the thought as she remembered how sorry her mother had been for the poor Queen. Was that why, because her husband didn't want her in his bed?

She pressed on to the shrine, trying to put all such thoughts out of her mind. '*Dios te salve, María,*' she began in Spanish, rolling the well-used words over her tongue in an effort to blot out the feel of another tongue against hers; '*llena eres de gracia; el Señor es contigo; bendita Tú eres entre todas las mujeres, y bendito es el fruto de tu vientre, Jesús.*' She shut her eyes, forcing herself to concentrate on what she was saying, remembering how as a child she had first said the prayer at her mother's knee, which was why it came more naturally to her in Spanish than in English.

She opened her eyes again and caught a glimpse of someone moving ahead of her through the trees. Recognition of the man's outline kept her rooted to the spot as she tried to convince herself she was mistaken. She knew of only one person who moved like that, but what could her cousin be doing here? And why now, of all times, when, for the first time, she had begun to believe that she might be able to forget all about him?

'*Santa María, Madre de Dios, ruega por nosotros, pecadores, ahora y en la hora de nuestra muerte. Amén.*'

The words came tumbling out with an earnestness that would have astonished both Miss Fairman and her mother. She meant every word of the prayer. Could it have been her cousin she had seen? She said another Hail Mary, and then another, recognizing that she had come to a moment of decision from which there would be no going back. Either she could marry Charles Arbuthnot with honour, or she could allow a moment's madness to ruin her whole life. It was as simple as that, except that now she knew that Charles had no intention of being her best friend, or a mere figurehead in her life. If she married him, he would demand her whole heart – and body. Was she prepared to give him as much?

It was a long time before she walked the short distance home, slipping into the house so quietly that not even the canaries were disturbed enough to announce her presence.

'Ah, there you are, my dear,' her mother greeted her. 'Did you have a nice time?'

Petronilla bent and kissed the cool cheek that was presented to her. 'I have been following Fabiola's example and saying my prayers,' her daughter told her gravely.

Doña Pilar's quick look was followed by a barely suppressed sigh of satisfaction.

'What example?' she demanded, her voice breaking between a laugh and a sob. 'When have you ever seen that child about her prayers?'

'More often than you think,' Petronilla defended her. 'She knows exactly what she wants, Mamá!'

Doña Pilar tapped her chin with her fan. 'And so do you, my darling! What's so wonderful in that?' Whereupon she seemed to lose all interest in the proceedings, much to her sorely tried daughter's relief.

Doña Louise Carr, widow of Francisco de la Tixera, was less indulgent in her assessment of Petronilla as a wife for Charles Arbuthnot. Childless, herself, and obsessed by nostalgia for her native land, she had been overjoyed when she had realized that Mr Arbuthnot had no ambition to be a sherry buyer for longer than a few years, that what he really wanted was to possess his own *bodega* and produce his own sherry. Since her husband's death, she had kept going out of habit, always meaning to sell when a likely buyer had come along but never finding quite the right person to meet her exacting standards of what was proper to her husband's memory.

There was an immediate rapport between herself and Doña Pilar as both ladies had married foreign nationals and had been obliged to live their whole married life in exile from their own family and friends. They understood one another exactly, though Doña Pilar had little patience for the sentimental reminiscences of the other for an

England she doubted had ever existed and which most certainly didn't exist now.

'The English are realistic,' she declared when she had heard enough. 'When Victoria came to the throne, she saw that if she behaved as her uncles before her, with court cases and rumours of bankruptcy, and having many lovers but no legitimate heirs, the English would wonder if the French were not right in their rejection of monarchy altogether! She is not by nature staid and dull, that one, but her Prince Albert is always earnest and always right! She would dance the night away, but he will not allow even that. No, no, the music must stop on the dot of eleven and everyone must be in bed by midnight! At first, this was only true of the Court, but now it is the same everywhere! It's only the English who would have the proverb that "early to bed and early to rise makes a man healthy, wealthy and wise"! In Spain, we put our trust in the Lord that he will supply these blessings, not in the hours we spend in our beds!'

Doña Louise murmured that there was a difference in climate, but Pilar dismissed that as a total irrelevance. 'If the English stayed at home one might believe it, but they seldom stay in their own country. Why, they now rule almost half the world, one way and another, and I am told they keep exactly the same hours in India and everywhere else! The truth of the matter is that they believe frivolity to be a sin!'

Only Petronilla laughed. Their hostess was more than a little shocked that not everyone took it for granted that respectability was the first virtue, making all the others more or less unnecessary. Then she remembered that Pilar was Spanish and, therefore, couldn't be expected to know any better, and the two were the best of friends again.

Of Petronilla, however, she retained her suspicions, finding fault with her free and easy manners which, she opined, were bound to lead her into trouble sooner or later. A gentleman, in her experience, always took his cue from the higher nature of the woman in his life, and, if he were not chastened by her love, supported by her courage, and transformed into a character of finer clay by her example, he would never respect her as a true woman!

Petronilla accepted the rebuke meekly, though privately she thought she had never heard so much nonsense in her life. For a little while she wondered if Mr Arbuthnot had told Doña Louise about the incident with her cousin, and she said defensively, 'Mr Arbuthnot will have to look elsewhere if he wants such a paragon for a wife! I'm afraid I fall far short of such an ideal!'

'We all do!' Doña Louise agreed with due modesty. 'But, I do wonder, dear, whether you have thought deeply enough of what Mr Arbuthnot's life will be, far away from his own land and with only you for company! They say that love overcomes all things, because love is blind to the weaknesses and failings of the beloved, as you know, but you *don't* love Charles, do you?'

'I like him better than any man I know,' Petronilla replied, longing to say a great deal more and only restraining herself with difficulty.

Doña Louise was far from satisfied. 'You mustn't mind me, my dear, but it isn't as though poor Charles has any family of his own and so I feel obliged – ' She sighed heavily. 'He deserves the very best! It's easy to see he has eyes for nobody but you, yet I can't help noticing that you don't feel the same way about him! I believe you are more than half in love with somebody else, only your mother won't even entertain such a notion.'

Petronilla gave her a level look, keeping a firm hold on her temper. 'I know you mean well,' she began, 'but that is something between me and Charles and nobody else. I will not pretend to you that I love Mr Arbuthnot as he deserves, but I have every intention of making him a good wife —'

'So you say! So you say, my dear, but what if this other man should come back into your life?'

'He won't,' Petronilla denied shortly.

'Is he dead?'

Petronilla's patience snapped. 'He never existed except in my imagination! I'm sorry, but I don't wish to discuss it! But if you want to know what I really think, there's no need to feel sorry for Charles Arbuthnot because he's tying himself to such a poor dab of a female as myself! It isn't only the woman he's marrying, it's my mother's Amontillado!'

'Petronilla Harris!'

But Petronilla was no longer listening. With a flurry of skirts, she was gone to her own room, slamming the door shut behind her.

'Well really!' Doña Louise exclaimed.

'What did you expect?' Doña Pilar asked her when the poor woman applied to her for her support. 'Petronilla is very much her father's daughter. She will do what she thinks to be right, whatever you and I may say.'

Doña Louise seldom considered herself to be in the wrong about anything she tackled. 'But is it right for her to marry poor Charles feeling as she does?' she demanded.

'She's the wife he wants —'

'Because of her dowry. That's what the girl told me and I see no reason to disbelieve her.'

Doña Pilar looked at the anxious woman and wished she had a little bit of common sense to leaven her concern and affection for Charles. 'I have often thought,' she said carefully, 'that as we grow older we forgot how difficult it was to sort out emotions when we were young. Nobody would have consented to my marriage to Tomás in the normal way and yet neither of us would have been as happy with anyone else. Wasn't it like that for you?'

Doña Louise relaxed, smiling. 'Indeed it was, though nobody believed I was the right choice for Francisco. The worst thing, from their point of view, was that I wasn't a Catholic and I refused to change my religion no matter what! Francisco didn't care, so why should they?' She took up her embroidery and put in a few stitches, examining the result with care. 'I believe you are right,' she said at last, 'that we should leave it to the two of them to make up their own minds. Charles has become very dear to me – I have no children of my own, you see.'

Doña Pilar put her head on one side, remembering also. 'Tomás would have liked to have had sons! Lots of them, to follow him into the stupid politics he loves so much! But we have only Petronilla, which is why her happiness means a great deal to the two of us. I think it must be always like that with parents in the last resort, that nobody is quite good enough to marry our own children, though Charles is the man I should always have chosen for her. He is a gentleman and she will make him very happy, I am sure of that, and we shall be very proud of them both!'

'Charles is in such a hurry,' Doña Louise began doubtfully.

'And Tomás is delayed again in England.' Doña Pilar's smile included the other woman as if she had indeed been a member of Charles Arbuthnot's family. 'If he doesn't come quickly, you and I will have to make all the preparations ourselves for, much as I would like to have him here, I agree with Charles that the sooner those two young people are married the better!'

A delightful feeling of importance took hold of the Englishwoman.

'I'm sure you're right!' she exclaimed. 'I have always thought this house cries out for weddings – and children —'

'It's certainly a beautiful house,' Doña Pilar was glad to agree. 'You will miss it when you go to England, won't you?'

But Doña Louise refused to admit as much. 'Yes, but England has always been my real home,' she said. 'I have stayed in Spain far too long already!'

'And I in England!' Doña Pilar sighed. 'If only my Tomás were here with me in Spain I should never want to move again. But there, England is his country and so it has become mine, and I love it too. I shall be content if he comes in time for the wedding.'

'Will he, do you think?'

Doña Pilar shook her head sadly. 'He will always do his duty, however long it takes him. That is the English way, is it not?' She forced a new, more cheerful note into her voice. 'And it's the Spanish way to enjoy ourselves, no matter what, so we'll both dance at our children's wedding and make the best of how things are, no?'

Doña Louise hastened to agree, wondering what the unknown Colonel could be like that his wife should miss his everyday presence to such an extent and felt herself at something of a loss for, if the truth were known, she had found widowhood a great deal more satisfactory than her own years as a wife.

'I'm sure he'll come as soon as he can!' she murmured inadequately.

Pilar would have liked to have left it at that, but Petronilla, too, was missing her father and wanted to talk about him and what it was that could possibly be delaying him in England.

'I never imagined being married without him!' she complained.

'Nor did I imagine I should have to be both father and mother at your wedding!' Pilar snapped back bitterly. 'That is what comes of being married to an important English politician! Be thankful that Charles is only a vintner and here in Spain with you!'

'I could scarcely marry him otherwise,' Petronilla pointed out with dignity. Then her sense of humour reasserted itself. 'Besides, if you ask me, they are both Government spies —'

Pilar put her fan up to her daughter's lips to silence her. 'Nonsense, child! I never heard of such a thing!' She spread the fan, her eyes sparking with a mixture of fun and excitement as her glance met Petronilla's. 'You have been listening to too many of Mrs Nightingale's old stories!'

'Perhaps,' Petronilla admitted. 'Only what was all that about Gibraltar in Seville? I think it was what Papa calls a "fishing expedition"!'

'Then the less we know about it the better!' her mother insisted firmly, and with that Petronilla was reluctantly obliged to agree.

Chapter Twelve

The day of her wedding dawned fine and clear.

Only the day before Petronilla had received a letter from her father giving her his blessing for a long and happy married life. He was obviously as upset as his wife and daughter were that he was still detained in England, but there was no way that he could be spared at the moment: what was going to be known as the Reaction of the Great Powers was following the eruption of the whole of Europe in revolution; and now the whole population was taking a great interest in British foreign policy where the Italian peninsula was concerned, as well as the unnecessarily harsh treatment the Austrians were meting out to the Hungarians. Indeed, he rather thought the whole government might fall if it didn't take more notice of what was becoming a veritable tide of popular unrest against the old order.

He had also taken care to express his concern that she might have been over-persuaded into accepting Charles Arbuthnot as her husband.

Sometimes, he had written, *your mother and I have disagreed on the subject of doing one's duty. She has always claimed that if we had been prevented from marrying, she would have obeyed whatever fate her father marked out for her. That is the Spanish way. I could see no reason then, and see no reason now why even a woman, in this day and age, should not choose for herself*

*the person with whom she wishes to live in what is the most
intimate relationship between any two people. Be very sure that
Charles Arbuthnot is your choice and don't allow your dear
mother's talk of being sin virgüenza, or any other such notion,
to distract you from following your own heart. This is what I
would say to you, were I able to be by your side, that even if
you were to change your mind walking up the aisle, my pride
in you as my daughter would be no less than it has ever been.*

Pilar had crumpled the letter angrily in her hand, only to
straighten it out again before returning it to her daughter.

'He was always the most stupid – the most —'

'Wonderful?' Petronilla had supplied helpfully.

Her mother's expression had changed instantly. 'Yes he
is, isn't he?' She had adjusted her daughter's veil. 'I wish
he could be here today!' She had glanced at the letter again.
'Have I over-persuaded you? I forget sometimes you are
as much English as you are Spanish. Nevertheless, we
Spanish are right, you know, because no one who neglects
their duty to other people as if they were of no account
in their lives can be truly happy. It is best, *hija mía*, to live
in the real world. Life is so short and we are dead for a
very long time, no?'

Petronilla had done her best to hide her quick
amusement. 'Dead, Mamá? It is supposed to be a better
life!'

'That is all very well, but this life is for living also – so
live it to the full, and not in your dreams. That is my
wish for you today, my darling daughter.'

Petronilla had been touched. 'Thank you, Mamá.'

When her mother had left her alone, she had spent some
time rereading her father's letter, only then noticing that
he had also seen fit to mention Charles in relation to his
interest in Gibraltar.

*Thank you for passing on Arbuthnot's messages. These may
be more important than either of us thought. The Rugged Rock
is a perilous place these days. Your affectionate father, T. Harris
(Col.)*

More than ever she wished he could have been there to

give her away into Charles Arbuthnot's keeping. She might have been able to ask him the question she had shied away from mentioning to her mother, dearly as she loved her. She could imagine her father's reaction, embarrassed and milking his whiskers for all he was worth; but he would have answered her as seriously as she would have asked the question. Did one have to be in love with a person before one could enjoy making love with them? Doña Pilar wouldn't have known the answer. Petronilla couldn't imagine that her mother had ever looked at another man apart from her father and so she wouldn't have known the answer anyway. Nor had Colonel Harris ever wanted anyone else but the woman he had married, but there had been a long time before he had ever known Pilar, when he *might* . . .

She put the letter away, catching a glimpse of herself in the glass. She was astonished to find she looked beautiful in her dress of gold. Her mother had called it the Pre-Raphaelite look, and had loosened her long dark hair, holding it back from her face with a simple golden veil, braided in the same colour as her bitter-chocolate eyes. The effect was startling to one accustomed to seeing herself in the pastel shades of English youth. The cloth of gold shone like a living thing in the sunlight and the emeralds her mother had given her, telling her they had always been in the Morena family, lent a touch of luxury that made her think of the gold encrusted Madonnas of the Spanish churches, who changed their dresses with the seasons and who were probably the best loved objects amongst the parishioners, men or women.

Would Charles Arbuthnot think her beautiful? Her mouth remembered the feel of his kiss, even while her mind was trying to school her thoughts into more exalted avenues. A great tide of warmth spread from her loins and she wished the ceremony over, so that she and Charles could be alone together as man and wife. She had very little idea what it was that men and women did together, but she would enjoy it if he were to kiss her again, more

than she had Diego's groping against her naked flesh at
the Medina Azahara, because she could never be afraid of
Mr Arbuthnot as she had been when she had found herself
alone with her cousin.

To give herself something else to think about, she
pushed open the shuttered french windows at the far end
of the room and went out on to the low balcony from
where she could see right across the vineyards. As in most
of the *bodegas* round about, Francisco de la Tixera had
built a great tower in the midst of the long lines of vines
so that a watch could be kept over the ripe grapes in
autumn. She saw that Mr Arbuthnot had climbed to the
very top and she had little difficulty in guessing at his
thoughts as he overlooked the whole property he was in
the process of purchasing. Did he regard her as part of the
deal? Petronilla frowned at his motionless form.
Somehow, she didn't believe she was. He would have
made his business deal with her mother anyway; with her
he had made a quite separate contract, one which she had
no doubt he would honour to the letter. She only hoped
she could find it in her heart to be as generous where he
was concerned.

Petronilla saw he had already changed into his wedding
finery, so he was probably filling in time, as she was,
waiting for everyone else to put on their best and ready
themselves to escort them to the church where they would
exchange the vows that would make them man and wife.

Quite when she became aware of another man's
presence in the vineyard, she could not afterwards have
said. One moment her eyes were fixed on the man she
was about to marry and the next, almost without her
being aware of it, there was a movement half-hidden by
the bare vines, pruned into the gnarled shapes of ancient
miniature trees, not yet green with the leaves of spring,
but a deep, rich brown that told that they were pregnant
with new life about to be revealed. Not really believing
what she had seen, Petronilla looked more closely at the

figure, bent almost double, as he picked his way towards the central tower. Where could he be going?

Charles Arbuthnot turned his head towards the house. For an instant Petronilla was distracted by the way the sun shone through his hair giving him a golden halo and the unearthly appearance of a medieval illustration, without any shadows to give contours to his body and face. He was a large man, larger than she had thought, and he seemed suddenly very exposed out there with the intruder getting steadily nearer by the moment.

Petronilla crinkled up her eyes to see them better. The stranger was getting closer. He straightened his back to see where he was going, and she knew immediately who he was and why he was there. There was no mistaking the way he moved, using as little effort as possible, a slight swing of his hips and a slight movement of one hand and he had moved from one of the long aisles between the vines to another. It was her cousin Don Diego.

She didn't have time to consider she would do better to stay where she was. She picked her skirts up as high as they would go, vaulted over the balcony, and ran as fast as her legs would carry her towards the unsuspecting Mr Arbuthnot.

'Charles!' she shrieked. 'Look out!' And then his Spanish name. '*Carlos!*'

He saw her coming, blank astonishment on his face, and came down the tower to meet her. A stork, her black-tipped wings flapping in indignation, resettled herself in her untidy nest, rattled that anyone had dared to come so close to her chosen spot. The movement caused Diego to hesitate in his progress and in the same moment Charles saw him.

Petronilla propelled herself through the vineyard even faster and arrived, breathless, just as her cousin broke into a run towards the tower. She hurled herself at him, in a fury that Diego should dare to ruin her wedding day, as he had done so much else. A glint of metal told her her cousin had a knife, but she was beyond being afraid for herself. She held out a hand to him, barely feeling the pain as the blade ripped through the gold material and into the flesh of her upper arm.

His left hand caught her up against him, his white teeth showing in what was more a snarl than a smile.

'What are you doing here?' she asked him furiously, unbearably relieved that, for once, she felt none of that fatal attraction he had for her, only a great irritation with him for disturbing her hard won self-control, mixed with a fear that he might use the knife on her again or, worse still, on Mr Arbuthnot, if he were to come into contact with him.

'Did you really think I would stand calmly by while you marry yourself to another man?' Diego taunted her. 'You were always meant to be my woman, Petronilla!'

The spirit went out of her, leaving her with no more strength than a rag doll, and she would have fallen if Diego hadn't flourished the knife in her face, arousing her anger to boiling point once again.

'I have made my choice!' she declared.

He held her closer and she could see in his eyes that he had it in mind to kiss her. Doubtless he thought it the best way of bringing her to heel – he had no reason to think otherwise, she acknowledged to herself but, this time, she was in better command of herself and had no intention of losing her self-respect to him again.

'Let me go, Diego,' she said quietly. 'You know as well as I do that I can never be yours.'

He made to kiss her, but she was ready for him, turning her face away and stamping hard on his toes. He let out a cry of agony and, taking advantage of his loosened grip, she wrenched herself free, as much hurt by the bewilderment on his face as she was by her now bleeding arm.

'Why, Petronilla?' he pleaded. 'What have I done to make you turn against me?'

Petronilla hardened her heart. 'Need you ask?' she said wearily. 'We're real people, living real lives, not puppets at the end of a string! What of Fabiola, or have you forgotten all about her? Will you treat her as casually as you did our *bodega*, bringing shame on yourself and our family?'

His eyes glittered angrily. 'Fabiola's family knows how I feel! She doesn't want to marry me any more than I do her! She wants to be some kind of nun! Is that the kind of wife you'd wish on to me? Well, I'm not accepting anything you've said! We're two of a kind, as you very well know!'

Guilt smote her. Was it possible that that was true? She shut her eyes, composing herself with difficulty. Her arm stung, bringing saliva into her mouth. It was a small thing compared with all the rest, but she had felt beautiful in her wedding dress and now that had been ruined too by Diego. She felt dishonoured by him inside and out.

'No,' she said at last, 'we are not at all the same! I shall keep my word to my *novio*, however you may treat yours!'

'If he still wants you – after this!'

The last time he had kissed her she had been caught up in the same demented nightmare that motivated his own life. She had been as much his victim as any fly caught in a spider's web, shining and beautiful in the morning dew. But she was not dazzled now. She was hurting, and his teeth were cutting into her fast-closed lips. This time she would not give in to him!

A rough hand pushed her cousin from her, flattening him with a single blow to the jaw.

'You should have left him to me, dear heart,' Charles Arbuthnot told her. 'Did he frighten you?'

'He hurt me,' Petronilla answered.

She thought she would never forget how solid and competent the Scotsman looked at that moment. He would never be romantic and beautiful, as a matador was beautiful in his 'suit of lights', but then neither was she a child any longer: since coming to Spain she had grown up into a woman who knew the value of kindness and steadiness in a man. Where once she had found her cousin's violence exciting, now she was as much repelled as she was awed by it. Nor could she forget how he had turned his knife on her without a moment's hesitation, as if his own pain was the only one to be real to him. Her only existence for him was for his own convenience.

Mr Arbuthnot caught sight of the blood running down her wrist and winced. 'I was going to let him go, but this is too much! Shall I turn him over to the authorities?'

Petronilla shook her head. The thought of having to answer questions as to what she was doing in the middle of the vineyard, a bare hour before she was due to set out for the church and her wedding, fighting with a man who was not her fiancé, was more than she felt able to countenance. It was bad enough having to explain her bleeding arm and the state of her dress to those who were predisposed in her favour, and even her mother was going to find it hard to believe her daughter to be wholly innocent in the encounter when she saw Petronilla's bruised mouth and blood-stained sleeve. Doña Pilar knew better than anyone else how dazzled Petronilla had been by her cousin's first attempts to seduce her, why should the second attempt have been any different?

'I thought he might kill you,' she said aloud.

'Me?' Mr Arbuthnot obviously thought the idea quite ludicrous. 'Don Diego would have to get up very early in the morning to get the better of me! He is – I'm sorry to say it, Petronilla – but he is such a little man!'

Petronilla looked down at her writhing cousin doing his best not to call Mr Arbuthnot's attention to himself again. Her own injuries were forgotten as she fought an urge to help him to his feet and wipe away the hurt from his face. Instead, she deliberately turned to Mr Arbuthnot.

'My cousin didn't really mean any harm —' she began.

Charles Arbuthnot merely looked at her and at the blood oozing out of her arm and down her sleeve.

'Probably not,' he said at last.

She looked as if she were about to faint. 'You're not afraid of him, are you?'

'Devil a bit!' he responded. 'Should I be?'

He took her arm in his two hands, examining the wicked looking cut down her arm. His mouth tightened ominously. 'I could kill him for this though!' he averred.

'I know.' Her voice shook. 'But you're too big a man to take such a petty revenge. It doesn't *matter*, Charles!'

He was absurdly pleased by the compliment; even so, he took care to stand between her and her cousin as Don Diego struggled to his feet, taking to his heels while the going was good, until he reached the edge of the vineyard, where he leaped over a ditch and disappeared down the road beyond.

'I will walk you back to the house,' Mr Arbuthnot said when he was gone. 'Is there someone who will bind up your arm?'

Petronilla nodded. 'Mamá will do it for me.'

He smiled slowly. 'The very choice! I would sooner have your Mamá attend my wounds than a hundred doctors!'

'Oh, me too!' she said. There was no one she would rather have than her mother to tend her wounds, but she could have done with a little praise from Mr Arbuthnot for her own fortitude at that moment, though she was not surprised that he should withhold it all the time she showed this ambivalent attitude towards her cousin. Surely, she marvelled, she could not be jealous of her own Mamá for her singleness of heart? Especially as Charles deserved so much better from her in every way. 'We may have more difficulty with my dress,' she added thoughtfully. 'She'll have something to say to me about that!'

'Well, you should understand that,' he said. 'You're half Spanish yourself, and just as outspoken!'

'And it's my dress! I thought I looked beautiful in it —'

'You look beautiful in anything to me!' he said simply. This should have pleased her but instead it only added to her irritation with him. She had given him every opportunity to make some romantic gesture of his own that would wipe all thoughts of her cousin from her mind and if the only thing he could think of to say was that she looked as beautiful to him in a rag as in her wedding dress, he didn't deserve any better from her than he was likely to receive in the near future! Didn't the silly man realize that it was for *him* she had wanted to look beautiful in her golden dress? Sometimes, she thought, the stupidity of men was too much for flesh and blood to bear!

'My dear child!'

Petronilla had never loved her mother more than when, after that first strangled gasp, she said no more, asked no questions, but set about doing what she could to repair the wedding dress with her own hands.

Petronilla bared her arm, wincing as Doña Pilar bathed it and bound it tightly with a clean bandage. One look at her mother's face made her bless such practical sympathy.

'I was afraid,' she found herself saying. And then, 'It hurt! Oh, Mamá, I thought there would be more gossip, but, truly, it wasn't my fault!'

'No, *pequeña*, it was not your fault and this time there will be no gossip. As far as everyone else is concerned, nothing has happened and nothing will happen. While I see what can be done with your dress, you will compose yourself and put your cousin completely out of your mind, no?' Her shoulders sagged a little. 'He is what your father would call a snake in the grass! I am certain of it! And what has he to do with Gibraltar? Whenever that place is mentioned there is always trouble! He hasn't involved you, has he?'

'Of course not!' Petronilla denied. 'It was something Papá asked Mr Arbuthnot to find out for him – and don't ask me what it was because I don't know anything more than you do! Mr Arbuthnot asked me to put a message to Papá in one of my letters, but I have no idea what it meant! Men like to keep their secrets to themselves – even the best of them!'

'And women do not?' her mother mocked.

'Not important secrets! We don't have any to keep!'

Doña Pilar looked thoughtful. 'Sometimes we do. Sometimes they are our own, but more often they are the secrets of someone we love and perhaps they are the more important when we don't realize we are privy to them. Your Papá has always interested himself in what is going on abroad – and he never plays games. But Gibraltar! That evil place! See that you keep his secrets, though and Charles's too if you should discover them, my darling – even if they concern the terrible Gibraltar!'

Petronilla shrugged. 'I don't believe Gibraltar is good for anything except smuggling!' she declared firmly.

'And who are the best smugglers in the world but the British?' her mother riposted.

'Papá a smuggler?' Petronilla's disbelief brought a smile to Doña Pilar's lips.

'He smuggled me out of Spain, once upon a time! But no, your father would not do anything dishonest, nor Charles either. They are both patriots and loyal to their own land, and Gibraltar is only a pimple on the coastline of Spain, *my* country, against which your Papa will never lift his hand in anger because of his love for me!'

Petronilla watched her mother's needle flying back and forth and marvelled at the tiny stitches that were rapidly repairing the knife hole in her dress so that even she, who knew how the sleeve had been ripped from elbow to wrist, could barely see where the tear has been.

'What can we do about the hem?' she asked. 'I must have dragged it in the dust as I ran through the vineyard. Can we wash it, do you think?'

'I will sponge it as soon as I have finished this. Don't worry, it will look as good as new before you show yourself in church. And that's another thing, my love! If my Tomás were here, I wonder very much if he would allow you to be married in such a church. It is very old, I grant you that, and the English think of it as their own because it was founded in the time of Henry VIII, before

266

he divorced poor Catherine of Aragon and married his English whore —'

'Hush, Mamá! She was the mother of Papá's favourite Queen Elizabeth.'

'Yes, well, perhaps she couldn't help being a whore,' Doña Pilar conceded. 'It was he who wasn't loyal to his wife, after all! But the British who came here were almost all Catholic and they wanted a church of their own. And now Father Mulholland has run away with the silver, but you are still to be married there because Mr Arbuthnot says it is the English church and he won't be married anywhere else! What is wrong with all the Spanish churches, I should like to know?'

'The priests don't speak English —'

'That is what I am trying to tell you! Father Mulholland is gone!'

Petronilla smothered a laugh. 'So I'm to make my vows in Spanish after all? Does it matter as Papá isn't here?'

'No, except the church is so poor and the only priest who is available speaks the worst Latin I have ever heard! There are so many beautiful churches, with splendid Madonnas dressed in the same gold as your wedding dress, and you must be married in what is little better than a ruin, with *nothing* to make it look pretty for you —'

'Oh, Mamá, why didn't you say so before if you mind so much?' Petronilla protested.

'Because I didn't know Father Mulholland would run away with the silver! It's very odd behaviour in a priest and not at all what one expects from such a person! I am glad your Papá isn't here, because you may be sure he would whisk you off to the Embassy in Madrid rather than consent to have his only daughter married in such a building, and then you wouldn't know if you were truly married or not!'

But Petronilla, when she finally arrived at the door of the church in the Calle Gonzalez Honoria, understood exactly why Mr Arbuthnot had chosen it for their wedding. It was very shabby and neglected, but the British community had filled it with flowers for the occasion, one of them even going so far as to put down one of their own carpets to hide the pitted floor of the stone aisle. It said much for the respect and affection the small community held for Charles Arbuthnot, Petronilla thought, for, on this occasion, it was not her mother's name which had brought about the transformation but his. He was liked wherever he went, this man of hers, and she was more fortunate than she deserved that it was he who was waiting for her at the altar and not *Señor* Don Diego Salcedo Morena.

The familiar Latin, even when rendered almost unrecognizable by the accents of the aged priest, was pleasantly soothing. Petronilla made an effort to concentrate more closely as he blessed the gold and silver that were the tokens of Mr Arbuthnot's wordly goods which from henceforth he would share with her, and their wedding rings, one for each of them, that symbolized their union. Petronilla had chosen to wear her ring on her right hand in the Spanish manner, as her mother always had. Her arm ached with a thudding rhythm as Charles went through the ritual of half placing it on her thumb, her forefinger, her middle finger, and finally pressing it home on her ring finger. 'In the name of the Father, and of the Son, and of the Holy Ghost. Amen.' For a terrible moment she thought she was going to faint, saw the horrified look on Mr Arbuthnot's face and wished she were anywhere else but there where she might shame him in front of his friends.

'I'm so sorry!' she said quite audibly.

Mr Arbuthnot put an arm about her shoulders. 'Is it such a dreadful prospect being married to me?' he whispered in her ear.

She was appalled that he should have misinterpreted her weakness in such a way. 'I'm honoured!' she whispered back. He winced as though she had hit him. 'My arm hurts!' she added hastily.

Her fingers trembled as she pressed home his ring in

turn. She was struck all over again by the pleasure his hands gave her and she took the opportunity to entwine her fingers with his, refusing to let him go, but when he released himself from her grasp she felt that his withdrawal was of his whole self.

They turned and faced the congregation together. Petronilla dropped a curtsy to her mother, her head held high. There was no reason for anyone else to feel the depths of despair that filled her own heart. Doña Louise, her previous disapproval forgotten, nodded her head and smiled rather nervously, her face flushed with the effort of overcoming her scruples and lending her consequence to the proceedings. As she had confessed to Doña Pilar, she had never set foot in anything other than an Anglican church in her life before and only did so now because her dear Charles, whom she looked upon quite as she might have done a son of her own, would have thought it a criticism of himself if she had stayed away.

'It doesn't seem quite – English not to worship in our own Established Church! Oh dear, I do hope it will be forgiven me!'

'And I wish Colonel Harris could have been here,' Doña Pilar had returned with some asperity. 'He would have understood your feelings exactly – and he could have supported our daughter much better than I can do, being only her mother!'

Doña Louise momentarily forgot her own troubles long enough to observe that Petronilla looked a trifle pale. 'I have told Charles, until I am quite weary of the subject, that he should take his bride away for a prolonged wedding trip instead of insisting that I should be free to leave for England as soon as I am ready to go. Much as I long for my own homeland and people around me, that young couple should have time to become accustomed to one another before they are obliged to settle down to the everyday business of running the *bodega*. But there! He wouldn't hear of my delaying my plans to suit him!'

'I should hope not!' Doña Pilar sighed. She, too, would

have preferred the young couple to have had time to get to know one another away from the interested eyes of their friends and, yes, relations too. At least that was one small problem she could solve by herself, she thought ruefully. She would take herself off, back to her own *bodega* in Montillo, and wait for her Tomás to come to her there, which would surely be quite soon now, for they had been apart for far too long already.

The reception was enjoyed by everyone. Petronilla felt beautiful in her golden dress, especially once she realized that no one had noticed her mother's running repairs. Once the first formalities were over, she was even able to forget the pain in her arm, enjoying the attentions her husband was receiving from all and sundry, standing by his side and taking such an obvious pleasure in the compliments that came his way that even Mr Arbuthnot began to relax.

'Feeling better?' he asked her, under cover of pouring her out a glass of sherry.

She nodded. 'Hush,' she added. 'I do believe Mamá is about to make a speech!'

Doña Pilar denied she was going to do anything of the sort. 'A quiet word with the two of you is hardly a speech, my love!' she retorted indignantly. 'Charles, it is about the Montillo Bodega. As you know Tomás and I have decided it will become the joint property of the two of you as part of our wedding present to you but, of necessity, there will be a delay until Colonel Harris comes to Spain and makes all the arrangements with Tío Ambrosio and the rest of my family.' She smiled, losing her seriousness and becoming once again her usual self, intent on enjoying the party going on about her. 'What are you going to call your new *bodega*, Carlos *mio*?'

Mr Arbuthnot grinned. There was no doubt about the love and admiration he bore his mother-in-law, Petronilla noticed. 'I thought Arbuthnot & Harris,' he suggested.

Doña Pilar's eyes flashed with quick denial. 'No, no, that won't do at all! My Colonel Harris would not want to give his name to a wine he never drinks! It will have to be Arbuthnot & Arbuthnot.'

To everyone's surprise it was Petronilla who vetoed that suggestion. 'There is only one Arbuthnot, my husband, and that is as it should be. I am proud to have his name as my own.' She lifted her glass, looking Charles straight in the eyes. 'To Arbuthnots,' she said. 'May God bless our marriage and our *bodega!*'

Charles Arbuthnot coloured up, his freckles standing out on his face as he regarded her. 'Amen to that,' he said.

Petronilla sat bolt upright in the centre of the bed, picking at the bandage on her arm. Under any other circumstances she would have gone in search of her husband to put an end to this waiting which was rapidly becoming unbearable to her.

Doña Pilar had refused to allow anyone else to help her daughter prepare for bed. With great courtesy she refused every offer, saying she preferred to do it herself.

'This is the last time we meet as mother and daughter,' she explained to Petronilla. 'Tomorrow, we shall know each other as friends, yes? When I married your father, the only other woman who was there was Mrs Nightingale. She was very English, very correct, and I was afraid she would be shocked because I wanted to be the wife of Tomás Harris more than anything in the world!'

'Mrs Nightingale?' Petronilla was momentarily diverted from her own anxieties. 'But she's a lovely person, Mamá! Wasn't she kind to you?'

'It wasn't kindness I wanted from her,' her mother remembered with a laugh. 'What I wanted was for her to go away so that I could be alone with Tomás! It wasn't my idea that we should wait until after the wedding ceremony to get to know each other, but he was determined to do nothing to shame me in case I should ever wish to return to Spain and find that my family would have nothing to do with me. Mrs Nightingale thought he was quite right. She told me the rustic manners of the English Court were all very well amongst a certain set, but that sooner or later the English would prefer not to see their monarch pursuing his wife through the House of Lords to punish her for her indiscretions! I remember very well how she looked at me, a twinkle in her eye. She had always been a most respectable person, she said, but she had never been dull.'

'Well, if half her stories are true, she certainly wasn't that!' Petronilla put in.

'No, she was never dull.'

Something in her mother's tone alerted Petronilla that there was some point she was supposed to understand from the recital.

'I don't find Charles dull!' she denied, chewing her lower lip.

'Are you sure, love? I've always thought the English stupid in that they tell their daughters nothing about anything that matters in life – I've heard more silly stories from English ladies than you'd believe about young girls travelling by train in the same compartment as some man and imagining themselves to be with child because of it! And sometimes the young women concerned were not so young! So I have always been frank with you about such things, hoping that when your turn comes, it would be with a man you could love as I have always loved your Papá. And now, Charles tells me that you were on the point of fainting in church at the thought of being his wife! Was your father right? Have I over-persuaded you to marry quickly because of that incident with your cousin?'

'No, Mamá, Mr Arbuthnot misunderstood. My arm was paining me, and there was the incense, and I was still shocked by what Cousin Diego had said and done in the vineyard. It had nothing to do with Charles!'

'I hope not, love, because a man wants more than a pillow in his bed on his wedding night! Marriage gives him rights you would be ill-advised to refuse Mr Arbuthnot, however you feel about him!' Doña Pilar shot a look at her daughter, sighing under her breath. 'You don't dislike him, do you?'

Petronilla looked away. 'No, I don't dislike him. I *wanted* to marry him. I *want* to be his wife —'

'Yes, but do you want him to make love to you?' Doña Pilar demanded.

Petronilla's eyes opened wide. 'Yes!' Her exasperation more than equalled her mother's. 'He has good hands,' she added with seeming irrelevance.

Much relieved, Doña Pilar crowed with satisfied laughter. 'I thought you might not have noticed!' she teased lightly. She kissed Petronilla's cheek. 'I am glad for you, *hija mía*! Though I think it might be a kindness in you to tell your Carlos that there is something you like about him when he comes to you tonight, no?'

'Yes, Mamá.'

Left alone, Petronilla began picking at the bandage on her arm and wondering how long she would have to wait for Mr Arbuthnot to make an appearance. It seemed a very long time and she was totally unprepared for his being still dressed in his street clothes when he did finally come.

'Is there anything the matter?' She had meant to sound both calm and confident, but her strangled tones betrayed her nervousness. She cleared her throat to give herself greater courage. 'I thought —'

He sat on the edge of the bed, his elbows on his knees, studying the pattern of the carpet between his legs.

'I know what you thought,' he cut her off. 'I've been thinking too, Petronilla. Your mother assures me you don't dislike me, but I saw your face in church and I don't think you're ready for marriage with anyone quite yet —'

'That isn't true!' Petronilla cut him off impetuously.

He didn't even look up. His study of the carpet seemed to go on for ever. 'True or not, when I come to you to make you my wife I want a willing woman —'

'I *am* willing!'

He looked at her then and she could read the hurt in his eyes and knew she had put it there.

'Not until you're as much in love with me as I am with you!' He clenched his fists and then deliberately relaxed them again. 'I'd rather wait until the time when you look in your heart and see only me there! Is that asking too much?'

Tears of frustration came into her eyes. She shook her head. 'I'm more than half in love with you now. I thought – tonight – Charles, I couldn't bear it if you never want me to be your wife!'

His good humour reasserted itself. 'I couldn't bear it either.' He took her hands in his, kissing first one and then the other. 'When you're absolutely sure you're ready for a husband, I'll be here beside you.' He squeezed her fingers between his. 'Don't let it be too long, *palomita*, because I love you very much!'

It was a long time before Petronilla slept that night. Torn between humiliation and an angry resignation, she punished her pillow as she would have liked to have punished her gentle, long-suffering husband.

'*Palomita*, little dove, indeed!' she said aloud. But she was touched by the endearment all the same. How could she have been so blind as to have thought her cousin Diego to be the more romantic man? Worse still, what did Charles Arbuthnot expect her to do to prove she was ready to be his wife? But to that, no matter how much she tossed and turned, there seemed to be no immediate answer.

Chapter Thirteen

Arbuthnots flourished. In the past, Petronilla felt she had worked quite hard for her father. She now knew that she had been seduced by the notion that real work couldn't be expected from a lady and that she had done only what she wanted to do, according to mood and the time available she could give to it after she had pursued her real vocation of being a social ornament and reflection of her father's status in the community. Charles Arbuthnot expected to find in her a real partner in his business, treating her in every respect as his equal in the daily workings of the *bodega* and, after her first surprise at how much she was expected to do, she found she liked the responsibility involved in taking the office work entirely on to her own shoulders. She enjoyed the planning, the neat rows of figures, and the social side of the selling of their product.

Most of the selling was naturally done by Charles, but it was she who prepared all the documents and organized the wine-tastings, and if her husband was away for any reason it was she who finally signed the agreements between the Arbuthnot Bodega and the wine merchants of London and, increasingly, all the major cities of Europe. Thus it was that Petronilla was alone in the office when they received their first firm order from an American Wine Company for what, for a ghastly moment, she thought was more barrels of sherry than they had any hope of supplying. Over-selling their product so disastrously was unlikely to appeal to the Mr Arbuthnot she was beginning to know so well.

Her first jig of joy came to an abrupt conclusion. Somehow or other, they were going to have to fulfil the order but, for the life of her, she couldn't see how. A quick consultation of the books she kept in such immaculate order confirmed her worst fears. They were over-committed already even without this American order.

Charles was in the vineyards and she went to find him, carrying the American letter with her. It was extremely hot. Not for the first time she wondered why nobody had invented a better garment for women to wear in the summer, one that would be sufficiently modest to be respectable and yet less suffocating than what they were forced to wear now. She no longer wondered why Spanish ladies entombed themselves in their houses for the greater part of the year, with the shutters closed against the sun, and with the constant opening and shutting of their flapping fans for company. She could have done with a fan now, but she was too English to carry one as matter of course, preferring to keep her hands free except on more formal occasions.

It always gave her great satisfaction to walk across their own land. If she worked hard herself, she had no complaints that Charles Arbuthnot didn't work as hard, or harder. Frequently he was to be found stripped to the waist like a peasant, revelling in the hard, physical labour that the vines entailed. Nothing was left to chance. Daily he examined the leaves and the budding fruit for any sign of disease or the pests that attack even the healthiest of vines and, just occasionally, she would accompany him on these tours of inspection, her own mind skittering over every kind of inessential as they walked together. When they were alone together, she was always careful to keep her thoughts well away from their personal life, lest she be overcome by the sadness that filled her whenever she realized how quickly time was going past, while they still had their separate bedrooms and their separate lives, with no more intimacy between them than there had ever been.

'Charles!' She waved the letter in her hand, hoping he would notice she had deliberately used his given name. She would have run if she hadn't been so hot and red in the face. Instead, she approached with a slow swing of her hips that she hoped would take his mind off his vines and put it firmly where it belonged – on herself. She was more successful than she had hoped, for she could feel him watching her every inch of the way and she felt a certain grim satisfaction that she could make him as physically aware of her as ever, even though he still refused to share her bed.

Strange that with his red hair his skin could nevertheless take a modest tan, though it was mostly freckles that met her eyes as she joined him where he was standing.

'Look!' She waved the letter in front of his nose. 'From America! Isn't it marvellous?'

He snatched the letter from her hand, eagerly perusing it. 'You can take the credit for this, my love! See, it says here that your costing and delivery dates were the thing that clinched the deal.'

'I know.' Petronilla made a face. 'Only we can't possibly deliver such a large order – and that was my doing also! It never occurred to me that they would want more than a sample order to begin with. What are we going to do?'

'Fill it,' he said simply.

'But how?'

'There's nothing here to say it has to be the undiluted produce of Arbuthnots.' He smiled at her. 'Most of our neighbours will be glad to have a share in this order. The American market is one we should all like to get into. We'll manage, honey – isn't that what the Americans call their women?'

She responded in kind, amused by the endearment. 'Are

you telling me not to bother my pretty head about it?' she accused him.

'Far from it. I'm suggesting you organize a social get-together amongst our friends and buy in enough wine from them to make up the order.'

'Are we going to tell them where it's going?'

'That's your decision.'

She was flattered, but it was in her mind that it ought to be a joint decision. She was not as experienced in the business as was he and, although she was accepted and liked as his wife, she knew she had a long way to go before the Jerez community accepted her as one of their number in any other role.

'Please, Charles, help me do the right thing!'

He read the letter again. 'Very well, we'll organize the party together. Will that satisfy you?'

'I shan't be satisfied until we do more than that together!' she burst out.

He gave her a quizzical look. 'The remedy for that lies in your own hands, my dear.' His look changed to one of concern as she flushed, wishing for the hundredth time that she could find the words to bring him to her side. 'It's too hot for you, standing out here in the sun. Shall I walk you back to the *bodega*?'

She was tempted to agree for she saw too little of him these days, but she shook her head, taking the American order back from him. 'No, there is no hurry for an answer today, is there? I'll make out a list of possible *bodegas* we could apply to and you can have a look at it this evening. It will be time enough to send out the invitations tomorrow.'

She had hoped he would overrule her, but he only stood and watched her walk away. It was at moments like this that she was at her most irritable where he was concerned. If it were only a business partner he wanted, he would have been more than welcome to have chosen her mother! She wanted to be much more than that to him, though she had to admit he had every reason for doubting her need for him and building a defensive wall about himself in case he should be further hurt by her indifference; and she could see no way of breaching it short of flinging herself on his mercy and begging him to make love to her. And that she would not do! If he had his pride, so did she.

The sun was blazing hot walking home. Once, she almost changed her mind and turned to call out to her husband to join her. He had already gone back to work however, his back to her, pointing out some vines that the men had missed as they went up and down the long lines, spraying the immature fruit as it began to appear.

Most of their soil was *albariza*, which she knew to be very high in calcium. She remembered that at their wedding reception, her mother and her husband had been deep in a discussion about whether agriculture would ever take over from the grapes around Jerez. Their grapes were too small and uninspiring to compete with those grown specially for the table, yet they were the ones that made the best wine.

Petronilla paused for a rest, looking about her. The name *albariza* came from *albo*, meaning snow-white, and the fields had looked like snow when she first came there, though the green leaves of the vines covered most of the whiteness now. The grapes of Jerez had a tough time to survive, which gave them their special quality, ultimately providing the unique blend of wine that has come to be known as sherry. When they had come to dig a new well for the house, they had found old roots from the earlier vines at least thirty feet down. She had seen the black streakers with her own eyes, not knowing at first what they were until Charles had told her that sometimes they would go even deeper in their search for water.

Walking through the vineyards, one could see that the soil was not as white as it at first appeared. There were plenty of greys, beiges and browns that made a fascinating pattern beneath her feet. Perhaps one day she would persuade Miss Fairman to execute a painting of the growing vines and she would hang it in the office for all to see, especially the representatives of these Americans whom she had heard were beginning to grow their own table wines on the west coast of their enormous country. It was hoped they would never produce their own fortified wines but, even if they did, Petronilla was confident they could never equal the magnificence of their own vintage.

As she walked on, she began to consider whom they should invite to their party. Many names occurred to her, for their social life in Jerez was extensive. She had even inveigled some of the more energetic neighbours into promising they would join her in a hunt when winter came round again, remembering how Wellington had imported his own hounds to make wintering on the Peninsula more tolerable when he had been engaged in wresting Spain from the unwelcome embrace of the French. She had few real hopes that it would ever come about, however, since she had discovered the local way of dealing with the foxes was to put down poisoned cheese for them to take. It seemed a poor sport to her who had been accustomed to hunting on horseback all her life. Indeed, she sorely missed the exercise that her father considered beneficial to everyone, regardless of their gender. Here, it was too hot to follow any of the amusements she had been used to in England. She was beginning to understand her mother's passion for dancing, especially in the cool hours of the night, the only time that the Spanish really came alive in the long, hot weeks of summer. Would a dance be feasible now, at such short notice, and when they had business to discuss with most of the people coming? Why not? If Charles would give his consent, she thought they would all enjoy such a gathering, especially if she could find one of the gypsy bands to play their authentic *flamenco* music for them.

Something moved in the vines closest to her. She bent down to take a look and realized she had stumbled across a small family of foxes, too young to feed themselves, sheltering beside their dead mother. The vixen, she had no doubt, was another victim of the poisoned cheese policy, and it was a miracle that her young had survived. They caught at Petronilla's heart, for they seemed completely confident that she meant them no harm. It was the closest she had ever been to their species and she was entranced by their dog-like expressions and, more than anything else, by their colouring that was so like that of her husband's that she laughed out loud.

'It's easy to see you are true Arbuthnots!' she said to them, and laughed again when they opened their mouths to reveal sharp little baby teeth and a flurry of pale pink tongues.

She gathered them up in her skirts, forgetting all about how hot she was, and hurried back to the *bodega* where she could find them some shelter and a leather glove from the fingers of which she hoped to persuade them to take some nourishment.

She was still giving them their feed when Mr Arbuthnot came to join her in the yard, intrigued to see what was holding her attention so closely. He was even more astonished when he saw the little foxes.

'Why don't you drown the lot of them and have done?' he asked her.

She turned furious eyes on him. 'What harm have they done?' she demanded.

'It was you who wanted to hunt them down,' he reminded her. 'Don't you hunt them to be rid of them?'

Petronilla was not prepared to face up to such a moral dilemma, however. Instead, she held out one of the foxes for him to hold while she placed the rest back in the box she had arranged for them.

'At least hunting is a quick death,' she defended herself.

'But these little ones are not to die, I take it?' he smiled at her.

'No,' she said briefly.

She wanted to tell him that they had gained her protection only because they shared his colouring and were therefore dear to her. As always, though, any such statement seemed silly even before she had uttered it, and so she kept silent until it was too late even to try and explain why she had saved their lives.

'What do you plan to do with them?'

She took the remaining pup from him and placed him amongst his brothers and sisters in the box.

'They're going to live here in the *bodega* as our mascots. I'm sure if they're treated well they'll respond just like dogs. They *look* like dogs! Lovely, *red* dogs and therefore quite suitable for our *bodega*, don't you think?'

'Why not a pair of real dogs?'

'I prefer these foxes!' she snapped, aware that he was teasing her, perhaps half-hoping she would admit that she wanted to keep them because he too had noticed they shared his own colouring.

It should have been an easy enough thing to say. What was there that was difficult about it? But she could not. The words stuck in her throat as she was overcome with guilt that she was still uncertain as to whether he could claim her whole heart, or only the greater part, the part that liked him better than any other man living, but whose love for him was something less than the all-consuming passion he demanded.

The next day there was a letter waiting for Petronilla from her father. Overjoyed to have real news of him at last, she rushed down to the breakfast room still clad in her night things, her silken house-gown negligently tied at the waist.

'Papá is coming at last!'

Startled as much by her appearance as by her news, Mr Arbuthnot rose to his feet. Petronilla's deep affection for her parents had endeared her to him from the first and had made him the more determined to have some of that wealth of devotion for himself. Surely, he thought again as he watched her excited face, that wasn't too much to ask of life?

'When is he coming?'

'As soon as he can book a passage! He has business in

Gibraltar as well, apparently, finding out why this feud has blown up between the Governor, General Gardiner, and the business men on the Rock. I didn't know there was any trouble, did you?'

'I had heard something about it,' Charles acknowledged.

'You didn't say anything —'

Mr Arbuthnot sat down again at the table. 'I wrote to your father telling him I'd heard this rumour that General Gardiner was the wrong man for Gibraltar just now.'

'Oh.' Petronilla was nonplussed. She sat down opposite him, feeling excluded and a little hurt. 'How long have you been writing to each other?'

Mr Arbuthnot's eyebrows rose. 'I wrote to ask his permission to marry you in the first instance. It's natural for a son-in-law to write to his father-in-law, surely?'

'I suppose so.' She still wasn't satisfied. 'Once, you used to trust me to forward messages to him.'

He saw immediately what was the matter with her. 'One can tell you're an only child! Why do you resent me having a small part of your parents' attention, their love for you isn't any the less?'

She was shocked that he should suggest such a thing. That it could be true, she acknowledged to herself only very reluctantly. She was used to being their only ewe lamb and it was hard to know that she was that no longer, that they liked and admired her husband quite as much as they did her. And why not? She wouldn't really have had it any other way.

She stuck her nose in the air. 'You're free to share your secrets with him by writing to him any time you please!' she said huffily. 'Spying is not a very attractive occupation, however!'

'Is that what you think I'm doing?'

She smiled slowly in response. 'No, I don't. I'm glad my parents like you, if you want to know. I just wish we could share everything else in our marriage as well. Is that selfish of me?'

He didn't answer. He never did when she referred to

the rift between them. Instead he changed the subject. 'Why don't you wait to have your party until your father gets here?'

'And Mamá? Nothing will keep her away once she knows he is expected! She has had to wait for him to get away for such a long time and they've never been separated before!' She didn't add that that was how she thought a married couple should be. She didn't have to. 'Can the American order wait so long?'

'It will have to wait until after the vintage, whatever response we get from the others. What else does your father have to say?'

As her husband he was entitled to open and read all her letters, yet he had never done so. They were always brought to her on her morning tea-tray, their seals unbroken, and she thought it would have been the same even if he were to recognize her cousin's handwriting on the envelope. Silently, she handed her father's letter across the table to him.

That Colonel Harris was missing his womenfolk was made clear from the very beginning. He was tired of London; he was even tired of Hampshire, though Mrs Nightingale had done her best to lighten his mood, arranging the most extraordinary entertainments for him, at some cost to herself, for she was frequently falling asleep in the middle of a dinner party these days, blaming herself for being such dull company, which she never had been and never would be as far as the Harris family was concerned.

Her mother's and Petronilla's absence had brought it home to him how much he was going to miss his daughter now that she was destined to live abroad. However, she was not to think that her choice of husband didn't meet with his approval. Her mother had written to him with all the details of the wedding, including what had passed between Petronilla and her cousin in the vineyard. He was glad Mr Arbuthnot had been there to put an end to the incident, for there was much to worry him about that

young man and he was glad Petronilla had thought better
of allowing him to interfere with her happiness with a
much better man. Suffice it now to say that he seemed to
be at the bottom of every unpleasant rumour to come out
of Spain recently, most of them centred on Gibraltar,
which made him as much Britain's business as he was
Spain's.

The rest of his news would keep until he saw her.
The Doña Louise Carr had not found England as she had
remembered it to be and he was to have the pleasure of
escorting her back to Spain on a prolonged visit. Privately,
he doubted she would ever settle anywhere and he thought
Petronilla would be well advised to plan on having an
extra house-guest for the better part of the coming winter.
The only point he had yet discovered in her favour was
her fondness for Mr Arbuthnot, but his daughter would
do well to be patient with her for he was beginning to
understand the corrosive effects of loneliness on even the
most stalwart character. She might even improve upon
further acquaintance, for Mrs Nightingale had found much
to admire in her, especially as she had been able to give
her an eye-witness account of the wedding and had had
words of praise for everyone concerned, even while she
had found the ceremony itself regrettable in that it had
been largely incomprehensible to her.

Finally, she was not to allow the fact that Don Diego
was a member of her Spanish family to spoil one moment
of her married happiness. She had always been a sensible
girl and he was certain that by now, with Charles
Arbuthnot's help, she had put everything to do with that
young man out of her mind once and for all. He realized
she might feel some sort of responsibility for him, but
she could safely leave him to others in the comfortable
knowledge that both her father and her husband would
do all in their power to protect their loved ones from
having any further contact with him. He hoped she had
made a complete recovery from her injuries by now and
had indeed forgotten all about the terrible business.

He was, as always, her affectionate father, T. Harris. (Col.)

Mr Arbuthnot refolded the sheets of paper and returned them across the table. Petronilla took the letter from him, refusing to meet his eyes. She had no answer for any questions he might ask about her cousin, not that she thought for a moment that he would ask any. Having delivered his decision that it was up to her to heal the breach between them, he had made it abundantly clear to her that no outside influence would make him change his mind and make it easy for her by leaving her complete submission unsaid. It should have been easy enough to tell him that she had forgotten all about Diego, but she knew she would never forget her cousin and the storm of emotion he had aroused in her. What she doubted was that it had ever been as important as everyone seemed to think. There was a difference, she thought, between the wild, painful reaction she had felt for Diego, which one part of her had never accepted at all, and the calmer, gentler love she felt for her husband. She had seen clearly the difference between the two on the morning of her wedding day, when she had feared for Charles's life at Diego's hands. In that moment, she had known Don Diego for what he was and the beauty of his body and his dancer's sense of movement and rhythm had counted for less than nothing with her.

She didn't think Mr Arbuthnot would believe her however, and she didn't blame him. How did one tell one's husband that one had been a child, seeing with the eyes of a child and therefore mistaking her joy in the beauty of the man, for love of the man himself? Would he believe her that the difference between the two was quite clear to her now that she had lived so many weeks in the same house as her husband? And if he did believe her, would it be the whole truth? She felt again the excitement she had always felt in her cousin's company and despised herself for being no better than a magpie, attracted by a surface glitter at the expense of the real worth of the man on the other side of the table.

'If we're going to have all these visitors to stay with us, we're going to have to build a larger house,' she joked.

'We'll manage.'

She couldn't imagine how. There were not enough bedchambers to go round, not if they kept to their present arrangements. She had Doña Louise's old room herself and she knew the Englishwoman would feel slighted if it were not offered to her during her visit. Her father and mother would share, of course, but she hardly imagined her mother would make the long journey from Montilla and Córdoba alone and everyone would have to be housed somehow. She gave her husband a speculative look through her lashes, wondering what he was thinking. And he still had made no comment on all that her father had had to say about her cousin!

She stood up, putting her letter away in her pocket. How glad she would be to see her darling Papá again!

'What has my Cousin Diego to do with Gibraltar?' she asked suddenly.

His start of surprise looked genuine enough. 'I imagine he thinks smuggling will provide him with some sort of an income.'

'Smuggling goods, or secrets?'

He gave her an interested look, as if he had not thought her capable of such clear vision where her cousin was concerned. For a long moment her question hung there between them as he stared at her. A smile began at the corners of his mouth.

'You look more beautiful every day, d'you know that?'

If he had intended to confuse her, he certainly succeeded. She clutched her négligé to her and hurried away back to her room, not daring to ask her question again. But she couldn't imagine her father would care, one way or the other, if Don Diego's interest in Gibraltar was merely in smuggling forbidden cargoes into Spain from Morocco. It was more likely that he thought Don Diego was up to something and that the French were interested in his activities so it behoved the British to be even more interested. But why Don Diego? Even while she acknowledged the excitement that her cousin could generate without even trying, she doubted he would be entrusted with anyone's state secrets, though he might provide an excellent diversion for somebody else. Had her father thought of that? Had Charles?

By the time she had dressed and reread her father's letter several times more, she had decided to take his advice and leave the worrying about her cousin to him. She was less inclined to approve of Charles Arbuthnot having anything more to do with Diego. She had been so afraid for him the last time and, if anything were to happen to him, she didn't think she would ever get over it. She felt enough guilt where he was concerned already.

The servants were delighted to hear they were to have visitors. There was no difficulty about taking on extra staff, everyone had a relation who could do with the work and who could be brought in in an emergency.

'It will be a pleasure to have the Doña Pilar, your mother, staying with us again,' Ignacio, their butler, assured her. 'How many persons will be coming with her?'

Petronilla confessed she didn't know. 'My father is coming – and Doña Louise.'

'*Sí, sí,*' Ignacio agreed impatiently. '*La inglesa* will want to stay in her old home, that goes without saying, but where are we going to put all these other persons?'

Petronilla didn't know. She spent most of the day at her desk, meticulously keeping the paperwork of the *bodega* up to date. She took a pride in the neat ledgers, filled with the figures that told their own story of how the *bodega* was progressing under the new Arbuthnot management. Today, however, she had found it difficult to concentrate. Her father would have written to her mother at the same time as he had to herself and, knowing Doña Pilar, she would set forth the instant she received the letter, not pausing for anything, certainly not her own comfort along the way. Petronilla thought Miss Fairman might come with her – and Fabiola, if she had not yet returned to her parents in Granada. Doña Rosa would stay put, the more especially if she were allowed to stay on at Montilla and not have to return to Tío Ambrosio's roof.

She was adding up the week's wages when the solution came to her. She felt hot all over, a light perspiration breaking out across her face. Deliberately, she recalled the way Charles had looked at her that morning, his eyes falling to the swell of her breasts, half revealed by her gaping négligé, and she drew comfort from the fact that he had been unable to drag his eyes away. It was equally obvious to her that by the time her mother arrived she would have to have done something to mend her marriage, or there would be a display of Spanish temperament. While Petronilla could sympathize with it, she had no desire to be on the receiving end once the questions began to fly. Nor did she think that Mr Arbuthnot would appreciate being called to account by his mother-in-law for not having consummated his marriage long ago. Far better that they should come to terms before that fate befell them!

Petronilla allowed herself a wry smile. Was she such a coward that she couldn't come to terms with Mr Arbuthnot without being prompted into it by sheer pride? Apparently not. But, if she were being driven into finding the remedy, at least she would do so with her head held high, before she could change her mind again and let things drift on as they had for far too long already.

She almost changed her mind again that evening as she made ready for bed. What was she going to say to him? What was she going to do? She sat down at her dressing table, staring at her reflection by the flickering light of the candle. He had called her beautiful, but she couldn't see it for herself. She had been out in the sun too long to have the milk-and-roses complexion that was so admired in England. She thought of the fruitless hours she had spent wishing her chocolate eyes would change to blue, her hair to gold, and the honeyed tones of her skin to the magnolia shade of her most admired friends. Was it possible that Charles Arbuthnot actually *preferred* her as she was?

She thought of the big-framed man she had married, with his fine hands and his rust-red hair. Such a man had never been her ideal, yet frequently she found herself comparing other men to him and never to his detriment. Even her cousin, beautiful as he was, had seemed slight and insignificant when he had stood beside him before being knocked to the ground. She had always thought of Diego as matador, *torrero*, who had only to wave his scarlet cloak before the enraged bull to tease the poor animal into allowing him to make his escape to fight another day. It hadn't been like that, that day in the vineyard, the day of her wedding, for that had been the moment when she had learned the true worth of the man she had married as well as the worthlessness of her Cousin Diego.

She stood up, blowing out the candle as she did so. If she waited any longer he would be in bed and asleep and she would have to screw herself up to approaching him all over again tomorrow.

His door was standing open. She hesitated in the doorway, uncertain how to announce her presence. She was just about to knock when her husband saw her standing there.

'Petronilla? Are you all right?'

There was only the blue light of the moon inside the room and he seemed bigger than ever as he got out of bed and came towards her. For a breathless moment she considered turning tail and running back to her own room, but she refused to be so poor-spirited.

'I – I –' she began.

His arms came round her, offering an unexpected comfort. She put her face against his bare shoulder and breathed in the scent of him.

'What do you want, Petronilla?'

She rubbed her fingers against his chest, liking to touch

him much more than she had expected. In the back of her mind she realized she had always wanted to know what the mat of red hair that covered his chest felt like and she was embarrassed to discover that that wasn't the only thing she wanted to know about him. There was so much more.

She kissed his neck. 'I want my husband,' she said simply.

He stiffened, holding his breath. Then he said, 'Are you sure, *palomita*? Are you quite, quite sure?'

'Yes, I'm sure,' she said.

Chapter Fourteen

Petronilla's ultimate reaction was one of surprise. Nothing she knew about Charles Arbuthnot had prepared her for what it would be like to be his wife in fact as well as in law. What was more, never once during the night had she thought to compare him with any other man. Mr Arbuthnot had had his own way of keeping her attention fixed wholly upon himself, and the astonishing thing was that she had revelled in every minute of his lovemaking, finding that she, too, had unexpected ways of adding to their mutual pleasure, ways which she had thought she knew nothing about, but which had seemed to come as naturally to her as eating or breathing. Not without amusement, she realized she had far more in common with her mother than she had thought, for Doña Pilar had always maintained that to be a woman, married to the right man, was to be the most fortunate creature alive. Only Petronilla had never been certain that Charles Arbuthnot was the right man for her – not until last night, that was.

Charles had been unstinting in his praise for her, telling her of his love for her at every stage in the proceedings and in words she had never thought to hear from him, not from the staid, rather dull Charles Arbuthnot! And if she had been less generous in return, it was largely because she hadn't been given the opportunity. Perhaps if she had been she would have given him some return of affection from her own lips, though, in the cold light of morning, she was glad she hadn't said the words in case they had been less than the truth. He didn't deserve lies from her, not even when she was striving to show him, in ways which didn't need any words, that she was no reluctant bride in his bed, but an eager, responsive woman who was wholly committed to their life together.

She had thought they would never sleep, but they must have done for when she awoke she found she was alone. Contentment seeped through her whole body as she rehearsed the events of the night in her mind. Would it always be like this? Would there be children? She tried to imagine Charles Arbuthnot's children, fox-coloured and sherry-eyed, but nothing seemed quite real to her where he was concerned. Her husband was at once a much more familiar and a much more mysterious being than he had been the day before. For instance, she had never thought about him and fatherhood before, but now she was hopeful that they would have children together, thinking what a marvellous father he would make for her babies, both the boys and the girls!

She wondered where he had gone and was grateful he had given her time to accustom herself to her new circumstances. It would be hard to make ordinary conversation with him quite yet. It was hard enough to face the coming day with any appearance of normality; she was stiff when she moved and that was Mr Arbuthnot's doing also. Who would have thought that he would do such a thing to her? And *with* her, for it had been as much her doing as his; she had been a great deal more than a pillow in his bed, in her mother's phrase – and she had enjoyed every minute of it.

Memories of her Cousin Diego and the fever he had induced in her didn't come to mind until the day was more than half over. Poor Diego, she thought, that he would never know the joy she had shared with Charles! There was so much of the little boy in her cousin that she began to wonder whether most of her feeling for him hadn't been more maternal than lover-like, induced by the sheer beauty of his body. When she shut her eyes, she could still see him as she had first seen him, a man who moved like a ballet dancer and who seemed to exist on a different plane of excitement and intensity of living to everyone else. For a brief moment she allowed herself to dwell on what her life would have been if she had married him instead of Mr Arbuthnot. It didn't take much imagination to know that Don Diego would have made a selfish lover, taking his own pleasure with the same careless brilliance with which he did everything else, but without any real concern for that of his partner. Fabiola, his reluctant fiancée, had known that instinctively and had rebelled in the only way open to her. Petronilla could admit to herself that she, on the other hand, had been foolish enough to be tempted by his brilliant exterior and the bewildered, unloved little boy she had glimpsed beneath. She had been fortunate that Charles and her mother had rescued her from such a fate, but she thought she would always feel a certain sympathy for Diego, no matter what. No one who looked so like an angel could be a complete devil. She would never bring herself to believe it to be so.

She turned her thoughts back to her husband. If Mr Arbuthnot's lovemaking had lacked a certain diamond-hard brilliance, she had no doubt at any time that he had been as much concerned for her pleasure as for his own. So to think of her cousin now seemed a kind of treachery, though if Charles were to occupy all her nights so happily, she doubted she would be thinking of Diego much in the future. Indeed, she was almost sure that once the children began to come, she would be free of her cousin's memory for ever. Life, indeed, was being very good to her!

Doña Pilar arrived in a matter of days, having set forth as soon as she had received the news that Colonel Harris was coming to Spain, leaving Miss Fairman to follow as soon as she could catch her breath. Surprisingly, Fabiola, as demure and virtuous as ever, and as devoted to getting her own way as she had ever been, had elected to travel with her and had done so with a minimum of fuss and trouble, making light of every adventure they had had along the way.

'I thought you would be at home in Granada by now!' Petronilla greeted the girl, pleased to see her.

'And allow Doña Pilar to make the journey here on her own? Anything might have happened to her!'

'Which you, naturally, would have prevented?' Petronilla teased her.

'Why not?' Fabiola demanded. 'Great things can always be wrought by prayer – even the conversion of bandits! All that is needed is faith –'

Doña Pilar chuckled. 'Faith in her own powers of persuasion! The Devil himself would give way to her through sheer exhaustion! What her parents will say to me if we should ever meet is not to be thought about! Would you believe that Tío Ambrosio agreed she should come with me, and Tía Consuelo actually *gave us her blessing* as she is certain Fabiola will be a good influence on us both!'

Petronilla burst out laughing. 'She never said so, Mamá!'

'I assure you she did! You may have overlooked it, as I confess I had myself, but the key to Fabiola's character is her obedience to God and authority and her willingness to sacrifice herself on the altar of duty!'

Fabiola managed to look smug and apologetic at one and the same time, shrugging her shoulders. 'Poor Doña Consuelo!' Her eyes lit with laughter. 'Me, I am sad for that one because she's never learned that God wants us to be happy, not crabbed and miserable. You see how right I am to say that no one should be forced to marry where there is no affection? Duty follows love, not the other way round!'

'Did you tell Tía Consuelo that?' Petronilla asked, interested. 'What did she say?'

'*Claro*, she said nothing, for we both knew I was right!

When I told her my parents would make me marry Don Diego if I went home to them, she saw immediately it was much better that I should come and visit with dear Petronilla!' Fabiola put her head on one side, smiling and very well pleased with herself. In the next instant she had somehow contrived to look very like Doña Consuelo. 'That any niece of mine should have met such a man under my roof! But how was I to know that he is without honour? The poor girl should have told me!'

Petronilla stared at her, awed. 'She's changed her mind about me?'

'Of course,' Fabiola said simply. 'She is sad, not bad, this aunt of yours!'

Doña Pilar and Petronilla exchanged glances.

'And how are you, *pequeña*?'

Petronilla blushed, but she was still smiling. 'I am well, Mamá. Mr Arbuthnot and I received our first order from America. We are planning a party while you're here to persuade our neighbours to help us fill it – and to welcome Papá to Spain. Won't it be marvellous to have him with us again?'

'It's been far too long!' her mother agreed grimly. Then with one of her swift changes of mood, she embraced Petronilla, kissing her first on one cheek and then on the other in the Continental manner. 'I am *pleased* with you, daughter. Colonel Harris and I are proud that you are such a help to your husband – and you are happy?'

'I am content, Mamá.'

Miss Fairman arrived one week later, flushed with all that she had seen of Seville.

'What poets they must have in this part of the world,' she said to Petronilla, 'if only one could only understand them.'

Petronilla agreed there must be a great many, only she couldn't at that moment think of any that she knew at all well. 'My mind is stuffed full of this party we are having,' she admitted apologetically. 'As soon as I can persuade

Mr Arbuthnot to agree to a date, we could make a start on the invitations.'

Miss Fairman struck a pose, looking as she imagined one of the great thinkers of old to have looked. 'The second of May, my dear, *that* is when you must have your party! Let's hope the dear Colonel will have arrived by then and all your Spanish friends can make him doubly welcome!'

It was, Petronilla saw at once, the complete answer to her problem. The *Dos de Mayo* was a great day in Spain, the day when they commemorated their heroic resistance to the French invasion of their peninsula. It was on the second of May that Spain had risen and had learned the savagery, brutality, hatred and courage that had been necessary to defend their homeland from the invaders. Once learned, however, these lessons had never been forgotten and they had turned on each other with equal savagery in a manner best summed up by the motto of their most famous regiment, the *Tercio: 'Viva la Muerte!'*. Ever since then, with the Carlist rebellions against Queen Isabella, endless civil war had stalked the land, swallowing up whole families as they lined up on one side or the other. Long live Death, indeed, Petronilla thought, but at least the *Dos de Mayo* was a date everyone could agree to celebrate with fervour, and it had never been forgotten that it had been the English who had come to their aid, expending their own blood and treasure in the cause.

'How clever of you!' she said to Miss Fairman, looking at her with a new respect. 'How did you come to know about *Dos de Mayo*?'

Miss Fairman reddened. 'Someone told me in Seville. Such an elegant gentleman, but I fear a traitor like your cousin Diego. If charm could decide battles, I'm afraid the Carlists would have won a long time ago, however, for the stories about the Queen, poor lady, are far from charming! But then what can you expect with such an upbringing? She would do well to learn from our own dear Queen, however. She and Prince Albert are the very model of respectable family life and there's no doubt the people like them all the better for it!'

'Don Carlos isn't a very respectable person either!' Petronilla retorted sharply.

Miss Fairman sighed. 'It's different for a man. A woman has a different nature —

> *a woman deck'd*
> *With saintly honours, chaste and good*
> *Whose thoughts celestial things affect,*
> *Whose eyes express her heavenly mood!*

Petronilla's eyes lit up with laughter. This was not a verse she had heard before, and she thought it the greatest nonsense, but she refrained from saying so, remembering belatedly that she was a married lady and that poor Miss Fairman was not.

'I don't think women, not even the Queen of England, are as different from men as all that,' she said aloud.

'You don't think women are made from a finer clay?'

Petronilla thought of her own eager response to Charles Arbuthnot's lovemaking. Sometimes she would even use one of the signs they had developed between them, asking for his attentions. It didn't seem to her that her nature was any higher than his, in fact there were times when she thought herself wanton in her need for her husband, because she had yet to learn to love him as he deserved to be loved.

'I think we're flesh and blood as they are.'

'Yes, dear, but a poet like Coventry Patmore must know what he is talking about.' She gave her ex-charge an anxious look. 'He married his Angel of the House, as he calls her, only weeks ago!'

'Poetic licence!'

Miss Fairman was more cross than disillusioned, for she was doubtful that Mr Patmore would ever be what she would call a *great* poet. 'There must be some difference!

Can you imagine *women* killing each other on the field of battle?'

'What about the Amazons? Weren't they women?'

Miss Fairman became crosser than ever. 'There are times when I regret your father insisted you should be instructed in such unedifying stories. *I* should not have repeated them to you otherwise!' Petronilla waited for the inevitable quote, but it was a long time in coming. '*Man has his will, – but woman has her way*. I'm afraid you're probably right, my dear: men fight and women nag!'

Petronilla made no effort to hide her astonishment. 'Who's been nagging you?' she demanded. 'Mamá's never nagged anyone in her life and I hope I take after her in that respect at least!'

'I wasn't thinking of myself,' Miss Fairman responded in selfless tones. 'I was thinking of the way Doña Rosa is treated by her family and she is not a poor relation, as I have always been! No, she has plenty of money of her own, but you wouldn't think it! Do you know, they flatly refused to allow her to come with me to Jerez? I thought Doña Consuelo would never cease her sneers at her poor cousin's expense! She would be at it now if Don Ambrosio hadn't suggested Doña Rosa went back to your mother's house.' Miss Fairman sighed deeply. 'I don't think your mother knows it yet, but she will be hard put to it to persuade Doña Rosa to leave her roof again! *Most* understandable, of course – who wouldn't prefer to live in such a courteous atmosphere – every attention! – and the *relief* of not being criticized all day long –'

She spoke with such feeling that Petronilla knew that she had been thinking of her own fate quite as much as Doña Rosa's. She wished she hadn't dismissed her illusions about women's saintliness so firmly, for what else had she to sustain her in her precarious existence, always at the beck and call of others, and without any real security for the future.

'Cousin Rosa will always be welcome to live at Montilla. The more the merrier,' she added gently. 'It wouldn't be home in Hampshire without Mrs Nightingale, would it?'

'*My* family would sooner forget all about me!'

Petronilla patted her governess on the shoulder. 'But, Miss Fairman, you've been with us long enough to know that we are your family now.' She saw the tears flood into the other woman's eyes and sought some means to distract her. 'I wouldn't dare ask you to help me with the invitations otherwise, would I?'

'No, dear. Always glad to make myself useful, as you know. Where are they? I'll get started on them right away!'

The invitations were sent out and the acceptances came flooding in. Doña Pilar prowled about the house, inventing things to do, anything that would pass the time until Colonel Harris arrived. Mostly she talked about sherry, until everyone else felt there was nothing more to be said on the subject and Petronilla felt obliged to hint her away from boring Fabiola and the rest of the household out of their minds.

'What else is there to talk about?' her mother insisted, fanning herself in a desultory way. 'I am tired of waiting! Why doesn't he come?'

Petronilla only looked at her.

'I'm sorry, darling. Only your father can turn me into such a rag-mannered, ungrateful, dismal woman! I am so glad to be here with you and Charles, but I want Tomás to be here too! We've been away from each other for much too long!'

'I know, Mamá. He's coming as quickly as he can.'

Her mother's fan flapped with greater vigour. 'And why was he kept in England all this time? Because of that Fat Rock, Gibraltar! He says Italy is on everyone's mind just now with their stupid plans for uniting under Victor Emanuel. What will happen to the Papal States, I ask you? Has anyone in England thought about that? And what about Austria? Does he plan to wave a wand and make them all go away – the French along with them?'

Italy? Why was it that politicians were only able to think of one thing at a time? She doubted if her father's interest in Gibraltar had been diverted by what was going on in the rest of Europe.

'What has Italy got to do with Gibraltar?' she asked aloud.

'Doubtless it will be the French again,' her mother answered. 'The Pope is right when he says these new liberal ideas turn to licence and godlessness! Protestants talk all the time about freedom and duty! The freedom to trade and the duty to make as much money as possible! What will the Pope do without his States?'

'Jesus managed without them.'

Doña Pilar laughed. 'How like your father you sound! But without me there to remind him, will Tomás think to ask if we can trust these Italians with the Pope? They are not all good Catholics like we Spanish!'

'Oh yes?' Petronilla rolled her eyes in pretended despair. 'Like the men who stand outside the church and gossip in the square, blessing themselves at the elevation bell, and thinking they have attended Mass?'

Doña Pilar preferred not to answer. She didn't mind losing the argument to her daughter, any more than she did to her husband, but she was in no mood to admit as much. She shut her fan with a satisfactory snap and rose to her feet.

'There, I feel better now!' she claimed. 'Let's go and see what kind of sherry that husband of yours has found for us to drink tonight!'

The Colonel had still not arrived when the first guests came up the tree-lined driveway of the *bodega*, dressed in their finest clothes for the party. Petronilla took her place next to her husband to receive their guests, her mother taking the third place which had always been her daughter's before and doing it with such grace that Petronilla knew she need never be afraid of being crowded out by Pilar's greater experience as a hostess in her own house. On the contrary her mother's presence gave her every confidence that her first large party was going to be a success. How could it be otherwise when she had been taught her own manners by Doña Pilar? Then her husband caught her attention, big and solid, his hair smoothed down and oiled to the colour of mahogany. He smelt like a Spaniard! Or was it that he had helped himself to her bath water in his anxiety to save as much water as possible for his precious vines.

She gave him an amused smile and he responded with a look that brought the heat rushing into her face. Her mother's chuckle only added to her confusion which was thankfully brought to an end by the sound of her father's voice outside, demanding that he and Doña Louise should be allowed to move ahead of the waiting queue of guests.

'Tomás!'

Doña Pilar was half-way down the steps before anyone could stop her, flinging herself into her husband's arms. A flood of Spanish was interrupted by calmer, English tones, and then the two of them reappeared by the front door.

'I hope I'm a welcome addition to your first formal party, Pet,' the Colonel said to his daughter.

'You don't know how welcome!' She noticed the way her mother was clutching at his arm, as if he might disappear at any moment again, and wondered if she would ever feel the same delight in Charles Arbuthnot's return to her. She felt again the heat his look had induced in her, the hardening of her nipples and the awareness of his presence she had felt in every part of her. She might not love him as her mother loved her father, but she was learning to appreciate this man of hers – even when he smelt like a bunch of roses! 'Oh, Papá, we were beginning to think you'd never come! You couldn't be more welcome to our *Dos de Mayo* party!'

He kissed her cheek. 'Whose idea was that?' he asked.

'Miss Fairman's. She feels very much at home in Spain.' Belatedly, she noticed Fabiola patiently waiting her turn to be introduced and brought her forward hurriedly. 'Fabiola, my father. Papá, this is the *Señorita* Doña Fabiola Ensenada y Lopez.' She watched the Spanish girl make her curtsy and saw her father's appreciation of the pretty smile she gave him. 'Her parents wish her to marry my cousin Don Diego,' she went on, 'but Fabiola has other ideas. She wants to be a Carmelite nun.'

The Colonel stiffened. 'A nun? In a nunnery? Poor child! Pilar, can't you do something to prevent —'

Mr Arbuthnot bent his head to his father-in-law's. The Colonel's nose twitched, but he said nothing. 'A nunnery is far from being a brothel in this country, sir,' Charles suggested respectfully.

The Colonel's nose twitched again. 'What about the priests —' He sniffed. 'Is it you or my daughter who smells heavily of roses?'

'Both of us,' Petronilla answered laughing. 'Mr Arbuthnot has a thing about saving water, so he followed me into my bath, into which my maid had already put about half a pint of rose-water!'

'Yes,' Fabiola agreed, much diverted by this interesting revelation. 'And when he is not talking about water, he, all of them, are forever talking about sherry! Me, I have no interest in sherry — absolutely none! Shall we go in a corner, sir, and talk about something quite different while your family finishes greeting their guests?'

Doña Pilar shook her head at their retreating backs, the pinched look of misery completely gone from her face now that her husband was back with her. 'That child flirts as naturally as she breathes! She'll be wasted in a convent!'

'If anyone can persuade her of that, it will be Papá!'

'I think not. She is quite decided. They say that when my cousin, the Dominican, was a young man it was just the same with him. The sisters of his friends all hinted they would like him to call on their parents — and he loved them all! He loved women and life, but most of all he loved God. *Claro*, it was no surprise when he became a priest!'

This was not a subject on which the Colonel's views met his wife's. He guessed Fabiola to be well below the age of consent, a pretty young girl with her whole life before her.

He pulled at his moustache, glaring at her, and was rewarded by a slight giggle. 'Petronilla is like you when you look like that! I should warn you that I know a great deal about you, because Doña Pilar and Petronilla like to talk about you all the time. They both missed you very much.'

'And you like to listen?' he suggested.

Her brow darkened. 'Not about sherry! Do you know, even this party is given because Arbuthnots haven't enough sherry of their own to send to America?'

'Don't you like sherry?'

'Not all the time. Morning, evening, noon and night, the talk is of sherry!' She covered her mouth with her lace fan, her eyes dancing with laughter above it. He was reminded of Pilar and felt he had known her all her life. 'I go to my room and pray,' she told him. 'That is my vocation. But when I come back, they are *still* talking about sherry!'

Colonel Harris found himself laughing. 'It's Doña Louise's favourite topic also. I think that's why she's returned to Spain, for there are few people who know much about such things in England.'

Fabiola chewed on her lower lip, staring up at him. 'You don't seem like an Englishman to me,' she confessed at last. 'I expected you to look more like a pirate! Doña Pilar says all Englishmen are pirates, but Don Carlos Arbootno doesn't count because he is a Scot!'

He grinned. 'You look very much the Spanish young lady to me! I can't imagine you wasting all that impudent charm in a nunnery!'

'Why waste? Nothing would be a greater waste than to marry Don Diego Salsedo. He is not interested in women, you understand, only himself. Don Ambrosio, your wife's uncle, is ashamed that anyone in his family should be penniless and a traitor. But Don Diego is worse than a traitor. He likes excitement – all the time! Do you understand what I am saying?'

'Yes,' he said, the amusement dying away from him. 'You're telling me to keep him away from my family. Is that right?'

She nodded quickly. 'Petronilla is happy now.'

'And what about you? There's no need for you to hide yourself away in some convent! I'll speak to your parents myself –'

She put a small hand on his arm. 'But I wish to give my life to God, *señor*! That is the only way I can be happy. Please believe me, because Don Diego is a dangerous man! Not dangerous to me, because I know what he is, and he has no attraction for me, but he is so beautiful that any woman would wish to be the one to tame his wild nature!'

'Petronilla is a married woman now!' the Colonel growled. 'She has her husband to look after her!'

'And you know bad things about Don Diego, no?'

'Possibly.'

'It's all right. You don't have to tell me, but it would be good to tell Petronilla – just in case. Even your Miss Fairman finds it hard to say no to Don Diego, and she approves of him even less than you do! It would be sad if he were to make Petronilla unhappy all over again, no?'

Thomas Harris gave her a thoughtful look. 'It would indeed,' he said.

The party was an enormous success. Spanish, British, Basque, whatever their nationality, they found a common language in sherry. Ignacio was kept fully occupied opening different bottles of *fino*, and the sweeter wines that many of them preferred. Everybody had an informed opinion on the quality and the differing subtle flavours that made one brand different from the next. They had all heard about the American order by that time and, although most of them were as unready as Arbuthnots to fill an order of that size, they were all of them interested in the possibilities of expanding their export trade.

Petronilla went from one group to another, introducing a lighter note whenever she had the opportunity. She was glad her father had Fabiola to entertain him because Doña Pilar was in great demand for, it had soon been recognized, she and Charles Arbuthnot both had good 'noses', being able to tell almost everything there was to know about a sherry merely from its aroma in the glass.

Looking round again, she saw her father was now reminiscing with an elderly Spaniard who had also been at Salamanca on that dreadful day of the battle. Today being the *Dos de Mayo* the Spanish gentleman was in a highly emotional state. Probably he had started drinking several hours earlier, but his back was as stiff as ever and his appreciation of the sherry he was being offered as selective as when he had got up that morning.

'You're not drinking, *señor*,' he said to Colonel Harris.

'I seldom drink sherry,' Thomas answered. 'At home I would ask for a whisky, or some other man's drink, but it doesn't seem quite the thing here.'

The Spaniard clapped him on the shoulder. 'A man who fought in our War of Independence is welcome to drink whatever he chooses, *compadre*! Your daughter will understand.'

Petronilla did. She brought her father his drink with her own hands. 'I do hope Doña Louise won't take it amiss, I have hardly spoken to her since your arrival, but there have been so many things to see to, and this party is very important to both Mr Arbuthnot and myself. Papá, we really are going to be one of the great *bodegas* of Jerez! We already sell in the Netherlands, as well as Britain, of course, and a bit in Germany, and now *America*! You know we use American oaks to make our butts? I am wondering if we couldn't make some kind of a deal with our American friends and bring back the oak in the same bottoms that we export our sherry. Do you think it would be any cheaper?'

'I don't know, child. I know nothing about winemaking. To tell you the truth, I didn't think your mother did either, but she seems to have remembered a great deal since returning to Spain.'

Petronilla nodded. 'She had to remember, Papá. Cousin Diego had done his best to bankrupt the family *bodega*. It will take years to bring it back into full production.'

For an instant the Colonel looked alarmed. 'None of your mother's business, surely? She won't want to be staying on in Spain for any length of time, will she?'

Petronilla's smile mocked him. 'With you in England?'

He took a sip of whisky. 'She won't like leaving you behind in Spain. It takes getting used to, to have one's only daughter married and living in a foreign country. I had always imagined you safely on a neighbouring estate in Hampshire – in and out of your old home all the time, that sort of thing! Are you happy with Mr Arbuthnot?'

'Very happy, Papá. He's a good, kind man and, if I thought I might be bored without reading all your blue books and helping prepare your speeches, I was quite mistaken. Mr Arbuthnot has set me up with an office of my own and we make all our decisions over the *bodega* together.'

'As long as you didn't take his offer because of that silly business in Córdoba? The Spanish make too much of too little – always have and always will! I wished I'd been here to set them all right for you!'

Petronilla forced a smile. 'I was young and silly. It's over now and best forgotten.'

'Can you forget him?'

Petronilla refused to meet the shrewd look in her father's eyes. 'I can try.' She bit her lip. 'Sometimes I think I have. I certainly don't want to have anything more to do with him. There's very little a man would find to admire in him, but Mama understood exactly. She was very kind – in her way –'

'Expected you to do your duty, no matter what, eh?'

The last of Petronilla's smile died away. 'She was right.

It was the only thing left for me to do, unless I were to offend beyond permission and, Mamá was right about that too, I could never have been happy, permanently rubbing against the grain where my family is concerned. Mr Arbuthnot says it's easy to see I'm a spoilt, only child, with you and Mamá loving me no matter what I do, but it doesn't seem to me that Charles has ever known much love and so he doesn't know how important it is to those of us who have.'

The Colonel milked his moustache thoughtfully. 'I never knew much love before I met your Mamá. There was never any doubt in my mind but that she loved me, right from the beginning, and I've always been grateful —'

Petronilla's face could have been carved from marble. 'I am trying to love Mr Arbuthnot as he should be loved. I think I do – most of the time. He is a very easy man to love!'

'And your Cousin Diego?'

'I think most people find him an easy man to hate!' She paused, finding it unexpectedly difficult to explain herself. 'Miss Fairman calls him the Shining One. And sometimes he is like a fallen angel. Most of the time he is more like a badly behaved little boy seeing how far he can go without being punished.'

'And you find that attractive?' He sounded surprised and she knew he was disappointed in her lack of judgement.

'It isn't something a man could understand, Papá. He is, as everyone says, a man without honour and, somehow, one never thinks of evil as being attractive, but it is, it really is! Only Fabiola seems to be unaffected by the lures he casts before all of us women. She was immune from the very first.'

Her father's eyebrows rose. 'Do you think him an evil man, Pet?'

Petronilla didn't answer at first. She pretended she was playing the hostess, looking about the room and making sure that none of her guests had been overlooked.

'I was hoping you would tell me that,' she said at last.

'Me? What makes you think I should know anything more about him than what you and your mother have told me?' the Colonel protested.

'You always know everything!' she countered.

'I know him to be in need of money,' he answered slowly.

'What's all this about Italy?' she asked baldly.

'Oh that! The Government thinks it important to keep Austria's position as a Great Power in Europe. The French think otherwise.'

'Naturally.'

'I think our Government might be distracted by this bid to unify Italy and forget the French are still interested in Spain, that's all, my dear. Austria won't give up their hold on Italy easily, but Spain is permanently on the boil and the French are always there, waiting for their opportunity.'

She gave him a considering, sideways look. 'Papá, I wish you could have been here for the wedding. I looked beautiful – thanks to Mamá —'

'In cloth of gold. Doña Louise told me.'

Petronilla pulled down the corners of her mouth. 'I'm afraid she doesn't approve of me. I don't mind, because she *does* approve of Charles and, oddly enough, so do I!'

She left his side almost immediately after that, her husband summoning her across the room to settle on the best method of delivery with one of their neighbours. After that she was immersed in the details of making up the order for America and had no time for her own personal considerations.

'We can only send them the very best quality,' she reminded the assembled vintners from time to time. 'I'm told Americans are very discerning and if we are to expect any repeat orders they must be made to think it worth their while to come back to us.'

There was a great deal of talk and even more tasting before they all reached agreement as to how many crates from each *bodega* should be shipped to America in the autumn. With the *solera* system it took a long time for a sherry to mature and take on the exact characteristics of the earlier wines with which the new wine was mixed. But in the end, each house could reproduce exactly their best sherries, year after year, in a way one could never be sure of doing with a single vintage.

'What about your mother's wines?' Doña Louise asked, astonished by the progress the Arbuthnots had made in such a short time.

'My wines no longer,' Doña Pilar reminded her. 'The Montilla Bodega is part of Arbuthnots now, though it will be some years before it'll be much use to them.' She took Doña Louise by the arm. 'How do you think our children are looking?'

Doña Louise bridled, pleased by the thought. 'I missed all this talk of sherry more than I thought possible!' she admitted in a rush. 'English women live very dull lives!'

'We do not!' Doña Pilar denied hotly. 'I am never happier than when I am dull in England, because Tomás is there. Everywhere else I find extraordinary dull without him, let me tell you!'

When all the guests were gone, Petronilla led the way into the *salon*, her hand lightly placed on her father's arm.

'How lovely to be alone at last!' she exclaimed. 'Papá, you and Mamá are going to stay with us for a few weeks now you're here, aren't you?'

'A few days,' he said regretfully. 'I must be on my way to Gibraltar after that —'

Doña Pilar caught up with them in a fury. 'What is that about Gibraltar?'

'Come with me,' Thomas coaxed her. 'We needn't stay there long.'

'I will not set foot on Gibraltar! *Absolutamente no!* And you, Tomás, are a great fool – *insensato* – if you think you can persuade me!'

The Colonel shrugged his shoulders. 'Then I must go alone,' he said.

Tears of fury came into Pilar's eyes. 'It is too much!'

she berated him. 'First it is England which cannot do without you – and now it is Gibraltar.' She pronounced it in the Spanish way, with a hard H at the beginning and a great rolling of the Rs. 'When does it become the turn of your family, *Señor Guerrero Inglés*? Do we have so much time left to us that we can *squander* it on the Fat Rock?'

He took her hands in his. 'Would you have me neglect my duty, *favorita*?'

'No. Duty is duty. But, Tomás, I cannot go with you to that place, not until Gibraltar is Spanish again.'

'Will you wait here for me?' he asked her.

'Yes,' she agreed. 'I shall wait here, but hurry back to me, *querido*. It has been far too long without you.'

Petronilla went and stood beside her own husband. 'Poor Mamá,' she said, 'I'm glad your duty doesn't take you away from me, Charles. My happiness depends on your being close by more each day!'

He smiled back at her, his whole heart in his eyes. 'I love you,' he said. But, even at that moment, she couldn't bring herself to answer him in kind. She still thought it might not be the whole truth and therefore unworthy of them both.

Chapter Fifteen

If Petronilla had seen little enough of her husband all through April because he had been out in the fields pruning the vines along with the other men, June was far worse. The fragile branches had to be propped up with sticks so that none of the grapes would lie on the ground and rot. Petronilla, who would sometimes accompany him, found it exhausting, backbreaking work and it was she who encouraged the other ladies to bring a picnic hamper out into the vineyards, thinking it was good for Charles to have an enforced rest in the heat of the day.

Doña Pilar, having made up her mind not to visit Gibraltar with her husband, did not refer to it again.

'I shall spend the summer in Jerez, visiting with my daughter,' she said a trifle defiantly to Petronilla. 'Your father may return here, or not, as he chooses!'

Petronilla was glad to have her company. Pilar had been right that now Petronilla was married they would meet as friends rather than as mother and daughter. There was a new quality to their relationship, culminating in Petronilla's realization that her mother was not nearly as old as she had always imagined. Indeed, sometimes she seemed to be more of her generation than her father's, and she understood all the better her mother's exasperation that he should waste the time they had together when, in the very nature of things, she was destined to many years of widowhood without him. Not that she lacked her own sense of duty, but it was family orientated and she had never been much interested in what he called the Balance of Power in Europe. She cared nothing for international politics, except that it was one of his major interests; she would listen to all that he had to say about it, pouncing on anything in his argument she felt was detrimental to her country, her Church, or anyone who was personally known to her. She saw government as a network of individual loyalties and responsibilities and was totally baffled by the party system, which she referred to as childish, as why should good, useful men be kept out of the ruling party just because they happened to be on the other side?

'Wouldn't Spain be better off with a party system?' Petronilla asked her one day.

Doña Pilar put on a doleful look. 'One side would soon think it better to murder the opposition and keep power in their own hands,' she said gloomily. 'That is the Spanish way.'

'Papá says one needs to keep a balance of power between the nations to avoid war – murdering each other on a grand scale!' Petronilla added for good measure.

'Yes, but he won't admit Spain to be a great power!' Pilar retorted. 'We are no more than a piece of land to be fought over by everyone else! He forgets that the Pope once divided the whole of the New World between the Spanish and the Portuguese. We were the greatest nation in all the world! Austria can be a great power, but Austria once belonged to us! Who kept the Turks out of Europe? Don Juan of Austria! And who was he? A Spaniard!'

Petronilla had some sympathy with this view. 'Papá hates war!' she said instead. 'He will do almost anything to keep Europe peaceful.'

Doña Pilar put a hand on her arm. 'That is very true, my love. He says only one who has seen war can know what a terrible evil it is. What do you think, Miss Fairman?'

The governess blinked, muttered something about women being incapable of understanding such things, and went on to say she believed war to be one of the Four Horsemen of the Apocalypse. As neither mother nor daughter had the slightest idea what she was talking about, she lapsed back into silence and it was left to Fabiola to bring them back to personal matters.

'*I* am very glad we are to spend the summer here, whatever the reason!' she said on a giggle. 'The longer I'm away from Granada, the more time my parents will have to understand I am not going to marry Don Diego, or anyone else!'

'Colonel Harris may have some ideas on that subject,' Doña Pilar warned her. 'We shall have to return you to your family sooner or later!'

'Later,' Fabiola preferred. 'Colonel Harris has no understanding of the religious life and I must have time to persuade him that it is what I truly want.'

'You'll never do that,' Petronilla smiled at her.

Fabiola gave her a pert look. 'You think not? He was determined I should return to Granada, but I am still here! Mr Arbuthnot agreed with me there are too many *bandeleros* on the roads, and Cousin Immaculada won't go by train because she declares it an unnatural way to travel, breathing fire all over the countryside, though I think she must go soon to explain why I am detained here —'

'Enough!' Doña Pilar begged her. 'Nobody will believe any other explanation except that my husband and I have decided it too dangerous on the roads for you to travel without an escort and none is available at the moment. That is what I have told your parents, and they are in complete agreement as far as I know, so let's hear no more on the matter.'

Charles Arbuthnot came to join them, overhearing the last remark. He squatted down beside Fabiola. 'You're not still worrying that Colonel Harris will perceive it as his duty to send you home, are you?'

She looked up at him, the picture of innocence. 'You will protect me from his duty, Don Arbootno?'

He rubbed his chin with a thoughtful finger. 'Probably.'

'Because you know how I feel?'

'No, *muchacha*, because we need your prayers for a bountiful vintage!'

'But, Charles,' Petronilla protested, 'it's bound to be a good vintage! You've worked so hard and Doña Louise said we can expect eight butts of wine per *aranzada* from this *albariza*-type vineyard. An *aranzada* is about one and three quarter acres, isn't it? You see, in a few years we'll have enough wine to supply our own orders. With Mama's wine —'

'Your wine, darling.'

'*Our* wine,' Petronilla amended.

Charles grinned at her. 'We can't fail,' he agreed with her. 'We have Fabiola's prayers, and the hoopoe sang in our fields before the vines budded —'

'Is that a good sign?' Fabiola was less than pleased to have her prayers compared with a bird's song.

'It's said to mean a good harvest. Probably because the hoopoe has a taste for small vermin and keeps the vines free of their infestations.'

'I think my prayers will do you more good,' Fabiola said, looking down her nose.

Mr Arbuthnot bit into a sandwich. 'I'll take any advantage I'm given. I mean to make Arbuthnots the greatest house in all of Spain!'

Walking home from the picnic, Petronilla had other things on her mind. She had been afraid that when Doña Louise had left them to go and stay with friends on the other side of Jerez her husband might expect her to return to her own bedroom. She had tried to make it easy for him by voluntarily going back to the room the Englishwoman had occupied during her visit. It had seemed like the end of the world, she remembered, but she had felt he was entitled to his privacy, even from her.

She remembered, too, her relief at seeing him in the doorway to her room and the way he had looked at her in silence, and then, when her nerves were stretched to breaking point, he had first smiled, then begun to laugh, and lifting her clear off the bed, had carried her into the next door room.

'This is where you belong, Madam Wife!'

She had been acutely conscious of the way his fingers had dragged across her cheek, forcing her to look at him. His hands could always give her pleasure, but that evening she had actually lifted her head and kissed them before he could say anything further. Immediately, she had felt the tension in him.

'You don't want to sleep alone, do you, *palomita*?'

'No.'

'Then why —?'

'I thought you might want your room to yourself.'

He had sat down beside her, hugging her closer to him. 'Are you sure you weren't looking for an excuse to free yourself from my attentions?'

Her eyes had opened wide, horrified that he should have such an idea. 'But, Charles, I thought you knew —' She had broken off, unsure of how to go on. 'I like being your wife,' she had said in the end.

'But not enough to tell me you love me?'

It had been a long time before she had answered. 'I do love you.' Her voice had sounded quite unlike her own and she had cleared her throat. 'I'm not sure I'm *in* love with you, that's all.'

'There's a difference?' he had muttered crossly.

'I don't know,' she had admitted helplessly.

'It sounds to me as though loving me is second best. Is that it?'

His misery had cut her like a knife. She had been trying to be truthful and, it seemed to her, all she had succeeded in being was needlessly cruel.

'You'll never be second best with me,' she had

whispered. 'You never were! I'm – I'm very *proud* to be your wife.'

'You'll be telling me next you're not worthy of me! Really, Petronilla, I expected better from you than that!'

'Better?' For a moment she had been quite indignant, then she had seen that he was laughing at her. 'I *like* being married to you! Will that do?'

'It'll have to.' He had kissed her very gently on the mouth. 'Until you're ready to admit you love me, I'll accept you on whatever terms you offer me, but don't try my patience too far, sweetheart. You may think you fell in love with that scallywag cousin of yours, but I know that for the illusion it always was – and you do too! You wouldn't give yourself to me so thoroughly, night after night, if you really loved anyone else. Sooner or later, you'll see that for the lie it is, and you've always been one for the truth, the whole truth, and nothing but the truth, or I wouldn't feel about you the way I do.'

She had felt a lump in her throat the size of a boulder. She had tried swallowing it in vain, had tried again, and had hoped she was not going to cry. That would have been the final humiliation.

'I want so much to love you!' she had said finally. 'I *do* love you!'

And he had smiled, looking suddenly smug and pleased with himself. 'Yes, I think you do.'

And he had done a great deal more than kiss her after that . . .

Her step as she walked home took on a new jauntiness as she relived how much it meant to her to be Mrs Charles Arbuthnot and nobody else in the whole world. The best part about it was that Charles was real, as real as the world in which he lived. Charles could be touched, and she could be as intimate with his body as she was with her own, and nobody, *nobody* could take that away from her!

Thinking of Mr Arbuthnot reminded her of her pet foxes. Since they had grown into sleek, red-coloured adolescents, they had been moved out of the inner courtyard and into an outbuilding that stood right away from the *bodega*, surrounded by a run of their own, which Petronilla had started to make herself but which, inevitably, had been finished by Charles. It had been he who had taken the trouble to find out what they ate, and everything else about them.

'You'd better watch yourself with them, Pet. They have sharp teeth – and they're enough like dogs to be subject to rabies.'

Petronilla didn't care; she loved them. She had given them names and had taught them to come when they were called. One day, she would teach them other things, for they were quite as intelligent as the dogs they so closely resembled.

She stood by their kennels and called them. There was no answer. She went closer and saw the first body, lying on the ground, a pool of blood by its throat. They were all dead, all of them, deliberately slaughtered. She ran from one to the other, going down on her knees in the dust, unable to believe her own eyes. Who would do such a thing?

A shadow crossed over the stiff body in front of her. Without even looking up, she knew who it was. She could tell by the way he walked – a ballet dancer's walk, or the step of a *torrero*.

'What do you want, Cousin Diego?' she ground out.

'We have unfinished business together, you and I, little English Petronilla. Your marriage hasn't changed anything between us!'

'I have no business apart from my husband's,' she answered, so calmly that she almost convinced herself she was unafraid of any revenge he might seek to inflict on her.

He stood negligently beside her, his riding whip beating out a pattern on the side of his leg. '*Our* business is between us and nobody else. You will always be *my* woman, we both knew that the first moment we saw one another! Why else would you give away my only source of income, if you weren't determined to show me I can't live without you. Well, my darling, you may have brought me to heel, but I won't take your trying to rule me lying down. You're only a female, my dear, and have no business trying to rule any man! How do you expect me to live?'

'How you've always lived – on your wits!' she retorted. 'You neglected the *bodega* so shamefully it wouldn't have kept you in small change for long. Neither my husband nor I have the slightest interest in your future! I wish you will believe me!'

'*You* would never have been left penniless by your family – even married to me, as I was promised you would be!'

She gave him look for look, and it was he who gave in first. 'My parents most certainly never promised you anything of the sort – and nobody else had any right to do so! You wouldn't have married me though, would you? If you were going to marry anyone, it would have to have been Fabiola, and not even her parents would find you an acceptable husband for her after the way you've behaved!'

She had the satisfaction of knowing she had annoyed him sufficiently to make him lose his temper. Her satisfaction was short lived, however. He prodded the dead fox beside her with one elegantly shod foot.

'You should have been warned on your wedding day,' he said. 'I mean to have you, one way or another, Doña Petronilla. Marry anyone you please, you'll always belong to me in spirit!'

Was it true? Nothing would induce her to believe it. She shook her head. 'I'm happy with my husband. Far happier than I could ever be with you!'

He laughed. It was a grotesque sound of complete disbelief. Somehow or other, it made her angry as the death of her pets had not. She had hardly taken in their cruel death, she had been so occupied with the perpetrator of their demise. Now she looked down at the unnaturally still carcasses of her dead pets.

'I don't find killing exciting!' she said abruptly. She rose from her knees, straight backed and with her head held high. 'And don't tell me their death is a "moment of truth" which will reveal some tie between us, because I don't believe a word of it! What truth am I to learn from the murder of my pet foxes? That you don't mind whom you hurt to get your own way? Or merely that you are capable of killing anything I choose to love apart from yourself?'

'I may kill you for your disloyalty to our love,' he said.

'What love? And how would my death prove anything except you can't bear not to have your own way? You don't know what love means, which is your misfortune. My husband has been my teacher and I am only now beginning to understand what it can mean between two people to really love one another.'

His smile became a sneer. 'The only thing that's Spanish about you, my dear, is your appearance. I'd thought better of you than to settle for dull matrimony with a foreigner, knowing every day what you're going to do tomorrow. Your Don Carlos will never give you the pleasure you could have had with me!'

'Being afraid isn't one of my pleasures,' she hastened to assure him. 'If you think it is, you've never really known me at all, Diego.'

His eyes glittered with disbelief. 'Are you sure?'

'Quite sure,' she said.

His languid stance changed to a more threatening posture, but she refused to cringe away from him, or to move so much as a muscle.

'You can take the foxes to be a message for your father, not your husband. Tell Colonel Harris that Don Carlos el Rey has need of Gibraltar and the British would be unwise to stand in his way. If they do, they will discover that British throats can be slit as easily as those of any other vermin. Tell him that!'

'Why should he accept such a message from you?' she demanded.

'Because of the rightness of the cause of him who sends me. It depends how urgently you give him the message as to whether he believes we mean what we say, Cousin Petronilla, so his continued good estate in our country depends on you as much as it does on me!'

It took great strength of will to walk away from him. It was only after she had walked the short distance to the *bodega* that she forced herself to take a deep breath and turn round to see if he was still there. He was gone. The relief of his going left her shaking from reaction and, leaning against the open door of the cool warehouse where the *criadera*, or nursery for the very young wine, was kept, she wept for the loss of her pets which suddenly seemed the greatest sorrow imaginable to her.

'What is it, Pet?' Charles Arbuthnot put his arm around his wife's heaving shoulders. 'It isn't like you to cry!'

'He killed the foxes.'

Mr Arbuthnot turned her to face him, his face grim. 'Who did?'

'Diego,' she whispered.

'Your cousin has been *here*? You saw him?'

'I went to visit the foxes. They were all dead, with their throats cut. I knew it was his doing as soon as I saw them.'

His hands clutched hers. 'Did you arrange to meet him there?'

'No. How could I?'

'You still think about him – dream about him!' He sighed at the look on her face. 'Did you imagine I don't know? How could I not know everything there is to know about you? You're my wife, aren't you?'

She returned the pressure on his hands. 'Yes, and glad to be! Don't scold me, Charles. I would never ask him to come here, or anywhere else! He frightens me, to tell the truth. And, whatever either of you think, I do not enjoy being afraid of anyone, or anything! Besides, the family *bodega* is *ours* – yours! – not his, and I'd never willingly put anything of yours in jeopardy, not even myself. I may not be able to love you as I should and as you deserve, but I would never betray you with anyone else, certainly not with someone I can only despise – ' She broke off, humbled by the doubt she had inspired in his mind. 'Do you think I don't hate myself for ever having been dazzled by a man I can't even like? Oh Charles, all my happiness lies in being your wife and it always will. Haven't I proved that to you yet? What should I want with such as he when I have you beside me every day?'

His face softened. 'Why should he want to kill your foxes?'

'Perhaps they reminded him of you,' she tried to joke.

He grinned, pleased by the thought. 'Did they remind *you* of me?'

She hung her head. 'In a way.' It was an ungracious admission, but it was the best she could do just then. 'He meant it as a message to my father.' She looked fully at him then, the tension between them forgotten for the moment. 'It all has to do with Gibraltar. I think my father may be in danger, Charles.'

'From the Carlists? Diego would be too unreliable an ambassador for anyone to trust him with a serious message, don't you think? He is more likely trying to frighten you. Put it out of your mind, dear heart. It will be soon enough to tell your father when he returns to us.'

Charles Arbuthnot didn't refer to the incident again. Petronilla had feared he might think it necessary to mention her cousin's visit to her mother, but he could see no reason to alarm his mother-in-law when there was nothing any of them could do to warn Colonel Harris of the threats he had uttered. Charles did, however, make sure a look out was posted throughout the vineyards in case Don Diego should come visiting again, and refused to allow any of the ladies to go out without an escort, making the excuse that it was getting too hot for them to go gadding about in the full sun.

'My wife doesn't mind being burned to a crisp,' he told

them laughingly, 'but I don't want any of you fainting
with the heat if you go too far away from the house.'

Doña Pilar crinkled up her eyes thoughtfully. 'If you
say so, Charles,' she agreed with unusual meekness. 'I will
make sure Petronilla goes no further than the office. It is,
as you say, far too hot to be comfortable in the vineyards.'

She waited until her daughter was busy elsewhere before
she gave one of her decisive nods of the head and said what
was really in her mind. 'Who killed the foxes, Charles? I
saw the blood on Petronilla's skirts. Why should anyone
want to destroy her pets?'

'You're very sharp, ma'am —'

'Was it Don Diego?'

He was silent and she made a little movement of
exasperation. 'Of course it was! Did my foolish daughter
send him away with a flea in his ear?'

'Something of the sort.'

Doña Pilar smiled a small, wry smile. 'Don't take it
amiss, *amigo*, but I shall be glad when we have Colonel
Harris safely back among us. When he comes, he will tell
us what to do, no? Meanwhile, we shall do our best to
forget all about it, though I must confess to some curiosity
as to why my daughter should have thought foxes a
suitable addition to a working *bodega*.'

Charles reddened. 'She claims their colouring reminded
her of me,' he explained. 'They were only a few weeks
old when she found them. The vixen had been poisoned
and she wouldn't let me drown them. She had them
trained like dogs. I think she had some idea of using them
as the Arbuthnot symbol – you know, on our labels and
advertising material, things like that.'

Doña Pillar nodded again. 'Foxes? To advertise good
sherry? Petronilla is my daughter, but she is much more
her father's over some things. You may be English
yourself —'

'Scottish!'

'— but, to the outsider, there is no understanding them!
She will adopt a parcel of foxes because they remind her

of you, but does she give serious thought to her feelings for you? No, she does not! What she needs is not foxes but children! Your children, Charles! Even Fabiola can see that she's head over heels in love with you, as she never was with that tiresome cousin of ours!'

'If you say so, ma'am.'

Doña Pilar regarded him with exasperation. 'And you are just as bad as she is, *mi yerno*, expecting her to know her own heart without any help from you! You make of this Diego something which is much too important to you both! It is in the marriage bed that a man and a woman forge the bonds which keep them together, not by dreaming romantic dreams of what can never be!'

'Is it too much to hope that one day she may dream romantic dreams of me?' Charles asked bitterly.

'Who wants to be a dream?' Pilar retorted. 'Me, I prefer a real man, here, by my side! I dream of Tomás all the time he is away from me, but it doesn't make me miss him any the less! Nor will I believe that Petronilla has time to dream of any other man when she shares the same bed with you every night! Foxes indeed! I expected better of you – even if you are not a Spaniard and therefore not at all practical in matters of the heart!'

Thomas arrived back from Gibraltar the very next day, his uncertain temper the most obvious sign that his visit had not gone as he had hoped.

'What did you expect?' asked his unsympathetic wife. 'Naturally, nobody will tell you anything! Why should they? It is Spanish business which goes on in the Bay, not British, even if it is smuggling!'

Colonel Harris recovered himself with difficulty. 'Who have you been talking to?' he asked. 'What's been happening here?'

Nobody answered him immediately. Petronilla would have done, but she didn't want to mention Don Diego's message in public. It was something that she felt was better kept for his ears only, especially after he had favoured them with an explosive account of what Gibraltar was like and how much he had disliked cooling his heels there, unable to persuade anyone of the urgency of his mission.

'I thought an English pirate would enjoy smuggling and making monkeys of the government men,' Doña Pilar murmured innocently.

'Possibly, my love, were I not on the government side in this business! I don't know why you must always have it that I have the instincts of a common criminal, for it would be hard to find anyone more respectable than myself, or so I flatter myself!'

'Papá,' Petronilla interrupted them, 'why did you have to go to Gibraltar? Does my cousin Diego have anything to do with it?'

Her father looked distinctly uncomfortable. 'He hasn't been heard of round here recently, has he?'

She made a noncommital remark, knowing he would take the hint and find some way of being alone with her, despite Doña Pilar's eagerness to have him all to herself.

When he did seek her out, Petronilla told him privately what had happened to her foxes. 'I thought you might know why Don Carlos thinks Gibraltar can help his cause.' she ended.

'Your foolish cousin will never take Gibraltar!' Her father had always looked younger than his years but, for once, he really did look old enough to be her grandfather. Petronilla put an anxious hand on his arm and was rewarded by a bleak smile. 'I can't tell you why he should kill your animals, other than that killing things seems to appeal to him, but someone is using smuggling in and around Gibraltar to raise funds for the Carlist cause, and he is one of the suspects.' He looked suddenly anxious. 'I'd rather your mother didn't know about this. I don't want her worried.'

'No, Papá.'

'And don't you go worrying yourself either, my dear. Your cousin is no longer any concern of yours. Leave it to me and your husband to deal with him. Whatever he's up to, he has the makings of a very dangerous young man!'

Petronilla chewed on her lip. 'Do you have to go back to Gibraltar?'

'Not immediately.' He hugged her to him seeing the expression on her face. 'I am in no danger, Pet. I have the advantage of being a British subject and that means something in this day and age, which is why I should have been less than happy if you had chosen to marry a foreigner, even a Spaniard like your mother!' He hugged her again, deliberately lightening their mood. 'I mean to spend the summer visiting my married daughter – if she'll have me?' he added. 'It's what your mother wants, bless her! We've been apart for more than a year and I want to make it up to her as much as I can in case I have to go to Gibraltar again.'

Petronilla's brow cleared, excited by the prospect. 'There's nothing Charles and I would like better!' she exclaimed. 'Stay for the vintage in September! Oh Papá, I wouldn't mind if you never went away again!'

Father and daughter laughed together, making the most of their moment together. Colonel Harris put a hand on either side of her face, forcing her to look him fully in the eyes.

'You weren't tempted to go away with your cousin when he was here?' he asked her.

'Not for a moment,' she assured him gravely.

'I'm glad,' he said. 'The fellow's a bounder and not worth thinking about! Your Charles is worth a dozen of him!'

Petronilla thought how nice it was to have her father back with them again. She couldn't remember a time when her father hadn't thought that the British way was the only way for a truly civilized man to behave, just as her mother was convinced that only the Spanish understood the practicalities of family life. It would be marvellous to have the two of them sharing the same house with herself and her husband for the whole summer and, better still, was the knowledge that Charles would welcome her parents' presence as sincerely as she did herself.

Towards the end of the month of August everyone's thoughts turned to the Fiesta of the Vendimía which marked the beginning of the vintage. It was earlier in Jerez than in Montilla, 8 September, the Birthday of Our Lady, as opposed to the Feast of St Matthew on the 29th. The fiesta went on for three days, starting with a grand procession on the Friday when the chosen queen of the vintage and her courtiers were driven through the town, throwing sweets to the *niños* who risked their lives, running in and out of the carriages in swarms, making the most of the break in their usually hardworking lives, for Spanish children were expected to earn their bread from a very early age.

To everyone's amusement, there had been some danger of Fabiola being chosen the fiesta's queen. Petronilla had been sorry when the girl had flatly refused the honour, saying it was unsuitable for someone with her aspirations to dress herself up and make a spectacle of herself in front of any number of men she didn't even know.

'I don't know how it is that you still do not take my vocation seriously!' Fabiola had answered crossly when she had first been approached. 'It is not respectable for someone in my position! Besides, everyone knows I don't care a button for sherry! The Jerez horses are a different matter! They are schooled to be as clever as the men who ride them. Why not have a fiesta for the horses?'

Petronilla had found herself laughing. She, too, loved watching the beautiful Spanish greys going through their routines, as elegant and knowing as if every move they made had been choreographed.

'But, of course!' Doña Pilar had said at once when told about the horses. 'Spanish horses are famous throughout the world! Everyone wants to see them! They are beautiful because they have so much Arab blood – like all we Andalucíans,' she had added on a mocking note, for not many of her compatriots were prepared to admit, even now, to the Moorish blood that flowed freely in their veins.

'They are the best thing in Jerez!' Fabiola agreed provocatively. 'Sherry – pouf! I prefer horses every time!'

'Do nuns do much riding?' Colonel Harris asked her, curling his whiskers innocently between his fingers.

Fabiola danced across the room towards him, delighted to have him join in the argument. '*Señor* Colonel, I am relying on you to save me from a much worse fate than being a nun! I don't wish to be a queen!'

'Understandable,' he agreed.

'Yes, *exactly*! How would I explain to the good sisters that I had been a stupid queen for a day? They would think me guilty of sinful pride – and a lot more besides!'

'Why tell them?' the Colonel asked. 'None of their business what you do!'

Fabiola chuckled. 'They are to be my family, *señor*. Is what your family does none of your business?'

He admitted defeat and delighted her still further by agreeing that someone else must be found for the part. 'You're a victim of your own popularity,' he told her. 'You're going to be missed in Jerez when we finally return you to your parents.'

'It will be much more fun not to be queen,' she declared. 'I want to see what everyone else is doing, not be stuck up on some carriage by myself.'

'Quite right, my dear,' he commended her.

Petronilla's attention was wholly on her husband. It was in his interests that their *bodega* should take a full part in the fiesta and she made every effort to see that they did. Even so, she was able to join all the others for the procession, admiring the young girls in their white dresses and blue scarves, representing the white fields of Jerez and the blue skies above.

On the Saturday there was a bullfight, to which

Petronilla refused to go. Miss Fairman, surprised into a tactlessness she immediately regretted, reminded her charge how much she had enjoyed the bullfight in Córdoba.

'And that was a very small one, my dear. This one is to be much better! Everyone says so!'

Petronilla excused herself, saying she was tired. There was a certain amount of truth in this for the celebrations of the day before had gone on for most of the night. After the procession, there had been the fireworks in the Plaza de Arenal. Neither Doña Pilar nor Fabiola had shown the least sign of wear at breakfast the morning after, but were very well satisfied at turning the night into day.

'We have plenty of time to sleep before the next event,' Doña Pilar said complacently. 'It was a lovely night! Dancing, fireworks, everyone having fun! How is it you're tired? Me, I am never tired when I'm enjoying myself!'

Her family had reason to know the truth of this. Her daughter and her husband exchanged glances. 'You forget I'm half English,' Petronilla reminded her. 'The English have something better to do with their nights than turn them into day!' Mr Arbuthnot's look of pure affection made her suddenly self conscious, and she blushed. 'I didn't mean —'

He came quickly to her rescue, but she could tell he was pleased by her gaffe, taking it as a compliment to himself, and she was saddened that since their marriage she had given him so little encouragement.

'You don't take advantage of the siesta, my love, unlike the other ladies – especially Fabiola!'

Fabiola's eyes snapped with amusement, enjoying the exchange as much as Petronilla was embarrassed by it. 'I go to my room to pray,' she said virtuously, lowering her eyes.

'And then dance the night away?' Mr Arbuthnot teased her.

She stuck her nose in the air. 'I am Spanish – like Doña Pilar! It is very sad, but the music only has to play for our toes to tap in time to it, and then we dance. It's one of the things I shall miss most after I enter Carmel.'

It was Fabiola, too, who seemed to understand why Petronilla wanted to avoid the bullfight. 'I shall stay at home also,' she decided, 'not because I am tired, but because the bullfight is an old pagan custom and I prefer to stay away.'

Thus it was that the two girls were on their own that Saturday evening. They saw the others off in splendidly decorated carriages, both of them surprised that Colonel Harris should choose to escort Doña Pilar to such an event.

'He'll hate every minute of it!' Petronilla said, watching the shining horses as they clip-clopped down the drive.

'No, he'll enjoy being with Doña Pilar,' Fabiola contradicted. 'She will explain everything to him and he will enjoy watching *her*. The poor bull will be nothing to either of them!'

Petronilla gave the Spanish girl an admiring look. 'Are your parents the same?' she asked her.

Fabiola laughed at the thought. 'No, after all these years they still hardly know each other. Their families arranged their marriage, ignoring the fact they had disliked each other as children and would as adults too! But they share a rigid duty to family life and on that they have a very good understanding. Most of the time they ignore each other, though there are enough of us children to prove they must have something to do with each other! They aren't daggers drawn like Don Ambrosio and Doña Consuelo. My father has never neglected my mother in that way.'

Petronilla raised her brows, not sure how to take this. 'Should you talk about your parents like that?' she asked.

Fabiola apologized immediately. 'People interest me,' she said by way of explanation. 'Even my own parents!'

The two young women were sitting in the main patio, sipping a glass of sherry that Petronilla wanted to try out, when they heard the carriages coming back up the drive. All the servants had been given time off to attend the bullfight so Petronilla went herself to welcome them home.

One look at their faces stopped Petronilla in her tracks. 'What's wrong?' she whispered.

Miss Fairman scuttled out of sight, knowing she would only be in the way if she stayed. Over her shoulder came the words, '*And the Lord set a mark upon Cain!*'

'What is she talking about?' Fabiola demanded.

It was Doña Pilar who answered. 'The matador was indisposed. Our Cousin Diego took his place and was gored.'

'Is he dead?' Petronilla asked.

Pilar shook her head. 'He was taken to hospital. Miss Fairman is right. The bull's horn caught his cheek and he's badly hurt —'

Thomas Harris took a step forward, his face grimmer than Petronilla had ever seen it. 'An impetuous young man, but still dangerous. He came with a message for me, but he couldn't resist showing off his ability as a *torrero* and suffered accordingly. There's nothing for it, I shall have to go back to Gibraltar.'

Doña Pilar clutched at his arm. 'Alone? No, Tomás, not again!'

'Arbuthnot has his hands full with the grape harvest —'

'That's true, sir, but until we know how badly Don Diego is hurt, the women would be better off with you in Gibraltar,' Charles said firmly.

Petronilla was outraged. 'I'm not leaving you!'

But, for once, Charles Arbuthnot refused to listen to her. 'You'll do as you're told!' he stormed at her, and then more gently, 'Petronilla, my love, I don't want to find *you* with your throat cut! Will you never understand that, without you, I wouldn't want to go on living?'

And to that she could find no immediate answer.

Chapter Sixteen

Colonel Harris would have been happier to have departed at once, but his womenfolk flatly refused to be rushed away from Jerez before the *feria* was over.

'What can happen to me with Cousin Diego in hospital?' Petronilla said lightly, prepared for battle. She thought she would never forget the agony in Mr Arbuthnot's voice when he had confessed his fears for her life. Her own heart had turned over within her, as much with guilt as with consternation that he should care so much.

'Why must you go to Gibraltar again?' Doña Pilar took up the cry. 'It is most inconvenient, let me tell you! And what do you propose should happen to Fabiola?'

Both men were inclined to be impatient. 'We can't afford to take the risk that Don Diego isn't alone in Jerez. Thank God he can't resist a good bullfight, or we might not have spotted him until it was too late,' Colonel Harris muttered.

'Of course he came alone!' Petronilla scoffed.

Charles hushed her with a gesture. 'I won't take that risk even if you're prepared to. You can stay until tomorrow for the end of the *feria*, and then you must go with your father!'

Petronilla threw him a speaking look, determined he should know the pleasure it gave her that his concern should make him so masterful. It was not a side of him she saw often and it gave her a warm feeling that her undemonstrative husband should be so protective towards her.

'What makes you think I shall be any safer in Gibraltar?' she demanded.

It was her father who answered. 'You're not safe anywhere, Pet.'

She was astounded. A shiver went down her spine. 'Why not?' she asked.

'You're my daughter,' he said drily.

Petronilla looked for her husband, seeking his help. She held out a hand to him and was glad when his fingers pressed hers reassuringly. Without thought, she leaned back against him, holding his hand tightly against her breast.

'But we're in Spain,' she said at last.

'As is also Gibraltar!' her mother pointed out with such disgust that Petronilla managed a shaky smile.

'I don't understand,' she said.

Her father cleared his throat. 'We didn't tell you your cousin threatened to take you hostage when he first came into the ring. He came close to where we were sitting and saluted your mother and I, just as if we were his personal guests at the affair. He wanted us to know exactly what he intended —'

'But *why*?' Petronilla broke in.

The Colonel tugged at his moustache. 'It won't come as much of a surprise to you to know that I went to Gibraltar on official business for our government. We've long been concerned as to what is going on there and now, at last, we have a Governor who sees it as his duty to put an end to all the illegal trading, instead of encouraging it for the benefit of his friends at home. It won't be a popular move in London, that goes without saying – a lot of people there are going to lose a lot of money —'

'English pirates!' Doña Pilar said, pleased to discover she had been right all along.

Thomas grinned at her. 'Corsairs, every one!' he confirmed. 'I'd like to think that would be enough to persuade the British Government to act, but I fear they are much more excited by a rumour Arbuthnot and I passed on to them that the Carlists are using Gibraltar to augment their funds. That they should do such a thing without their consent has angered them far more than a bit of harmless smuggling.'

'What is harmless about ruining Spanish trade?' Doña Pilar exploded, angry, as she always was at any mention of Gibraltar.

Petronilla gripped Charles's hand more tightly. 'Is that what Don Diego has been doing?'

'Probably,' Thomas Harris acknowledged cautiously.

'You must know more than that!'

'I *know* very little more than you do,' her father assured her. 'My guess is that Diego is merely a diversion. I can't imagine anyone putting such an impetuous young man in charge of fund raising, can you?'

Petronilla was silent, her eyes enormous, as she thought about her cousin. He had a most persuasive silver tongue and he would be able to make out a good case for his employment at such a task. That the excitements of smuggling would appeal to him she had no doubt at all, but she still couldn't see what advantage he could get from abducting her away from her family – from her *husband* – unless it was because he still had some idea he could force her to consent to some sort of relationship between the two of them. She burned with indignation at the thought. How *dared* he think she would allow him to hurt Charles?

'Yes, I can imagine it,' she said at last. 'It's always been the same in Spain that they take their leaders from the highest in the land. Isn't that so, Mamá? People are always saying that Don Carlos failed to convince the *hidalgos* of his claim, right from the start. Don Diego is very presentable, whatever else may be said against him.'

Her mother gave one of those characteristic nods of her

head. 'That is true. In England your generals become dukes; in Spain our dukes become generals. If there is no one else, Don Carlos may be forced to depend on Cousin Diego to do his smuggling for him!'

'Yes, but what makes him think I would go with him?' Petronilla wailed.

Her father heaved a sigh. 'You were to be his insurance that the British Government would keep their nose out of his own and his master's affairs. He could have taken you the day he killed your foxes, but his sense of drama wanted me to be here to applaud his cleverness.'

So much for any hopes she might have had that her cousin had any real affection for her! She turned in her husband's arms, spreading her fingers across the hard wall of his chest. He was so dear and familiar to her that she hated the prospect of having to leave him on his own, but how to tell him so?

'I'd rather stay here with you!' she told Charles abruptly.

He bent his head to hers. 'We'll talk about it,' he promised. 'We have tomorrow's excitements to get through first. Unless you mean to go tomorrow, sir?'

'I want to find out how badly hurt that young man is before we leave,' the Colonel decided. He turned to his son-in-law. 'It might be better to surprise any sympathizers he might have in Gibraltar by going by land. We can take Fabiola home to Granada, leave Pilar at Montilla —'

'You will not!' the last named lady told him flatly. 'If you must go to Gibraltar, then Petronilla and I will go with you. I am tired of this so called cousin of ours putting us all on edge. It is time to put an end to his games, no? And who better to do it than you, Tomás? Then we can all be safe again and Petronilla can have more little foxes —'

'Whatever for?' her husband asked.

'Because it amuses her to have little red animals with the same colouring as Mr Arbuthnot! Later, there will be children, please God, but I have decided the *zorros* will look pretty on the Arbuthnot labels after all! Our daughter is very clever to have thought of it, yes?'

Colonel Harris looked less than convinced. 'Foxes!' he snorted.

Petronilla tried to move her thoughts away from the foxes, wishing she could get the picture of their poor little dead bodies out of her mind. How like Diego to allow himself to be diverted by a bullfight! She wondered how he had persuaded the other *torreros* to permit him to don the 'suit of lights' and take his part as matador in the ring. He had probably spun them some story of his own abilities and they had believed every word of it!

Then a new thought came to her. Had he threatened the Arbuthnot *bodega* as well as herself?

'Charles,' she whispered. 'I'm going to bed.'

He smiled and nodded, already deep in conversation with her father. How irritating men could be, always thinking that only they could make sense of the politics which her father considered to be the most important thing in life, when really, as Doña Pilar was always insisting, they hardly mattered at all when one came down to real life. Didn't Charles realize that she needed to talk to him?

She exchanged a small, wry smile with her mother. 'Are you coming?' she asked with a small sigh of annoyance.

Doña Pilar shrugged. 'Give them time, *hija*. Your father will solve everything in the end!'

'But they don't *listen*,' her daughter complained.

Her mother laughed. 'You have all night to make Charles listen! Do you want to stay here with him so much?'

Petronilla stopped still on the stairs, her head bowed. 'I'm afraid to leave him.'

'Then I should tell him so,' her mother returned lightly.

That, Petronilla discovered, was easier said than done. She undressed, putting on her prettiest nightgown, and settled down to wait for Charles to join her. When he finally came, she had fallen asleep, the lamp beside the bed spluttering in the first stages of extinction. He sat down on the edge of the bed, looking down at her, wondering how she managed to sleep so peacefully when he felt sick at heart at the thought of her going away from him. She looked as Spanish as her mother, but she was her father's daughter underneath. The combination had always delighted him. From the very beginning he had been desperately in love with her, willing to take her on any terms he could get, and now she was going away and she still hadn't told him she loved him, though once or twice lately he had thought she had been on the point of uttering the words.

He brushed her hair back from her face with gentle fingers and she stirred under his touch. His muscles hardened with longing for her. If she refused to lie to him about the way she felt about him, her body was less scrupulous and welcomed him with a matter-of-fact delight that was all Spanish. If she had been less honest with herself and him, she might have deluded them both into thinking that it was out of love that she welcomed his lovemaking with such satisfaction, but she had refused point blank to make such a connection. Since a boy he had been told that women had no sexual appetites of their own, merely suffering the act for their husband's pleasure. Doña Louise had been the last to go out of her way to warn him not to expect too much from a bride she had been convinced would be both ignorant and frightened.

Petronilla had been neither. When his curiosity had got the better of him and he had confessed his surprise, she had giggled, half embarrassed by his confused enquiry and half delighted that she had exceeded his expectations as a wife. She had been totally unashamed of her naked body, he remembered, her dark brown eyes brimming with laughter as she had answered that she was glad she meant more to him than the pillow in his bed, for *she* had been told she had a duty to be more to her husband than that! Then the laughter had been gone, replaced by a sadness that had put paid to his hopes. She had lifted his hand from her breast and kissed his fingers, one by one.

'I will try to be a good wife to you,' she had promised.

Looking down on her now, he wanted to tell her that she had succeeded beyond either of their dreams. He would be desolate without her . . .

She woke and sat up with one of those sudden movements she shared with her mother. The reflection of the light shone like diamonds in the blackness of her eyes, her lashes long and casting shadows on her pale cheeks. To him she had never looked more desirable. He wanted to make love to her very badly.

'Was I asleep? You were so long! Are you coming to bed now?'

He tumbled her back against the pillows, holding her a prisoner by putting a hand on either side of her slim body.

'What I'd like,' he said, 'is to keep you in bed all day tomorrow!' His eyes crinkled at the corners as he smiled at her in open invitation. 'Shall we make our own celebrations and leave it to the others to represent us at the public events?'

'I wish we could.' She stared up at him. 'Charles, I'm not going with my father on Monday. I'm going to stay here with you.'

His eyebrows shot up. 'Are you now?'

She pleated the front of his shirt between her fingers. 'I'm afraid to go without you —'

'*Afraid?*'

She refused to meet his eyes. 'I feel more secure when I'm with you. I'm afraid of what may happen if I'm away from you.'

His mouth tightened. 'Your cousin?'

'I suppose so,' she admitted. 'I can't explain it – I wish I could! Please keep me here with you!'

His retreat from her wasn't only physical, it was also in his mind. She saw that she had succeeded in hurting him again and ached inside, wishing she could say something to reassure him that this had nothing to do with her cousin, at least not in the way he was thinking. All she knew was that she was afraid without the emotional anchor of his presence, they might lose even the affection that had always bound them together. She trusted him, but she had little cause to trust herself, not since that one disastrous day when she had been tempted by her cousin Diego and had gone alone on a picnic with him.

'Charles, please!' she appealed to him.

He stood up, turning his back on her. 'Your cousin's in hospital for some days at least. You'll be better off in your father's care.'

'That isn't true! How can I be better off away from you?'

'There's more to life that making love,' he threw at her, wanting to hurt her as she had hurt him.

'And are you to work yourself into an early grave on your own here?' she asked him coldly.

'What's that to you?'

Irritated, she started up out of the bed. 'If you don't know, I'm not going to tell you! Suppose, instead, *you* think about what will happen when Cousin Diego gets out of hospital! I have cause to be afraid —'

He glowered at her over his shoulder. 'I'm not afraid of your Shining One!'

'Nor am I for myself! But what if he destroys the *bodega*? What then, Charles?'

His red hair shone like a halo about his head. He rocked back and forth on his heels. 'I hadn't thought of that,' he said slowly. 'I wonder if your father has!'

She was immediately concerned. 'You don't really think he could hurt us here, do you?'

'No, Pet, I don't. I don't think he'd waste any time here, knowing you to be gone with your father. It would be a different story at Montilla though, with only your mother there to try and stop him.'

Petronilla blenched. 'Mamá?'

He turned back to her, sweeping her off her feet and

throwing her back on to the bed, following her with a great whoop of triumph.

'I'm coming with you, my sweet! Doña Louise will look after the vintage for us here and be glad to do it! You and I are going to accompany your parents to Gibraltar!'

She couldn't have been more delighted. 'Truly? You'll come with us?'

He buried his face in her shoulder. 'Shall we make love?' he asked her. 'Isn't that what you really want from me?'

Her relief brought an added zest to her consent. She watched with a pounding heart as Charles Arbuthnot stripped his clothes from his body and came to join her in the large bed. In this respect as least, she and her husband were made for each other, two halves of a perfect whole and she welcomed him as eagerly as she always had. She remembered how once she had wondered whether all men looked stronger and more manly without their clothes. It was something to which she would never know the answer and it made no difference to her appreciation of Charles's naked body and the way his muscles moved under his skin which was quite different from her own soft curves. He was as hard as if he had been carved from wood. The dawn was breaking when she realized he had fallen asleep by her side, relaxed and happy. Surely, she thought, when they could give such joy to each other, there had to be some kind of love between them – perhaps the only kind of loving they'd ever know.

They were late coming down to breakfast the next morning. Charles made light of it, bidding her send for her maid straight away to get her ready for the great Mass which was to be the highlight of the day.

'What are you going to do?' she asked, a naked invitation in her eyes.

He slapped her on her rump, grinning. 'I, my dear love, am going to speak to your father. I can't walk away from here without making certain preparations!'

'At least we shall be together,' she sighed.

He paused, looking at her. 'You don't have to be afraid of your cousin, you know. There isn't much he can do while he's in hospital.'

She sighed again. 'He'll have healed up by the time we get to Granada, if we go by road as Papá means to. I wish we had seen the last of him. One thing I promise you, he won't get at my family again through me!'

He smiled, thinking how voluptuous she looked as she waited for him to remove himself. 'Not your favourite character?'

'Mostly I hate him,' she said with feeling. 'I don't think you'll ever understand how I feel about him!'

He came and stood over her, bending down to kiss her. 'Sometimes I wonder if *you* understand how you really feel about him – or me.'

It was her turn to smile. 'Do I seem like a reluctant wife to you?'

'No, never that,' he admitted.

Her maid came at once. 'Your mother left instructions you had decided not to breakfast because you are going to Communion, or I should have woken you earlier!' She was plainly impressed her mistress should be so devout. 'You must wear your very best dress today! Today is the first time your grapes are being blessed at a High Mass, no? The *Señor* Don Arbootno says we are all to go, whether we work with the grapes or not! And Doña Louise is returning after the ceremony! God is good to give us so much happiness!'

Petronilla had marked out her dress days before. She wore an underskirt of horsehair, a fully flounced skirt of scarlet taffeta and a matching jacket. She thought she looked very well in it, though she hoped it would not be too hot in church, what with the incense and the crowds of worshippers who were sure to be there. Her hair was parted in the centre and drawn smoothly back, a few locks gathered up from the rest and crimped into ringlets. It was a very fashionable style and she thought she looked very well by the time her maid had finished. Her hair was too heavy to submit to the forced curls for long and the ringlets were already falling out when she took a last look at herself in the glass.

Her maid clucked her tongue. 'You are too Spanish for such an English style, *señora*. Why not wear the mantilla and the comb your mother gave you?' She leaned forward, poking a finger under her mistress's nose. 'Perhaps your husband will pick a flower for you to wear in your hair?'

Petronilla gave way without argument and she was very well pleased with the results. The seams of her dress were piped in black, and the black of her mantilla and the gold and tortoiseshell of her comb gave her an elegance that reminded her strongly of her mother. She had never looked more Spanish, but then why should she look anything else on such a Spanish occasion? Arbuthnots might be British owned, but it was being built on Spanish earth, with Spanish workers, with grapes maturing in the warm Spanish sun.

Charles was obviously delighted with her appearance. He handed her up into the carriage and sat beside her, the two of them leading the procession of carriages to the Collegiate Church that stood on a hillside just below the gardens of the Alcázar in Jerez. It was a golden church that gleamed in the sunlight, the statues of the saints standing about the dome. Like so many churches in that part of Spain, it had been built on the site of an old mosque, of which the Mudejar tower still survived, standing a little apart and much, much older than the nearly new church.

In front of the church a rectangular wooden press, called a *lagar*, had been set up and filled with grapes. They all went to examine it more closely, enjoying the scene as four of their best workmen, in short trousers and the famous nailed boots of sherry-making fame, stood by to jump in and start treading the grapes.

The Arbuthnot contingent was joined by Doña Louise, exultant that she was to be left in charge of the *bodega* again, a *bodega* which she still considered partly her own.

Even though she knew it was actually Charles's property, bought and paid for, which was what she had wanted at the time, she had forgotten all about that now and was eager to return to her own land. She bristled with an importance that was only slightly modified by having to endure another Catholic Mass in which she refused to take any part whatsoever, apart from being bodily present. Pleased to see Colonel Harris kneeling beside his wife, she pushed her way past the others, settling herself on his other side.

'I wonder if they would pay us the same compliment if we were in England,' she said in a harsh whisper.

Thomas Harris muttered under his breath and, thus encouraged, Doña Louise continued more loudly, 'A lot of pagan nonsense!'

'Sherry is a pagan drink!' Colonel Harris grunted. 'You should know that if anyone does.'

Doña Pilar glared at them both. 'And what is pagan about thanking God for the birth of the new wine?' she demanded. She shrugged indignant shoulders. 'It is pagan *not* to thank God!' she added. She leaned over to address Doña Louise more directly. '*Señor el Draque* was pleased to steal our sherry – as the English steal everything in the end!'

'Including you!' Thomas retorted.

Delighted, Doña Pilar laughed, hiding her face in her hands. '*Sí, Señor Inglés*, including me!'

Petronilla's eye fell on Fabiola lost in her prayers. She had so much to be thankful for herself that she applied herself more earnestly to giving thanks for the new vintage and for seeking the Divine Protection for her whole family and everything that was dear to her.

When the Mass was over, the entire congregation swept out of the gloomy interior of the church into the sunshine beyond, bearing the image of San Gines de la Jara, the patron saint of the vintage.

'Who is he?' Colonel Harris asked his daughter.

She suppressed a smile. 'He isn't in the Roman missal.

I've looked,' she answered. 'There's a San Gines who was martyred in Arles, but this San Gines belongs to the Jerez vintage. Charles says he was a nephew of the great Charlemagne and was born in France. He went on pilgrimage to the shrine of Santiago el Major, in Compostela, and became a hermit. Who knows who he really.was?'

Her father looked her over. 'You become more Spanish every day, my dear.'

Amused, she smiled up at him through her lashes. 'Is that a compliment, Papá?'

'Ask your mother!' he retorted.

She chuckled. 'I will,' she promised.

The queen of the vintage, surrounded by her courtiers, took her place on the steps of the church, awaiting the blessing of the priest, before she deposited the first bunch of grapes into the *lagar*. The waiting workmen jumped in and began to mark time, crushing the grapes under their feet.

Petronilla was so busy looking at all the activity that she was unaware of Charles coming up behind her.

'Well, *palomita*?'

At the same moment a cloud of white doves were released over their heads and the choir began the first notes of a *Te Deum* of praise and thanksgiving. Petronilla stood completely still, allowing the moment to take possession of her. So that was why Charles called her *palomita*, little pigeon. *Palermos blancos!* The cry went up all round her as the doves circled above them. It was such a graceful endearment for her husband to use that tears of gratitude started into her eyes. She reached out a hand to him.

'I wish we could stay and see our own vintage in,' she said.

'Next year.'

And all the years after that. But it would never be this year again, the year of their own first vintage, and the first of their marriage and their partnership.

Long after the ceremonies were over, everyone in Jerez

who had anything to do with the making of sherry stood around, watching the grapes being trodden by teams of workmen from the various *bodegas*. It was a great social occasion and they made the most of it, discussing their plans with one another, for they all realized that what was good for one *bodega* would be good for all the others. Many of them were ex-patriots, from Britain, from France, from everywhere, speaking a mixture of languages that finally resolved itself into a mixture of Spanish and English.

As always, Charles was in great demand. He had the great advantage that he knew the business from the first to the last, from the planting of the young vines to the selling of the finished product to the British merchants of London, who were still their greatest customers. His advice was eagerly sought by anyone who had run into difficulties, as he always knew the answer to their shipping problems and who to contact in London to obtain a better price than the one they had been half promised by one of the fly-by-night dealers who were always looking for something on the cheap.

Petronilla watched Doña Louise follow him from one group to another, pushing her way into the centre of each gathering, her head bobbing up and down as she interrupted what he was saying, eager to explain that she would be back in residence at her old house while everyone else was away.

'You're going away? Now?' Their next-door neighbour was appalled. 'Surely not?'

Charles Arbuthnot remained cheerful. 'Doña Louise is going to oversee the vintage. It won't be the first time for her, though she hoped to have all that behind her now that she's retired —'

'Very kind of her, I'm sure!' the man muttered.

Fabiola, who had been talking to one of the priests, came drifting down the steps of the church, her face bright with happiness. 'Isn't it grand to be alive?' she said to Doña Louise. 'God is good!'

Doña Louise looked at the girl with acute suspicion. 'If my fiancé were lying, wounded, on a hospital bed – ' She hurried on to the next group without waiting for an answer.

Fabiola's calm was impregnable. 'Yes, but he has gone from the hospital,' she went on cheerfully to Petronilla. 'It was only a flesh wound and he refused to stay any longer.'

'But, Fabiola, that's awful!' Petronilla exclaimed.

Fabiola hugged herself with glee. 'No, no, it's marvellous news! The good father saw him earlier this morning and, guess what, Petronilla, Don Diego told him he wants to marry me as little as I want to marry him! He said he may be leaving Spain altogether to go and fight in Italy. Most of all, he was angry with himself for stepping in front of that bull and letting him rip his cheek open. That is like Don Diego, no? That a man should be so vain of his good looks!'

Petronilla tapped her foot impatiently, wondering how to extract her husband from his admirers long enough to tell him what had happened. She could tell her father, of course, but he was popular also, as was Doña Pilar who was never at a loss in a crowd, enjoying everything as she always did.

'Have the doves been released yet?' Fabiola enquired.

'A little while ago,' Petronilla told her, not really listening.

The Spanish girl made a little *moue* of disappointment. 'They carry messages from our Andalucían poets to the whole world. They tell the whole world the new vintage has begun here in Jerez. Isn't that beautiful?'

'Who told you that?'

Fabiola fluttered her eyelids. 'A man!'

'What man?'

'A friend of Don Diego's. He was in the church, talking to the good father. I didn't know who they were talking about at first. It was only when they began to discuss the bullfight yesterday that I realized he was another *torero* come to make his peace with God. Naturally, I was going to leave him alone with the priest, but he suddenly turned to me and asked me if I had been at the Plaza de Torros yesterday. I said no, I never went to the *corrida* these days. He was very handsome, *mire*, so I didn't mind talking to him. He was so exactly the kind of man my parents would *not* wish me to get into conversation with, winking his eye whenever he thought the priest wasn't looking. I asked him if he were the matador who had been ill the day before and he said he hadn't been sick precisely, that Don Diego had paid him to allow him to go into the ring in his place, which was no more than I'd expected —'

'Fabiola, my love,' Petronilla interrupted her, 'matadors don't allow amateurs to take their place in an important *corrida*! There must have been more to it than that!'

'There was! Don Diego threatened to kill him,' Fabiola said simply.

Petronilla gave her a shocked look. 'Are you sure?'

Fabiola shrugged. 'It's like Don Diego, no? That's why no one would help him with the bull. That's what the *torero* wanted to tell the priest. He was afraid Don Diego had been badly hurt – on his orders, you understand, because he felt his whole reputation as a matador was at stake. He had trained for years, starting with the smaller fights and progressing to the better known venues. To be chosen for Jerez on the Saturday of the Fiesta of the Vendimía was what he had been working towards, and then along came this man who stuck a knife in his ribs and demanded he be allowed to wear his *traje de luces* and kill the bull! He said he could be his *mozo de estoques* —'

'His what?' Petronilla asked.

'His sword boy – his off-stage assistant – every matador has one! But Don Diego would have none of it! He wanted to kill the bull himself!'

Petronilla could believe it. It was exactly what her Cousin Diego would want to do, and it was exactly the way he would have gone about it.

'I wish the bull had killed him!' she exclaimed.

Fabiola was unmoved. She slapped at Petronilla's hand with her fan. 'Naughty!' she rebuked her, gurgling with laughter.

'At least I can think beyond the present moment!' Petronilla retorted. 'If Cousin Diego isn't in hospital, where is he?'

A look of horror crossed the younger girl's face. 'I'm sorry! You're right, I didn't think! It was such a relief that he doesn't wish to marry me – you must understand that! Think how terrible it would be to be married to such a monster –'

'I prefer not to,' Petronilla said coldly. 'More to the point, I think we should tell Mr Arbuthnot –'

'Yes, indeed!' Fabiola approved. 'If you will stay here, I'll tell him you have need of him – or your father.' Her eyes widened innocently. 'I adore your father! If he weren't married to your Mamá – ' Her tongue protruded between rose-red lips, her eyes roguish over her spread fan. 'He is – *muy hombre* and very brave, no?'

Petronilla looked up towards heaven, seeking inspiration. 'Fabiola,' she began sternly. But the girl had already gone, looking the very picture of decorum and innocence. Petronilla shook her head at the girl's retreating back, rather hoping that no one at Carmel would try to quench her bubbling high spirits.

In a matter of moments both her husband and her father were making a determined effort to reach her side through the crowds. They arrived together, with Doña Pilar only a few seconds behind them.

'What is it now?' Colonel Harris asked wearily.

Petronilla explained how Fabiola had learned that Don Diego had left the hospital.

'I thought you ought to know,' she said awkwardly. 'If he comes looking for us, I'd sooner be already gone. He may go straight to Gibraltar –'

Her father put an arm about her shoulders, not deceiving her for a moment with his nonchalance. She knew him to be as worried as she was herself. 'Don't worry, love,' he said. 'We'll soon find out where he is, and where he's going next. He's in too much of a hurry to pay proper attention to intelligence – and I'm too old a soldier not to have learned my lessons in that respect! Your cousin is no match for anyone who's served in the British Army! Can you be ready to leave tonight?'

'If Doña Louise —'

Charles Arbuthnot shook his head at her. 'I'll leave a letter for her to read in the morning. The fewer people who know which way we have gone the better.'

Doña Pilar gave her husband's arm a squeeze. 'It will be quite like old times, *Señor* Pirate, will it not? Almost I am reconciled for having to visit your beastly Gibraltar because we shall travel there like gypsies, across my beautiful Spain —'

Petronilla was caught up in her mother's words. 'And Granada? Is it as beautiful as everyone says?'

'More beautiful!'

Fabiola strolled back round the *lagar* to rejoin Petronilla just in time to hear what had been said. 'Granada is beautiful because the Moors made it so, but where are they now? Sometimes I wonder if anyone who creates beauty can ever be truly lost to God. Me, I would sooner go to Gibraltar!'

'You'll do as you're told, young lady!' Colonel Harris growled at her.

'But, of course, *señor*! Don't I always?'

'Hardly ever!' Doña Pilar told her briskly. 'Now, be quiet, children. If we are to pack our things and be on our way before nightfall, we must make our excuses and explain that we are expected home for luncheon at three o'clock. Nobody will be surprised as it will be supposed Mr Arbuthnot is entertaining some of his old friends amongst the London buyers who have come to Jerez for the celebrations. Is it understood?'

The local band, enthusiastic rather than tuneful, started up, drowning the last of her instructions. Simultaneously, shouts of triumph at the *lagar* announced that the butt had been filled with must and was ready to be carried off to the Bodega of San Gines. Colonel Harris and Mr Arbuthnot exchanged glances and hurried the womenfolk away towards their waiting carriages.

'As Disraeli says: Never explain, never apologize!' Colonel Harris said with a grin. 'At this rate we'll be twenty miles away by nightfall!'

Petronilla, changed into her habit and mounted on the *jaca* her mother had picked out for her what seemed so long ago, looked back towards her husband's *bodega*, thinking that she was the only one of them who seemed at all reluctant to be leaving. There was a picnic atmosphere about the others, as though they were embarking on nothing more than an occasion of social pleasure.

'We'll be home again before you know it!' Charles said, bringing his mount in close beside hers.

She looked at him, her eyes as shadowed as her thoughts. 'I've brought you nothing but trouble, haven't I?'

'You're my wife, Petronilla,' he answered her.

'And that makes me less of a bad bargain?'

He smiled, saying nothing for a long time. She gave him an irritated look, wishing he would go away and leave her alone – anything rather than be so long-suffering and self-righteous and *nice*!

'Bad bargain or not, trouble or not, it means I shall always hold you to it, Mrs Arbuthnot, no matter how far we have to travel for me to prove it to you,' he said at last.

And with that she had to be content.

Book Four

Gibraltar and the Mature Wine

Round and round the rugged Rock the ragged rascals ran.

SIR JOHN FALSTAFF: *If I had a thousand sons, the first human principle I would teach them should be, to forswear thin potations and to addict themselves to sack.*

William Shakespeare, *Henry IV, Part 2* Act IV, Scene III, lines 133–6.

Chapter Seventeen

The journey was an uncomfortable one, especially in the beginning. Colonel Harris had made many a forced march in his youth, but never with women in the party, unless it were his wife; women, moreover, who were accustomed to a gentle morning's trot in the park rather than day after day of hard riding across unsympathetic terrain. Miss Fairman, for one, was exhausted almost before they had begun, bemoaning the fact that nobody had seen fit to bring a carriage for her own and Fabiola's greater comfort.

'It's all very well for you,' she flung at Petronilla, 'you were practically born on a horse like your mother before you! I was spared for more ladylike pursuits!' Her mount stumbled over a half-buried root, causing her to cling on to the saddle pommel for dear life. '*O for a horse with wings!*'

Petronilla chuckled. She would start to worry about her governess when she had no apt quotation with which to make her point. When that happened, Miss Fairman would really be in trouble. Petronilla knew her to be far too spirited to give in easily though; she would back Miss Fairman to be well up in the front by the time they reached Córdoba and probably devoted to her horse as well!

Everywhere there were rumours of bandits travelling the same road as themselves.

'Pooh!' Doña Pilar belittled their fears. 'We have guards!

And we have Colonel Harris to lead us! Why should we be afraid of a few bandits? I'll hear no more complaints from anyone until we see these bandits with our own eyes!'

They didn't have long to wait. Rounding a corner in the rough, stone-strewn road, it was obvious that the previous party of travellers had been set upon some time earlier, two of their number left for dead. The few guards they had went to take a look, spreading out on both sides of the road to make sure there was no danger of a second ambush. Reassured, the guards rejoined the others.

'It would be better if the ladies waited here until we can clear the path,' it was suggested.

Colonel Harris readily agreed with this plan. He and Mr Arbuthnot helped the ladies dismount and then went to see what they could do to help.

'Nothing seems to have changed since I first came to Spain,' he grumbled to his son-in-law. 'The roads are a disgrace and it doesn't seem to be anyone's job to see they're repaired and policed. We wouldn't stand for such conditions for long in England, let me tell you! Best administrators in the world, the British! They could do with a spell of having us in charge over here —'

Charles Arbuthnot lifted an eyebrow. 'The Spanish have a very old civilization of their own. Do you think they'd appreciate being organized by a lot of Protestant upstarts from the North?'

Thomas Harris pulled on his whiskers. 'Mebbe not. It might unite them as nothing else seems able to do, but a lot of British lives would be lost. The truth is, I shan't be happy until we get the ladies safely to our destination. We could have done with half a dozen extra guards along this road!'

Charles suppressed a smile. 'Don't let Doña Pilar or Petronilla hear you calling their abilities into question, sir! They are, both of them, convinced that we couldn't manage the journey without them!'

'Or without Fabiola's prayers!' Colonel Harris grunted.

'That minx will be wasted if she gets her own way and enters Carmel.'

Charles grinned. 'I wonder. She has you more than half convinced that she knows what she's doing, and neither my wife nor I ever expected that!'

'Humph,' The Colonel thought about it. 'I always imagined girls were forced into those places. Shouldn't care for it for any daughter of mine, however devout she turned out to be —'

His son-in-law laughed out loud. 'No danger of that!'

'Glad to hear it,' Thomas responded. 'Marriage is the natural vocation for any woman. Always has been, always will be. She's got a good head on her shoulders, though. I don't mind telling you I miss having her helping me with my speeches in the House. However, her life out here seems to suit her very well. Taken to the sherry world like a duck to water, if her mother is to be believed.'

'Yes, I think she has,' Charles confirmed.

Neither Doña Pilar nor Petronilla had any time for Miss Fairman's complaints about the long ride. Fabiola listened sympathetically for a while, but then she, too, wanted to know what was keeping the men.

'It will be dark in a moment,' she pointed out impatiently. 'Has anyone given any thought as to where we are going to sleep tonight?'

By the time the men returned it was too dark to go much further in any safety. Colonel Harris declared there was a village only a few miles down the road where he had been told there was a *fonda*, a kind of inn, where they would be able to spend the night.

'Good,' Doña Pilar approved. 'Miss Fairman will feel better when she has had something to eat, no?'

Only Petronilla was inclined to argue that she would sooner stay in a *posada* than any *fonda*. 'It's where you'd stay if you were alone, Papa, you know it it!'

'If I were on my own I should probably camp out under the stars! As it is, Mr Arbuthnot and I have your comfort to consider, my dear, and we can't approve of ladies staying in the same establishment as their horses!'

'Not even if the horses are better housed?'

Her father glowered at her. 'Now, now, no impertin ence, young lady! Since when have you ever stayed in either type of establishment?'

'I've heard the comments of some of our wine buyers who travel back and forth across the country all the time —'

'Nevertheless, you will leave it to your father to decide where we stay, *hija mía*,' her mother interrupted smoothly. 'You and I have our husbands to guard us at night; Miss Fairman and Fabiola may well be nervous by themselves. If Tomás says a *fonda* is more suitable, then that it where we shall stay!'

Petronilla said nothing more. The *fonda* was just about as unwelcoming as she had expected and, taking a look round the accommodation, she waited confidently for her father's explosion of disgust when he acquainted himself with the so-called sanitation. It was not long in coming.

'We haven't even got the place to ourselves!' he groaned. 'It's more like a rabbit warren than any inn I've ever been unfortunate enough to patronize!'

'It will do for the one night!' Pilar soothed him. She, too, had surveyed the three main bedchambers with dismay, finding that they all led out of one another, the stairs from down below being at one end of the building and the only private room at the other. 'Who is in that room?' she demanded imperiously.

Petronilla had already discovered a villainous looking character in the end bedchamber. He had come to the door and stared at her with amazement when she had moved her own and Mr Arbuthnot's bedding into the room next door.

'What's a party of gentry doing on the road?' he had asked her. 'Where are you going?'

'We like the exercise,' Petronilla had answered.

He had stared at her harder than ever. 'It's dangerous

on the road these days,' he had given it as his opinion. 'Ladies are better off at home!'

'Tell that to my husband!' Petronilla had invited him cheerfully. 'Are you going far yourself?'

'Far enough,' he had grunted.

Petronilla had decided the man to be a 'gentleman of the road', as she had heard them called in England. When Charles came to inspect their quarters, having agreed with his father-in-law that he and Petronilla should be allotted the room next to the stranger, Miss Fairman and Fabiola the one in the middle, and the Harrises the one next to the stairs, Petronilla lost no time in introducing the two men, longing to know what her husband would make of her 'highwayman'.

'You want to be careful,' Mr Arbuthnot told the stranger. 'We came across the remains of an ambushed party of travellers a few miles back.' He glanced significantly at his wife. 'This isn't the time to be travelling alone!'

The man's lips parted to show a row of rotting and yellowed teeth. 'Better alone, *señor*. I come and go as I please, disappearing like a shadow in the night if need be. That's my trade, as you might say.'

A highwayman indeed! Petronilla congratulated herself. She was more intrigued than disapproving.

'Is it in places like these that you select your victims? It would be easy enough to discover if they were carrying any valuables.'

His jaw dropped. 'I'm an honest man, *señora*, and a patriot!'

'Oh.' She didn't bother to hide her disappointment. 'I thought as you came and went like a shadow —'

Mr Arbuthnot stopped her with a look. 'In England such gentlemen are considered romantic,' he said by way of explanation to the stranger.

'I thought you were both Spanish?' The man's eyes darted from one to the other. 'Truly, you are English? I thought you might be from Compostela way. There are plenty with your colouring up there – and they speak with a funny accent too!' he added to Charles, still suspicious.

'*Claro*,' Petronilla said comfortably. 'My father is the English Colonel you can hear shouting at the landlord downstairs.'

'*Sí, sí*, I hear him!' The man relaxed his guard. He smiled ingratiatingly at Petronilla. 'I am much more romantic than any *bandido*, you can imagine, *señora*, I am what some people call a spy! I buy and sell information to anyone who is prepared to pay for it.'

Petronilla was suitably impressed. 'A spy?' she marvelled. 'I had no idea anyone could make a living from such an occupation. You must meet a lot of interesting people and have a great many stories to tell! How lucky you are staying in the same *fonda* as ourselves! I have always wanted to meet a spy!'

The man was delighted at her interest. 'I have never met any foreigners before,' he confided. 'I am from Barcelona, the greatest city in the world! Have you ever seen my city?'

Petronilla confessed she hadn't. 'It's possible my father has been there. You must talk to him about it.'

'It is a much greater city than Madrid.'

'I haven't been to Madrid either,' Petronilla confessed.

'You don't want to go there! The usurper whore, Isabella, holds court in Madrid —'

Petronilla's innocent expression disappeared at the mere mention of the Doña Isabella. 'You spy for Don Carlos!' she accused him sharply.

He nodded, dismayed to be suddenly confronted by a virago who knew much more about Spanish politics than he thought any foreigner had any business knowing. 'Don Carlos is the rightful King of Spain,' he offered in placating tones. 'We don't have females on our throne!'

'Since when?' Petronilla's voice shook with anger. 'The French may have introduced their stupid Salic law here, but Spain will never be a part of France while there are loyal Spaniards to fight for the independence of their country.'

Mr Arbuthnot put a warning hand on her shoulder. 'England has a queen, which is why my wife is so heated on the subject. Women have little understanding of any country's politics, but how many of us men can convince them of anything they don't want to believe?'

The spy gave Petronilla a sidelong glance, noting the angry look she gave her husband. 'Spain needs a king, whatever may be the case in England. That is why I am here, to see if Andalucía will rise if Don Carlos should call on them to do so. The sooner, the better, if all we hear from Madrid is true!'

'It's outrageous! Is that poor woman never to have any peace?'

'She should abdicate in her uncle's favour,' the man insisted. 'We'd be better off without her – *and* her mother –'

'And would Don Carlos be any better?' Petronilla demanded scornfully.

'He could get his own heirs!'

Petronilla blinked at the vulgarity. She was beginning to think Charles was right and she would have done better to keep a still tongue in her head. 'I don't wish to hear any more!' she declared rather more grandly than she felt. 'I'm going downstairs to join the others.'

'Good idea!' her husband said drily. He shook his head at her retreating back. 'Are you married, *señor*? No? Then you won't understand, any more than I do, how it is that our wives always know better than we do ourselves!'

The man grinned slowly. 'She's a handsome woman, whatever her politics. I thought all English women were blonde with blue eyes, but she has the black eyes and straight back of a Spanish lady. You're a lucky man, *señor*! I'm sorry I shan't be staying the night but must be on my way before midnight. It won't do you any good to try to follow me, for I shall be long gone before you get that parcel of women back on the road. If you're wise, you'll forget you've seen me!'

Mr Arbuthnot nodded gravely. 'I'll pass the message on to my wife and make sure she listens! You don't need to worry about her telling anyone she's seen you. She'll have forgotten all about you by morning when some new diversion takes her fancy.'

The man sniffed, wiping his mouth and nose on the back of his sleeve. 'Like any woman, *señor*,' he grunted. 'I wouldn't have believed she was English though if I hadn't heard her father speaking Spanish. *He's* a foreigner right enough – and so are you!'

Petronilla, overhearing this exchange as she made her retreat, was at first indignant and then amused. It would obviously be much better if the spy didn't meet either her mother or Fabiola, but there was no harm in telling her father of his presence. She had an idea that Colonel Harris would be more than interested in this strange character.

He was. She could tell by the sudden brightness in his eyes and the sidelong glance he gave towards the other women.

'I suppose you want me to keep them out of the way while you have your conversation with him?' she agreed with resignation.

'It might be better,' he agreed.

'It would certainly be better! He thinks we're an English party having a look round Spain the hard way. Charles had some difficulty explaining my Spanish looks to him; I don't think his reputation for veracity would survive an introduction to Mamá and Fabiola. My husband is quite clever sometimes,' she added thoughtfully, 'though he might have thought of something nicer to say about me than that I'm given to female flutters of high fancy!'

'Aren't you, if only sometimes, where he's concerned? Be off with you, my dear!'

Shaken by her father's sly teasing, Petronilla gathered up the other ladies, suggesting they should oversee the cooking of their evening meal. Doña Pilar, seeing the sense of this at once, led the way into the kitchens, poking the fire, glancing in every cooking pot, berating the unfortunate girl who was preparing some rotten vegetables, and finally undertaking the preparations herself with the same thoroughness with which she did everything she tackled.

It could not have been a more Spanish scene, Petronilla thought with some amusement. She hoped the spy would not take it into his head to come and find out what all the noise was about.

'This fire is only cold-hot!' her mother declared. 'It must be hot-hot! Blow on it, girl! And you,' she commanded the reluctant innkeeper, 'why is there no bread for us? Bring flour and salt! Go, go, we wish to eat before morning, not tomorrow night! Fabiola, see if there are any melons and maybe some olives!'

'Not melons,' Fabiola complained. 'Melons in the morning are pure gold; at midday, silver, but at night, they are lead!'

'You are too young to suffer from indigestion!' Doña Pilar declared roundly. 'You don't hear Miss Fairman complaining —'

'I'm too sore to complain!' the governess wailed.

Doña Pilar didn't even look up. 'Petronilla will go and see the horses are properly fed. If this is the best the village has for human beings, that is one thing, but if the horses are to go all day tomorrow, they need *cebada y paja*! How do you say *cebo* in English? Fodder, is it not? The horses must have the best fodder you can find! You hear me, daughter?'

'Yes, Mamá.'

Petronilla was not averse to leaving the cooking in her mother's capable hands. She had never seen her parent in better spirits, rushing about the kitchen with little dancing steps, becoming more Spanish by the moment as she shrieked her instructions in the Andalucían dialect, making use of anyone and everyone who came within her range. At another time, she might have been surprised that Doña

Pilar knew how to cook a whole meal for so many, for she had never done any such thing as Mrs Harris in England, but she had learned to know her mother better since coming to Spain and she had little doubt that she could turn her hand to most things if it involved her own comfort or survival. What was more, she would do it well, better than many of the cooks she had employed from time to time, and certainly much better than Petronilla could ever do.

The village was bigger than she had expected. A few black-clad old crones stood in their doorways and watched her pass in the moonlight. She felt as though she was being watched every inch of the way and she began to wish she had not set forth alone, but had waited until Charles had been free to go with her. Two men came rushing towards her, slapping each other on the back, both of them rolling drunk, bottles of cheap liquor in their fists, the only thing that prevented them from knocking each other's heads off. Surprised to see such violence in two villagers, Petronilla looked at them more closely and saw they wore the tattered remains of army uniforms – whose it wasn't light enough to see. She was grateful when they had passed her by without noticing her and she hurried her footsteps towards the stables, hoping not to meet anyone else.

Their own guards had joined the local grooms for a game of cards and were far from pleased to see her.

'Can we not be trusted to feed the beasts? Would we let our own animals starve, let alone yours?'

'Of course not,' Petronilla sought to reassure them. 'My mother had enough help in the kitchen —'

'Ah, the Doña Pilar would want to know her *jaca* is well looked after!' Petronilla wondered why it was acceptable for her mother, but not for herself, to be interested in the welfare of her mount, but she said nothing, for all their lives might depend on these men sooner or later.

'She sent me to find out if you were being well looked

after too,' she smiled at them. 'She's cooking enough food for everybody.'

But they refused the invitation, preferring to stay where they were, relaxing amongst their new friends. Only their leader, a young man who had trained as a soldier himself, walked with her back into the dusty street.

'We are not the only people staying in the village, *señora*. An ugly lot of vagabonds by all accounts. Their leader is staying up at the *fonda*, so be careful, Doña Petronilla, and warn your father, will you?'

'My father is talking to him now. He's a Carlist spy — '

'Hush.'

'You're quite right!' She lowered her voice to a conspiratorial whisper. 'He's leaving before midnight. He said so.'

'His horse is saddled up and waiting for him. Tell the *Señor* Colonel, or the *Señor* Arbootno, that I am watching him.' He opened the barn door for her. *¡Buenas noches, señora!*'

She replied in kind and was about to depart when he pulled her back inside again. 'Is that the man?'

She marvelled at his sharp eyes for she could see no one in the shadowed street. Then she heard his footsteps and nodded her head, pointing towards the stables at the back where she could hide herself until he had gone.

She didn't have long to wait. The man was up on his horse and gone almost before she had hidden herself away. He rode like a madman, sawing at the reins to his horse's distress, and the dislike Petronilla had felt for him from the first, took shape in her mind and in the bad taste in her mouth.

'Are all Carlists mad?' she asked in a whisper.

'All Spaniards are mad if they think it'll make any difference to who is on the throne,' the guard sighed. 'The woman or the uncle, we still have to eat and bring the next generation into the world, and we need peace and quiet to do that, not fighting each other to the death.'

'My uncles died in the cause,' Petronilla told him.

'So the Doña Pilar told me. Maybe it's different for you *hidalgos*, you don't have to work to survive like the rest of us, but I have my family to think of and how my wife would manage without the money I bring home.'

'Have you been married long?' Petronilla asked.

'A few months only. I remember the day you were wed,' he added shyly. 'I had no work then, but Don Arbootno took me on to keep an eye on you when you went out into the vineyards —'

'He didn't tell me!' Petronilla said indignantly.

'No, I was to keep out of sight, unless your cousin came back and attacked you again. It was the first work I'd had for a long time and my *novia* and I asked permission to marry also. Don Arbootno said I could always be sure of work in the *bodega*.'

'I see. Did anyone else know you were keeping an eye on me?'

'Your mother knew, *señora*. There is very little that escapes her where her family is concerned. Many times she has asked me to see you don't work too hard in the vineyards.'

Petronilla was astonished. He was a burly young man, with the looks that went with his Moorish ancestry. 'What's your name?' she asked him.

'Pablo Rodriguez.'

'Well, Pablo Rodriguez, will you walk me back to the *fonda*? I think I've had enough excitement for one evening.'

He left her at the door to the *fonda* yard, sketching her a salute as he watched her go inside.

'Where have you been?' her anxious father greeted her. 'And who was that with you?'

'Pablo Rodriguez.' She sniffed the air. 'Is dinner ready? I'm ravenous!'

'I suppose you went to check on the horses? Was that your idea?'

'Mamá's.'

Her father looked grim. 'I'm glad Pablo was there to

see you safely back here. I didn't like the look of that Carlist fellow. He asked how you came to speak Spanish like a native. I told him the language was close enough to Italian for you to have picked it up very quickly. I only hope he believed me!'

'I don't see why not,' Petronilla murmured. 'He knows Charles and I are married because we were together in the room next to his, and he could hardly mistake you for anything other than an Englishman, so I must be English also!'

She made to go towards the kitchen, but her father put a hand on her sleeve to hold her back, frowning.

Petronilla stopped willingly enough, putting her own hand over her father's in a gesture of the affection that had always lain between them.

'What is it, Papá?'

'He asked me if I had anything to do with Gibraltar. Like them all, he wants an early return of the Rock to Spanish control, but he seems to know more about it than he should if he had never been there. Love, I asked him if he knew anything about Don Diego Salcedo Morena, saying I'd been told by the Gibraltarian authorities that he's a Carlist also. He knew him right enough. Said he was supposed to be raising money for the Carlist funds. Everybody smuggles everything in and out of Gibraltar! I pretended the only time I'd seen the place was when I arrived in Spain because I don't want any trouble until we have Fabiola safely back with her family, and the rest of you —'

Petronilla lifted her chin. 'We always knew Cousin Diego had declared for Don Carlos,' she reminded him.

The pressure of her father's fingers increased. 'Gibraltar is my business, Pet. *British* business.'

Petronilla forced a smile. 'Don't let Mamá hear you! She won't admit the Fat Rock has anything to do with the British!'

'No Spaniard does,' her father sighed. 'Nevertheless, all the while we hold Gibraltar, we hold the entrance to the

Mediterranean. She wouldn't really want us to give that up with Europe in the state it is.'

Petronilla marvelled that any man, even her father, could be so blind. What did Doña Pilar care about the rest of Europe? She cared only for Spain's honour and the affront that British control of Gibraltar offered to that honour. Petronilla thought she'd care a lot less whether the Carlists or the Cristinos held the Rock, anything would be preferable to having another nation insisting on remaining on their doorstep.

'Smuggling would appeal to Cousin Diego almost as much as bull fighting,' she said aloud. 'I only hope, for his sake, that he's better at it!'

Her father gave her a satisfied look. 'Give me Don Arbootno every time!' he glinted at her.

In that moment she looked so like her mother that he gasped. The smile held that same hint of mischief and something more, something he had never expected to see in his daughter. She walked ahead of him, a slight swing to her hips, looking back at him over her shoulder. '*Muy hombre* that Don Arbootno,' she mocked him.

He choked. 'Petronilla!'

But she had already glanced round the kitchen, seen her husband wasn't there, and was making for the stairs to see if he was still upstairs in their room.

There had been a new arrival since she had been gone. She heard their voices from the top of the steps and hurried to see who it was her husband was talking to. She recognized the stranger at once, a smile of pleasure breaking over her face.

'Mr Clarke!'

Mr Arbuthnot turned to face his wife. 'You know each other?'

Petronilla nodded enthusiastically. 'Mr Clarke represents Berry Brothers, in St James Street. He came to see us in Montilla, but we had very little to offer him. Mamá will be delighted to see you again!'

'As I am you, Miss Harris.'

'Mrs Arbuthnot now,' Petronilla said simply. 'Do you two know each other also?'

'By reputation,' Mr Clarke answered her. 'Your husband was telling me he's bought his own *bodega*. I can't tell you how much I envy him – envy you both, for Arbuthnot tells me you're his partner in everything, ma'am! I hope to do business with you. You won't do any better in London than to deal with Berry's of St James!'

'True.' Petronilla knew it to be a very good offer, but she was afraid of having an exclusive contract quite yet. It would be different if she could be sure they would always have enough of their own sherry to fulfil the bargain, but that wouldn't be this year, or next. 'Come back in a couple of years' time and we'll have a deal!'

Mr Clarke's eyes slid from her to her husband. 'Arbuthnot and I can sort it out when I next come to Jerez, though I gather things are vastly improved at Montilla!'

'Have you been there recently?'

'I was there last month. I'm on my way to Jerez now.'

Mr Arbuthnot came to life. 'Good, I can ask you to call in on Doña Louise? She's keeping an eye on the vintage for us —'

Mr Clarke's eyes gleamed. 'Could she do with a hand? I mean, I'm a bit ahead of myself to do much buying for this year's vintage. Would she mind if I spent some time at Arbuthnots? I've had enough of the road for the time being?'

'You'd be more than welcome,' both the Arbuthnots agreed in unison. Petronilla swallowed down her irritation of a moment earlier when she had felt Mr Clarke would have done better not to have made it quite so clear that he planned to do business only with the male partner of Arbuthnots. She rather looked forward to disillusioning him if ever they did do business together! 'You're welcome to dine with us also,' she added, 'though quite what my mother has found to cook for us downstairs, I don't know!'

Both men were amused by her description of her mother rolling up her sleeves and organizing the kitchen as a general would his army.

'And I'll tell you something else,' Petronilla went on, making sure she had her husband's full attention, 'this is the last time that any of us stay in a *fonda*, no matter what my father says! The *posadas* may have fewer members of the gentry knocking on their doors, but I'll not be separated from the horses again. I was frightened out of my wits walking down the road in the dark —'

'You did what?' Charles Arbuthnot demanded.

'It was all right, your "watch-dog" walked me back again, but I don't fancy running into Carlists in the dark – or in the daytime, for that matter!'

Charles's eyes narrowed as he looked at her. 'Wherever we stay, you're not to go out alone again – anywhere!' he commanded.

She smiled at him through her lashes. 'Will you come with me?'

'No, baggage, I'll keep you chained to the bed every night!'

She giggled, forgetting all about Mr Clarke. 'Is that a promise?' then she sobered up, biting her lip. 'As long as you help me persuade Papá about the *posadas*, I'll do anything you ask. Perhaps we could tell him they're more hygienic, what do you think?'

Mr Clarke stifled a laugh. 'Sharing the facilities with the horses?'

'Better than with the Carlist spies!' Petronilla insisted.

Doña Pilar was as pleased to see Mr Clarke again as Petronilla had been. 'You went by the *bodega* at Montilla? Did you see all the work we have done since you were last there?'

They sat round the scrubbed wooden table in the kitchen while the innkeeper, now completely reconciled to Doña Pilar's unorthodox methods, brought the food to the table. A brace of plump chickens formed the centre of the dish, bedded on saffron rice, flavoured with walnuts, dried figs and anything else that had been lying round the kitchen. Seeing the inn's servants were holding back, Doña Pilar made room for them round the table herself, bidding them join the feast. Colonel Harris was less happy with this arrangement, but Petronilla had already learned that this was the Spanish way and she approved of it, knowing that nobody would respect her mother any the less because of her easy ways.

'You don't have to worry they'll take advantage of her, Papá,' she tried to comfort him, dismayed by his obvious discomfort.

'You, both of you, look and behave more like Spaniards every day!' he complained.

She was glad he had spoken in English. 'We're living in Spain,' she pointed out quietly. 'She'll be as English again as you could wish when you take her back to England.'

'She looks completely happy where she is!'

'She's always happy when you're with her. She looked more "penny plain" than "twopence coloured" before you joined us. Poor Mamá! She can never be truly happy away from you!'

Colonel Harris had always enjoyed his family's re-enactments of any play he had taken them to see. He had made Petronilla a small cardboard theatre with his own hands, treating her to the cast list of characters that were often to be obtained after a successful run, twopence for the coloured variety and only a penny for those that came in black and white. He smiled now at Petronilla's allusion.

'And you? Do you feel "penny plain" when you're away from Charles?'

Petronilla considered the question, a little surprised to find it might be true of her just as much as it was true of her mother. Yet how could it be? Her mother had always been in love with her father, but she . . .

'I like things just the way they are, when we're all together!' she claimed.

'Hmph, your mother's love of adventure! I've been

meaning to warn you all, whatever you do, *don't* drink the water unless it's been boiled first. I have a friend in London who insists that dirty water is the source of cholera amongst other things. Did you hear me, Pilar?'

His wife smiled at him across the table. 'Of course I hear you, Tomás, because I like to listen to every word you say! Only, this time Petronilla is right and we shall stay in *posadas* from now on. When I am obliged to relieve myself I prefer the company of horses to that of vermin. We can boil the water equally well wherever we are, no?'

The Colonel's ill-humour vanished as if it had never been. 'Yes, dear, it will make it even more of an adventure to stay in *posadas* – our adventures always turn out to be uncomfortable –'

Doña Pilar broke the wishbone off one of the chickens and held it out to him across the table, her eyes gleaming with laughter.

'I remember only the best times, *tirano odioso, mi esposo!*'

There might as well have been no one else there at all.

Miss Fairman refused to go any further than Córdoba.

'You'll make much better time without me,' she said firmly. 'I shall probably join Doña Rosa at Montilla –'

'Yes, and I shall go with you,' Doña Pilar decided unexpectedly. 'Petronilla will chaperon Fabiola, and we older ladies shall be comfortable together until you come back for us.'

'I believe you'll do anything not to be obliged to accompany Papá to Gibraltar!' Petronilla accused her.

Her mother flushed, looking both cross and stubborn. 'And what business is that of yours?' she demanded.

Petronilla hugged her. 'Papá will be disappointed.'

Doña Pilar shrugged. 'He knows where I am,' she said firmly.

Petronilla had not been to Granada before and sometimes it seemed to her they would never get there, travelling day after day across the hot, golden land that was Spain. Fabiola insisted her city was the most beautiful of them all, which Petronilla and her father both found difficult to believe. Only Mr Arbuthnot nodded and told them to wait and see, that it was everything the young girl claimed it to be.

Then, when they had practically given up hope of ever reaching the ancient Moorish capital, there it lay before them, nestling under snow-capped mountains.

Mr Arbuthnot halted his mount beside his awed wife.

> '. . . *and look around you;*' he quoted softly,
> '*The city is a lady whose husband is the mountain.*
> *The river's girdle clasps her hand, and the flowers*
> *Smile like the jewels that twinkle at her throat.*'

'Whoever said that?' Petronilla asked him.

'Ibn Zamrak, a long, long time ago, when your ancestors were fighting the War of the Roses, and mine were busy murdering each other also.'

It was several minutes before Petronilla answered, and then she said, 'How much he must have loved it here. How sad it must have been when they all had to go.'

Her husband gave a sideways glance. 'That, too, was a long time ago,' he said.

Chapter Eighteen

The Moors might have been expelled from their last stronghold in Granada long before, but their presence was as real as if the Catholic Kings had never been. The cathedral belonged to the Catholic Kings, Doña Isabel I and her husband: the Alhambra, crowning the hill that looked down on the rest of the city, was a splendid legacy of the last flowering of that Islamic civilization that, in one of those paradoxes of history, had restored to Europe much of the Classical learning that had begun in Egypt, Greece and Rome, adding the foundations of modern mathematics and medicine to that store of precious knowledge that had made it possible for the countries of Western Europe to climb out of the Dark Ages into the industrial present.

Petronilla had always understood from her mother that this was the explanation for the explosion of energy that had led to Spain and Portugal colonizing so much of the world, before the gold of the New World had brought about the debilitating inflation that had dissipated their power, leaving them with a glorious past and an uncertain, precarious future, at the mercy of other, younger powers who had little love for those who had thwarted their own dreams and ambitions for so long.

Granada brought all this back to her, like an illustrated

history book she had long ago discarded thinking she had no further use for it. She turned eagerly to her father.

'It's a beautiful city – it reminds me of Mamá, though she always claims Córdoba to be her city!'

'Very Spanish,' he commented wryly. 'A ruined paradise.'

She put her head on one side, considering the matter. 'The British would rebuild it, no doubt, but it wouldn't be the same. It would be efficient, but much less beautiful, don't you think?'

He snorted a protest. 'Some of our landowners are constructing ruins in their grounds because they think them romantic. There's nothing romantic about a collection of useless buildings!'

But Petronilla refused to be put down. 'Perhaps they'll find a use for it – one day. Meanwhile, whatever you say, I'd sooner live here than in many places in England! You know they say in Spain that every man is a king; we can't make that claim at home, can we?'

'Being poor is the same everywhere.'

Petronilla looked about her. 'That I don't believe. It must be easier where it's warm and where one can grow something to eat, even in the winter.'

Colonel Harris set his shoulders against such an idea. 'And what is there to spur them on to bettering themselves? If you mollycoddle the poor they'll never do anything for themselves, but expect those who've made a better go of things to give them hand-outs for the rest of their lives!'

Petronilla gave him an exasperated look. 'Is that what you're saying in the House these days?'

'More or less. Don't you approve? The Irish come flocking over —'

'Would you rather they died of starvation at home?'

His smile was reluctant. 'Like your mother, *you'd* rather they all sat round the table with us, but it wouldn't do in the long run. It would be patronizing to expect another able-bodied human being to acccpt charity when he can work for a living!'

Petronilla remained unconvinced. 'Must it be charity, Papá? It might be justice —'

Mr Arbuthnot shook his head at them both. 'If you'd stop arguing for a moment, Fabiola is trying to tell us we're going the wrong way for her parents' house.'

Petronilla turned back at once. 'Is it far?' she asked the Spanish girl. 'It will be dark in a minute.'

'It's dark now,' Fabiola pointed out.

'Why didn't you tell us we were going the wrong way?'

Fabiola tossed her head. 'I don't care how late we arrive! Besides, I like to hear you and your father arguing! I *never* say anything to my parents if I can help it. Not that they'd listen, they never listen to anything I say.'

Petronilla laughed. 'Poor Fabiola! Your filial piety is so inspiring! What will your parents do without you?'

Fabiola pulled down the corners of her mouth and Petronilla saw to her surprise that she was very close to tears. 'It isn't my fault I don't want to go home!' the Spanish girl declared. 'Who knows what Immaculada has told them about me! They sent for her to go home to look after my sisters, but me they only want to marry off to someone I don't like —'

'They may have changed their mind by now,' Petronilla sought to comfort her.

Fabiola looked at her with tear-drenched eyes. 'They think him a hero, fighting in the cause of Don Carlos. Why should they change their mind? What do they know of him as a *bandido*? They won't listen to me! To them I am still a child, with no mind of my own, someone to be dismissed back to the nursery whenever I tell them something they don't wish to hear!'

'We'll see,' said Petronilla. 'Perhaps my father will persuade them —'

'Your father is a foreigner and a heretic.' Fabiola ran her reins through her gloved fingers, giving herself up to misery. 'It isn't because they support Don Carlos that they think well of Don Diego. It's all the same to them if Don Carlos or Doña Isabella is on the throne. Our family is far older and more illustrious than anything of which they can boast. They admire Don Diego because they think he is like them, from an old family – *blue-blooded* and as proud as they are themselves.'

'My mother will have told them differently.'

Fabiola brightened. 'And that she approves of my entering Carmel next year?'

Petronilla doubted that very much. Doña Pilar would expect Fabiola to do her duty, whatever her parents decided for her, and whatever she wished for her herself. Her father would be far more likely to intervene on Fabiola's behalf, but even Fabiola could see that her parents would be unlikely to listen to him.

It was really dark by the time they reached the street where the Ensenadas made their home.

'I wish we could have arrived in daylight,' Colonel Harris worried aloud. 'I sent them warning of our coming some days back, but who knows if they will have received my message.'

Fabiola, however, was in no doubt about her welcome. She clapped her hands together and shouted for the *soreno*, greeting the man who came running down the street towards them, a huge bunch of keys in his hand, and bidding him help her dismount.

'Doña Fabiola! Do your parents expect you tonight?'

'Open the door and we'll find out,' she commanded him, offering him a coin from her purse.

It was immediately clear that not only were they not expected, they were not welcome either. Petronilla had her first glimpse of Fabiola's father, a stiff, straight-backed gentleman, as he came to the door himself, nodding the two footmen to go about their business.

'So you have decided to come home at last,' he said to his daughter.

'Yes, Papá. Didn't you get Doña Pilar's letter?'

'I received a letter from a Mrs Harris —'

'Doña Pilar Morena,' Fabiola confirmed. 'This is her daughter, Doña Petronilla Harris y Morena, the wife of Don Carlos Arbootno. My father, Don Lorenzo Ensenada.'

He bowed gravely to Petronilla. 'I thank you for bringing my daughter back to me.' He hesitated. 'Forgive my confusion, but I thought it was you whom my daughter's fiancé had determined to marry in her stead?'

It was Mr Arbuthnot who answered for her. 'There was little danger of that, sir. Unfortunately Don Diego is my wife's cousin, but, as my father-in-law will confirm, neither she nor my mother-in-law have anything to do with him.'

'Are you a Spaniard, sir?'

'I'm a Scot,' Charles answered.

'A Catholic?'

'As is my wife.'

The old man frowned out into the darkness. 'Her English father is a heretic?'

Petronilla gave him look for look. She was not accustomed to being kept waiting on anyone's doorstep. 'My father fought at Salamanca in the War of Independence. My mother and I are very proud of him.'

'Nevertheless, I have my younger daughters to consider. I cannot expose them to the company of an English heretic. Perhaps your husband and he can find lodgings somewhere else in Granada. You, yourself, are welcome to our hospitality, Doña Petronilla, for Fabiola's sake —'

'I prefer to be with my husband!' Petronilla declared roundly.

Fabiola stole a hand into hers. 'Please, Petronilla, stay with me! Please don't leave me!'

Petronilla's good nature had no defence against such an appeal. She was, however, deeply offended by the welcome they had received and, whereas when she had first come to Spain she would have lacked the confidence to make any complaint, she was well equal to the task now.

'I haven't the least intention of abandoning you on the doorstep like an orphan in the storm. If we are not to be invited in, you will naturally remain under our care until we are able to restore you to your family in a more seemly fashion. You tell me this is your father and so I am forced to believe you, but I am at a total loss as to why he sees fit to act as his own butler, nor why he should deal so discourteously with his daughter's friends, no matter what the circumstances. No doubt we shall receive some kind of an explanation when we return in the morning.'

She thought, not without amusement, that Fabiola had never heard anyone address her father with such evident disapproval. At first, she was so pale that the girl looked about to faint, then her colour came flooding back into her face, as she grasped Petronilla's hand with a new resolution.

'I am so ashamed, Papá. Doña Pilar —'

'You may well be ashamed!' her father returned grimly. 'Your behaviour is not what I expect from a member of my family, though I am well aware you have been led astray —'

Petronilla cut him off with an imperious lift of one eyebrow. 'By my mother, Don Lorenzo?'

'I have no complaints —'

'I should think not!' Petronilla retorted. 'She had no hesitation in taking your daughter in when she arrived unannounced, escorted by her *accompañadora*, it is true, but scarcely an adequate chaperon for a young girl destined to enter Carmel as soon as she is allowed to do so. You are very fortunate we are able to return her to your care alive, in these days when the roads are full of bad men intent on mischief – my cousin, Don Diego, amongst them, I regret to say.'

Don Lorenzo's complacency was shattered. 'Doña Petronilla, I must beg you to come inside with my daughter! By tomorrow, I promise you, we shall be better organized to receive your father and your husband, but for tonight there is only my wife and daughters at home.'

He wrung his hands together in distress. 'I can't expose them to the danger of a heretic going about the Devil's work amongst them – oh dear, your father! Forgive me, you have reason to complain of your welcome, but what am I to do? You're accustomed —'

Petronilla took pity on him. 'My father will quite understand your difficulty,' she assured him. 'He feels exactly the same way! He was deeply upset to know of your daughter's vocation, I may tell you, and not just because he's a Protestant and has some very curious ideas about the tasks nuns are expected to perform. I'm afraid he's still of the opinion that she thinks it the only alternative to a marriage she can't like! He's positively explosive on the subject and so I warn you!'

Colonel Harris watched his daughter's performance with a grudging appreciation. He felt a foreigner in her presence and suspected that Charles Arbuthnot did as well. The younger man had been silent throughout the interchange, standing negligently to one side as if the whole affair had nothing to do with him.

'Well I'll be damned!' Thomas swore under his breath as Petronilla marched down the front-door steps.

'Probably,' his son-in-law murmured. 'She's very much your daughter, isn't she?'

'I was thinking how very Spanish she's become!'

'On the contrary, sir, Spain is in full retreat!'

Petronilla wondered why the two men were laughing. It didn't seem a laughing matter to her that they should be obliged to find alternative lodgings after dark in a strange city. Her father was no longer a young man and she thought that their travels across Spain, with him insisting on being responsible for all the arrangements, had aged him still further. How much better it would have been if she could have gone with Charles, leaving her father to a comfortable early night inside.

'Please look after him,' she whispered to Charles. 'He's tired. It's disgraceful he should be treated like this, but I can't abandon Fabiola after all this time.'

'He'll be all right with me,' her husband promised. He touched her cheek with a gentle finger. 'It would have rejoiced your mother's heart to see you tackle that *beato*, my love!'

'I hope so,' she responded gravely. 'But it's your opinion —'

'Petronilla!' Fabiola's voice came to them. 'Do come quickly! Mamá is waiting dinner!'

'I wish I were coming with you both!' Petronilla said rather forlornly.

Her father was the first to turn away. 'Your first duty is to that child,' he said gruffly. 'We'll see you tomorrow, Pet. Goodnight.'

By the time dinner was over, Petronilla wished more than ever that she had gone with the others. Don Lorenzo spent the meal glaring at his unfortunate daughter. Petronilla wondered what the voluble Immaculada had told him of their hasty departure for Montilla and what she had learned about Don Diego since arriving there. She thought it would have had very little relation to reality for poor Immaculada would have been terrified that she might be blamed in any way for the escapade by her so-called relations. She had her own future to consider, a future she intended to be as comfortable as that of anyone in her position. Nor had she much relished being sent back to Granada by train for no better reason that she could see than that Fabiola had wished to be rid of her in order to accompany her hostess on a headlong ride to Jerez to greet Colonel Harris at last.

Fabiola's mother, Doña Teresa, never uttered once throughout the whole meal. She ate in a stolid silence, without interest either in the food or the others at the table. Only once the ladies had retired to the *salon*, and were awaiting Don Lorenzo, did she say to Petronilla – after spreading her fan and flapping it to and fro for a whole minute – 'You will have to share Fabiola's room. It is the only one we have kept aired. In Granada everything becomes damp – even in the summer. The humidity is terrible!'

Fabiola's lips trembled mutinously. 'Granada has a beautiful climate, Mamá!'

Doña Teresa ignored her. 'My husband tells me you are married, Doña Petronilla?'

'To Charles Arbuthnot, of Jerez,' Petronilla confirmed.

'We had heard you were to marry your cousin, Don Diego Salcedo Morena.'

Petronilla waited for her usual reaction to the mention of her cousin to hit her. To her relief, she felt absolutely nothing at all.

'There was never any danger of that,' she said aloud. 'Even if I had been willing, my parents would never have given their consent to such a match. Don Diego is a cross my family has to bear, not someone we welcome willingly into our homes. Both my uncles died for their support of the Queen.'

Doña Teresa's fan never paused in its movements back and forth. 'He is an old-fashioned gentleman, no? A soldier —'

'And a traitor!'

'A traitor to whom? Not to Spain, surely?'

Petronilla refused to be intimidated. 'To his family. His latest escapade was to get himself half-killed in a bullfight. Even Tío Ambrosio will find it hard to forgive his nephew playing the matador!'

'He wasn't killed?'

'No.'

Fabiola made another attempt to join in the conversation. 'He tried to murder Doña Petronilla —'

'Nonsense, child!' her mother cut her off. 'You are speaking of your *novio*, the man your father has chosen to be your husband.'

Petronilla looked at Fabiola's quenched expression and decided nothing could be gained by continuing this conversation. She rose to her feet, stifling a yawn.

'Forgive me, Fabiola my dear, but I shall be falling

asleep where I sit if I stay here any longer! Besides, you will wish to be private with your parents —'

'No, no,' Fabiola said in a hurry. 'I shall come with you! Goodnight, Mamá!'

Doña Teresa didn't even look up when the two young women left her alone in the room. It was almost as if she didn't notice their going.

Sitting up in the middle of the large box-bed that dwarfed the tiny bedchamber, which Fabiola had chosen to make her own sooner than share with any of her younger sisters, the Spanish girl watched Petronilla as she brushed out her hair for the night. 'You see how it is?' she demanded. 'They haven't even provided you with a maid to help you to bed!'

'I imagine they thought that if you can manage without assistance, so can I!' Petronilla answered smoothly. Inwardly she doubted if her hosts had thought about the matter at all.

'It's humiliating! I told them how kind you and your mother have been for *months*, and how comfortable you both made me!'

'Don't think about it,' Petronilla recommended, climbing into bed. 'Move over, will you?'

Fabiola settled herself down to sleep, the tears forcing a path between her lids. She sniffed pathetically.

'They're going to make me marry him, aren't they?' she whispered at last.

'Certainly not! Mr Arbuthnot will speak to your father in the morning and, if that doesn't answer, we'll take you away with us again and return you to my mother until you're old enough to enter Carmel.'

Delighted, Fabiola flung her arms about her friend. 'You mean it? Doña Pilar will keep me with her?'

'She won't have to,' Petronilla answered sleepily, 'Charles will arrange everything, you'll see!'

She was almost asleep before it occurred to her to wonder how her husband was going to carry out such a feat. And why him, and not her father? She hugged herself under the bedclothes, wishing Charles were beside her, for she was lonely without him. *She loved Charles Arbuthnot!* The idea smote her like a sledgehammer, driving all thoughts of sleep out of her mind. Married to him, she had finally grown up, she thought, wondering how she could ever have been so young and heedless as to imagine herself to be dazzled by her worthless cousin when Charles had been waiting for her, solid, serious, and the best thing that had ever happened to her! Darling Charles! She thought back to the last time they had made love and marvelled at the hunger her whole body felt for his touch and the whispered endearments that had become so precious to her. She would not, willingly, spend another night away from him, she vowed, and so she would tell him at the very first opportunity she had! And at last she slept.

Fabiola brought her a cup of chocolate and a buttered roll in the morning, explaining that she had no confidence in her mother having made any other arrangements for Petronilla's breakfast.

'Where have you been so early?' Petronilla demanded.

'Hush! I slipped out to Mass.' Fabiola sat down on the edge of the bed. 'It isn't that I don't believe Mr Arbuthnot will do everything in his power to help me, but only God can decide if he will be successful.'

Petronilla grinned. 'So you thought you'd give him a push in the right direction?'

Fabiola shook her head. 'I might have done yesterday,' she admitted. 'Today, I am resolved to carry out his will, whatever it may be.' Her voice shook dangerously. 'Only, I don't think I could bear it if he wants me to marry Don Diego! I have always disliked your cousin —'

Petronilla was impressed. 'And were never deceived by his charming exterior as I was,' she ended for her. 'I can't dislike him, you know, even now, but I should hate to be married to him also!'

'Oh, I've known that for ages! Your husband is just

right for you, but it's your father I adore! I know he is a Lutheran —'

'He's nothing of the sort! He's Church of England! Most English people are.'

Fabiola creased up her brow. 'There's a difference between one kind of a Protestant and another?'

'Yes, of course!'

'Oh, I didn't know. Never mind, God will forgive him. He is a very good man, I think.'

'I think so, too,' his daughter agreed, as solemn as her mother was when discussing her father's faith. 'Mamá says she has done her best and the rest is up to God. She thinks he has a pretty good chance of getting to heaven despite his religion. It has something to do with a Samaritan woman in the Bible – and don't ask me who she was because I don't know. Miss Fairman would be able to quote you chapter and verse —'

Fabiola looked at her with big eyes. 'The Samaritans were as bad as heretics?'

Petronilla didn't know that either, but she refused to admit as much. 'Have I time to find out where the others put up for the night before your parents will expect me to wait on them?' she asked instead.

Fabiola cleared the empty cup away. 'If you hurry! I'll come straight back in case you need any help.'

So there was to be no maid this morning either. Petronilla was thankful that her clothes were on the simple side. Even her boots, though extremely fashionable, had been chosen with the use they would be put to in mind. Petronilla had been greatly taken with the new toe-caps and heels made of leather that were far more long-wearing than any kind of cloth could be. Better still, they were shaped for her left and right foot, giving a comfort for which she had been grateful during the long days in the saddle as they had ridden across Spain.

When she was ready, she went in search of Fabiola. The two of them crept outside as if they were thieves rather than going about their lawful business. Indeed, Fabiola was so nervous that they might be discovered that, as soon as she had found out how far they were from what she presumed to be the centre of the city, Petronilla determined they should turn back.

'It isn't as though we know where they are so that we can go straight to them. Let's hope they lose no time in coming to visit us.'

'Yes, but we won't be able to speak to them properly with my parents there,' Fabiola objected dolefully.

Petronilla's spirits sagged. 'Nonsense,' she said briskly, as much to reassure herself as Fabiola. 'Your parents may have authority over you, but they have none over *me*.'

'You wait and see,' Fabiola returned gloomily.

Nor did they have long to wait. Don Lorenzo and Doña Teresa presented a united front when they were finally ready to see their unwanted guest. Fabiola, they instructed to return to the schoolroom to join her sisters, refusing to say one word until she had done as she was bidden. Not wanting to antagonize them unnecessarily, Petronilla made no protest, aware that it was none of her business, no matter how much she might like to make it so. Instead, she thanked God for the wisdom of her own mother who had never dismissed her as if she were of no account, not even when she had been a sore trial to her, always wanting to trail after her father, earnestly discussing the affairs of the world, more like a son than a daughter. When her mother had wanted her daughter to herself, she had found other ways of gaining her attention. Seldom criticizing or showing any sign of disapproval of her masculine interests, she had nevertheless seen to it that her daughter had learned all the gentler arts in which ladies were supposed to be proficient, though not even she had been able to teach Petronilla to sew a fine seam, or embroider with the dainty, tiny stitches that she herself had learned from the nuns as a child.

'Doña Petronilla,' Don Lorenzo opened the proceedings, 'my daughter had no right to involve you in what is a private family matter. I was most displeased that she should so far forget herself as to go rushing off, without a "by your leave", telling you and your mother fantastic stories about how her mother and I were forcing her into a marriage against her will. She is far too young to know her own mind! And with five daughters to find husbands for, was I to reject Don Diego, a gentleman from an impeccable family and of whom I had heard nothing but good?'

'Don Lorenzo, please! None of this is any affair of mine. When Fabiola came to us, she had it in mind that Don Diego and I were wanting to marry, but that couldn't have been further from the truth. However, she did succeed in convincing my mother she has a genuine vocation to Carmel. Needless to say, my whole family has become very fond of her while she was with us. If we seem to presume, it is only because we want her happiness as much as I'm sure you do.'

Don Lorenzo looked down his nose. 'Quite so.'

Petronilla managed a small smile. 'I can't help thinking you would be happier discussing this with my husband rather than with myself,' she said hopefully. 'Or my father —'

'Is your husband acquainted with Don Diego?'

'Indeed, he is! It was because of their concern as to what damage Don Diego might inflict on my family's *bodega* in Montilla, as well as the possibility of your daughter and I being held hostage to gain funds for Don Carlos's cause, that my husband refused to allow us to travel before, or come without their escort. My father is on British Government business and should have been in Gibraltar long since. You have no need to fear his not understanding our Spanish customs, I promise you. He has never stopped either my mother or I from practising our religion.'

Don Lorenzo's disbelief was obvious. 'Why hasn't he become a Catholic himself?' he demanded.

'It's difficult to understand,' Petronilla said drily, 'but he thinks us backward with our unreformed religion.' Her dark eyes became bright with suppressed laughter. 'The idea that anyone should voluntarily enter a convent he found particularly hard to understand. It's amazing what the English think the Spanish are capable of doing. He had some idea that our priests run riot in every nunnery —'

'He must be mad!' Don Lorenzo exclaimed.

'More mistaken. The Spanish believe all sorts of peculiar things about the English also.'

'But they are true!'

Petronilla shook her head. 'A few of them maybe, most of them are as much nonsense as what the English believe about the Spanish.'

He gave up the argument reluctantly. 'They still hold Gibraltar, which is rightfully ours!'

'My mother would certainly agree with you about that!' Petronilla sighed. 'My father is the servant of his government, however, and has other ideas on the subject. I refuse to make up my mind, one way or the other.'

That struck a chord with Don Lorenzo. 'I feel the same about Spanish politics,' he confessed. 'Some are for Doña Isabella, and some for Don Carlos. My family is older than theirs and I am a true Spaniard besides. Why should I accept either of them as king?'

Petronilla began to understand him as she had not the evening before. She even felt sorry for him. Here, in Granada, the arguments probably did seem remote and not worth all the fuss and bother.

'And what if Don Diego succeeds in persuading Granada to rise against Doña Isabella?'

Both Fabiola's parents went grey at the thought. 'Is that likely?'

'In my father's opinion, no. It's his belief that Cousin Diego's interest in the Carlist cause is mainly to raise funds for his own use now that he is denied the benefits of the Montilla *bodega* —'

'I understood it was his own property.'

Petronilla's surprise was completely genuine. 'Oh no, it came to my mother on the death of my grandmother. Both my uncles were killed fighting the Carlists. My mother made it part of my dowry when I was married. My husband and I are living at Sanlúcar, near Jerez, but once the Montilla vineyards are productive again, we hope to mix the wines —'

'Your husband is in the sherry business?'

'Yes. Didn't Fabiola tell you?'

It was obvious that neither of them had given themselves time to listen to anything their daughter might have said. Petronilla would have pressed them further but, at that moment, a footman came in announcing the arrival of Colonel Harris and Mr Arbuthnot, his tongue tripping over the foreign names.

'Show them in,' Don Lorenzo ordered him wearily. 'No, wait a moment. Tell Padre Pedro that they're here first, will you?'

Thus it was that Don Lorenzo received the two men, his chaplain supporting him on one hand and his wife on the other. Petronilla was hard put to it not to laugh as she saw the disbelief on her father's face as all three of them solemnly crossed themselves at his entry.

'What nonsense is this?' he asked his daughter in English.

'They're afraid of you,' she explained simply. He nodded, pulling on his whiskers, seeing some sense in this. 'Nor do they like you having anything to do with Gibraltar,' she added with resignation.

'Yes.' Don Lorenzo pounced on the one word he could understand. 'What is this business you have in Gibraltar?'

'To put an end to the worst of the smuggling there,' Colonel Harris told him.

Don Lorenzo shrugged his shoulders. 'Is that all? I thought it might have something to do with young Don Diego.'

'It has,' Colonel Harris agreed.

'If he wishes to harass the British by raising funds for a Spanish cause by a bit of smuggling, where's the harm in it? Gibraltar has been a centre of smuggling since you British stole the Rock from us!'

Petronilla's eyes flashed. 'Spain already has a monarch,'

she declared violently, 'and the Constitution of Cádiz, which the Queen would support if only she were left alone long enough to do so! What good will another civil war do anybody in Spain?'

Don Lorenzo stared at her, unable to credit that any woman should have addressed him in such terms. Twice he opened his mouth, shutting it again with a snap of disapproval. 'What do you, or any woman, know about such things?' he demanded at last.

'I hold by the Constitution of 1812!'

Colonel Harris silenced her with a look. 'My wife's family have suffered much in Doña Isabella's cause, though I think we could all forgive Don Diego if he were sincere in his support for Don Carlos. His profits from smuggling go into his own pocket, however. Doña Pilar says all her family has a taste for excitement —'

'He's young. He'll grow out of it!' Don Lorenzo said hopefully.

'He's more likely to end up at the end of a rope. The Governor of Gibraltar would overlook a bit of harmless smuggling, but this goes beyond everything, endangering innocent lives, Spanish as well as British. He is a thoroughly dangerous young man!'

'I can't believe anyone of his breeding, his —'

Charles Arbuthnot took a step forward. 'He tried to murder my wife, his own cousin —'

'To murder her?' Don Lorenzo's horror was reflected in his wife's expression. 'We didn't believe Fabiola when she told us something of this!'

'I wouldn't be here otherwise,' Charles went on grimly. 'Nothing else would have made me miss our first vintage, I assure you, but I wouldn't trust anyone else with my wife's life.'

'You go to Gibraltar with the English heretic?'

Mr Arbuthnot nodded. 'Doña Louise, the widow of Francisco de la Tixera, is managing the *bodega* while I'm away. The last we heard of Don Diego he was playing the matador in the bullring at the Fiesta of the Vendimía.

We saw him gored and taken to hospital, but he was out again the next day – I fail to see such a flamboyant gesture could benefit any serious cause!'

For the first time the Spanish *hidalgo* and the Englishman understood one another exactly. Within half an hour, the two men were as comfortable as two old friends, the defences they had erected around themselves completely forgotten.

'Did you have any trouble finding somewhere to spend the night?' Petronilla asked her husband under cover of their conversation.

'Wait until you see it for yourself!'

'Tonight?' she said hopefully.

'Miss me?'

'Oh, Charles, you'll never know how much!'

But any hopes she might have had of joining Charles and her father that night were doomed to disappointment. At Colonel Harris's behest, Fabiola was summoned to join them all for a glass of sherry, greeting both men with such affection that Don Lorenzo's attention was well and truly caught.

'Were you there when Don Diego tried to murder his cousin?'

Fabiola nearly spilled her drink. 'Yes, Papá. Petronilla, show him the scar on your arm!'

Obediently, Petronilla did so, making as light as she could of the whole incident. 'I must confess I am afraid of what he will do next,' she murmured to Don Lorenzo. 'It was the foxes —'

By the time he had heard all about the death of Petronilla's pets, Fabiola had forgotten all about the awe in which she had always held her father and was plucking at his sleeve, demanding that Petronilla should be invited to stay with them a few days longer.

'I suppose you hope she will persuade me to let you have your way and enter Carmel?' Don Lorenzo asked her fondly.

'No, Papá, only if you and Mamá agree that it is what

God wants for me. If you say I must marry, then so be it. I have never wanted to disobey your wishes, only I want so much to enter Carmel and I could never find the right way of telling you how much!'

Don Lorenzo said nothing for a long time. 'It would seem you've grown up while you've been away, Fabiola. If Doña Petronilla will consent to saying with us for a few days, I should like to talk to you both about this vocation of yours.'

Fabiola bobbed a curtsy, her face aglow with happiness. 'Yes, Papá,' she whispered.

Petronilla didn't have the heart to disappoint her. She hoped her father would insist that he must press on for Gibraltar, but both he and Charles seemed pleased to be spending a few more days in Granada.

'Bear up, my love,' Charles Arbuthnot smiled at his wife. 'A few days won't be the end of the world.'

It wasn't, of course, but it certainly felt like it. Petronilla's manners were too good for her to let it show, however, and Fabiola was perfectly certain that she wanted to remain with the Ensenadas just as much as Fabiola wanted to have her.

Chapter Nineteen

Petronilla had been prepared for boredom, what she had not been prepared for was the suffocating tedium in which the Ensenada daughters were expected to pass their time. The *Señorita* Immaculada Lopez ruled over the schoolroom with a lazy contentment; her charges existed on the edge of hysteria, seeking diversion from any excuse that presented itself: a quarrel, an unexpected female visitor as young as themselves, or a brief walk outside on the rare occasions when Immaculada felt the necessity of some exercise. It never occurred to either Don Lorenzo or Doña Teresa that their eldest daughter was now of an age when she might be included in more adult pursuits, and so inevitably Petronilla was also subjected to the schoolroom regime, despite being a married lady who had been out and about in society for well over a year.

Fabiola was apologetic but disinclined to risk antagonizing her father at a time when he finally seemed to be coming round to allowing her to enter Carmel as soon as she turned eighteen. Fabiola, herself, had hoped to get the bishop's permission to enter even earlier than that, but had been wise enough to give way before her parents' very real consternation that she should have a vocation for anything other than the wedding they had always planned for her.

'I'm sorry, Fabiola, but I must be allowed to see how

Papá and Mr Arbuthnot are getting on. I'm worried about my father. He looked so tired after our journey here. I'm beginning to realize he's an old man.'

'I don't think they'll let us go without Immaculada in attendance,' Fabiola answered. 'And since I talked her into going to Córdoba with me, they probably won't even allow us out with her!'

'But that's ridiculous! I'm a married lady —'

'I know. I'm awfully sorry, truly I am, but you see you came here as my friend and they don't think I'm grown-up at all!'

'Then it's time they learned differently,' Petronilla said with decision. 'You and I are too old for the schoolroom, and I, at least, refuse to be cloistered here a moment longer! I am going out to find my father and to learn from him when he intends to set forth for Gibraltar!'

Immaculada, when appealed to, agreed they should all venture out in a group. 'I shall be glad of your help in keeping an eye on the younger girls,' she said to Petronilla. 'Cousin Teresa is very strict with them, as you have seen, and it really doesn't answer. But there, what can I do? I am lucky Don Lorenzo didn't cast me out entirely when he heard I had permitted Fabiola's flight to Montilla. As I said to him, wasn't it better I should accompany her than let her go alone? Thank God, your mother's family is held in such respect! Anyway, here I still am, and thankful to be so!'

None of the girls were allowed to dawdle along as they usually did, giggling as the *piropeadores* called out their outrageous compliments as they passed by. A furious Immaculada panted after them, bidding them not to swing their hips, or indeed show by so much as a quiver of a muscle that they had heard what was being said.

'You see how it is!' she moaned to Petronilla. 'Whatever is the world coming to when respectable ladies are submitted to such insults?'

Petronilla had never grown used to what she took to be an entirely Andalucían custom, and it was left to Fabiola truly to enjoy the ritual. With her head bowed in modesty, the glances she exchanged with the young men were every bit as hot and wicked as theirs. 'I do so enjoy receiving *piropos!*' she sighed. 'I'm sure I should never be able to invent such imaginative compliments. The young gallants bring it to a high art, don't you think?'

Petronilla smothered a laugh. 'Do you ever believe anything they say?' she enquired.

Fabiola's eyes flashed. 'Of course! Every word! It makes one feel good to know one is beautiful and desirable —'

'Now that is enough of that!' Immaculada cut her off.

Confused, Petronilla's asked her point-blank. 'But what about Carmel? I thought you were going to give up all that sort of thing?'

In Fabiola's mind, however, there was no contradiction between the one thing and the other. 'Should God only have the undesirable and dowdy?'

'I suppose not.'

'Everything comes from God,' Fabiola insisted gently, 'even the love you have for Mr Arbuthnot. Would you have me offer God less than you do your husband?'

Petronilla only hoped the Spanish girl wouldn't take it into her head to say anything of a similar nature to her father, for she was absolutely certain that all his doubts about nunneries would immediately be revived. Her mother would understand better for her relationship with God was an intimate, everyday affair that had nothing to do with best clothes on Sunday and rented pews, but Petronilla still wondered that anyone who could enjoy masculine appreciation with such gleeful zest was really cut out to be a nun.

They had walked quite a long way before she recalled the purpose of the outing. 'Do we know where they're staying?' she asked Fabiola.

'I asked the *soreno*. Look up there and you'll see their *posada!*' Fabiola giggled with delight. 'I've always wanted to visit the ruins – they're said to be full of desperate characters, but I care nothing for that! My brothers have always insisted the Alhambra to be the most beautiful palace in the whole of Spain, even if it is falling down. It must have a splendid view over the city, don't you think?'

Petronilla did. The glimpses she had of the red-gold walls and buildings that crowned the hill above the Alhambra forest had appealed to her sense of romance. Whilst they had still been at Jerez, and more to amuse her mother and Fabiola than because she had any expectation of going there herself, she had read aloud to them in the evenings from the American writer Washington Irving's *Tales of the Alhambra*, and they had exclaimed over the illustrations, which had looked better even than anything that was to be seen in Seville.

It was cooler under the trees. Immaculada, exhausted by the uphill path, elected to rest with her younger charges beside the Tomato Fountain in the middle of the wooded slopes.

'Everyone says the Generalife gardens are better than these old trees,' Fabiola tried to persuade her, but the *dueña* could go no further.

'If I'd known we were coming such a long way I'd have asked Cousin Teresa for the use of the carriage!' she puffed.

Fabiola fussed about her, seeing to her comfort as best she could. 'You're not to worry about a thing,' she assured her. 'I shall be quite safe with Doña Petronilla, and I've told the girls not to leave you alone for a second!'

The Spanish girl executed a little skip of pleasure as she and Petronilla made their escape, hastening their footsteps as they neared the road on which was the inn where Washington Irving had actually stayed some decade earlier.

'Isn't this fun?' Fabiola exclaimed. 'How do you suppose we get inside?'

Petronilla hadn't the least idea. She looked about for somebody to ask and was delighted to recognize Pablo Rodriguez coming round the corner towards her.

'Allow me to escort you ladies to the Colonel's camp.

The best way is through the courtyard of the Palace of Charles V. They say he found the old Moorish palace too draughty and built his own modern place in one corner of it. A mistake, to my way of thinking, though I have to admit it to be a handsome building.'

It was indeed, a very grand building, though it lacked the romance of its near neighbour where, Petronilla was convinced, the ghosts of the last of the Moorish kingdoms still walked.

Pedro led the way inside through a magnificent circular courtyard, open to the skies above.

'But what was it used for?' Fabiola whispered, awed by its sheer size.

'Couldn't say what it was used for once, but it's our front door in a manner of speaking right now. We go down here.'

The two women followed him down some stone steps into a darkened chamber from which they emerged into the Court of the Myrtles, the two ladies dragging behind, looking at everything as they wandered slowly through the ruined palace. Petronilla went from room to room, exclaiming her pleasure at the arabesques and countless quotations from the Koran written in the ornamental kufic script.

'I wonder what it all means?'

Pablo shook his head at her. 'Nothing good! The Moriscos used sorcery and all kinds of foul spells to entrap good Catholics into betraying Christ. If it's beautiful, it's because sin is beautiful! You'd do better to look the other way, *señora, señorita!*'

It soon became clear that wherever the roof was remaining in one of the towers whole families had moved in, amongst them the hero, if such an obvious rogue can be accounted a hero, Mateo Jímenez, who had made a bloated living from his appearance in Washington Irving's famous book, his stories becoming more and more obscure and unbelievable as he made the most of his moment of fame.

They had reached the Hall of the Kings when Petronilla caught sight of her father, standing in the so-called gallery and looking out across the city. She went and stood beside him, glad to see his shoulders as straight as she remembered them, without the slight sag that had worried her so much when they had first arrived in Granada.

'What a marvellous place, Papá! Where's Charles?'

Her father embraced her, his face lighting up at the sight of her. 'And how's my favourite daughter?'

She pulled a face at him. 'All the better for seeing you. Fabiola and I longed to see a little of Granada – but this is beautiful beyond anything I could have imagined! I'd love to spend the night here with you!'

Her father pulled on his moustache, bowing to Fabiola. 'There are some mighty strange characters making their homes amongst the ruins –'

'Oh, do tell us about them,' Fabiola begged.

Colonel Harris smiled back at the girl. He thought she looked peaked and wished there was some way he could convince her parents that young girls needed a certain amount of space to grow, exactly as their brothers did. Pilar would tell him it was none of his business, and she was undoubtedly right, but he had grown fond of the Spanish girl and, although he still couldn't bring himself to approve of her vocation, her sincerity had earned his respect.

'It's unnatural for a young woman to shut herself away for the rest of her life!' he had grumbled to his wife.

Doña Pilar had laughed at him for his concern. 'Nobody will ever persuade her against her will,' she had reassured him. 'Already she has you admitting it will be herself who does the shutting away, a little while ago you were blaming the whole Church for it! She reminds you of somebody, no?'

Well, so she did! She had some of that fire and spirit of his Spanish wife, but he couldn't imagine Pilar ever wanting to be a nun!

'Where's Charles?' Petronilla asked again.

Her father's eyes twinkled at her. 'He was amusing himself trying to get some of these writings round the windows and doors translated. Go and find him, my dear; Fabiola and I can amuse each other until you get back.'

Petronilla needed no second bidding. She found Charles not far away, his drawing book in his hand, frowning at an intricate pattern beside one of the main doors.

She linked her arm with his, smiling at his neatly drawn, faithfully executed copy. 'Have you found out what it means?' she asked him.

'I'm told that if you follow the line you never get to the end, so I think it must mean eternity.' He finished a final flourish and turned to her, his pleasure at seeing her breaking over his face. 'Darling!'

She rubbed her fingers against his, leaning her head against his shoulder and shutting her eyes. 'I love you!' she said with a sudden burst of courage.

His smile grew broader. 'Was that so hard to say?'

'Not really,' she admitted. 'Not now I know it to be the truth.'

'I love you too,' he said.

She was confused for a moment, not knowing what to say next. It was far too public a place for such an intimate conversation.

'Charles, I wish I could stay here with you. It's such a beautiful place! I'm hardly allowed out of the schoolroom at the Ensenadas – not that that would matter if I weren't separated from you.' She saw by the expression on his face that he thought it her duty to stay with Fabiola a while longer and was seeking the words to tell her so. With a sigh of resignation, she saved him the necessity. 'May I join you for one night here before we go?'

He threw his drawing book to one side, seizing both her hands in his. The look in his eyes took her breath away. She felt a heaviness in her breasts and a hot molten need for him in her loins. The intensity of the moment was such that she had never experienced before. She had never been so aware of another human being, feeling in her own person the lines of humour that were etched at the corners of his eyes, the way his ruddy hair grew out of his scalp and, most of all the remembered feel of his strong yet gentle fingers against her flesh. Laughing somewhat breathlessly, she looked down, seeking to recover her poise.

'So, that's how it is, is it?' he teased her, very well pleased.

She was not sure she liked him knowing how vulnerable she was to him. Her acknowledgement of her love for him was still too new for her to feel at her ease with it herself, let alone with him.

'I'm your wife, Charles, not a young girl who has to ask permission to come and go!'

'Not my permission?' he pressed her.

'Well, yes, but not Don Lorenzo's!'

'I will do what I can,' Charles promised. 'Your father won't be ready to leave Granada quite yet. He moves around from group to group, looking every inch the English traveller in search of romantic adventures to tell his grandchildren, but he knows what he's doing. There's a fellow living here called Jesús whom he talks with more than most. He's a *flamenco* singer and a sometime *torero*. Better still he's done a bit of smuggling around Gibraltar. I think he may be going with us when we leave.'

'Oh? What else is he?'

His eyes narrowed. 'You know,' he said, 'there was a time when I thought beautiful women shouldn't have brains in their heads —'

Her mouth quivered with amusement. 'And now?'

'You're my partner, aren't you?'

'Am I?'

'You were my partner *before* you were my wife!'

'Then tell me properly about Jesús. What else is he besides a smuggler? My father wouldn't have much interest in him if he were only that!'

'He was born and bred in Gibraltar. A British trained soldier of sorts. He's been a mercenary in Spain also, loyal to the *Reina* la Doña Isabella II. He's a very interesting fellow.'

'He sounds it.'

Colonel Harris and Fabiola came and joined them, Fabiola bubbling over with interest in the strange stories Thomas was telling her about the other people who had found a home in the Alhambra Palace.

'Don't you wish you were staying here with them?' she asked Petronilla, and was immediately overcome by the tactlessness of the question. 'Oh dear, of course you do! It would be a splendid adventure for you! But I'm afraid my parents would never understand why you should prefer to leave their roof for this. They would never willingly come here, you know. I sometimes wonder why we of the true Faith have to be afraid all the time of those who know nothing about God, but so it is.' Her mood changed suddenly, her doubts dispelled by her next train of thought. 'Petronilla, I have invited your father and husband to honour us with their company for dinner tonight —'

Petronilla gasped aloud. 'But what will your father say?'

Fabiola tossed her head. 'I don't care! It is only proper to make them welcome, don't you think? I'm sure your mother would say so!'

Petronilla looked at Fabiola's flushed, determined face and thought how difficult it was when people refused to accept the usual norms of behaviour and what distress it inevitably caused to those around them.

'You are quite right, my dear,' she approved, doing her best to hide her own misgivings. 'But, if we are to prepare your parents, we had best be making our way home, don't you think?'

Fabiola's lack of enthusiasm was the mirror of her own. Petronilla threaded her fingers through her husband's, giving him a silent message of how much she would have preferred to have stayed and talked to him for a little while longer.

He brushed her cheek with his free hand, bending his

head to salute her with a chaste kiss on the cheek. 'Cheer up, lass, I'll get you here for at least one night, by hook or by crook, I promise!'

She gave him look for look. 'A honeymoon?'

'It's a romantic setting,' he acknowledged, 'but don't build your hopes up too high. We'll make our own time, even if it isn't here.'

And with that she had to be content.

Petronilla was proud of the two men when she saw them. Both were immaculately turned out despite having been on the road for so long and their manners, whilst easier than those of the stiff Spanish, were calculated to put their hosts at their ease, especially Fabiola, whose pleasure in their company was so unaffected that even her parents began to unbend, a little astonished to find their daughter transformed from goose to swan before their wondering eyes.

'Another party of Englishmen have joined us at the Alhambra,' Colonel Harris told them. 'If we'd expected to have much in common with them, however, we were doomed to disappointment. One of them is an artist fellow, I believe. He dressed himself and his whole party in Moorish costumes, or what he imagined they would have worn, and then, just as we were getting used to that, he had them all change into Spanish period costume and we left them, strutting around as though they owned the place!'

This brought a smile even to the Doña Teresa's face. 'Why do they want to pretend to be somebody else?' she asked, bewildered.

'I think, when they've made up their minds, they plan to paint each other in costume,' Charles supplied. 'Apparently, it's the latest thing in London to execute paintings of the mysterious East, or to paint one's sitters in various costumes.'

'What I don't understand,' Don Lorenzo said at last to his guest, 'is why you should want to return to your foggy island? You have a Spanish wife, and a daughter who lives here in Spain. Why do you punish yourself by living in the rain?'

Colonel Harris coughed, casting an imploring look at Petronilla, who willingly took up the cudgels on his behalf.

'You wouldn't ask if you could see my father's home,' she told them. 'It is the most comfortable dwelling I know, with large, well-appointed rooms and, best of all, it has piped water! All one has to do is turn a tap and out comes the water. I've seen nothing like it in Spain!'

'Indeed not!' Charles Arbuthnot chimed in. 'My father-in-law is of the opinion that piped clean water will put an end to cholera and other similar water-borne diseases once it becomes universal.'

The Colonel tugged on his whiskers, not ill-pleased to have one of his favourite hobby-horses brought out for an airing. 'Birmingham is the best place to see the advantages of a modern water system,' he growled. 'I was proud to bring their efforts to the notice of the House —'

'My father is a Member of Parliament,' Petronilla put in by way of explanation.

Doña Teresa, her fork caught half-way between her plate and her mouth, creased her forehead and addressed Colonel Harris directly for the first time. 'Have you no servants in England to carry the water?' she asked him.

It wasn't long before the Colonel was deep in an explanation of the advantages of the modern plumbing that was so dear to his heart. Seeking the occasional word from Petronilla, he launched into a dissertation of how piped water and proper sewerage was the answer to all the ills of urban living.

It was not a subject that Petronilla would have expected to appeal to her hosts. She could not have been more mistaken. Don Lorenzo might affect to despise the Moors who had built Granada and had made it the city it was, but he had inherited enough from their history and culture to have a positively Arab appreciation of water and its importance for gracious living. He had long understood the importance of personal hygiene, which had always been a fetish of the whole of that part of Spain that had been the last to be subdued by the Catholic Kings, and was quite prepared to believe that a great many diseases were water-borne.

After his guests had departed, Don Lorenzo expressed his amazement to Petronilla and his daughter that any Englishman should have the address and *educación* he discerned in Colonel Harris, and declared him to be almost a Spaniard such was his understanding of the things that really mattered in life – all except his regrettable religion of course! One way and the other, it was a most successful evening.

Petronilla and the young Ensenadas had only just finished breakfast the following morning when the message came up to the schoolroom that Don Lorenzo wished to see his eldest daughter in his study. If the Doña Petronilla would care to accompany her, he would be even better pleased. Coffee would be served, or chocolate, if that was the ladies' choice, and some of Fabiola's favourite almond biscuits.

The two ladies looked at each other in mutual inquiry. 'What can he want with me?' Fabiola asked herself, examining her conscience minutely for something she might have done to offend him.

'There's only one way to find out,' Petronilla answered, impatient with herself for being almost as nervous as Fabiola at the summons. 'Besides, he wouldn't want me to be there if he were annoyed with you, would he?'

Fabiola brightened somewhat. 'Oh, Petronilla, I don't know what I'm going to do when you go and I am left here on my own!'

Petronilla felt a spurt of sympathy for her. She didn't pretend for a moment that she thought anything else but that Fabiola's existence amongst her family was drab in the extreme. 'I'd ask your father if you could spend another few months in the care of my mother,' she began doubtfully, 'but she did say that if you were serious about entering Carmel the best thing you could do would be to convince your father that he has a vital role in that decision because of his natural authority over you. Mamá always says that one's duty must come first, no matter how hard it seems, because it's the only way one ever achieves happiness in the end.'

'Oh, I know that!' Fabiola muttered. 'She told me she thought it must have been the Devil who had put it about that anyone had a *right* to be happy, because she had never known that philosophy lead to anything else except unhappiness and a great deal of unnecessary pain. Only, I don't want to be left here on my own!' She took a deep breath, controlling herself with difficulty. 'What am I to do?'

'Your duty, my love.'

Don Lorenzo greeted them both with an expansive smile. He served his startled daughter with her chocolate and biscuits with his own hands, just as if she were an honoured guest in the house, smiling at both ladies and making the lightest of conversation as if he had nothing better to do than entertain them both.

'Seeing you in company yesterday made me proud to be the father of such an adult young lady,' he said to Fabiola, when everyone had partaken of all they wanted. 'Our English visitors obviously think very well of you and I thought you behaved just right, my dear.' He turned to include Petronilla. 'I think I owe you an apology, Doña Petronilla. If I had known your menfolk better I should have been proud to have had them as house-guests. I must admit your father is the first Englishman with whom I have ever had any conversation. A most interesting man! A Member of Parliament! Does he support the party of your Queen?'

Petronilla managed to keep a straight face. 'Queen Victoria doesn't have a party of her own. She is obliged to invite the leader of the party who has the most members in the House to be her Prime Minister. She may have her own private preferences, but we know nothing of those!' May God forgive me, she added silently, because, of course, everyone knew the Queen's preferences in these matters, whether they agreed with her or not.

'I have heard tell of a Mr Gladstone,' Don Lorenzo frowned at her.

'Not her favourite person,' Petronilla couldn't resist remarking. 'Nor one of my mother's either!'

'Indeed? because he is a Protestant?'

Petronilla did laugh then. 'No, though I have heard it said that if he were ever to convert to Rome, he would spend so much time justifying himself in the confessional that it would be the priest who would abdicate!'

Slightly shocked, Don Lorenzo tried to make sense of this peculiar way of looking at a great man. 'Nevertheless, your father has a respect for him?' he asked almost hopefully.

'He admires some of his ideas.'

'And your husband?'

Petronilla was forced to admit she had never discussed Mr Gladstone with her husband. 'Mr Arbuthnot has very little interest in politics. We live in Spain —'

'Ah yes, your husband is almost a Spaniard! I had some conversation with him also. He told me you are his partner in the Arbuthnot *bodega*, a great honour for such a young woman!'

'I am fortunate in my marriage,' Petronilla acknowledged.

'As I have always hoped all my daughters will be!' Don Lorenzo commented. 'A father wants only his daughter's happiness and, although she may think she knows what she wants from life, his is the ultimate responsibility that the right choice is made. It would distress him greatly if he should make the wrong choice – something he would always regret!'

It plainly hadn't occurred to him that it would be the daughter who would have to live with the consequences of that 'wrong' decision and, even if it had, Petronilla doubted he would see any point in consulting the daughter concerned.

'My father's only regret was that I married younger than he would have liked and while he was still in England,' she said aloud. 'We have always been such good friends that he had hoped I would make my home near him, so that we could visit practically every day. Spain is rather far for that!'

Don Lorenzo nodded gravely, though he had never felt the slightest urge to have anything to do with his own daughters. Indeed, it was his firm opinion that women were incapable of friendship and were without any interest for most men except for the single purpose of mothering the next generation.

'Fabiola is younger than you were then,' he said abruptly.

'A few months only,' Petronilla pointed out.

He was silent for so long that she began to wonder if she should have said something more on Fabiola's behalf.

Then, making both ladies jump, he leaned forward and barked at his daughter: 'I've been thinking about this Carmel nonsense! I had breakfast with the Cardinal Archbishop and told him you wanted to enter as soon as I saw my way to give my permission. Seems he knew all about it! Padre Pedro had mentioned the matter to him some time ago. We agreed you should seek admission in six weeks' time. What do you think about that? Mind you, it wouldn't surprise me in the least to see you back amongst us by Christmas – There's no need to cry about it, child! I didn't know it meant so much to you!'

Fabiola stood before him, her face ablaze with happiness even while the tears poured down her cheeks.

'Oh, thank you, Papá!' she exclaimed. She curtsied to him, turned and cast her arms about Petronilla. 'God is good! How could I ever have doubted he would find a way?'

Petronilla gave Fabiola a quick hug, marvelling that anyone could look so exultant at the prospect of the spartan existence of life as a Discalced Carmelite, but glad for her for she knew that nothing else could satisfy her.

Soon after a footman came to tell the Doña Petronilla her husband was waiting to see her down below. She followed the man down the stairs, trying to pretend that she wasn't glad to get away from the emotional atmosphere upstairs. In the doorway she could see Mr Arbuthnot waiting for her, reassuringly solid in his English-cut clothes, his hat and crop held in one hand and a frowning expression between his eyes.

'I give you good morning, Charles!'

He turned, spreading his arms out to receive her. The footman disappeared with a quick nod of his head, a broad grin on his face, as Petronilla went to her husband in a rush, throwing herself into his embrace.

'You taste of chocolate!' he murmured fondly, kissing her a second time.

'And of almond biscuits! Don Lorenzo has given his permission for Fabiola to enter Carmel!'

He didn't look nearly as surprised as he should have done and she wondered what had passed between the men after she, Fabiola and Doña Teresa had retired after dinner the night before. That something had, she had no doubt, for she couldn't think it was often that Don Lorenzo bestirred himself to attend the Cardinal first thing in the morning.

'Glad to hear it!' Charles responded. 'Best thing for her.'

'Yes. What did you have to do with it?'

'I? What makes you think Don Lorenzo would listen to anything a foreigner has to say?'

Petronilla rapped him on the cheek with her fan. 'Darling Charles! You and Fabiola make a fine pair! You always get your own way, both of you!'

He grinned slowly, his eyes narrowing, but not before she had seen a new expectancy in their depths. 'And you don't, my love?'

She laughed. 'If you could see Fabiola's delighted

response to the *piropos* she received in the street yesterday, you'd wonder about our little nun!'

'And what about the ones you received?'

'Me? An old, married woman? Not that it has felt much like it these last few days. I'm so glad to see you I could burst!'

'So I see! I came to tell you we leave for Gibraltar in the morning. Apparently we are to pick up your mother on the way —'

'She'll never set foot on Gibraltar!'

'Your father seems to think she will. Jesús and Pablo have turned up some pretty nasty rumours about your cousin's activities over there and that makes it family business as far as she's concerned.' He stood back from her, the glint in his eyes more apparent than ever. 'Do you still want to come to the Alhambra for the night?'

'Tonight?' She waited for his nod, her whole body tingling with suppressed excitement. 'May I really join you tonight?' She rubbed his fingers against her cheek, smiling at him through her lashes.

'All you have to do is to make your farewells to Fabiola —'

'Does Papá know I'm coming?'

'He has other plans for this evening. Jesús has located a group of smugglers who have worked with Don Diego. They're a close-knit lot these Gibraltarians! According to Pablo, they don't speak Spanish or English, but some kind of mongrel language of their own, which none of the rest of us can understand.'

Petronilla blenched. 'It's dangerous, isn't it? Surely Papá can leave it to the others to find out whatever it is he wants to know?'

'My dear girl, you know your father better than that!'

'Yes, but if it's dangerous he's not as young as he was —'

'If there were any real danger, sweetheart, I'd go with him, even if it meant disappointing your hopes of a "honeymoon". Satisfied?'

She was. She trusted Charles Arbuthnot as she trusted

no one else. It gave her a nice feeling to know she was fortunate enough to be married to him and she was on the point of telling him so when he put it completely out of her mind by offering her another piece of information for her to think about.

'By the way, I had a letter from your friend Mr Clarke. He's going to stay on with Doña Louise until we get back to Jerez. there's no one I'd sooner have keep an eye on the place. He's a good man.'

Petronilla wasn't quite so sure she liked that. 'We can't afford to pay anyone else to do our work for us! Doña Louise is different because she wants to stay on in her old house anyway. The only difficulty there will be is to get her out again because I'm convinced she doesn't really want to live in England at all! I refuse to have anyone else living with us, especially someone we know nothing about except that he works —'

'For one of the best respected wine merchants in London.'

'I didn't realize he meant to move in with us!'

'Petronilla! Just because he's keeping his hand in while we're away doesn't mean he's going to be there for ever!'

Upstairs, Petronilla said her goodbyes to Fabiola. 'I am so glad for you that your father has given way,' she told her sincerely.

Fabiola was inclined to be tearful. 'I may never see you again! You won't forget all about me, will you? You'll know where I am?'

'Of course! I suppose one is allowed to see you where you're going?'

'Oh yes. There's a grille, you know, but that is more to keep the world out than to keep the nuns in. I shall pray for you every day!'

'And you can receive letters?'

'Yes, but I don't know how often I may be able to write back. I shall want to hear all about what you're doing, however.'

Petronilla agreed to write. She enjoyed writing letters

to her intimate friends and Fabiola had, over the weeks she had spent with her family, become one of her very dearest friends.

'What did you think of Mr Clarke?' she asked her.

It was a moment or two before Fabiola could put a face to the name. 'Oh you mean the wine merchant, that first night, who took the "spy's" room after he had left? He was nice.'

'Yes, I thought so too,' Petronilla admitted, determined to be fair. 'Mr Arbuthnot has asked him to help Doña Louise while we're away.'

'Would it be such a bad thing?' Fabiola asked. 'With him on hand you may even have time for a social life – and to come and visit me!'

'I'd like children — ' Petronilla began, and then stopped. She had told no one, not even Charles, how disappointing she found it not to be expecting after all this time.

Fabiola smiled a wise little smile. 'Of course there will be children! Just as soon as you stop riding all over the countryside and live the life of a lady of leisure! And the first girl you will call after me, no?'

It was much easier to make her adieus to Don Lorenzo and Doña Teresa. Both said everything that was proper, thanking her for all her family had done for Fabiola and asking her to pass on their grateful greetings to her lady mother, which Petronilla consented to do with a graciousness that brought a smile to her husband's lips, who had never quite accustomed himself to Petronilla in her Spanish mood, when she both looked and behaved as if she were wholly a product of the *hidalguía*, instead of the English daughter of an English military colonel.

Petronilla renewed her acquaintance with her *jaca*, blowing up her nostrils as she had seen her mother do, delighted when the little mare returned her caresses with a whinnied welcome.

Fabiola stepped forward, putting a hand on the bridle. '*Vaya con Dios*, Mrs Arbuthnot!' Her tongue stumbled over the English title. 'Don't forget your promise! Your first daughter is to be called after me!'

Petronilla's last sight of her was with her hands clutched together, her lips moving in silent prayer and she made a silent vow to do her best to visit Fabiola in her convent as frequently as she was able, and certainly when she made her final vows, giving herself wholly to God, having found the pearl of great price for which she was prepared to give up everything else in this world for the next.

There was a moon that night. It turned the water flowing from the fountains into cascades of diamonds, an endless stream of beauty that was never still, the breeze catching the drops of water from time to time for altering the rhythm of its passage.

Petronilla went and joined her husband, leaning against him as they looked across the city below, little pin-points of light shimmering amidst the blackness of the mysterious, narrow streets, the tree-lined squares, the countless churches, many of them built on the site of the old mosques which had preceded them, and the simple enclosed dwellings that were still built in the old Moorish style, another legacy of the former rulers of Andalucía.

From the promenades of the hill of Sabika, extend your gaze across the city, a lady betrothed to the hill . . . for Sabika is Grenada's crown, the very stars of heaven its jewels; And the Alhambra, may God protect it, is the central ruby of that crown.

Petronilla looked about her as the poem bade her. 'The Moors did love it, didn't they?'

'In a way it will always belong to them,' Charles answered. 'They conceived the city and brought it to birth. No one can ever take that away from them. Their memorial will remain for as long as these buildings stand.'

Petronilla shut her eyes, summoning up a mental picture of the palace, the graceful forest of slim pillars, the filigree work on walls and ceilings, probably spelling out words to anyone who could read them, but still making exquisite patterns for those who could not. She had come across her father's group of English painters, attired in Moorish costumes that slipped about their persons as they walked. She had thought them to be ridiculous, but she had changed her mind when she had seen some of their careful paintings, capturing the spirit of the palace in ways no words ever could.

Charles had introduced her to the Gibraltarian Jesús who, apart from lisping a heavily accented '*Buenas tardes*', had shifted from one foot to the other in an agony of embarrassment until she had taken pity on him, and suggested they should move on to the small tower that Charles had marked out as their own for the night.

Her father had joined them for dinner. There had been some *flamenco* dancing and singing from a group of gypsies who were passing through Granada on their way to the horse fair at Seville. The haunting sound of their strange melodies still echoed in her ears, mixed with the complicated patterns of the drubbing heels of the dancers, so fast that she had been unable to follow the speed of their feet with her eyes.

'Well, my dears,' her father had said at last, 'Jesús and I are about to complete our round of the local inns, but Pablo will be around somewhere if you should need anything. We must get away before noon tomorrow, so be ready, won't you?'

He had kissed his daughter a fond goodnight, giving her an approving glance for he had thought she was looking very well indeed, a Spanish comb in her hair and her mantilla flung back to show off her black, glossy hair and dark good looks. She might have been considered too sunburned to be considered a beauty in England, but marriage evidently suited her, bringing more mature lines to her face and figure, and a glow of well-being to her complexion and expression that was better than the rosebud mouths and golden hair that were fashionable in the more northerly climes of his homeland.

Petronilla, full of Trevelez ham cured in the snow-covered Sierra, and a traditional Moorish delicacy made from almonds, the *torta real* from Motril, had made no objection when her husband had led her by the hand, bringing her to this hidden room beneath the tower. It was ridiculous, she thought, to be shy with her own husband, but she could think of nothing to ease the atmosphere that had suddenly come alive between them. One moment they had been discussing the beauties of Granada and the next there was only silence and a trembling in the pit of her stomach that refused to go away no matter what disagreeable thoughts she brought to mind, hoping to dispel it. She sniffed, deciding it was a waste of a perfectly beautiful evening to think about anything but love and that she was finally reunited with her husband.

She leaned against a pillar, shutting her eyes, wondering how to bring him to the point. She need not have worried. His fingers on the nape of her neck sent a shock of awareness down her spine, turning the trembling into a whirlwind of desire.

'Charles?'

He took the comb out of her hair, tangling his fingers in its long tresses. She turned towards him, a smile at the corner of her lips.

'Why don't you get sunburned?' she asked him. 'Most red-headed people do.'

'I have freckles,' he answered. 'Haven't you noticed?'

She licked her lips. 'I've noticed everything about you.'

He grinned. 'And you're in love with me?'

She blushed. 'Yes.'

His hands had reached the buttons of her bodice. 'And you remember your father's rose garden in England?'

'Yes.'

He pushed her dress off her shoulders. 'That was when

you fell in love with me. That was when we fell in love with each other.'

She gave a start of surprise. She turned to look at him. 'Then?' she wondered. 'It couldn't have been then!'

'Why not?'

'I would have known it!'

'I think you did – then.'

She could not deny it, not entirely. 'I was a child!' she excused herself.

'Half and half,' he acknowledged. 'It was the child who was dazzled by the beautiful feathers of a peacock, but it was the adult who didn't like the raucous note in his voice.'

'True,' she agreed, glad that he understood so well.

'How do you feel about the peacock now, my love?'

A glimpse of humour lurked at the back of her eyes. 'He moulted. Without his feathers he was a very poor sort of bird!' She hesitated, feeling braver in the face of his gentleness. 'And I grew up. I'm sorry it took me so long.'

He bent his head, touching his lips to hers. 'I kept telling myself that all I had to do was wait until you were old enough to read your own feelings. I'd have waited all the years of my life for you.'

The kiss was not enough for her. She ran her fingers through the springing growth of his hair, pulling his head down to hers and opening her mouth eagerly to his. But he drew back, his sherry eyes grave and wary.

'When you came to my bed you didn't know you were in love with me, did you?'

'Not then. I knew I liked you better than any other man.'

'And you liked to make love with me —'

'You're my husband, aren't you?' He smiled at the unexpected naïvety in someone he had come to think of as being as wise as her mother. 'I love you, I love you, I love you! Isn't that enough for you?'

They were both completely naked when they made love. It was both shocking and delightful to feel his skin

413

against hers, with nothing between them, as if they were two pagans instead of a Christian man and woman. But if Charles could see nothing wrong with it, then neither would she, Petronilla decided. His pleasure was her pleasure; his happiness her happiness.

'I never want to be apart from you again!' she told him when it was over, already half-asleep.

'Nor I from you, my darling wife,' he whispered back, and his words were like an accolade, filling her cup of happiness to overflowing. That night there were only the two of them in the whole world.

Chapter Twenty

Doña Pilar rode out to meet them when they drew close to Montilla. She sat her horse with the nonchalant ease of one who has always ridden, her hand shading her eyes as she watched them approach. Seeing her in the distance, Petronilla urged her *jaca* into first a canter and then a headlong gallop, coming to a breakneck halt within inches of her mother as she had seen bull herders do in the fields.

Pilar greeted her with one of her decided nods of the head. 'You look well, child!' She surveyed her from head to foot. 'Have you come to terms with Charles at last, or are you expecting?'

'I'm not expecting – as far as I know.'

'But not because Charles has been neglecting you?'

'N-no. We were separated in Granada —'

'Yes, I received a long, incoherent letter from Fabiola.' Doña Pilar didn't bother to hide her amusement. 'She is successfully settled, I gather? You have done well, daughter!' She laughed at Petronilla's expression. 'Was it very boring in the Ensenada household? I was afraid it might be. But I'm sure it was worth it when Don Lorenzo finally gave Fabiola his consent. That girl is a child after my own heart!'

'I've never seen anyone so happy, Mamá!' But she was talking to thin air, for her mother had spotted Colonel Harris in the distance and, with a whoop of joy quite at odds with her normal dignity, she was off her horse and dancing over the ground towards him. 'Tomás! How *good* it is to see you! At last we are all together! We shall have a holiday, no? You, me, Charles and Petronilla!'

Colonel Harris put his arms about her. 'We're on our way to Gibraltar.'

Pilar stamped her foot. 'Gibraltar! I think nothing of Gibraltar! I prefer you not to mention that place again! You hear me?'

'Can't help it, *enamorada*. That's where we're going. We don't have any choice in the matter.'

'The others are going too?' Doña Pilar kicked out at his shins. 'How dare you take them there, *Señor Robar*?'

Colonel Harris caught her by the waist, a broad grin on his face. 'It's not me who's robbing the Spanish government blind, so I'll thank you not to call me that! Either you come with us, Pilar, or you wait for us here! Which is it to be?'

'I will go with my family!'

'As far as Algeciras?'

She resigned herself to her fate. 'Wherever you go, Tomás, I go! Gibraltar is worse than another woman in our lives! Whichever way we turn, there is that Fat Rock coming between us! I'll have no more of it! If it means going with you to Gibraltar, then that is where we'll go!'

'Good!' He hugged her tightly against him.

Petronilla averted her eyes, pointing towards the homestead with her whip. 'I'll race you home, Charles Arbuthnot!' she called over her shoulder. 'Are you coming?'

'After you, ma'am,' he replied, doffing his hat with the same formality with which she had addressed him.

She was hard put to it to keep ahead even so, and she only did so because it annoyed her very much to be beaten, even by him. She steadied her little mare as they approached the high gates that marked the entrance to the homestead and *bodega*, bowing to the guard who opened the gate for her. Charles rode in beside her, leaping off his horse and going straight to help her from the saddle.

'Very gallant!' she approved.

He grinned. 'Any excuse to get my hands on you, woman!'

'Hush,' she rebuked him. 'We're not on "honeymoon" now.'

'More's the pity!'

She gave him look for look before going inside to greet Cousin Rosa and Miss Fairman. Charles watched her go, leaning against his mount. When she was out of sight, he handed over the horses to the waiting groom, and took himself off to take a look round the *bodega* sheds to see what was going on there.

Miss Fairman rose to her feet, taking both Petronilla's hands in hers and looking her up and down with delight.

'*Marry first and love will follow?*' she quoted the old seventeenth-century proverb hopefully. 'I was sure it would be so, but one can't help worrying, can one? I was so hopeful all summer long, but you *look* like a bride now, my dear!'

'Charles is the very best of men,' Petronilla answered, not really wanting to reveal quite how happy she was, not even to her old governess. She might have added that her only sorrow at that moment was that they still hadn't succeeded in making a child between them, but no doubt Fabiola was right and that would come when she was no longer living half her life on the back of a horse. The older woman took the hint, though she couldn't resist exchanging a look of triumph with Doña Rosa, with whom she was on the very best of terms.

'Are you here to stay?' Cousin Rosa fussed in her turn. 'Cousin Pilar has been on hot bricks for days against your coming! And, oh Petronilla, she has told me you won't mind at all if I make my home here, rather than with Cousin Ambrosio in Córdoba – The *Señorita* Fairman is to stay here also, so that we can be company for one another! What do you think of that?'

'An excellent idea!' Petronilla said warmly. If she were surprised that Miss Fairman should be contemplating spending the rest of her life in Spain, she said nothing.

'It seems we're only spending the one night,' she told them both, 'before going on our way to Gibraltar.'

Cousin Rosa pinched up her mouth in distress. 'Cousin Pilar will be so upset to see Colonel Harris leave for that place again!'

'She's coming with us,' Petronilla announced, eyebrows raised.

'Never!'

'Fancy!' Miss Fairman exclaimed, for once no quotation coming to mind. 'Well, I for one think it a very good idea! She does so hate to be parted from her husband! She's been as close to being bad-tempered as I've ever seen her these last few days!'

Petronilla was amused. 'Has she made your lives intolerable?' she enquired basely.

But Miss Fairman wouldn't have it so. 'A little on edge is how I would have described it, dear. And, really, one can't wonder at it! I always thought our government was on the side of law and order, not making their fortunes out of smuggling! Your father should be ashamed!'

'You've been listening to Mamá,' Petronilla accused her. 'What about Nelson and the Battle of Trafalgar? Do you think Britain could have won that without Gibraltar?'

Unfortunately, her parents chose that moment to come and join them, looking for all the world like well-bred strangers rather than the laughing, battling couple Petronilla had last seen.

Her mother snorted her contempt. 'Me, I am sick of that battle! Are we to live on its glory for the rest of our days? Must Spain wait for ever for justice?'

'While Gibraltar remains the key to the Mediterranean, yes,' the Colonel answered her. 'The Balance of Power —'

Pilar groaned aloud. 'No, no, it's too much! Whenever That Place is mentioned everybody begins to quarrel! It's bad enough we must go there, without having Gibraltar,

Gibraltar, Gibraltar rammed down our throats every minute of every hour! Is it understood?' Somehow the Spanish pronunciation of the hated name, drawled over the tongue with a contemptuous droop of the mouth, coupled with a very Spanish shrug of the shoulders, reduced it in importance to a tiresome boil on the rump of Spain.

Petronilla giggled, caught her father's eye and bit her lip. 'I'm sorry, Papá.'

'*You* ought to know better!' he barked at her.

'Why? You've never succeeded in convincing Mamá —'

'Your mother's knowledge of politics could safely be written on a threepenny bit! I had hoped you would have had a better understanding of the consequences of our giving up Gibraltar.'

Pilar gave his arm a shake. 'Tomás, really! None of us has the least interest in that abominable place! We have consented to go with you, and that must be enough for you. It seems to me quite fitting that Cousin Diego should find this Rock compatible, for it is perfectly clear that anyone who has anything to do with it has no morals, no manners and no proper feeling for their country at all!'

Colonel Harris forgot his complaint in the face of this attack. His whiskers quivered. 'Pirates can be quite amusing people at times,' he offered thoughtfully.

Pilar's delighted laugh rang out through the patio. 'Yes, my darling *Señor Pirata*, who stole my whole heart, you have always amused me excessively, *except* when you talk about Gibraltar, so it's better we don't discuss it any more, no?'

'Much better,' he capitulated with a sigh.

He kept his word all evening, so it was only when Charles had joined Petronilla in their bedroom that she warned him that, even while Gibraltar was their destination, it might be better not to mention the Rock too often in her mother's presence on the way there.

'There's plenty of other things to talk over with her,' he answered. 'She hasn't been wasting her time while we

were in Granada! The vintage is going very well here.'
His enthusiasm lit as he joined her on the bed. 'I've been
thinking, Pet. We could send Mr Clarke over here when
we get back to Jerez —'

Petronilla pursed up her lips. 'No,' she said.

'What do you mean, no? It would be convenient —'

'I said no,' she reiterated.

He considered her determined expression for a long
moment. 'I'm not asking your permission, I'm telling
you,' he said at last.

'And I'm telling you no. The *bodega* at Sanlúcar is yours,
and you may do as you like there, but this *bodega* belongs
to me, through my family, and I say no. I'll not have Mr
Clarke here.'

'In the last resort, you don't have any choice!' he
grunted. 'However, I've noted your protest —'

Petronilla only smiled. 'No, my love, it's you who
doesn't understand. In Spain, a woman has control over
her own property. One day I hope to hand on *my bodega*
to *our* daughter as part of her dowry! Like you, I shall
make a note of your protest if you don't happen to approve
of the proposal.'

Charles eyed her in astonishment, noting her raised
eyebrow and her deliberately pleasant tone of voice. 'You
mean it, don't you?'

She nodded. 'It means a lot to me to be a partner in
Arbuthnots. I know it's not an equal partnership, nor
would I want it to be, for I realize there are many things
I can't do as well as a man, but I don't fancy being replaced
by any Mr Clarke, without a "by your leave" —'

'He won't be replacing you, darling!'

She saw that she had his full attention now. 'Are you
sure? It sounded very like it to me!'

He rubbed the back of his fingers against her cheek. 'I
admit I'd forgotten that what's yours is not automatically
mine in Spain. You've made your point and, if you
become half the winemaker that your mother is, I shan't

be sorry you made it. I was only trying to make things easier for you – you work harder than many men I know!'

'Women are stronger than you think!' she retorted. 'I haven't complained, have I?'

'No, nor would you, if I know anything about it! However, a husband is meant to look after his wife. Would you agree with that?'

She was cautious. 'Yes.'

'Then you must agree I'd be a poor sort of husband if I expected you to be wife, mother and a full-time partner in Arbuthnots as well —'

'Mother?' she interrupted sharply.

'Is there any reason why we shouldn't have children?'

'I am still not with child – after all this time! Charles what if we never do have any children?'

'They'll come in time —'

'I hope they will! But please don't shut me out, Charles. Not even our children could compensate me for that.'

He leaned up on his elbow, looking down at her. 'I love you,' he said. He bent his head and kissed her, gently at first, and then with increasing urgency, his tongue slipping between her teeth and sparring with hers in a game of passion that soon had her inviting him closer still.

'Love me?' he asked her.

'You know I do.'

They were the last words either of them were to utter until the stroke of midnight reminded them they had another long day in the saddle again on the morrow, and every day until they reached Gibraltar.

Petronilla's first sight of the Rock was disappointing. It stood proud of the surrounding coastline – a huge, rugged grey rock, sitting oddly in the red sand around it that edged the natural bay which made Gibraltar so important strategically. From that part of Spain, all along the coast to Tarifa, the Atlas Mountains on the African side of the narrow strait were clearly visible. The currents that churned where the cold waters of the Atlantic met the warmer, less salty waters of the Mediterranean had been feared and respected by the ancient world, for so many ships had been lost in their turbulent depths. This meeting of the two waters meant that it was rare indeed for Gibraltar to be seen in its entirety. More usually, a cloud sat on its summit, disguising it from where Spain glowered across the bay towards the British held isthmus, tethered for all time to the Spanish mainland, a constant thorn in the flesh of Spanish history and honour.

Doña Pilar took one look and turned away, not speaking again until Colonel Harris had them all safely ensconced in the new Reina Cristina Hotel that stood on a hill to the south of the town of Algeciras, overlooking the sea.

'Very nice,' she approved, glad to be out of the saddle. 'I have not been so far south before. It is a very pretty place this, with its gardens and shady trees. Petronilla and I will await you here while you go to Gibraltar.'

'Good idea,' the Colonel agreed. 'It'll do you good to have a whole day of peaceful inactivity in pleasant surroundings.'

Charles was less sanguine about leaving Petronilla behind the next day, however. 'Won't the Governor take it amiss? I mean, a courtesy visit from at least one of the ladies – he must know they are with us!'

'He will understand.'

'Oh well, another time.' Charles still wasn't happy about it. 'Petronilla is a British citizen —'

'Legally, so am I,' Doña Pilar muttered. 'But not on Gibraltar! There, I am always Spanish and affronted that my own people do not rule there!'

Charles gave his wife a resigned look. 'And you're half Spanish, I suppose?'

She nodded. 'Ambivalent,' she declared. 'I refuse to take sides!'

'Is that what I'm to tell the Governor?'

'Tell him we're exhausted from the journey, what else?' Petronilla advised, amused by her mother's languid air of innocence. She wondered what her parent was plotting, and whether her father was merely turning a blind eye to whatever it was she had in mind, or whether he innocently supposed she was indeed tired and in need of a rest.

It was only when the two men were mounting up for the ride to Gibraltar that Colonel Harris beckoned her over to where he was adjusting his stirrup.

'Stay with her, love. She doesn't mean any harm, but we can't afford any trouble just now.'

'What sort of trouble?' Petronilla asked.

'There probably won't be any. Family means a great deal to your mother though and Don Diego is her cousin!'

Petronilla gave her father a speaking look. 'How dare you? She's *your* wife and that's always meant more to her than family, country or even her own life!'

'She won't want to see me running into any danger,' the Colonel offered apologetically. 'I don't mean anything more than that.'

'I should hope not!'

'Stay with her anyway, Pet. She's more vulnerable than she knows – and so are you! Stay out of trouble, and keep your mother out of trouble too! That's all I'm asking of you!'

'All?' She thought about it a moment. 'I thought you wanted us with you, Papá? Would you rather have come alone?'

'I wanted you both where I can keep an eye on you, but it's no good expecting your mother to set foot on Gibraltar until she's good and ready to do so and so I'm reluctantly asking you to keep an eye on her and *don't* believe any messages you may receive unless you know the bearer, all right?'

She nodded. 'I'll do my best.'

'Good.'

If Charles was curious to know what had passed between father and daughter, he made no reference to the hurried exchange when he kissed Petronilla goodbye.

'It's unlike your mother not to put good manners above her own feelings,' he muttered uneasily. 'I could wish you at least were coming with us to pay your respects to the Governor. He is Queen Victoria's representative and any slight to him is a slight to her.'

Petronilla smiled up at him. 'Mamá'll come round to paying her respects to him *and* to Gibraltar in her own time. She's come this far, hasn't she?'

'I'm beginning to wonder why,' he answered grimly. 'I'll make your excuses today, but the next time you're coming with us, whatever your mother does!'

'Yes, dear.'

She watched the men ride away and then went in search of her mother.

'Have they gone? Have they truly gone?' Doña Pilar waited for her daughter's confirmation with an eagerness that belied her former languid indifference. 'Come, I want to show you something! I have ordered a carriage to take us to San Roque, because I want you to know the true story of Gibraltar before you go there. Then, when you know what really happened, we'll go together.'

Seeing her mother's set expression, Petronilla agreed meekly to accompany her wherever she wanted to go. She insisted on their being served with tea in the garden before they set forth, however, to which Doña Pilar made no objection. Indeed, her spirits seemed to be reviving miraculously now that they were alone together.

'It was all the fault of that terrible British mercenary, Rooke,' she began, sipping her tea contentedly. 'He was fighting for the Prince of Hesse-Darmstadt, who was the agent of Charles, Archduke of Austria, and pretender to the Spanish throne.'

Petronilla groaned aloud. 'Has there ever not been a pretender to the Spanish throne?'

'It was inevitable,' her mother answered simply. 'There was a time when Spain was everywhere: Austria, the Low Countries, the New World, everywhere. Spain, alone, protected Europe from the Turks and Islam, but that is all long forgotten! But that is not the point now! This Rooke, you understand was not fighting for the British, he had sold his sword to another and had no business there for Britain at all! It was during the War of the Spanish Succession in 1704. The Dutch were in Gibraltar also but once they had done their duty for the Hapsburgs they sailed away again, as was right and proper! But this Rooke did not sail away again! At first, it was not a matter of great consequence. The first two governors were Spaniards and were appointed in the name of "Charles III" and not in the name of the British Crown. You understand what I am saying?'

Petronilla wondered what title Rooke had been given by the British, if any. It was hard to believe they had been interested in Gibraltar at that time. It was all so long ago!

'When did Gibraltar become British?' she asked.

'But this is what I am telling you!' her mother responded furiously. '*Never* did it *become* British! It was *stolen* by the British when they realized Charles had no hope of gaining the Spanish throne, and that anyway he had succeeded his father to become the Emperor of Austria, so nobody wanted him to have Spain as well! Well, when that happened, suddenly your Queen Anne decided Gibraltar was a British conquest, because the mercenary Rooke was British! But even that was not the end of the matter! The rest I shall show you when we reach San Roque.' With trembling hands, she took another sip of tea. 'You did not think the British could be so base, did you? That they could behave so, without any honour? They are not all like your father, let me tell you, though even he prefers that the Fat Rock should remain British, because he thinks that if nobody is too powerful in Europe then we shall all live in peace. It's ridiculous, no? With nobody else to fight, we all fight each other at home, like here in Spain!'

Petronilla smothered a laugh. 'It sometimes seems that way,' she acknowledged.

Doña Pilar shook her head sadly. 'Your father works so hard to make peace that we must help him, no? Only, I remember you are my daughter also and you must know the truth about Gibraltar before we go and honour the representative of the British Crown who has no business ruling in Spanish Gibraltar, even though we are now poor and without influence in the great congresses of Europe.'

So this was the compromise her mother had decided upon. It seemed harmless enough to Petronilla. She had little doubt her father would tell another story as to how Gibraltar came into Britain's possession, but which of the two versions would come nearer to the truth of what had actually taken place nearly a hundred and fifty years before, she would probably never know.

'Then let's go,' Petronilla said.

The carriage was comfortable, the driver keeping up an endless commentary on all the major sites of the town and the countryside through which they passed. He was a native of Tarifa, he told them, the town that had given its names to the tariffs the excise men charged and which the *contrabandistas*, of which there were many, many on this coastline, did their best to avoid. He knew so much about their activities that Petronilla began to think he was probably one himself when he was not being employed by the hotel to transport their guests hither and yon.

By the time they had gone right round the bay, both ladies would have preferred their own conversation, but neither of them could bring themselves to be cruel enough to put an end to the unlikely stories he insisted on regaling for their entertainment.

'San Roque!' he announced at last. 'You wish to go up into the village?'

Doña Pilar brightened visibly. 'Yes, we wish to go to the Town Hall.'

She could hardly wait for the carriage to draw up before she was down on the ground, sweeping Petronilla inside as if she had been there a hundred times before instead of only having heard the story from others, largely from her brothers when they had all been children together. She seemed to know exactly where to go, crying out with triumph as she found what she was looking for.

'See! This is the pennant, and this is the image of

Nuestra *Señora* de la Coronada, which will one day return in triumph when Gibraltar is Spanish again! That will be a glorious day, the most glorious day in her life!'

Petronilla was filled with sadness at the sight of these mementoes; Doña Pilar, however, was far from showing any signs of patriotic nostalgia. On the contrary, she was thoroughly enjoying herself with a truly Spanish intensity of emotion, exclaiming over every detail. A little amused, Petronilla recognized the attraction of a lost cause, the more heroically out of reach the better.

'¡*Mire!*' Doña Pilar instructed, her English deserting her in the agony of her distress. She pointed with a small, plump finger at the report the parish priest had written in his parish register on the 8 August 1707. 'Read it aloud!' she commanded.

' . . . *this unhappy town having been seized by British arms, and according to the stipulations, permission being given to those who wished to leave the town with their belongings, many of us abandoned our country, homes and goods —*'

'You see? You see how it was? This was the whole population of Gibraltar! Now they live here, waiting for the day of their return. Read some more!'

' . . . *What a miserable spectacle to see women and children fleeing panic-stricken through the fields in the heat of August! The English looted the churches and our houses as soon as, and sometimes before, we left them.*'

Petronilla stopped reading, not wanting to know any more. This was what her father had told her was what was meant by war. What took place on the battlefield was permissible, he had said, but the suffering of the innocent was the worst part, made worse by badly-paid soldiers seeking the spoils of war and the high spirits of others, glad only to be alive when so many others had fallen beside them.

Doña Pilar, by now thoroughly enjoying the retelling of the old story, was not yet satisfied that Petronilla understood that Spain had been the innocent party in everything that had happened.

'The true inhabitants of Gibraltar now live here, *in honour*, in San Roque, while there are no Spaniards left in Gibraltar. There are only British soldiers, Genoese, Maltese, even Jews and Moors, though both of those are forbidden to dwell there under the Treaty of Utrecht, which the British pretend gives them the right to hold the Rock! It is very sad how they can be so two-faced, no?'

Petronilla made a move to escape, but Pilar had by no means finished with her.

'We go now to see more! You see that stained window? Read what is written on the marble slabs on either side!'

Petronilla reluctantly did so, recognizing that they rehearsed much the same story as the one her mother had told her. That Gibraltar had never surrendered to the British, but to a group who professed to be defending the interests of the archdukes of Austria to the Spanish throne, during the War of the Succession.

The surrender was effected in the most honourable conditions after a desperate and heroic battle. When the English flag was unexpectedly hoisted on the Rock, the Council, councillors, and with them the entire population, expatriated themselves, preferring the loss of their goods and homes to the foreign yoke; they settled here without losing their identity as a town, where they have remained ever since and will do so until the inevitable hour of their return.

'Huh!' Doña Pilar cried in triumph. 'How I should like to make your father read that! He wouldn't dare come home and tell me William Pitt had once said in the House of Commons: "Gibraltar! The most inestimable jewel in the British Crown!"'

'William Pitt, Mamá?'

'But yes, William Pitt! He was alive when Lord Nelson

was fighting the Battle of Trafalgar not very far from here. The Lord Nelson was killed, if you want to know —'

'I don't!' Petronilla decided.

'You don't?'

Her mother's disappointment made Petronilla want to laugh. She went over to the second marble slab and started to read that also. It informed her that the loss of Gibraltar had been a glorious as well as a lamentable page in Spain's history. There had been only seventy soldiers holding the town, augmented by some four hundred citizens, before their communications had been cut off by the besieging forces. Nevertheless, the inhabitants had fought with an epic stoicism, refusing all demands for surrender, until Gibraltar was destroyed in a duel of honour. It was indeed a sad story, but not one that she would allow to ruin her life.

She turned and faced her mother, to find her quite restored to normal, a mischievous smile lightening her previously stony-faced hatred for the Fat Rock, as she called it.

'I can't be sorry the British hold Gibraltar today,' Petronilla said, waiting for the inevitable explosion to follow.

There was none. Doña Pilar didn't even blink. 'Much better!' she agreed smugly. 'Better still, though, that your father shouldn't know I think so. It isn't good for him to be always right about everything!'

Petronilla trembled on the edge of laughter. 'I'm sure he'll never guess,' she murmured.

'No, much better not! You see, *hija*, the Spaniard is taught to put nothing above his honour, only God, and Gibraltar must always be a stain on our honour. That's why you had to know how it really was, so you would know that, although Gibraltar was lost and is still lost to us, nevertheless, our honour is intact. People may tell you otherwise, but you will *know* and will never be ashamed of your Spanish blood, yes?'

Petronilla's laughter was forgotten. 'Yes, I'll always know,' she agreed very gently.

After that, her mother was in the very best of spirits. She was graciousness itself to the various officials who had come to see who these strangers were who had insisted on entering their *ayuntamiento*, without warning or seeking anyone's permission. The Mayor, at first suspicious of these two strange women, was completely won over when Doña Pilar explained her mission to him, introducing Petronilla to him as her daughter, Mrs Arbuthnot.

If there was a slight, remaining tension at the mention of such a British name, it was soon forgotten when he found that Petronilla spoke Spanish as well as he did himself and was completely in sympathy with all he was doing to hold the people of San Roque together in a single community ready for their return to the Rock.

'One day it will be ours again!' he sighed.

Petronilla was less sure of that, but she saw no need to say so. Instead, she took the opportunity to ask him if the smuggling around the coast was really as bad as she had heard.

'It is very bad these days. Stories abound everywhere, but that is normal. More disturbing is when my own people are involved. We do all we can to protect them and to dissuade them from having anything to do with such a thing. It is better not to have anything to do with the Moors, we tell them. And better not to antagonize the British, not now they are at last trying to put a stop to this ill-favoured business. Now we have something new, however, not poor people seeking to make a little money, not even some big fish in London and Madrid and Tangiers employing little fish to take their risks for them. No, no, this is an appeal to patriotism, to make money for the Carlist cause —'

'Ah,' Petronilla encouraged him, 'who would disapprove of that?'

His dignity was touching. 'I do, *señora*. We have had two men killed, leaving widows and small children to be provided for by the rest of us. When these things happen there is no sign of the man who promised them vast sums if they would work for him. What use is a king like that?'

Doña Pilar drew herself up. 'Don Carlos is employing these men?' she demanded.

'So it's said. I don't know what to believe! Whoever he is, he's a man of rank, someone born to command! He comes and goes, telling everyone that the fewer people who know where to find him the better. He is much admired, *señoras*, as being without fear for himself. I've heard he was wounded himself recently —'

'Where?' Petronilla asked point-blank.

The Mayor stared at her in surprise. 'I am told a bullet grazed his cheek. Is such a man known to you?'

Petronilla did her best to recover herself. 'I'm a stranger in these parts. My mother is from Córdoba – Montilla – though she lives in England these days. My husband and I are travelling with my parents so that we may see something of the country where my mother was born.' She broke off, becoming aware of her mother's astonished gaze. 'We know very little of all that is going on in Spain these days,' she added with determination. 'I had quite thought Don Carlos to be a thing of the past, but there, what do women know of these things?'

The Mayor escorted them back to their carriage, exchanging a few words with their driver who was able to confirm that they were staying at the Reina Cristina in Algeciras, and that both their husbands were foreigners, exactly as Petronilla had said.

'So,' Doña Pilar said, when the carriage was rolling down the hill to the coastal road again, 'you think this smuggler is Cousin Diego?'

'Possibly,' Petronilla said. She put a finger to her lips and pointed towards the driver. 'I'm curious to know why you're resigned to the British holding Gibraltar?'

'Resigned is the right word,' her mother answered. 'If the Spanish cannot have their own, then it's better the British should have it. Besides, I have to admit it was good the British won Trafalgar, no?' Her eyes lit up with laughter. 'Did you know that the dead Lord Nelson was brought ashore at Rosia Harbour on Gibraltar? It was important he should be taken back to England for a proper State funeral, but they were at a loss to know what to do with him!'

'What did they do?' Petronilla asked, knowing her mother would enjoy the telling of what she plainly considered to be a good story. Besides, she was curious, never having heard it before.

'They put him in a cask of cognac, which was stupid, because everyone knows that rum is better! It was disastrous! The expanding gases from the body mixed with the vapour of the spirit and blew the top off the cask in the middle of the night. The guards nearly died of fright to see Nelson trying to climb out, as they believed! After this, they changed the brandy for rum. It was ridiculous, no?'

Doña Pilar began to laugh even while she was speaking. In a moment or two, Petronilla, too, was helpless with mirth. Her mother had never been more dear to her than she was in that moment, her hearty, earthy laugh ringing out in a manner that was very seldom heard amongst English ladies in Victorian England.

Petronilla turned a laughing glance at her. 'They should have had you to tell them what to do!' she observed.

'¡Claro!' her mother agreed calmly. 'To waste all that good brandy is not something any good vintner would want to see!'

And they started to laugh again, making the most of the moment, as if they both knew this could only be an interlude before the men returned from Gibraltar and the serious business of their visit began.

Chapter Twenty-One

Charles had the grace to be apologetic.

'The Governor has called a meeting for this morning and your father accepted for both of us to be there.'

'You mean,' Petronilla said, sucking in her cheeks to keep herself from laughing, 'that you don't want Mamá and I to go with you to Gibraltar after all?'

'The meeting can't go on for ever! Why don't you come and have a look round until after the meeting is over?'

'Yes, I think I'd like that. I've been reading all about it in the guide book. It isn't solid at all! Did you know that?'

Charles looked thoroughly disgruntled. 'It isn't my sort of place,' he confessed. 'Apart from the military, everyone seems to be trying to sell you something!'

Petronilla gave him a thoughtful look. 'The man behind the smuggling has a scar on his face these days,' she told him. 'People around here think he got in the way of a stray bullet, but you and I know it were far more likely that he was caught by a bull's horn.'

He didn't ask her where she had heard the rumour. 'Have you told your father?'

'No, I thought you'd better do that – if Mamá hasn't done so already.'

'Right.'

She saw that in his mind he was already at the morning's meeting only paying her a very small part of his attention.

Really men were all the same when they were asked to partake in any adventure, she thought. Their first thought was always to keep the women out of it and keep all the fun for themselves, but with her mother as ally she was quite complacent that she would get the better of them yet. Once in Gibraltar, they would have a hard time getting rid of either of them because there was a great deal she wished to see. Until she had been loaned this guide book by the hotel owner, she had had no idea Gibraltar was such an interesting place.

She found her mother a much better audience for the odd bits and pieces she had discovered about the Rock. Both ladies found it remarkable that Neolithic man had inhabited the smaller caves and caverns many thousands of years before. Doña Pilar had been inclined to doubt that this could be so, but Petronilla was quite happy with the idea.

'They found the skeleton of a cave-dweller in 1848,' she declared. 'Gibraltar Man! Only it happens to be a female. The caves are about eight hundred feet above sea level. They must have been like mountain goats to have got up and down from such places! Or do you think the sea is lower now?'

'I think Gibraltar is as God made it,' Doña Pilar maintained stubbornly. 'I have never believed in these old bones people discover, especially not when they are conveniently found a few weeks before someone brings out a book on the subject. That time it was Mr Darwin and his *Origin of the Species*. Your father met him once and said he was a modest man, unwilling to thrust his ideas on anyone, but everyone knows when man was created, and not even the modest Mr Darwin can change that!'

'Did you read his book?' Petronilla asked.

Doña Pilar was shocked by the idea. 'Of course not! Even if I had wanted to, I'm sure the Church would have forbidden it.'

Petronilla lost interest. 'There are wild simians to be

seen. They say here that the local people refer to them as
apes, but they are really monkeys who have no tails.
Apparently they are very bad-tempered.'

'Why should I wish to see some bad-tempered
monkeys?'

'They are the only ones of their kind in Europe. They're
under the protection of the Army because if they should
leave the Rock, so will the British. Some of the males are
dangerous as well as bad-tempered.'

Doña Pilar gave her daughter a speaking look. 'What
else is there in Gibraltar?'

'Let's go and take a look,' Petronilla suggested. 'I'll
bring the book with me and we can make up our minds
what we want to look at when we get there.'

Once she had assured herself that neither monkeys nor
ancient skeletons would figure on their agenda, Doña Pilar
was pleased with this idea. She went herself to hire the
same carriage that had taken them to San Roque the day
before and then went to make herself ready, putting on
one of her prettiest dresses in case she should be invited
to meet the Governor after all, once the men had finished
their meeting.

Petronilla, too, spent a long time before her glass, trying
to decide whether she should wear her mantilla, which
was both comfortable and practical, or resort to an English
bonnet, which might be safer under the circumstances.
She really didn't know. Digging around in her
portmanteau, she discovered her bonnet to be crumpled
and sadly the worse for wear, and so she settled for the
Spanish look and hoped Charles would approve when he
saw her.

A number of ships of the Royal Navy were tied up in
the natural harbour for which Gibraltar is justly famous.
Their masts rose and fell with the slight swell, their sails
neatly furled away whilst they were in port. Other, smaller
fishing vessels came and went. Were they all based in
Gibraltar, or did some of them come from across the bay
from Algeciras? There was no way that Petronilla could

tell, but she thought them very pretty as they sped across the deep blue of the sea.

Less beautiful was the single street that ran the whole length of Gibraltar. Some of the shops smelt of the East and were full of exotic Indian dresses and even more exotic looking people trying to sell hand-carved ivory elephants and all sorts of extraordinary ornaments and bits and bobs. Yet it also had the look of every English town she had ever seen. Perhaps the fashions were dowdier and the uniforms less well-turned-out, but the soldiers who stood guard outside the Governor's residence were as smart as any she had seen parading in Winchester. She felt sorry for them sweltering under the hot sun, but no doubt they preferred it to the winter's drizzle they often had to contend with at home.

Doña Pilar was soon bored by the few shops that had managed to attract her interest. 'How terrible it must be to be obliged to live here any length of time!' she exclaimed. 'I expect they would all much prefer to be in Spain.'

Petronilla found herself agreeing with her. She remembered how much she had longed to disembark at British Gibraltar when they had first come to Spain and was at a loss to know now why she had thought it would be reassuringly familiar in a strange world. Despite the many British touches on the Rock, it was still far more foreign to her than Spain had ever been, mostly because of the difficulty she had in understanding anything anyone said to her. Worse still, she found the only street that they could find as boring as did her mother.

'There must be somewhere where we could have a dish of tea,' she began doubtfully.

'You think so?' Doña Pilar was even less convinced. 'I shall go to the church and say my prayers. You remember, Fabiola especially asked us to pray for her?'

Petronilla couldn't think of anything better to do. They walked down the street again and walked into the first church they came to. It was very modern, of a Moorish design, and almost completely empty.

'What is this church?' Doña Pilar asked the single woman she could see. The only answer was a blank stare. She repeated the question in Spanish, only to be met by the same response. 'You ask her!' she commanded her daughter. 'She doesn't understand me.'

Petronilla was soon given to know they were in the Anglican cathedral which had been built only a few years before for the British community.

'Is there another church?' she asked the woman.

The old lady pointed further down the street and mother and daughter set forth, Doña Pilar looking back over her shoulder with disbelieving eyes.

'It is bizarre, no, to build a church to look like a mosque? What has this to do with England?'

Petronilla didn't know. It was difficult not to laugh at her mother's face when they finally reached their own cathedral and found that it was, in fact, the converted mosque the other cathedral was pretending to be, perhaps because so many Andalucian churches are built on the ruins of the mosques that had served their Moorish ancestors before them.

Inside a priest was celebrating Mass, his congregation whispering to one another in a bastardized Spanish, interspersed by an incomprehensible English that was the official language of the Rock. Doña Pilar ran her beads through one hand, lazily fanning herself with the other, while Petronilla fidgeted at her side, feeling no urge to pray, or to sit quietly doing nothing as her mother was able to do. Now that they were here in Gibraltar, she was more than a little dissatisfied not to know what was being done about her cousin's smuggling ring. More than that, she wanted to know what was being said at the Governor's meeting and whether her father would be able to hold the ring between the new Governor's determination to put an end to the whole unsavoury business and the City of

London who made a great deal of money from it and who were also in part the Government's paymasters.

'If you can't sit quietly, go outside!' Doña Pilar broke into her thoughts. 'What's the matter with you?'

'Nothing,' Petronilla whispered back, not liking to admit to her utter boredom.

'Then sit still, or go!' her mother commanded.

Petronilla chose to go. She walked restlessly up and down outside the cathedral, working herself up into a fever of indignation that her husband and father should have effectively excluded their womenfolk from what she had managed to convince herself was a meeting to decide the fate of her whole family.

Most people had gone inside, leaving Main Street empty and sweltering under the midday sun. She thought she would walk up to the Convent, the Governor's residence, and see if the meeting were over yet. Even if it were not, they would soon be changing the guard and that would be a distraction to keep her occupied until lunchtime.

She flapped her fan with more nervous energy than dignity and felt hotter then ever. The feathers in her fan drooped in sympathy with her spirits and she plucked at it with her fingers, trying to restore it to its former beauty. The feathers started to come out, the glue that had held them disintegrating in the heat. It was not a valuable fan, but it had been a pretty toy and Petronilla had been fond of it. Perhaps, she thought, she would buy another while she was in Gibraltar. If nothing else, it would give her something to do until her mother finished her prayers.

The shops were shutting for the lunch hour as she walked along. In one of the Indian shops, she saw a fan made from a peacock's tail and wondered if it would suit her purpose, or even whether she really liked it. She took a step inside, blinking at the sudden change from bright sunshine to shade.

'Petronilla!'

She was first startled, and then infuriated, to hear her name being called in the street, just as if she were some trollop to have her name shouted abroad by all and sundry. She turned and went outside again, meaning to give the perpetrator of this insult a piece of her mind, but as far as she could see there was no one there.

'May I help you, madam?'

The sing-song voice of the Indian woman made her turn again. At least she spoke English.

'I need a new fan,' she began.

'Petronilla!'

'Did you hear that? You know I have the strangest feeling I know that voice —'

The Indian woman smiled and nodded. 'One hears many strange sounds in Gibraltar. *¡Ni habla inglés ni español tampoco!* I'm told the Spanish call our Gibraltarian Spanish *Llanito*, because nobody understands it save those of us who live here.'

'My name sounds the same in any language!' Petronilla said drily. 'Especially when shouted out in a public street by my own cousin! What I want to know is what he is doing here in the first place!'

'Your cousin? Shouldn't he be in Gibraltar?'

'No,' Petronilla said, 'he should not.'

The Indian woman tried to hide her surprise. 'Many ships call in at Gibraltar these days,' she began hopefully. She had had the greatest expectations of selling one of her most expensive fans to this aggressive young woman, who looked Spanish but spoke English with such a pure accent that it had to be her mother tongue. Now, she saw the sale slipping away as Petronilla glowered out into the street through the open door. 'Perhaps your cousin —'

'My cousin is a smuggler and a traitor to Spain, not a tourist!' Petronilla informed her loftily.

The Indian woman merely looked prim. 'Gibraltar is British, not Spanish,' she pointed out. 'If he is your cousin —'

Petronilla swept her a haughty look, regretting ever having stepped inside the shop. 'That is the trouble! Gibraltar is British, but my cousin is Spanish and, if he is here, my father should know of it. I must go to him at once!'

It took her a little while to convince the shopkeeper that she meant to go straight to the Governor's residence, no matter what temptations the Indian woman offered her from the Aladdin's Cave that was her shop.

'Nobody goes to the Convent without an appointment, *señora*.'

'No? But I have no wish for another priest —'

'A priest?' The Indian lady was as confused as Petronilla for a moment. 'The Governor's residence used to be a Franciscan convent. There are guards outside. Let me show you some fans, *señora*, before I close for the *siesta*, and you can find your cousin after that.'

But Petronilla had already retreated back into the street. Looking first one way and then the other, she chose the most likely route and was relieved to find she had made the right decision when she saw a sign pointing to the Convent and soon came up to a pretty building, nestling behind a small square, planted with trees and creepers. She was about to make her presence known to one of the guards when she was struck hard on the side of her head. For a moment, she was completely aware of the empty street, the smart marines standing to attention only about a hundred yards away from her, and then she felt herself falling into the blackness of unconsciousness and knew no more.

She had a headache. She opened her eyes, wondering where she was. It was beautifully cool. It was also dark and mysterious. Forcing herself up on to her feet, she found herself in a cave from which she could look out if she stood on tip-toe. There was nothing between the opening and the minute harbour a long, long way below. Petronilla judged herself to be in a cave on the north side of the Rock. She tried to remember what she had read about the many caves which riddled the interior, some of them used as gun emplacements and some carved out by

the British Sappers at the time of the Great Siege of
Gibraltar in the eighteenth century. She wished she had
paid greater attention to her guide book. She felt *terrible*!

'Cousin Petronilla!'

She had been right about knowing his voice, she
thought, when he had first called out to her in the street.
She didn't even look round, but went on staring out at
the sea beneath.

'Cousin Diego.'

He advanced into the cave, putting a hand on her
shoulder and turning her round to face him. The scar
pulled at the corner of his mouth, ran right across his
cheek and ended somewhere by his right ear. It had healed
up, more or less, but it still had a red and ugly look to it.
Knowing how proud he had always been of his handsome
good looks, she was surprised that he could bear anyone
to see him like that.

'They told me at San Roque you'd been shot,' she said.
'Why didn't you tell them you were playing at being a
matador when you got that scar?'

'I'm an important man in these parts!'

She nodded. 'A smuggler.'

'We need the profits! It costs a lot of money to raise an
army, cousin; more than you'll ever see in your lifetime!'

She nodded again. 'More than Don Carlos will ever see,
I dare say!'

He stood in silence for a moment, then he said, 'You
used to like me. I liked you, too! That's why I brought
you here to give you a last chance to throw in your lot
with me. We were made for each other!' His fingers
touched her cheek. 'I love you, Petronilla!'

'Is that why you thought I wouldn't mind your shouting
my name in the street like that? *Petronilla!* Not *Doña*
Petronilla, not even *Cousin* Petronilla! It would have been
more fitting to have called me Mrs Arbuthnot —'

'Never!'

She looked at him, brows slightly raised, every bit as

proud as he. 'Mrs Arbuthnot is who I am. Mrs Charles Arbuthnot. Had you forgotten!'

'How could I forget? You should have come with me on your wedding day and then I shouldn't have been put to all this trouble now. I could have killed you that day for pretending to prefer him to me! A fine dance you've led me, one way and another! But you couldn't keep away from me in the end, could you? You came to Gibraltar, as I always knew you would!'

Her head pounded and she felt physically sick. 'Diego —'

He ignored the interruption. 'You are *my* woman! I shall never allow you to go back to *him*!'

'You mean to keep me a prisoner?'

His smile was distorted by the new, livid scar, but there was no mistaking the look in his eyes as his glance dwelt on her ashen face. 'A prisoner of love!'

Petronilla shook her head. 'Don't be ridiculous, cousin! I suppose this egg on the side of my head is meant to make me forget all about my husband?'

He shrugged. 'A little pain —'

Petronilla took a step away from him. 'I told you once before that I have never been in love with pain – or with you!'

'Little liar! You were nearly mine on that picnic at the Medina Azahara, only your English blood came between us —'

Petronilla essayed a laugh. It was a feeble attempt and it made her feel iller than ever. 'It was my very Spanish Mamá who brought it home to me what a silly little fool I had been to allow myself to be dazzled by my heroic cousin! My English father was much more concerned about the hurt you might inflict. How glad I am I'm Spanish enough to put my duty to my family before my own childish inclinations – for it would have been a disaster for both of us, my dear Diego, if I had let you have your way with me!'

'I wanted you!'

'Oh yes,' she agreed. 'I thought I wanted you too, but

we've both grown up since then. You have your Cause, and I have my darling Charles! God was good to us, was he not?'

His outrage made him more ridiculous than the personification of a romantic dream that she remembered and which had haunted her for so many months after their picnic together.

'Your stupid husband had no right to take you away from me! You are lucky I didn't kill him before he could touch you!'

Petronilla looked out across the sea again. 'Charles is more than a match for you – or any other man,' she declared softly. 'I owe him all my happiness.'

He took a step towards her and, perhaps because she wasn't looking at him, she could feel his ill-temper in his every movement.

'You haven't been listening, Petronilla. You're *my* woman and I mean to have you! That's what we both want –'

She turned her head, the light from outside hurting her eyes. 'No, my dear, it isn't what I want at all. I doubt it ever was. I was dazzled by your beauty for a while, but love is something different as I hope you'll one day know for yourself. Believe me, Charles would never have hit me over the head –'

'Are you telling me you don't love me?' he pressed her, his lower lip as sulky as a small boy's.

'I'm telling you that you don't love me either – you've never given yourself time to get to know me! I misled you into thinking I was as much a romantic as you are, longing for revolution and derring-do, but the truth is that I'm perfectly happy as a staid, married woman, who wants children far more than death or glory; I would bore you into leaving me long before we had finished quarrelling over your support for Don Carlos and mine for the Doña Isabella.'

The quizzical expression in the back of her eyes made

him think about the truth of what she was saying. 'I shall never love any other woman!' he vowed extravagantly.

'Nonsense, you'll probably love half a dozen! But don't, I beg of you, hit them over the head to gain their attention because nothing could be calculated to put them off you quicker! I have the most abominable headache —'

'I didn't think you'd make such a fuss about nothing,' he frowned at her. He caught her up against him with a sudden lightening of mood. 'Shall I kiss it better?'

'Certainly not!'

A muscle twitched in his cheek, pulling at his scar and giving him a dangerous look. 'Why aren't you afraid of me?' he asked her.

Her head pounded painfully, but she knew better than to show him any weakness. 'Should I be?' she countered.

'As you say, I have my Cause.' He hesitated, taking her hands into his own and staring at her with a wild, lost look that made her wonder if he hadn't been fonder of her than she had known. 'I thought you'd want to help me. I thought you *loved* me?'

'I'm sorry,' she said helplessly.

'Sorry! You don't know what the word means! If you're not on my side, you're one of the enemy. You do see that, don't you?' His hands clutched hers, hurting her fingers. 'I'm told your father is in Gibraltar,' he said. 'You may not love me, but you love him, don't you?'

It felt as though her heart had stopped beating. 'You know I do!'

'Then you had best do as I wish, my Petronilla, if you don't want harm to come to him.'

Petronilla blenched. She was too proud to show him she was afraid, however, and tried to pass it off as an unsteadiness caused by the blow to her head. If she could be kidnapped on the Main Street of Gibraltar in full daylight, with the marines standing on guard within sight, what might not be arranged for a man who, no matter how gallant he had been in the past, was now old and tired and more in the need of his wife's loving care than

444

another adventure? Her mouth trembled despite herself
and she turned away, putting her hand up to her head as
if to ease the pain.

'Leave my father alone!' she bit out.

He laughed. It was an ugly sound. 'My dear girl, if I
were to kiss you now —'

'I very much hope you won't!' she exploded.

'Why do you think you would dislike it? You didn't
before! Is your reluctance now because of this?' He pointed
towards his scar. 'I don't believe it has anything to do
with your "happy marriage"!'

She refused to look at him. 'Charles Arbuthnot made a
woman out of the child you kissed on that picnic. What
would you make of me?'

'Once, you wouldn't have cared. You preferred me to
that husband of yours! You found him boring then, don't
pretend you didn't! And don't expect me to believe you
don't still find him boring more often than not?'

Petronilla's head began to ache again in earnest. It
seemed incredible to her that there had ever been a time
when she had thought Charles to be merely worthy and
rather dull. She knew much better after Granada!

'I don't see him in quite the same way since I became
his wife,' she said with such satisfaction that Diego was
both convinced and infuriated by her smugness.

He looked sulkier than ever. 'I took a lot of trouble to
bring you up here and have you to myself for a while!'

'What I don't understand is why you should have done
so,' Petronilla said flatly. 'All you've done is to give me
a headache —' One glance was enough to see that his
interest in her welfare was strictly limited. She tried
another tack. 'It may seem dull to you, but I assure you
I've never enjoyed myself more than now I am Charles's
partner at the *bodega*, and in his life. Mamá was quite right
when she said one would never be content if one snatched
one's own happiness at everyone else's expense. Selfishness
is a very hard cross to bear.'

'You think me selfish?'

Petronilla wished she could say she didn't. She not only thought him selfish, she couldn't even bring herself to dislike him; instead she only felt sorry for him and she knew enough about men by now to know there was nothing he would hate more than to be pitied by her.

'Not deliberately selfish,' she said aloud. 'To be that you have to be aware of other people, but none of us mean anything more to you than what you can get out of us. I find that sad.'

'I have other interests beside winemaking!' he declared.

'Don Carlos? Don't deceive yourself! Your cause is your own. The money you smuggle goes into your own pocket. Isn't that the truth?'

He began to laugh. 'I have to live. What have you and the rest of my family ever done for me? When I've made my own fortune, I'll pass the rest on to Don Carlos, never you fear, and that may be sooner than you think!'

'Oh?' It was obvious she didn't believe him, which made him angrier than she had ever seen him.

'What do you know about anything?' he taunted her. 'You *look* Spanish,' he complained, 'but you don't understand, do you? You don't understand anything! I'm a *hidalgo*. Blue blood runs in my veins. How should I soil my hands with work like a *peón*? I'm entitled to command, to give orders, not to have to take them as if I were a nobody!'

'So you turned smuggler?'

'It costs money to be a gentleman.'

She hardened her heart. 'Smuggler and traitor!'

'Because I don't acknowledge the Doña Isabella to be Queen? Why does that make me a traitor? Because your uncles died on the other side? Neither pretender to the throne is Spanish, so what do either of them matter to me?'

'That won't make it any easier for you if you're discovered in Gibraltar!' she warned him. 'The British have promised the Spanish Government they're going to put an end to all the smuggling that passes through the Rock. They're not going to make an exception for you!'

He managed a glassy smile. 'I have you,' he said.

'Me? What good will that do you?'

'My dear Petronilla —'

'*Cousin* Petronilla!'

'I don't think of you as a cousin,' he objected.

'Then you'd better address me as Mrs Arbuthnot for that's how I think of myself!'

'An English name for an English woman!'

'I was born and brought up in England, but I feel quite at home in Spain too.'

'It makes no difference to me. You're still your father's daughter and that's the one thing that matters. As long as I hold you, my dear, I hold Gibraltar, and he who holds Gibraltar holds all Andalucía! I have no need for Don Carlos any longer! I have no need of anybody! All the time I hold you, your father won't let any of them touch me!'

So that was what he intended by her, despite all his talk of love and his need for her. She could have wept when she thought how easy she had made it for him. Belatedly, she remembered her father's warning and wished he had been franker with her from the very beginning. And yet she should have been able to work it out for herself, and she might have done, if she hadn't been so busy thinking of herself as Charles Arbuthnot's wife rather than Thomas Harris's daughter.

'You underrate my father,' she said aloud.

He shook his head violently. 'With Cousin Pilar insisting you must be rescued at all costs?' He laughed, a raucous sound that had nothing to do with amusement. 'What will the British Government think you're worth when they realize you're my prisoner?'

The mention of her mother stiffened Petronilla's backbone. If her mother would be angry with anyone, it would be with her stupid daughter for getting herself into this pickle. She certainly wouldn't allow her beloved husband to risk his neck in any attempt to rescue her. She was less sure of what her husband might do, but she prayed Charles would stand firm and refuse to deal with Don Diego, taking his cue from his father-in-law. She swallowed, pretending to herself she wasn't afraid. She felt suddenly alone and vulnerable.

'I have nothing to do with the British Government so why should they care what happens to me?' Her voice shook a little. She cleared her throat, hoping her cousin hadn't noticed. Her eyes smarted with tears, but she refused to allow them to fall, thinking how ashamed Charles would be of her if she showed any female weakness in the face of her cousin's threats.

She tried not to listen as Don Diego went on, 'You think I don't know all about your father? Everyone knows Gibraltar has always been a centre of smuggling and will be again, as soon as all the good citizens can persuade Colonel Harris, MP, to go back to England, taking his wife and daughter with him. This Governor won't last two minutes without your father's personal backing as soon as his policies are seen to have failed. I'm not the only one to make a little money smuggling in these waters. The English are not above turning a dishonest penny – providing there's no danger of their being caught of course!'

Petronilla tapped an impatient toe, working herself up into a fury that would help control the fright that threatened to paralyse her mind and limbs. 'You can't keep me for ever against my will!' she said out loud.

The scar on his face showed livid and angry. 'You'll do as you're told!'

He went to the entrance of the cave and she saw for the first time that he was limping. Was that also the result of his playing the matador? She shut her eyes, forcing herself to think. Was there some way she could use that to her own advantage? She could think of nothing and that was an added disappointment to her.

Her cousin came back into the cave, walking right up to her, the jauntiness back in his step. 'You may have met

448

the man who'll take the message down to your father where you are!'

She had indeed! The man was her father's Gibraltarian friend from the Alhambra, Jesús!

Petronilla froze.

It was Jesús who broke the silence in the cave. 'Is the Doña Petronilla staying with us?' he asked.

Her cousin hunched his shoulders. 'Not willingly. She claims to have fallen in love with that husband of hers! I should never have let him live!'

Petronilla met Jesús's eyes, unsure of herself. How could her father have been so mistaken in this man? She had always known Thomas Harris to be an excellent judge of character – but this! Could they trust no man on this *Piedra Gorda*? Perhaps her mother had known instinctively something about Gibraltar her father couldn't recognize, seeing it only as a British possession?

'I am surprised to see you here,' she said to the man. 'I shouldn't have thought you'd have any interest in who sits on the throne of Spain. I was told you are a Gibraltarian.'

'Sometimes,' Jesús muttered. 'Money has no nationality, *señora*, as the gentlemen of the City of London will tell you.'

'I have another name for such activities!' Petronilla shot back at him. She was more afraid than ever now, afraid for herself and afraid for her father. Her only hope was that Charles would take command of the whole situation. He, she knew to be more than a match for her blackguard of a cousin!

Was it her imagination, or was Jesús more nervous of her cousin's volatile temper than he was of her knowing his true allegiance? Did that mean that he thought she would never be able to reveal her knowledge to the Gibraltar authorities? She felt her flesh creep at the thought. She was not like her mother, facing death with equanimity. She wanted to live long enough to be the mother of Charles Arbuthnot's children – indeed, she was again counting the days to find out if she were not already in the family way.

'What do you intend to do with me?' she asked.

Jesús blinked. Don Diego's love of inflicting pain had lit up his whole face, the scar making it grotesque in the half-light that filled the cave. 'You were always meant to be mine!'

She was reminded of a cat playing with its prey and wished she could hate him, or despise him as some kind of evil monster, but she was consumed with a sadness that he was unable to live up to the vision she had once had of him. Great physical beauty should have an inner beauty to match. Once, she had thought he had both and she would never quite forget the magical effect he had had on her before she had left such childish dreams behind and had settled for the vastly more satisfying love she had for Charles, in which there was more reality than romance, as befitted two adults who liked as much as they loved each other.

Jesús grimaced. 'No one is going to hurt you, Doña Petronilla. If you'll write a note to your father, I'll see that it's delivered to him. Nothing will happen to you if you co-operate in persuading your father that General Gardiner is the wrong Governor for a place like Gibraltar.'

Petronilla's eyes widened. 'You're going to hold me to ransom? You won't get one penny out of any member of my family, neither my father nor my husband!' She stuck her nose in the air, pursing her lips together lest their trembling should betray her fears.

Her cousin produced a pad and pencil, pushing them into her hands.

'Write!' he commanded.

'I won't!'

'I think you will, my Pet, or do you want me to kiss you?'

She shivered. 'Never!'

'Don't worry yourself, *señora*,' Jesús said roughly. 'Governor Gardiner will want to get you back as quickly as possible. whether you write him a letter or not. Everybody in Gibraltar knows he has your father visiting and reporting back to London on every move he makes.'

'Because you betrayed him, I suppose!' she retorted.

'Shall we say, your father and I see Gibraltar's future rather differently?'

'You'd do better not to say anything at all,' Petronilla observed. 'I shall look forward to reporting everything you do say at your trial!' She turned away and went to look out at the sea again, struggling to keep an appearance of calm such as she knew her mother would have maintained. The whole world was empty as far as she could see. She had only herself to depend upon if she were ever to find a way out.

Thus she never saw exactly what happened next. She heard a scuffle behind her and the next minute she knew Jesús and another man had lifted her cousin bodily off his feet and had deposited him on the floor, the stranger sitting on his chest, a great booming laugh coming out of his face.

Horrified, Petronilla ran towards them. 'Don't kill him!'

'He might not have spared you!' Jesús said over his shoulder.

His brother laughed again. 'Shall I tie him up?'

Jesús got slowly to his feet. He smiled across the cave at Petronilla. 'It's as well the future of Spain doesn't rest on this one's shoulders! Or the future of Gibraltar either!' He bowed his head politely. 'Here is no place for you, *señora*. Follow me, and I'll take you down below. My brother Ireneo will stay and guard *Señor* Don Diego —'

Bewildered, Petronilla looked from one to the other of them. 'I don't understand,' she began.

'Your husband will tell us what to do with him.'

Petronilla put a hand up to her head. She didn't know what to do for the best. She had no reason to trust Jesús – indeed she thought any reliance on him was probably misplaced, for it was obvious that both he and his brother were smugglers long before they were anything else.

'Was it you who hit me over the head?' she asked, not wanting to go with him, little as she wanted to stay behind.

'And face your husband's fury for mistreating you? No, it was not I. Your cousin is easily provoked, *señora*. You should have answered your name when he first called you, before he lost his temper with you. Didn't you know it was he?'

Petronilla managed a brief smile. 'There was a time when I would have gone anywhere with him, but that was before I married my husband —' She broke off, biting her lip. 'I can't dislike him even now, you know. Your brother won't kill him, will he?'

Jesús shrugged. 'It makes no difference to me.'

'Then why do you follow him?' she asked him.

'Did he tell you he was our leader?'

She nodded. 'They told me so at San Roque too.'

'Because somebody shot at us and he was the one who got hit?'

'He got that playing the matador during the Fiesta of the Vendimía in Jerez!' she retorted. 'I don't believe he makes a better *contrabandista* than he did a *torero*! I almost wish there was a proper war going on for him to fight in it and gain the glory he seeks!'

Jesús merely grunted. 'Be glad he's your cousin, Doña Petronilla, and not your husband!' he said.

Chapter Twenty-Two

Jesús knew the caves like the back of his hand. He found ways, some of them only narrow crevices, that led from one cave to another, until they came out into the huge cavern known as St Michael's, the size of which convinced Petronilla, as her guide book had not, that the whole of Gibraltar was riddled with caves – both natural and man-made – and far from being the solid rock of legend.

Petronilla followed Jesús as closely as she could. Now that she was no longer as afraid as she had been, she had time to think about her aching head and the soreness of her limbs. She wondered if her cousin hadn't bodily dragged her up to the hidden cave where she had regained consciousness. She ought to have been glad that Ireneo was standing guard over him, but she knew, if it had been up to her, she would have let him go despite his treatment of her.

'Are you for or against my cousin?' she asked.

He stared at her over the flickering flame in the lamp he was holding. 'My brother and I earn our living by smuggling,' he said at last. 'We can't afford your cousin's interference in our trade because he attracts too much attention to us, but, in return for your safety, my brother and I can expect your father and the Governor to look the other way, no?'

He lifted the lamp he was carrying so that she could see

the enormous stalactites and stalagmites that descended in great coloured pillars from the darkness above them, or grew like great trees as if they had no beginning and no end.

'What makes you think my father would accept such a bargain?' she demanded.

Jesús swung the lamp back and forth. 'Your father and I understand one another. He understands that a man has to live.'

Petronilla wished he'd hold the light still. Her head ached worse than ever. 'What about my husband?' She had thought until recently her father to be the soldier and politician and therefore the natural leader of their party, but since Granada she hadn't been so sure. Charles Arbuthnot had a way of thinking things through which always seemed to work to his own advantage. Yet he must have thought it safe for her and her mother to venture on to Gibraltar for he had made no move to stop her from joining the menfolk after their meeting.

She probed a little further. 'I suppose what he does will depend on what you do to me?'

'We intend you no harm, *señora*, only to keep you safe until we have the Governor's agreement to make no more trouble for us. You have nothing to fear from either my brother or myself.'

Somehow the way he said it revived the panic she had felt earlier and all her distrust of the smuggler she had once thought to be her father's friend. Indeed, she might have been better off with her cousin.

However, she had no choice for the moment but to follow Jesús down several more secret passages until they reached yet more northern galleries that had been cut into the northern face of the Rock during the Great Siege, which had begun on 11 July 1779 and had continued unbroken for three years and seven months.

Petronilla thought of the people who had withstood that siege and wondered what they had done to keep their spirits up during such a long time. She had been a prisoner for at the most a couple of hours and already she was at a loss to know how to revive her spirits sufficiently to put her mind to a proper plan for her escape. What she really needed was time to think, but she couldn't think of any subject that would sufficiently interest Jesús to slow down his headlong progress through the Rock.

'Why did the Siege go on for so long?' she asked suddenly.

It was something which he had studied in detail ever since he was a boy. 'The Royal Navy was busy with the American War of Independence. They came once a year and relieved the Rock, otherwise it was left to the Gibraltarians themselves to defy the combined might of the French and the Spanish!'

She saw that this was one of the occasions when the smuggler was a Gibraltarian. He spoke with pride, almost as if he had been there himself.

'What happened in the end?'

He stopped for a moment, only too glad to relate every detail to her. 'It was the tedium that was the main threat to their resolve to hold out. Their commander was a man called Eliott, who must have known the British were so stretched in America there was little chance of their coming to Gibraltar's aid for many a long day. To give them something to do, he organized that the two thousand British should walk out of the gates one night, spike all the enemy guns, and walk back in again.'

'And was that the end of it?'

'It made them feel like men again,' he insisted, 'instead of rats caught in a trap. Gibraltar is too small a place for its citizens to be confined on the Rock for long. They call it a kind of island fever. But no one complained about the length of the Siege then, any more than we would today if things come to that. There were ten Spanish and French to every one of them, but they never surrendered.'

And nor would she! She would win her own victory with the same panache that Eliott had shown.

'If this it to be my prison, I should prefer to be alone,' she told Jesús proudly. 'I have things to think about!'

He was immediately suspicious. 'What have you got to think about?'

'How to get out of here,' she said frankly. 'Was it the Siege that started the Gibraltarians off as smugglers, do you suppose? Owing no allegiance to anybody, they'd see no harm in trading with both sides, just as you do today!'

His indignation rewarded her better than she had hoped. 'We were the victims of the Siege! We were the ones who withstood it!'

'Not the British Army?'

'We're all British who live on Gibraltar, as British as you are!'

'Oh? I thought you were a Spaniard when it suited you, working for my cousin and the cause of Don Carlos?'

'Your cousin has never been one of us!'

Petronilla put her head back and looked at him. 'I don't see that you're any better than he is. Please go away!'

Jesús was clearly undecided. He decided to stay and justify himself. 'It's easy for you to look down your nose at us,' he complained. 'Gibraltarians have always made their money from smuggling. We're *paid* to smuggle as often as not by respectable British citizens. How else are we to make a living? It isn't we who make our money from bunkering the Royal Navy, or supplying the military. Some of us may work on the ships —'

'My father wants to put an end to the London connection.'

'And do us out of a living altogether? A fine reward that would be for saving you from your cousin! We do no harm to anyone!'

'There must be something else you could do?'

'Would you have us become farmers, each of us with a couple of yards to cultivate?'

'I don't know what you can do,' she admitted. 'What about fishing?'

'We call it fishing that we do now!'

Her laughter was hollow. What else would they call it? She sat down on a ledge that had been carved out of the wall and put her head in her hands. She no longer cared whether he went or stayed, all she wanted was the pounding in her head to stop. She felt his hand on the back of her neck and started back, hitting her head on the uneven wall of the cave.

'What do you want?' she asked in fright.

'That devil-may-care cousin of yours hit you harder than he should! Are you sure you'll be all right here until I get back?'

'I'll do my best not to be here!' Her wry humour brought an unwilling smile to his lips. She thought she read concern in his eyes and then he stood back and she determined she had been mistaken. It was easier to think of him as being as big a villain as her cousin.

'Don't go looking for Don Diego, will you?' A muscle jerked in his face. 'You can get lost in these caves and, if you do find your cousin, neither he nor Ireneo will help you. You may have been safe with Don Diego when he thought you were his adoring admirer, but you've made him think of you now as Mrs Arbuthnot and that's a different matter! If I thought you'd go looking for him, I'd have to lock you up somewhere. You're in no fit state to go prowling about these caves by yourself!'

It was a good half hour before she realized that he had indeed left her alone. She couldn't remember his going, only opening her eyes and finding that he was gone. Had she slept? She thought not. One didn't fall asleep sitting bolt upright, not in her experience. She thought it more likely she had been unconscious for a moment and felt her head with cautious fingers, alarmed to feel the matted blood in her hair. However, she felt no worse than she had before. Indeed, she was feeling better for the pounding in her head had ceased for the time being. She thought she might have slipped into unconsciousness before Jesús had left her, thinking her safely disposed of until he got back. She was as much a prisoner as she had been before.

Or was she still a prisoner? The first thing to do was to find out and see if this wasn't 'the opportunity she had been seeking to make her escape. She stood up with resolution, expecting her head to hurt again. It did, but it was no longer unbearable. Jesús had taken the lamp with him, leaving her in darkness, but it was not the impenetrable darkness that it might have been, hidden away in a cave without any access to the light of day outside. She looked about her, accustoming herself to her surroundings by straining every sense until she thought she could hear the very substance of the rock, a rock she now knew to be more like a sponge than impregnable granite. She saw it in her memory as one cave after another, some natural, some man-made, some much larger than others, but nevertheless all linked together – and, sooner or later, leading to freedom.

Petronilla found her way through the first few caves by following the ruts in the floor, which must have been made by the dollies that were employed in bringing up the heavy ammunition. Then she found the painted marks that had once marked the positions of the stores that had been kept in the caves.

She was naturally attracted by any shaft of light she could see. Heading for one, she realized with a fright she was outside the cave where Ireneo was still watching her cousin, the two men chatting as if they were the best of friends. She paused, her breath coming in gasps from her exertions, and tried to listen to what they were saying. The shape of the caves distorted the acoustics and she found it difficult at first to understand Ireneo's thick dialect. When she did begin to make out the mixture of Spanish and English he favoured, she realized how fortunate she had been that Jesús had transferred her to another cave, as far away from her cousin as possible. She had never heard women discussed in such terms before and was at first shocked that her cousin should do so with a man he considered so far beneath him in every other way.

'That vixen should have been mine —'

Ireneo laughed. Half his conversation seemed to consist of loud bursts of laughter. 'You should have taken her while you could. Jesús probably has her now!'

Petronilla backed away, upset by the reference to herself. She had thought she meant more to Diego than some whore he had fancied and had almost charmed into being his. She had thought they had shared a dream together such as only comes once in a lifetime and it hurt to know that while she had been enthralled by his beauty and his sad, romantic circumstances, he had seen her as nothing more than an innocent he would allow to worship at his shrine for a while, until he had wanted someone else to reflect his glory in his bed. She saw clearly now why her mother had been so angry that she should have picnicked with him alone. What a narrow escape she had had – and that had been largely due to Charles, who had understood, as so many of their compatriots did not, the difference between innocence and ignorance, and who had left her to make her own discovery of the tawdry subterfuge for love which was the best her cousin had to offer. Charles could have demolished what she felt for her cousin in a few words, but would he have won her heart for himself so completely if he had? She could thank God for his wisdom now!

She fell into the next cave, landing in a heap on the floor. The jolt started her head throbbing again. She remembered her mother saying that all her family loved adventure and wondered if it were her English blood that set her apart, longing only for Charles and the security he gave her. And what if she were pregnant at last? Would her cousin have respected such a possibility? For that, if for no other reason, she had to find her way out of this labyrinth and regain her freedom.

She struggled back on to her feet, forcing herself from cave to cave to get as far away from her cousin as she could, regardless of where her route took her. And then, almost before she was ready for it, she found herself back in the enormous cavern of St Michael's. She had no doubt that she would find her way out from there and her triumph warmed her. She couldn't wait for her own adventure to be at an end and for her to be safely held in Charles's arms once more.

It took her a long time to find the right exit that took her out into the open air. The sun was shining as brightly as ever, carving black shadows into the buildings that were spread out at her feet. A monkey, one of the famed Gibraltar apes, swore at a nearby female. Looking at it, Petronilla struggled against bursting into tears of relief, forcing herself to note the animal's wicked-looking dirty teeth and evil temper. She stood still, giving it time to get used to her presence on the steep slope on which she found herself.

She never took her eyes off him for a moment as she edged her way round him, not even when she almost fell down some roughly cut out steps that led down to the first of the houses that had been built into the steep side of the slope. There was a fortress close by which she discovered also served as the gaol. It was a solid-looking building, its windows shuttered and secretive. She walked past it, disconcerted by the sound of people walking about and talking that came up from the Main Street below when, only a few moments ago, she had wondered if she would ever see the outside world again. She slithered down some steps and found herself in a small cobbled street that led directly down past a few tenement dwellings and into the mile long Calle Royale below. She was free.

Petronilla recognized the figure of her angry mother at once. She was standing in the entrance to the Convent, her parasol held over her head and her rosary still wound about her fingers, looking at once furious and very, very Spanish.

'You have a town of only one street and yet you have

still managed to lose my daughter? It is exactly what I should expect from *bandaleros* – thieves and braggarts, such as I have always known Gibraltarians to be! What have you done with her?'

An anxious subaltern danced about Doña Pilar's angry figure. 'Who is your daughter, ma'am, *señora*, my lady?'

Pilar turned upon him. '*Who* is my daughter?' Her English deserted her for a moment and she muttered to herself in Spanish, her frustration showing in every quivering muscle. 'Ah, who is my daughter?' she repeated at last. 'She is Mrs Charles Arbuthnot, the daughter of Colonel Harris! Now do you know who she is?'

Petronilla ran the last few yards, catapulting herself into the centre of the dispute.

'Mamá! Here I am!

Doña Pilar turned and saw her, disbelief written all over her face. 'You look terrible,' she vouchsafed at last.

'I feel terrible!'

It was comforting to be taken into her mother's cool, scented embrace. Pilar's fingers found the gash on her daughter's head in a trice, but her touch was so gentle that Petronilla hardly noticed.

'Mamá, I must speak to Charles!'

The subaltern stepped back, coming to attention with such vigour that he nearly lost his balance. 'Is your husband Mr Charles Arbuthnot, ma'am?'

Petronilla nodded wearily. 'I need to speak to him,' she reiterated.

'I don't believe he's here, ma'am. He was here, with your father —'

'*¡Dios mío!* And where is my father now?'

'Petronilla, tell me at once what happened to you?'

But Petronilla wasn't listening. 'If Charles isn't here I must see my father! Is he still with the Governor?'

The young man's Adam's apple rose and fell as his consternation grew. 'Ma'am, are you expected by the Governor?'

'I shouldn't think so,' Petronilla returned impatiently.

'Certainly we're expected!' Doña Pilar added, drawing herself up to her full height and putting her head so far back that she managed to look down her nose at the unfortunate young man, looking for all the world like an indignant pekinese. She caught the subaltern's surreptitious look at her daughter and saw her for the first time through somebody else's eyes. Petronilla's dress was torn and filthy, her hair hanging down her back, the comb in two pieces with half the teeth missing. Worst of all, there were bruises all over her face and hands and, she had no doubt at all, all over the rest of her body too. Doña Pilar was horrified by the sight.

'Never again shall Tomás tell me this is a civilized British colony!' she raged. 'One cannot even go into a church to say one's prayers in peace! First, no one knows what has happened to my one and only daughter, and then you appear from nowhere, looking like last year's scarecrow! It is too much! Now it is *I, hija mía,* who wishes to know exactly what happened to you, and then we shall see this person who pretends to govern this Rock and find out how he means to put an end to this outrage – and so I shall tell your father, if we are ever to see *him* again!'

'Mamá, I am trying to tell you! It was Cousin Diego —'

'That *desgraciado*! It is all of a piece that he should come and go as he likes! I will not permit that he, a foreigner, should come here, on British soil, and molest my family in broad daylight! We shall see the Governor at once and find out what he intends to do about it.'

Petronilla's sense of the ridiculous got the better of her. 'On British soil?' she repeated in marvelling tones.

'Of course on British soil! We are not in Spain now, are we?' Doña Pilar turned on her heel and marched towards the front door, lowering her parasol as she did so. 'And if you repeat one word of what I said to your father, I shall never speak to you again!' she added with a finality that defied any argument.

Petronilla followed her to the closed front door. 'Where

can Charles have gone?' she sighed. 'Papá should never have let him out of his sight! He might have known we need him with us!'

Her mother gave her a quizzical look. 'What makes you think poor Tomás has any control over your Charles? More often, these days, it is the other way about, but do you hear me complaining?'

Petronilla put a hand up to her head. It made her feel better to know that she was not the only one who looked to Charles for guidance and the natural leadership he seemed to have assumed almost without anyone having noticed. She doubted if anyone would resent his taking the reins into his own hands, least of all her father, whose affection for Charles could not have been greater if he had been his son rather than his son-in-law.

The door opened and Colonel Harris emerged. As in Granada, he seemed to have aged in the few hours since they had last seen him.

'Tomás!'

'Papá!'

It was hard to know who had spoken first. Colonel Harris was astonished to see them both. His face lit up as he embraced his wife, putting his other hand out to include Petronilla.

'Papá, do you know where Charles is?'

'As long as you are safe, my dear —'

'But what about Charles?'

'He will look after himself.'

Petronilla stamped her foot, looking as Spanish as her mother. 'If you won't help find him then I must go alone!'

Pilar frowned. 'You will do as your Papá tells you!'

'And what if Diego kills Charles?'

She had the full attention of both her parents then. Colonel Harris made a move towards her. 'I'm sorry, child. I was so surprised to see your mother actually standing on British Gibraltar that everything else went out of my mind. Now what's all this about Don Diego? Is he responsible for your battered appearance because, if he is,

463

the Governor will want to hear all about it. That cousin of yours isn't safe to have around. I think we'd better go inside —'

Petronilla felt close to tears. 'I'd rather go to an hotel! I refuse to present myself to the Governor looking like a gypsy!'

'Quite right,' her mother approved.

Petronilla grabbed her father's arm. 'How long has Charles been gone?'

Colonel Harris pulled on his whiskers, glowering at her. 'Nobody has gone anywhere, my pet.'

'Then where is Charles?' she insisted.

'Talking with the Governor. He'll be with us in a moment. Ah, here comes Charles now!'

At the sight of her husband, Petronilla finally burst into tears. She threw herself into his arms, uncaring how many people should be watching. 'Oh, Charles, I'm so glad to see you!'

He tried to hide from her the shock her tattered appearance gave him. First he was alarmed until he had reassured himself she was not badly hurt, and then he was blazingly angry that anyone should have dared to touch her.

'Darling heart, what happened to you?'

'I was abducted —'

'By whom?'

Looking at her husband's frowning face, she was suddenly reluctant to tell him the whole story. She knew it to be a mistaken loyalty but, somehow, she had no ambition to see Diego captured and humiliated after all. Instead, she said, 'Don't trust Jesús, whatever you do! He's a smuggler —'

It was Pilar who took up the story. 'Petronilla was worried for your safety. She thought you had gone alone in answer to a message from our cousin and that you would be killed. It seems to me that Gibraltar is exactly as I always said it was, a nest of smugglers who would murder their own grandmothers for a few pence!'

Charles hugged Petronilla close against him, now

completely confused. 'Look, my dear, let's find a hotel and you can tell me the whole story,' he suggested. 'Shall I send to Algeciras for a change of dress for you? What did you do? Crawl the whole way up the Calle Real on your hands and knees?'

Petronilla was not amused. 'Believe me, Main Street is the only level bit of this Rock! And no, there isn't time to send to Algeciras for anything! I thought you'd try to rescue me and get yourself murdered by Diego! Doesn't it matter to you that Jesús is his accomplice? That he and his brother are both smugglers, just like Diego is? And Diego certainly has murder in his heart and, let me tell you, I have no mind to be a widow quite yet!'

Mr Arbuthnot looked for help from Doña Pilar. His mother-in-law's response was immediate.

'First, we shall find an hotel, where we shall order a small luncheon and have time to compose ourselves. Then we shall make a plan to put an end to Cousin Diego trying to murder everyone —'

'Yes, but I'd much rather we captured them before they make widows out of either, or both of us!' Petronilla interrupted. She leaned closer against Charles. 'Diego is in love with Death. I don't think he can help it.'

The two men exchanged glances. 'And you think Jesús to be his man?' her father asked her.

'He and his brother Ireneo. Cousin Diego thinks he's their leader, but I think it's the other way about. Jesús took me away from Diego and put me in another cave. Diego would rather have killed me than let me go. Charles, I think Diego is mad!'

Doña Pilar patted her Petronilla's hand, determined to remove her from such a public place before a crowd gathered to see what was going on.

'You shall tell us all about it over lunch,' she said firmly. She shook her head sadly over the state of Petronilla's dress. 'A private room would be the most suitable if it can be arranged, Tomás. The poor child is exhausted and her head hurts. Me, I am not at all enamoured of your

Gibraltar, let me tell you! To smuggle is one thing and quite understandable, but to hit my daughter over the head is something else and altogether abominable! This Governor of yours must be made to do his duty and put an end to this business, don't you agree?'

'Yes, dear,' her husband agreed, glad to see that one of his womenfolk was back to normal, even while he thought Petronilla to be still in shock from whatever her cousin had tried to do to her. He winced, feeling his age and wondering what had happened to his sense of adventure. What he wanted was a quiet half hour alone with Pilar, and to leave Petronilla to her own husband's care, but he was accustomed to having his family look to him for guidance and he was not quite ready to relinquish the reins to the younger man – not quite yet.

Thomas was glad of his military training as he led his family away from the small square, going before them to make the necessary arrangements for their reception at the nearest convenient hotel. He was well pleased when he found a respectable looking hostel, not too large, but with everything his wife had stipulated as being necessary for their comfort. He was unaccustomed to his daughter giving way to her emotions, for she was the least missish female he knew, never complaining in his hearing about her circumstances – though maybe that particular honour should be claimed by Pilar, whom he would rather have by his side in an emergency than most men he could name. Shocked by his daughter's pallor, he had recognized all too clearly that her incoherence was a symptom of the fright her cousin had given her, and he was now as convinced as Pilar that something would have to be done about that young man, and done quickly, whatever the details of his latest escapade.

Colonel Harris was soon being ushered into the two best bedrooms, a third being hastily transformed into a private dining room. A large *gratificación* changed hands to ensure the landlord kept a still tongue in his head over their movements and, in a matter of minutes, he was helping his son-in-law to help the two ladies up the stairs and into their respective rooms.

'See if you think Petronilla should have a doctor,' he murmured to Charles. 'That's a nasty gash she has on her head.'

'Right you are, sir.'

Her husband's cheerfulness and determined normality were the best medicine Petronilla could have had. As soon as they were alone she took a step towards him.

'I'm so sorry, Charles. I should have been more careful!'

'It doesn't sound as if you had much choice in the matter.' He led her over to the bed and sat her down on the edge, fetching some water in a pitcher from the washstand. 'I'm going to clean up that scalp wound, Pet. I'll be as gentle as I can, but there's a great deal of dried blood in your hair and it's bound to hurt you. Or would you rather your mother did it?'

'I'd rather you did it. I'm afraid I may cry again —'

He began examining her head. 'I'd say you have something to cry about, my love. Suppose you tell me exactly what happened to you.'

It took some time for her to recount all that had happened since she and her mother had arrived in Gibraltar. By the time she had finished, she was weeping again, the tears dripping through her fingers as she tried to wipe them away.

'I was so afraid for you when I thought you had gone to look for me!' she confessed. 'And nobody would listen to me!' She took a deep breath, facing up to the real anxiety that underlay all the rest in her mind, if not in her heart. 'What will happen to Diego?'

'If he's captured on Gibraltar he will have to stand trial. I can't hold out much hope for his future. Sir Robert Gardiner means to put an end to Gibraltar as a centre for smuggling in the area, one way of another. Your father is behind him in that, as you know.'

Petronilla winced as his fingers caught in her hair. 'They'll hang him?'

467

His silence answered her.

'He may think he's their leader, but it is just his fantasy. They make use of him, as he thinks he's making use of them. What they hoped was that Papá would come after me. With an English MP in their clutches, they thought they could persuade the Governor to turn a blind eye to their activities. It was Cousin Diego's idea, and I have to admit it to be a good one, but Jesús made it quite clear that was their only interest in him.' She made a face. 'Diego is quite ordinary really, but I didn't always think so. I must have taken leave of my senses —'

'You were young in years and experience.'

She turned and faced him. 'I hurt you and I'm sorry for it. You didn't deserve that from me.' She began to cry again. 'If he hit me over the head it was no more than my deserts, but if anything had happened to you, I don't know what I should have done! Oh Charles, I love you so much!'

He kissed the tears from her face. 'My darling wife, you've proved that to me time and again —'

'In Granada?' She managed a rather tearful smile. 'That's what I'm trying to tell you. You know what is said about Granada? ¡*Dale Limosna, Mujer, Que no hay en la vida nade Come la pena de ser Ciego en Granada*! That there is nothing crueller in life than to be blind in Granada. Well, before Granada I was blind to all that you mean to me, but I never shall be again! Never!'

He kissed her lips. 'Goose!' he said lovingly. 'You were mine from the moment I kissed you in the rose garden. I knew it even if you didn't. Feeling better?'

'Yes.'

'Then I'd better have a word with your father. You're sure it was your cousin who hit you?'

Her pleasure dissolved into renewed agitation. 'What are you planning to do? Papá looks so much older than he did. It would break Mama's heart if anything were to happen to him.'

Charles nodded, his face stern. 'I had a word with the

Governor and we agreed your father should stay down below while I —'

'I shall go with you!'

'Darling —'

'I mean it, Charles! You're not going anywhere without me! Not alone! And not before the Governor finds someone who can find his way through those caves, and who is not one of the smugglers! There must be a plan of them and where they all lead! The cave where I was put by Jesús is on the north side, one of the galleries the British troops carved out during the Great Siege. The man Ireneo stayed with Cousin Diego. I think they were afraid he might do something rash and spoil all their plans.' She shivered. 'I thought he meant to kill me – I think Jesús thought so too, or he wouldn't have taken the risk of separating us.'

'It may have been out of respect for your father —'

But she was no longer listening. She sat up very straight and looked him in the eye. 'I mean to come with you,' she announced, a stubborn set to her mouth and chin. 'It seems to me it would be much better if Diego were to escape from Gibraltar, and Papá won't like it if Jesús is arrested in his stead, so he had better go with him.'

'You're not going anywhere with that bang on your head —'

'Well, it did hurt, I'm not going to deny it, but you've managed to make me feel quite comfortable again, as you always do, and now I feel ready for anything!'

'And if I decide your place is down here with your mother?'

Petronilla only shrugged a shoulder. 'Who else can show you the way into the caves? Be thankful that Mamá will prefer to stay with Papá, or she might have insisted on coming with us also.'

'A family affair?' he said wryly.

'Yes, but it will be you who will decide what's to be done with my cousin and Jesús when we catch up with them,' she replied soothingly. 'I wouldn't be able to manage any of it without you.'

Charles pursed up his lips to keep himself from laughing. 'I doubt your father will approve your ideas of justice, Pet,' he warned her. 'He has a liking for Jesús. Apparently he once served in the British Army —'

'He's still a smuggler!'

Charles's lips twitched. 'Now and again. But he also served in your father's old regiment. That counts far more with him than a spot of smuggling.'

She sniffed. 'It seems to me,' she said firmly, 'the fewer people who know our plans the better. Papá will be quite happy to leave everything in your hands, and so will Mamá, because she'd never be happy knowing that a cousin of ours had been forced to a reckoning by anyone who governs Gibraltar in the name of the British Crown.' She gave him an anxious look. 'You do see that, don't you?'

'I don't know that I can go all the way with you down that path,' he retorted. 'Your cousin has threatened a member of *my* family for the last time, no matter what claims he has on your sympathy. If that means bringing him to justice here, on the Rock, then so be it. You'll have to leave the final decision on that score to me.'

'He's my cousin —'

'I know that,' he answered sharply. 'He's also a dream you're reluctant to let go, no matter how much you know yourself to be my wife. If you were the only one involved, I might take the chance of giving him his freedom, but are we still to go in fear of our lives when the children start to come?'

Petronilla had no answer to that. She presented him with a white, strained face, lowering her eyes before his. 'But I may go with you?' she said at last.

'Yes, my love, where I go, you go! Shall we join your parents for luncheon?'

Doña Pilar took one look at her daughter's appearance and found she had a great deal more to say on the subject of Gibraltar despite having just finished telling Thomas she would never soil her lips with the Fat Rock's name again. She motioned an indignant hand in Petronilla's direction.

'This is your Gibraltar! Look at our daughter! What kind of a place is this where *contrabandistas* come and go as they please, where your daughter is hit over the head and abducted – it is intolerable! First we shall have lunch and we shall *both* go and see General Sir Robert Gardiner and that will be an end of the matter, no?'

The two men looked at her with amused trepidation. 'My dear,' the Colonel began.

But Doña Pilar was far from finished. 'I never thought to have anything in common with this man, but now I find I have! He, too, says there must be no more smuggling, no matter what the City of London says, and I agree with him! The British must find another way to finance their ridiculous conquest of a Rock!'

'A Rock with holes in it,' Petronilla supplied, enjoying this tirade.

'They should know that smuggling is contrary to the Treaty of Utrecht!' Doña Pilar finished awefully.

'What is this Treaty of Utrecht?' her daughter asked her.

'Who cares?' Pilar snapped back. 'It was promised there would be no smuggling! I wish to see the Governor to tell him that if anything more happens to any member of my family through British stupidity, I shall have a great deal to say about the matter when I get back to London! You think that I cannot, but I assure you that I can!'

No one was in any doubt that she meant exactly what she said, nor did they doubt that she was able to carry out her threat. There was no doubt that many a powerful guest who had accepted her hospitality in Hampshire from time to time would be pleased to do her a favour in return, making mincemeat of a government that had been unable to protect the daughter of one of their own in a Crown Colony.

Thomas Harris eyed her with respect. 'You'd be better

employed taking Petronilla back to Algeciras. She looks like a ghost.'

'That is what I am telling you, *mí esposo*. Only it is for Charles to tell her what to do these days, no, not her mother, or her Papá? And none of us is going to do anything on an empty stomach or we shall all end up as ghosts as likely as not, and that is not a fate that appeals to me at all!'

She rang the bell and oversaw the arrival of a dish of cold cuts of meat; a tomato and onion salad; a solid cake of egg and vegetables, known for some reason as a Spanish omelette; some freshly grilled sardines; a bowl of fruits: oranges, pomegranates, passion fruits, both black and green grapes, persimmons; and some of the tempting sweets made by the nuns of the Order of the Comendadores of Santiago and Santa Isabel, which caused a scandalized exclamation from the still angry Pilar, who recognized one of her favourite sweetmeats from childhood and could only wonder at how they had made their way across the bay to Gibraltar. What nuns were there on the *Piedra Gorda* to make them? Worse still, was the quality of the sherry which was all that the hotel had to offer them, which they one and all indignantly rejected as being beneath contempt. Colonel Harris would have preferred a whisky, but that proved as impossible here as it frequently was on the Spanish mainland.

'If you don't mind my saying so, sir,' Charles addressed his father-in-law when they had finished eating, 'I am of the opinion it would be better if you all returned to Algeciras and left me to acquaint the Governor with the whole story of Petronilla's abduction. I imagine he'll have the Army round up everyone concerned —'

'Charles!' Petronilla exploded. 'I told you. I mean to go with you! I will not wait at home and worry about you, whatever you may say!'

Pilar came to life, poking Thomas in the ribs with the point of her fan. 'She is right! Imagine how it will be for them, Tomás! When did we ever not want to have a fine adventure together?'

He was caught up briefly in the same memory, his eyes gleaming back at her, but then he remembered Petronilla's bruises and his concern overcame his memories.

'Not this time, *favorita*,' he sighed.

'No, no,' her mother agreed with unusual submissiveness, 'you and I had our adventures when we were young, the very best of times, which neither of us will ever forget. It's the young people's turn to be uncomfortable and make all the decisions. At our age we need tranquillity and time to spend together!'

Petronilla eyed her mother with foreboding. 'You mean I may go with Charles?' she asked with disbelief.

Pilar's placid smile told its own story. 'As far as I am concerned, I hope very much you will go away and leave your father and I to make the best of this terrible hostelry! The decision is not mine to make, however. You must ask Charles to take you with him – if you are feeling well enough to go anywhere!'

Petronilla's smile reflected her mother's. 'Charles would not be so unkind as to deprive me of my own adventure!' she declared. Only she knew, deep inside, that she was dreading what might happen in the caves that afternoon.

Thomas was silent for a long time after the younger couple had left them, shifting from side to side in his upholstered chair.

'I'm getting old,' he said at last. 'I don't even want to go with them. I never thought I'd be glad to be left behind and have someone else take the responsibility of putting an end to your murderous cousin. It's a good thing I became a politician, my dear. The House is about all I'm fit for these days!'

But Pilar refused to be downcast by such gloomy thoughts. 'I can think of something else you've always been fitted for, only we are never alone for long enough these days for me to feel like a proper wife to you.' She held out her hand to him, her face full of the same gentle mockery he remembered so well from the days after he had effected her rescue from another lieutenant of Don Carlos, and a much more dangerous one than Don Diego would ever turn out to be. He felt an answering surge of desire for this woman he loved so well. 'Have we time?' she asked him on the edge of laughter.

He was on his feet in a trice, feeling as young as he had felt old a moment before. 'We have all the time in the world,' he answered her, and followed her into the bedroom.

If Sir Robert Gardiner was appalled by Petronilla's appearance, he gave no sign of it. That he was determined to rid Gibraltar of the pestilential smugglers who plagued the whole coastline, he left them in no doubt whatsoever. 'I care nothing for opinion in London who would have me turn a blind eye to the smuggling in the Bay – *whoever* may be involved in it. I am sorry, Mrs Arbuthnot, that your cousin should be numbered among these villains, but that doesn't excuse me from doing my duty as I see it. If there are smugglers in the caves of Gibraltar, they must be flushed out at once. That's why there are troops garrisoned here, and why I was chosen to be Governor —'

'Of course, sir,' Petronilla retired into the background, leaving it to her husband to talk Sir Robert into giving them a few hours before a clean sweep was made through the caves. Jesús would have been long gone, she thought, taking his brother with him. But what of Diego? Would they show any loyalty to him, or would they abandon him to his fate?

Charles was more successful than she had been. He had the Governor laughing with some story and he looked exactly as a dependable, solid citizen should look. Only she knew what that red hair denoted and how his sherry-coloured eyes could soften first into warm affection and then into blazing passion. He was a hidden person whom it had taken her a long, long time to get to know. Was she being unfair to him now because she wanted Diego set free? She threaded her fingers together, worrying about her motive in wanting her cousin to escape the gallows when he had wished her nothing but harm in the past and probably would again in the future.

The Governor addressed her directly only once more. 'You are more fortunate in your husband than you are in your cousin!' he said. And it was only when the door had closed behind them that she realized he was congratulating her on her British husband, her cousin being the natural consequence of her Spanish heritage, and that he had thought she would be complimented by his strictly English point of view and his expectation that she would share it to the full, finding the Spanish as incomprehensible as he did himself.

The caves were so confusing that Petronilla was surprised she had ever managed to escape from them in the first place. It took all her courage to go back down into the darkness, even with Charles holding her by the hand as if she had been his child rather than his wife. The further they went, the more guilty she felt.

'Charles, let's go back!'

'Having come so far?'

She tried to pull her hand out of his, but he held her fast. 'I had no right —' she began unhappily.

'Oh, this is none of your doing,' he reassured her. 'I've been waiting for the opportunity to come face to face with your cousin on my terms for a long time now. He has done enough damage to me and mine for me to look forward to giving him a bloody nose!'

Oh yes? And what then? Would he help her cousin to his feet and shake him by the hand? And what of Jesús and Ireneo? They might be more of a danger than Diego had ever been.

She would have argued with her husband further, now badly frightened as to what might happen to him because of her foolish ambivalence where her cousin was

475

concerned, when they heard voices coming from one of the other caves and she froze where she stood.

'I'm not going any further!' she whispered.

A slight pressure from Charles's fingers answered her. 'Is that your cousin?'

She shook her head, forgetting he couldn't see her. 'Jesús.'

He lowered his head to hers. 'Is there another way round without running into them?'

Petronilla forced herself to think. She would have turned and gone back if it hadn't meant leaving Charles on his own. She leaned back against the cool, jagged wall and shivered. Of course there was another way round! She remembered the way exactly. If they hadn't moved Diego from where she had last seen him, with Ireneo apparently guarding him, she thought she knew exactly how to get there.

Her skirts hindered her as she led the way through the narrow crannies that led from one cave to another, tracing her way back along the way that Jesús had brought her earlier that day. The sound of the men's voices was distorted and came at them from unexpected angles. Once she heard Ireneo's inane laugh as if he were standing beside her and the next moment as if he were too far away to bother about. Two minutes later, she and Charles had arrived at the entrance of the cave where she had last seen Diego.

There was only silence ahead of them.

'He was in there. Ireneo was guarding him —'

Charles stepped forward into the cave, motioning her behind him.

'Don Diego!'

Petronilla's cousin turned round from looking out through the only outlet that looked straight out across the sea. It offered a view that could only be seen ordinarily by one of the seagulls that nested on the cliff, far away from the interference of men.

It was Petronilla's face Diego saw. He didn't hear

Charles's voice at all. He reached across the cave towards her, the livid scar distorting his smile of welcome. He was indeed a fallen angel, she thought, and she was no longer surprised that her younger self had longed to be the one to save him from himself.

'You came back to me!' he exclaimed.

'No, no, I haven't! You must leave here at once! If the British catch you, they'll hang you!'

Diego saw Charles then. 'And what will your husband do to me?' he drawled.

'Diego, please go now, before they send the troops in to get you!' she begged him.

He had himself under control now. The brief feeling for herself that she had read on his face was gone.

'Aren't you going to call me to account yourself?' he taunted Charles. 'If Petronilla were my wife, you'd have been a dead man long since!'

Charles looked as solid and as – *dull*, as he ever had. For the last time in her life, Petronilla was to wish he were more romantic and exciting. She couldn't admire her cousin, but she could still feel that magnetic, defiant, devil-may-care quality in him that had attracted her from the very beginning.

'Please, Diego! Please go for my sake!'

His laughter reverberated round the cavern. The pounding footsteps of the smugglers came running towards them, followed by the more solid steps of the Governor's troops closing relentlessly in on them.

Diego bowed to Petronilla with a flourish. 'It would seem time is running out for me,' he said. 'Come with me, Petronilla, and we'll be together for all eternity!'

Petronilla gave him a wide-eyed, frightened look, retreating against Charles's reassuringly familiar frame. 'I want to live —'

Diego's eyes glittered, she thought with tears. 'You look Spanish,' he said sadly. 'I was misled by that. You have an English soul!'

'I love Charles!'

'And duty!' he sneered. 'Husband, children and home! With me, you could have reached for the stars and heard the music of the universe in your ears. God help you, cousin, for he abandoned me many years ago!'

Petronilla turned her back on him, hiding her face in her husband's shoulder. The footsteps came even closer. 'Fabiola says he never abandons anyone!' she said, her voice muffled. 'That it's never too late!'

Diego was very still, listening with his whole body to the approaching smugglers and troops. His face took on that mask of cruelty she had seen before, the first time when he had tried to whip his horses into submission.

'I would have sent you on ahead – to wait for me, if Jesús hadn't taken you away. It's too late now. It was always too late for me with you, wasn't it? You come from the *respectable* side of the family, a conventional, respectable marriage the height of your ambition! No wonder you didn't want to die with me!'

Petronilla pushed herself away from Charles, making a last bid to save Diego. 'Run! They'll catch you otherwise!'

'They won't catch me.' His voice was firm, almost exultant. 'This is my "moment of truth"! Don't look like that, my dear. You have your Carlos, surely you wouldn't deny me my moment of glory?'

She watched with unbelieving eyes as her cousin pulled himself up on to the narrow ledge and sketched her a last, graceful salute.

'¡*Viva muerte!*' he cried out to the sky and the sea, and he was gone, falling down and down on to the rocks below, the seagulls screeching about him as he went to his death.

The silence stretched into an eternity. Even the boots of the soldiers were quiet, their task complete.

Petronilla moved into the circle of her husband's embrace, content to be held tightly against him for a long, long moment. Later, she would cry for her cousin and that part of her youth which had died with him and, later still, she would rejoice in her love for Charles and in the life she was alive to share with him into a contented old age.

'Darling Charles,' she said, 'please take me home.'

Epilogue

Petronilla had little memory of the sea trip from Gibraltar to Cádiz. She was distressed to discover that she was still as bad a sailor as ever. One look at the sea and her stomach began to turn over in the most alarming manner. Worse, if she had expected any sympathy, she received none. Her parents were otherwise occupied, taken up entirely with one another, which, at any other time would have met with her complete approval, but as the conviction grew upon her that she was about to depart this life at any moment, she felt a little interest on the part of her forebears was the least she could expect from them.

'If I die before we get to Cádiz, please don't bury me at sea,' she begged Charles when he came to visit her. 'It would be to add insult to injury!'

'I think you'll live.' His tone of voice, with its faint quiver of laughter, was worse than casual, it was *unfeeling*. 'Your mother thinks you may be *encinta*,' he added, holding a handy bowl out to her.

She shut her eyes. 'She thinks I'm *encinta* every time I'm a little off-colour —' She opened her eyes again – wide. 'Tell her I'm suffering from *mareo*! No, don't tell her anything as my welfare is of so little interest to her! Just go away and let me die in peace!'

When he had gone she had something else to do other than feeling sick and sorry for herself. She rushed over to the mirror, taking a good look at herself, counting on her fingers as best she could at the same time in a revival of hope that her mother might be right.

She looked dreadful. Her skin was yellow and the bruises on her brow, which had produced a splendid black eye, was now at the green and purple stage. It was as well, she thought, no one could see the back of her head for she thought it must look as decadent as the rest of her. An unlikely looking future mother, she told herself. She looked more as though she had been engaged in one of those awful prize fights that gentlemen sometimes talked about when they thought no ladies were present.

The ship rolled beneath her and she made a rush for the refuge of her bunk. How many more hours did she have to endure before they reached Cádiz and she could once again step on dry land? Half of her longed to get home as speedily as possible, the other half dreading the comments her appearance was likely to bring forth, especially from Doña Louise who had never been known to turn a tactful blind eye to anything. Nor had Petronilla forgotten that Mr Clarke would be there also, still hoping Mr Arbuthnot would offer him a partnership in the *bodega*. She sighed. If she were indeed in the family way, she would lose much of the advantage she had wrested from Charles in her battle for retaining her own position in Arbuthnots.

Cádiz was just as she remembered it – and completely different. The physical features were the same, the harbour, the ships riding at anchor, the smaller fishing boats with their crews sitting on the quayside mending their nets. The town, too, was just as she remembered it. The small square houses, all of them painted white, with their wrought-iron security bars outside their windows, the grey dust lifting and falling down the streets whenever a breeze ventured further inland than the harbour itself. The last time she had seen it, she had been disappointed. She had wondered at the shimmering horizons, the huge stacks of salt reclaimed from the flats beside the sea, and the fantastic display of birds, from flamingos to the familiar storks, but they had all been strange and unfamiliar to her. She had longed for the security of Hampshire and for the private conversations she had shared with her father in front of the fire in his study. Even her mother had seemed a foreigner, living a different existence altogether from the one in which Petronilla had always seen her before.

This time, she stood on the deck beside her husband, relishing their closeness to home.

'Glad to be going ashore?' Charles grinned at her.

'Glad to be alive!' she responded with feeling.

'You look a bit better. Your father is unbearably proud of you, telling everyone you would have been a fine soldier if you'd been a boy.'

She arched a brow, amused and a little touched because she had a great affection for her father. 'I'd have been a rotten soldier!'

'I confess I'm glad you're his daughter and not his son.'

She laughed. 'So am I!'

It was strange to be on dry land again. For a while she could still feel the water rising and falling beneath her feet. She was glad to be handed up into the waiting carriage beside her mother, Charles and her father sitting opposite, their luggage following behind in another carriage.

Doña Pilar clicked her tongue. 'You look like one of Tomás's ragged rascals,' she declared. 'It is true what he says, no? Round and round the rugged Rock the ragged rascals ran!'

'Very true,' Petronilla murmured, 'but I had hoped for a more dignified epitaph than to be included amongst the rascals.'

'It is bad to be a rascal?'

'I think I may grow used to it,' her daughter answered. 'I certainly look the part! *Bribon, picaro*,' she translated, laughing. 'I can expect nothing better, having an English pirate for a father and an *aventurera* for a mother!'

Doña Pilar's eyes sparkled, highly complimented. 'Yes, but this time it was you who had the adventure, you and

Charles together, which is nice. Tomás and I are too old to have adventures any more!'

The journey by carriage that took them the rest of the way to Sanlúcar was exactly as Petronilla remembered it. She couldn't get enough of the now familiar scenery as she watched the gold-and-silver countryside pass by.

'I never thought to be so glad to be home!' she exclaimed to Charles. 'I enjoyed being away, of course, because of Granada and being with you, but I prefer the sherry-maker I married! It will be nice to be quiet again, with no one trying to murder us and only the *bodega* to worry about!' It seemed to her she was even more impatient than he to be home again as they came within sight of Sanlúcar, and it came as an unpleasant shock to her when Michael Clarke came running out to greet them as their carriage turned into the drive of the Arbuthnot *bodega*.

'Welcome home!'

Petronilla had forgotten that he would be there. 'How are you?' she asked him.

'Marvellous! Doña Louise and I have a surprise for you!'

Petronilla sighed. 'Will we never be alone here together?' she murmured in an aside to her husband.

'I'll get rid of them,' he promised.

Doña Pilar had other ideas, however. 'No, *amigo*, I shall get rid of them. You take Petronilla to her room and fuss over her a little. One can't be too careful when one is *encinta*: one needs rest and special foods, and so on.'

'Particularly "and so on"!' Petronilla chimed in, laughing. 'Mama, I don't yet know that I am in the family way.'

Doña Pilar put her nose in the air. 'A mother always knows! You must go straight to bed and stay there until morning! I shall be very disappointed, let me tell you, if I am not to be an *abuela* at last!'

Petronilla accepted the inevitable and allowed herself to be swept off to her room. It was marvellous to be back in her own bed and to be allowed to sleep with no dark shadows hanging over her.

'Are you coming to bed too, Charles?' she asked hopefully.

His smile was diffident. 'As soon as I've taken a look round the *bodega, bienquista.*'

That's how it would always be she thought, but aloud all she said was, 'Don't be too long, will you?'

When she awoke it was already tomorrow and her husband had come and gone, leaving no more than the imprint of his head in the pillow beside hers. Her maid put her head round the door to ask whether her mistress would have her breakfast in bed or whether, seeing the advanced hour, she would now wait to have luncheon with her mother, the Doña Pilar, and Doña Louise? Petronilla chose the latter. She was astonished that she could have slept so long, but she felt all the better for it, better than she had for a long time. In a matter of moments, she was out of bed and dressed, eager to see the *bodega* again for herself. It was so good to be home!

She wandered through the 'cathedrals' of wine, casting an eye over the way they had been stacked, knowing the importance of the exact angle. It was all exactly as she would have wished. Her eye was caught by a *venencia*, one of the long sticks with a small tasting cup at the end which the *capataz* used to test the contents of the individual butts, to see if they were ready to pass on to the next stage of the *solera* system. She picked it up, remembering how badly she had managed her first attempt at using it. Practice, her mother had told her, was the only way to master the art, and practice she had, but not recently. She took it down and dipped it into the nearest butt, drawing it back and safely depositing the golden liquid into the glass in her other hand. She had managed it!

'Well done!'

She looked round to see her husband watching her with lazy eyes. She executed a little dance of joy. 'It was well done, wasn't it?' Her eyes filled with laughter. 'I was beginning to think I would never learn!'

'It's a knack, like any other,' he said in his prosaic way. 'Mr Clarke has a surprise for you, by the way.'

She pokered up at the mention of the buyer's name, but she went with him because she could think of no reason why she shouldn't. In the pen where her pet foxes had once lived, a new family had been installed. They stood up on their back legs, clamouring for her attention through the paling fence that had been erected to keep them in. Her reservations fell away from her as she fell to her knees, returning their greetings with the same loving laughter she had kept for her former pets.

'They're very well trained!' Mr Clarke assured her eagerly. 'They come when they're called – most of the time – and I think they could be persuaded to walk at the end of a leash –'

'They're beautiful! Thank you very much, Mr Clarke.'

'Yes, well, as long as you don't think I've overstepped the mark. Your husband says I can only stay on if I have your approval. You've always run the office, haven't you?'

Petronilla turned her attention back to the foxes. 'I'm proud of being my husband's partner as well as his wife.'

Mr Clarke squatted down beside her. 'The thing is, Mrs Arbuthnot, your husband has been telling me how it is in Spain, that women here manage their own affairs. I wanted to assure you that if you take me on to help with the *bodega*, here and at Montilla, we'd both know who is the senior partner –'

Petronilla suddenly realized what was happening – and who had stage-managed the whole business to gain her approval.

'Mr Arbuthnot is the senior partner of both our *bodegas*, Mr Clarke,' she said in her most forbidding tones.

'Yes, but –'

He looked so distraught and anxious that she felt sorry for him. She put her hand in her husband's and allowed him to pull her up on to her feet.

'Mr Clarke, welcome to Arbuthnots. I'm sure my husband and I will both be very glad to have your help.

I know I shall be, because I'm beginning to think my mother may be right and that I shall have other things on my mind in the near future. And thank you for the foxes. It was a kind thought and much appreciated. I plan to have them on all our labels! Don't you think they fit in well with the Arbuthnot colour scheme?'

The young man laughed. 'If you are to appear on the labels too, ma'am.'

She accepted the compliment with the new maturity she had learned in the last few months. 'You don't think me too dark and Spanish-looking?'

'Sherry is a Spanish drink,' he answered her.

'What do you think?' she asked her husband.

He didn't answer her then. He didn't answer her until many hours later when she was changing her dress for dinner that evening. She had chosen a dress of the new purple that could now be made from chemicals instead of from the expensive dyes that had formerly been used. It suited her well and she thought she looked very well in it.

'That's just the right colour!' Charles exclaimed. 'I never would have thought it, but it's exactly right against the red of the foxes!'

She looked at him, startled. 'My purple dress?' she asked, confused.

He grinned happily at her. 'For our labels. You, and the little foxes on your knee. Arbuthnots Sherries!'

She turned towards him, taking both his hands in hers. 'It may be Arbuthnot & Son someday soon. Have you thought of that?'

'I've thought of little else all day,' he admitted, 'but nothing and nobody can ever take your place, my love, not in my heart and not in our *bodega*. Do you know that now?'

She leaned against him, well content. 'Please God we shall always have each other,' she said softly, 'because, no matter how many children we may have, or what blessings come our way, all my happiness will always be in being your wife.'

He went away for a moment, returning and setting two crystal glasses before her. With enormous care, he poured some of their own wine into each of the glasses. He put one of the glasses into her hand, lifting the other in a toast.

'To Arbuthnots!' he said.

'To us,' she amended, clinking her own glass against his, and drank deeply. And to real life, she added silently to herself, remembering it was what her mother had wished her on her wedding day. 'To Arbuthnots and my husband!'

He grinned, his sherry eyes gleaming with a promise of things to come. He put down his glass and kissed her on the lips. '*Favorita, bienquista, enamorada!* My very dear wife! We'd better go down to dinner.'

It was hard to believe she had ever thought him dull, even more impossible that there had ever been a time when her flesh hadn't quickened to his touch, nor her spirits revived at the very sight of him. He had always been the most comfortable person she had known, but she knew him better now, and what she had always liked, she now loved with her whole heart.

'Yes,' she said, 'but I think I'll leave the accounts until tomorrow. I want to spend tonight in my husband's company!'

'And he in yours!' His smile was slow as his fingers brushed against her cheek. 'You must wear that new purple dress more often, my dear. It is most becoming!'

She almost laughed. 'Do you really think so?'

'There is only one dress I prefer and that is none at all,' he added thoughtfully.

She laughed out loud then, not at all embarrassed. 'I knew we'd get back to Granada sooner or later! What a good thing it is we have most of our lives before us, or we'd never go down to dinner at all, and I'm more hungry than I've been for a long, long time – for food as well as for you!'

A smile tugged at the corners of his lips. 'Then by all means, let us go down and eat,' he said. 'The sooner the better,' he added with such a wealth of meaning that she blushed despite herself.

'Yes, Charles,' she agreed demurely, and walked with him towards the stairs, to join their extended family down below.

Elizabeth de Guise's new novel is a powerful story of love
and intrigue set against the beauty of nineteenth-century
Venice and the darker side of Victorian England.

Bridge of Sighs is now available in hardback from Macmillan and will be a Pan paperback in 1993.

Here follows a short extract . . .

1849

Venice at last! It was Thursday the 12th of July and every
citizen was abroad, celebrating the *festa* of the Madonna
della Salute. The tall, thin woman, dressed in widow's
weeds, turned to her small stepdaughter with a sigh. She
was worn out with the difficulties of travel in these days
of wars and rumours of wars. She had known weeks ago
that the Austrians were blockading her native city, but she
had never imagined that she wouldn't find some way of
passing safely through their lines. In the event she had had
to hire a fishing vessel to bring her and the child across
the Lagoon – and even that had cost her more than she
could easily spare because everyone seemed to believe that
the Austrians were about to drop bombs on their defenceless heads. She had laughed when she first heard the story,
but she wasn't laughing now. Huge placards had appeared
all over the city, emblazoned with evil-looking people
whirling their mustachios as they dropped huge bombs
from various ridiculously shaped balloons. Someone in
Venice was taking the Austrian threats seriously, even
whilst the rest of the citizenry laughed and made mostly
obscene jokes about the incompetence of the Croats and
the Austrians themselves.

The child looked up at her expectantly. She was dirty
and smelled of fish. Her stepmother sighed again.

'Someone is coming to meet us directly,' she encouraged

both herself and the child. 'Why don't you go and look at the gondolas, Nell, until I call you?'

It never occurred to her that an 18-month-old might fall into the water. The woman was totally unaccustomed to children, regarding them as diminutive adults well able to look after themselves. Not even the journey from England had disabused her of this idea. It was perhaps fortunate that Nell was more than a little awed as well as excited by her new surroundings. The huge square in which she found herself fascinated the little girl. She blinked at the strange buildings and pointed with a fat finger towards the pigeons, familiar to her from those she had seen before in England.

'Birds!' she said with satisfaction.

'Go and look at the gondolas,' her stepmother advised her again. 'Gondolas mean Venice to the whole world!'

A slight frown appeared on the child's forehead. The word gondola meant nothing to her. 'Birds!' she said again.

The woman pointed towards the black gondolas, bobbing gently on the water as it slapped against the wooden moorings that edged the square.

'Boats!' Nell pulled herself up on to her feet and walked with the rolling gait of the very young towards the water. Once there, she sat down hard on the dusty flagstone, pleased with her achievement, and waved her fists at the dipping profiles of the gondolas. 'Boats! Boats! Boats!' she chortled.

'Gondolas,' her stepmother corrected her.

Nell rubbed her fingers in the dirt, then wiped them on her skirt. That was more fun than anything else she had done for a long time having been cooped up on board ship for so many weeks. Her stepmother had proved to be an indifferent sailor and had kept Nell in her cabin with her, out of the way of any trouble as she put it. The child rubbed her fingers in the dirt again, chuckling and talking unintelligibly to herself. She was glad to be free of the confines of the ship which had brought them here from England.

Soon she grew bored with these games of her own devising and, with a sudden, fastidious dislike of having dirty fingers and a dirty dress, turned back to the only person she knew on the square, but her stepmother was no longer watching her. Someone had brought her a chair to sit on and she had her eyes tight closed against the future, as if she were afraid it would be even more unbearable than the past.

Nell was too young to know that now was not the time for any reasonable person to have returned to Venice, but the awkward, angular woman knew the greater dangers they would have suffered if they had stayed in England. She had known – of course she had known – in her *mind* that Venice, once so proud, was now no more than a pretty bauble for other nations to quarrel over, but in her heart it meant home and safety, no matter how formidable was the army that was standing at its door. Napoleon had called the Piazza San Marco the 'drawing room of Europe'. He had demolished one end of the square to make his own mark upon it, destroying Sansovino's Church of San Giminiano to build a royal palace, surmounting which he had intended to raise a huge statue to himself. Thankfully, the woman thought, the statue had never come into being, even though, thanks to him, Venice had lost her proud independence, never to be free and sovereign again. There had been talk in London of unifying the whole peninsula of Italy into one kingdom; that had been a plan of which she could have approved, but talk was all it was ever likely to be while the Great Powers found it convenient to parcel out all the lesser powers to suit their own ends. Which was why Venice was now to be restored to Austria, courtesy of the British Government, as her English friends had taken such pleasure in telling her. And now, looking about her, at the shabbiness of her buildings and the weariness of her citizens, she wondered if Venice might not be sufficiently tired of being ruled by others and if some of the old spirit might not be reborn and create again the days of the Serene

Republic under her Doge and council, with all her old splendour and magnificence.

But that was an idle dream and she knew it. She opened her eyes, noting the grey, anxious look on the faces of her compatriots who gathered in the square. No one here seemed to have any more confidence in the future than she had herself.

She looked about her, trying to dismiss her recent disappointments from her mind. The best antidote to thinking recently had proved to be her little stepdaughter. Where was the tiresome child? It would be just like her to disappear now that they were so nearly home.

Nell pulled on the woman's skirts, pointing up into the skies.

'Pretty!'

The woman didn't bother to look up. 'Pretty birds,' she agreed, as her own sour thoughts rushed back, unbidden, into her mind.

Nell pulled harder, determined to have her stepmother's full attention. 'Pretty!' she said again.

The woman looked up and saw the balloons as they floated through the air towards the city. One by one they exploded as they hung in the sky, beautiful against a blue background broken only by fluffy little clouds, long before they could come close enough to imperil the great St Mark's Basilica and the magazines that contained the stores of weapons, all of them on the main island.

'What—?' she exclaimed. Who could have imagined that such a ridiculous idea could actually have been brought about? It must be true that those wretched Austrians really were intent on murdering innocent women and children from the skies. She turned to the frightened people who had run into the centre of the square to see what was going on. None of them had ever seen anything like this before, nor, despite all the warnings, had they really expected the murderous Austrians to carry out their threats.

'What are they trying to do?' someone demanded.

'Set fire to the city!' someone else gasped.

'But those aren't guns, they're balloons! They can't harm us with balloons, can they?'

'The Austrians really do mean to bomb us into oblivion! We shall all be killed!'

The panic began with a murmur and grew louder and louder. Only Nell was unmoved, enjoying the sight of the balloons drifting towards them, their baskets exploding one by one and harmlessly falling away into the waters of the canal.

'Pretty!' she reiterated, delighted, stamping her feet up and down. 'More, more!'

The woman eyed her stepdaughter's delight, meaning to rebuke her. Instead, her lips curled into a reluctant smile.

'You don't want Austrians soldiers here, do you?' she asked her.

Nell clasped her hands together, shaking them excitedly up and down.

'More b'loons!'

Many years later that was to be Nell's sole memory of the first aerial bombardment the world had ever seen: the great globes of the balloons and their exploding baskets, and the panic all about her as the Venetians believed their city was doomed, and then the excited relief as they realised that they were in no immediate danger. There were twenty balloons in all, far more than the three that the Austrians later pretended was all they had sent winging their way over the city from vessels anchored some way off the Lido. The great majority exploded in the air or fell harmlessly into the Lagoon, though one dropped into St Andrew's Castle, adding to the general excitement, and some dropped back on the besiegers themselves as the wind changed, causing a roar of delight amongst the frightened Venetians. At the time, the child knew nothing of all that. She thought of it as a spectacle put on specially for her and her stepmother's arrival in Venice and she loved the city from that day onwards. To her, it was always to be the most beautiful place in the world.

★